# HERO

# THE LEGEND OF DRIZZT

Follow Drizzt and his companions on all of their adventures
*(in chronological order)*

# Prelude

M OSTLY HUMAN BANDITS, TO BE HONEST," REGIS TOLD
Wulfgar. The two were relaxing in the back of a wagon as
it rolled southeast from Daggerford down the Trade Way
that late spring day of the Year of the Nether Mountain
Scrolls, or 1486 by Dalereckoning. "You would expect more
monsters to prowl the area, what with the land being so
sparse of true settlements, but the trouble was mostly the making
of humans." The halfling ended with a sigh.

Beside him, Wulfgar nodded and glanced out over his arm,
which was thrown up and around the wooden rail of the wagon,
at the rolling hills to the north of the road. Somewhere up there,
his friends were on the march at the head of a vast dwarven army,
likely heading east to the Sword Coast before they began their
southern turn to the ancient dwarven homeland of Gauntlgrym.

Wulfgar knew Bruenor would get the place back. With Drizzt
and Catti-brie at his side, the determined dwarf would not be
denied. Surely they would encounter great dangers, and just as
surely they would find their way through, even without him.

That thought hung with him, for what surprised Wulfgar
most in thinking about the coming trials his friends would face
was his own lack of guilt in not being there beside them.

There was so much more of the world that he wanted to see!

He hadn't returned to life again simply to replay the events
of his first existence. And in that spirit, he had come south from
Mithral Hall to Silverymoon, and then to Waterdeep where they

1

had spent the cold winter, with Regis and the strange monk Afafrenfere. They rode along the Trade Way bound for the port city of Suzail on the westernmost expanse of the Sea of Fallen Stars, where they would sign on with a ship to Aglarond, to the city of Delthuntle, where Regis's beloved Donnola Topolino headed the formidable rogue's house of the same name.

"Plenty o' monsters about, don't ye doubt," the grizzled old driver called back. "Were it just human folk, I'd've not paid ye so well for yer guarding!"

"Paid?" Wulfgar quietly echoed with a laugh, for their pay was a ride, nothing more.

"Yes, but I find human bandits the most troubling along the road, don't you?" Regis answered the man. "At least between Daggerford and the Boareskyr Bridge."

The driver looked back, his face twisted in cynical skepticism. He was sorely in need of a shave, Wulfgar noted, with gray stubble sticking straight out of the many warts on his face. Wulfgar got the impression that the man hadn't cut the scraggly beard that length, or that he hadn't cut any of his hair in a long, long while. But still, the longest hairs on his wide, round face were those sticking down from his huge nostrils.

"Bah! Are ye the herald o' the Trade Way now?" the driver said to the well-coifed and rather foppish looking halfling. For indeed, Regis was the height of fashion, with his grand blue beret; black, stiff-collared traveling cloak; fine clothes; and the brilliant cage of the fine rapier showing in front of his left hip.

"I rode with the Ponies," Regis responded, no small amount of pride in his voice.

Wulfgar almost expected his diminutive friend to twirl his mustache.

"The Ponies?" the driver replied, and there was no missing the change in the timbre of the man's voice, which dropped low as he turned a bit farther around to study Regis. Had he scrutinized Regis more carefully back in Daggerford, the man would probably have guessed that truth about the cultured halfling before it was announced. With his neatly trimmed goatee, his long and curly brown locks, and splendid garments, it was obvious that Regis was an adventurer of some importance and accomplishment. And the three-bladed dagger on his right hip, the fabulous rapier on his left, and the hand crossbow slung across his chest just under the folds of his fancy cloak were worn in a way that bespoke experience and not mere ornamentation.

Wulfgar carefully watched the driver, then turned back to Regis as the two locked their measuring stares.

"Yes, the Grinning Ponies," Regis said. "Perhaps you have heard of them."

The driver swung back around—quite rudely, Wulfgar thought. "Aye, they're about," he said without looking back again. "A lot more in their tales than in truth, but them little ones're about." And under his breath so that Wulfgar could barely hear, the driver added, "Causing more trouble than they be fixing, to be sure."

Wulfgar arched an eyebrow as he glanced at Regis, who motioned for him to hold silent.

"Aye," Regis replied to the driver. "They called themselves grinning, but I always secretly put the word 'giggling' first in the title. The Giggling Ponies! Fancy enough riders, but not much for the fight. 'Twas why I left them. They so dearly wanted to be counted as heroes, but never earning the title, and oh, how gleefully did they cut down men whenever they found the easy kill!"

The driver grumbled something inaudible.

Regis tossed a wink at Wulfgar. "Men not deserving the blade," the halfling went on, dramatically. "Men just wanting to make a bit o' bread for their families, was all."

Wulfgar scrunched up his face at the curious words, for never before had Regis spoken of the Grinning Ponies with anything less than grand praise. But the big man stared even more curiously at the accent his halfling friend had suddenly affected, one more common to the peasants of the region and one he had never heard from Regis before.

"Bandit," Regis silently mouthed to Wulfgar, subtly pointing to the driver, their current employer.

"Aye, them lords and ladies steal, but it's all legal, and just the sword for a man takin' what he's needing just to fill his own belly and them o' his family," said the driver.

"Taking by the sword, and so the sword returns," Wulfgar said.

"Bah!" the driver snorted. "Well, by the sword and by the hammer if them bandits come for me, then what? Ye just remember who's payin' ye!"

Neither of the companions thought that the driver had said any of that with conviction or with any fear at all that they might soon be accosted.

The halfling and the barbarian exchanged knowing nods. They had been hired by a bandit who was taking them, no doubt, into a hornet's nest of thieves. And likely soon, they each realized. They were moving out well beyond the patrolled lands around Daggerford.

Wulfgar pointed to the trail in their wake, and Regis nodded.

"How long are we for the road this day?" the halfling asked.

"To the sunset. I'm lookin' for the Boareskyr Bridge in a tenday, no more, and that's twenty-and-five or more miles a day."

Regis looked at Wulfgar and shook his head, confident that they weren't getting anywhere near the Boareskyr Bridge with this particular driver leading them.

"Then we'll be long into the night with our watches, and so I'll find me some sleep now," Regis announced. He began shuffling boxes about and from his magical pouch produced a heavy blanket.

"Aye, road's clear enough," said the driver, without even glancing back. "Ye both might be taking a good afternoon nap."

"Afafrenfere?" Regis mouthed.

Wulfgar shrugged. The monk had remained behind in Daggerford, following a lead regarding a missing companion named Effron, but had promised to catch up with them on the road. They could use him now. That one could fight well, and a battle was likely very near.

At the same time Wulfgar slid a bag of apples under the blanket, which was suspended between two crates, Regis slipped off the back of the wagon, disappearing into the tall grass so quickly that Wulfgar couldn't even follow the halfling's movements beyond the first few hunched steps.

A few moments later, Wulfgar gave a great, feigned yawn, and rested back, conveniently obscuring most of the halfling's bedroll from the driver.

"Aye, but you scream loudly at any sign of trouble," he said to the driver. "My little friend here is known for his great snoring."

"The littlest ones always are!" the man said with a laugh, and soon after, tellingly, he began to whistle.

And Wulfgar began to snore.

The barbarian knew that Regis's guess was correct very soon after, when the wagon slowed and lurched a bit as it went off the side of the trail. Wulfgar opened his eyes just enough to see that they were moving into a copse of trees.

He heard the footsteps of approaching men, heard the driver suddenly scrambling down from his bench.

Up popped Wulfgar to find himself surrounded by a trio of bandits centered by a man with a fine-looking sword. A woman stood to his right, holding a sturdy spear, and to his left was a second man with an axe so heavy Wulfgar was amazed the flabby-armed, round-bellied fellow could hold it up and remain standing. The driver was just off to the side of the cart, huddled on the ground. An archer stared down at Wulfgar from above, and he noted a second, bow drawn, behind a wall of planks covered in leaves and set between two oaks.

"Here now, big fellow," said the swordsman, a tall, slender man with long, curly blond locks. "No need to be getting excited here. You're caught, as you know, and so there's no need for us to spill your blood all over the ground."

"Might be fun, though," said the woman standing beside him, and she leveled her spear Wulfgar's way.

"Caught?" Wulfgar asked, as if he had no idea what any of this could mean. He turned his head to the right, glancing over the side of the wagon. "Driver?"

The man whimpered.

"You just keep yourself curled and face down, or you'll feel the bite of my blade!" the swordsman, apparently the leader, ordered.

Wulfgar knew better.

"Your pouch," the swordsman demanded, holding out his free hand.

"You would take my last copper?" Wulfgar asked.

"Aye, and that pretty hammer, too," said the axe-wielder, as dirty a human as Wulfgar had ever seen. He wasn't as tall as the swordsman, though quite a bit heavier, and as he motioned for Aegis-fang with his bulky axe, Wulfgar was struck by the clumsiness of the movement. Of the three in front of him, only the swordsman seemed to handle his weapon with any aplomb.

And the archer above him, he noted, was leaning so heavily and so forward against a branch that he'd never be able to properly adjust his shot quickly to either side.

Wulfgar reached to his belt, broke the tie on his small pouch, and tossed it to the swordsman.

"And the warhammer," the swordsman demanded.

Wulfgar looked at Aegis-fang. "My father made this for me," he answered.

The man with the axe giggled and spat.

"Then perhaps he will make you another," said the swordsman. "We are not murderers, after all."

"Unless we have to be," said the woman, and she rolled her spear over in her fingers.

Wulfgar put on an expression of regret and looked down at Aegis-fang yet again.

"Now!" the swordsman yelled, trying to startle him, trying to get him to hand it over before he could even consider anything else. And so Wulfgar complied, tossing Aegis-fang to the ground at the man's feet.

The ruffian with the axe was fast to it, and he dropped his own weapon happily as he picked up the magnificently balanced Aegis-fang.

"Good choice," said the swordsman.

Wulfgar shrugged.

"Aye, but we have to kill him anyway, eh?" said the woman.

"Nay, just tie him and leave him," the swordsman replied.

The ruffian with Aegis-fang had moved off a step to the side, near to the driver, to put his new weapon through some practice swings. Wulfgar noted that the driver kept peeking up at the bandit, apparently trying to get his attention. He whispered something along the lines of ". . . his little friend."

"And your fine hat, please," the swordsman asked politely.

Wulfgar turned to his left, where Regis's splendid blue beret lay at the top of the blanket suspended between the crates.

"It's not my hat."

"Then whose . . . ?" the swordsman started to ask, but the man with Aegis-fang cried out, "Eh, take care! He's got a little rat friend hidin' under there!"

The spear-wielder's eyes widened with alarm and she reflexively thrust forward the spear.

"No!" the swordsman cried, but too late.

An arrow dropped harmlessly to the ground beside her, and as Wulfgar dodged the thrust and grasped the spear just blow the tip, he managed to glance up into the tree to see the archer fully slumped over the branch, one arm and one leg on either side.

Silently thanking Regis, Wulfgar grabbed the spear shaft with his second hand and shoved it back at the woman, driving it past her right side. Then, with frightening strength, he casually flicked it—and her—into the air. She tumbled into the swordsman and knocked him aside.

Wulfgar rolled into a back somersault, his hands planting and pushing off to throw him up to his feet, and over the right side of the wagon he went, landing next to the huddled driver, who looked up.

Wulfgar kicked him in the face, sending him sprawling in the dirt.

But on came the bandit wielding Aegis-fang.

"What have you done?" the swordsman cried as he extracted himself from his female companion. Both turned to help their friend, but a voice from behind stopped them before they took their first steps.

"Nothing wise."

The two leaped about, trying to bring their weapons to a defensive posture. Regis sent in his rapier, prodding the woman in her leading hand, going right through her palm as she tried to swing her spear across her chest. She yelped, lost her grip with that hand, and fell back defensively, her spear angled to the ground.

At the same time, the swordsman took the opening to leap forward with a strike. But the dagger neatly picked it off and turned the blade out wide. The bandit disengaged skillfully and spun to square up against his diminutive foe. He found the halfling holding the dagger in front of him, but with only one of its serpent-like side blades now apparent.

"Good sir, I fear you have broken my fine knife," the halfling said.

The swordsman smiled—but only until the halfling threw the "broken" tine at him. It struck him on his blocking forearm, doing no immediate harm, but the piece transformed from a metal side blade into a tiny living serpent. Before the surprised bandit could react, the snake rushed along with incredible speed, up his arm, over his shoulder, and around his neck, and there it circled and tightened. The swordsman clawed at it with his free hand, working to keep his sword up in an attempt to ward off the halfling.

But this was more than a small magical serpent. It was a garrote, and one that summoned a most awful specter right behind the victim, an undead entity that tugged with such tremendous force that the swordsman was yanked off his feet and sent flying backward and to the ground.

And there he lay, writhing, choking. He dropped his sword and grabbed at the serpent with both hands, but to no avail.

And then how the bulky man roared, lifting his beautiful new weapon up over his head with both hands, charging for the unarmed barbarian, determined to crush the fool's skull with a single, mighty downward chop.

It took him a couple of long strides to realize that he wasn't holding the warhammer any longer, and a couple more halting steps to come to the realization that the barbarian now had the weapon securely back in hand.

And by that time, of course, the portly bandit found himself standing right in front of the huge, muscular—and *armed*—barbarian.

"Huh?" the ruffian asked, clearly at a loss.

Wulfgar stabbed the head of Aegis-fang forward into the man's fat face, cracking teeth and splattering his nose, stopping the attacker in his tracks. The portly bandit stumbled back a step, staring at Wulfgar in disbelief, unable to sort out how that warhammer could have possibly been taken from him so cleanly, and from several strides away.

He didn't understand Aegis-fang, and its connection to Wulfgar, son of Beornegar and son of Bruenor, and how the simple whisper of "Tempus" would magically teleport the hammer to Wulfgar's waiting hand.

The bandit staggered. He shook his head. He fell over onto the ground.

Wulfgar couldn't watch that descent. A thrumming sound from the bluff alerted him to danger. He threw himself back, turning his head and sweeping his arms up in front of his chest and face—and a good thing he did. When he hit the ground in a roll, he had an arrow sticking out of his muscled forearm!

He paid it little heed, coming around and to his feet then in a fast half-turn from which he sent Aegis-fang flying for the hidden archer.

The warhammer hit the wooden blind and blew apart the planks, driving through in an explosion of splinters. Wulfgar heard a cry, a woman's voice, and the female archer went flying out the back of her ambush spot.

"Tempus!" Wulfgar roared, though he really wasn't even certain if that name meant anything to him anymore.

Still, the hammer appeared in his hand, and so his battle cry was one well-chosen.

The woman grabbed up her spear again, wincing with pain but with no choice but to battle through it. She thrust ahead, more to keep the halfling at bay than in any hopes of scoring a hit, but Regis was far too quick for that.

In perfect fencing balance, left foot trailing and perpendicular to the fight, he quick-stepped a retreat, then came rushing ahead. Seeing her error, the woman tried to send her spear forward again, but Regis was inside the head and the strength of the thrust then, and a fast down-and-out sweep of the rapier turned the spear out wide.

The dashing halfling stepped in behind, and, one-two, stabbed the woman in her shoulders.

He swept out to the side, toward the man being choked to death on the ground by the spectral apparition.

A quick stab of Regis's splendid rapier ended that drama, the simple hit on the apparition making it disappear to nothingness. The swordsman fell flat, gasping.

"Do stay down," Regis warned him, rushing back the other way, sweeping his rapier in circles around the stabbing tip of the woman's spear. And when her eyes, too, began to spin as she tried to keep up with the movement, the halfling reversed the flow, driving his rapier down and across his body, taking the spear inside while he stepped outside and forward.

Now his dagger came in, catching the spear fully, and he

lifted it high, waded in underneath the lifted tip, and brought his rapier's point in under the woman's chin.

"Oh, dear lady, I do not wish to end your life," he said graciously. "So please do drop your nasty spear."

Head tilted way back, nowhere to flee, she looked down at him and swallowed hard—and did indeed let go of the spear.

Regis flicked it far aside, then called over his shoulder to the swordsman, who was stubbornly trying to rise.

"I am sure I told you to stay on the ground," he said.

The man paused, but then started up once more.

"I have another . . ." Regis started to explain, but he just sighed and sent his dagger's second magical snake flying at the man.

Regis didn't even watch the result. He didn't have to.

He turned his attention back to the woman at the end of his rapier, and her eyes told the tale, as did the swordsman's desperate gasp, when a second apparition appeared at the back of the new garrote and began choking the life out of him once more.

This time, Regis let the undead fiend choke the man unconscious before he calmly walked over and poked the specter, dispelling the deadly magic.

Regis heaved a great sigh. "Sometimes, they are so stubborn," he said to Wulfgar, his complaint interrupted by the crack of a tree branch up above. The archer, sound asleep from Regis's poisoned hand crossbow dart, fell heavily to the dirt right beside the barbarian and the female prisoner.

Regis looked from the groaning, broken man to Wulfgar, and shrugged.

Wulfgar motioned to Regis's magical pouch, where he kept his potions, salves, and bandages. The barbarian hoisted his warhammer up on one shoulder then kicked softly at the man on the ground in front of him. "If you stand up," he warned the portly bandit, and then extended the warning to the wagon driver as well, "I will crush your heads."

To emphasize his point, he sent his hammer swinging down, the head driving deeply into the ground right in front of the prone bandit's face.

"Stay down and right there," Wulfgar reiterated. Then he stalked off, breaking through the remaining splinters of the blind between the oaks and moving into the brush to find the second archer, the woman. He carried her out over his shoulder, with her groaning in agony with every step. One of her arms hung limp and twisted, terribly shattered, and her breathing came in gasps. The hammer had driven through her arm and collapsed half her chest.

Without magic, she would surely die in short order. Fortunately for her, and for the other archer, Wulfgar and Regis were not without magic. Even as Wulfgar moved over to lay the wounded woman on the back of the wagon, Regis had his portable alchemy lab set up, and the spear-wielding woman he had captured was moving from one fallen bandit to another with potions of healing.

"These unguents and potions are not cheaply made," Regis grumbled to Wulfgar. He reached for a potion bottle, but noting the extent of the woman's wounds, went instead to a small jar of salve.

"What gold value is too much?" Wulfgar asked.

Regis smiled and began applying the healing salve.

A rustle caught their attention and they turned to see the other woman, the one Regis had captured, rushing away through the underbrush.

Regis looked up at Wulfgar. "Do you think she has more friends?"

Wulfgar looked around at the motley crew scattered all about. These were farmers, or perhaps tradesmen, dirt poor and desperate.

"Should I catch her, that we can hang the lot of them together?" he asked.

Regis's horrified expression lasted only the moment it took for him to realize his large friend was teasing. But even in that jest, Wulfgar had set out a perplexing question. Whatever were they to do with this group? They had no intention of executing them, for clearly these were not hardened murderers and thieves.

But still, could they leave them alive and free here on the road, where they might bring more mischief and even harm to the next unwary travelers who got into the back of the treacherous driver's wagon?

"Justice can be harsh on the Trade Way," Regis remarked.

"Would the Ponies execute this bunch?"

"Only if they were found to have killed someone."

"Then what else?" Wulfgar asked. The man choked unconscious by Regis's garrote awakened then, coughing and sputtering and struggling to sit up. Wulfgar stepped over and helped him, grabbing him by the front of the tunic and hoisting him to his feet with just the one arm.

"Thieves are put to work for merchants or craftsmen," Regis explained. "Hard labor until their debt is repaid for the trouble they have caused."

"I . . . We . . . we . . . we could have killed you," the swordsman sputtered.

"No, you could not have," Wulfgar replied, walking the fellow over to the wagon. "Nor did you want to when you thought you had me helpless, and that is the only reason any of you are still alive."

"So then what do you mean to do with us?" asked the leader of the group.

"We hired a wagon to take us to the Boareskyr Bridge," Wulfgar explained. "And so you shall do exactly that. All of you."

He shoved the man away. "Go and find your woman who tried to stab me," Wulfgar instructed, nodding to the brush where the woman had run. "Bring her back. If you return, you will ride with us to the bridge. If you do not return, you will find your four friends dead right here, and we will be gone with the wagon. And know that if you do not return to us quickly, if I ever see you again, I will kill you."

"Do you think he'll come back?" Regis asked when the man disappeared into the underbrush.

"Are you asking for a wager?"

The halfling grinned.

◆ ◆ ◆

SOON AFTER, THE sun beginning its western descent, the wagon once again rolled down the Trade Way toward the Boareskyr Bridge, with Wulfgar sitting on the bench beside the bruised and terrified driver and Regis right behind him, keeping an eye on the two archers, the most badly wounded of the bandit group.

The portly man who had foolishly thought to wield Wulfgar's hammer sat on the back of the wagon, his legs dangling.

They had barely begun to roll out when the other two bandits appeared on the road behind them, running to catch up—and with a familiar robed figure right behind them, prodding them along.

"Bah, a gold piece for Wulfgar, then," Regis grumbled.

But he was glad that his big friend had guessed right, and glad, too, to see that Brother Afafrenfere had come at last.

◆ ◆ ◆

"BUT I WOULD be foolish to try, yes?" the swordsman, Adelard Arras of Waterdeep, said to Wulfgar soon after they broke camp the next morning.

"Yes," Wulfgar replied.

"And since I know this, I would not try!"

Wulfgar looked at him skeptically.

"I am no fool!" Adelard protested.

"But you are a highwayman. And not a very good one."

Adelard sighed and shook his head. "The road is dangerous, my friend."

"Never confuse me as your friend," Wulfgar warned.

"But you did not kill me, nor any of my companions," Adelard protested. "Yet you are a fierce warrior, of course, and would not shy from such extreme retribution. Indeed, by your own admission, you spent a great deal of wealth in the form of potions and salves to save us."

"She shot me with an arrow," Wulfgar reminded him, nodding back at the woman who rode, much more comfortably now, in the back of the wagon.

"And yet we live! All of us! Because you see in us—"

"You are not getting your weapons back," Wulfgar declared with finality. "In the time between here and the bridge, prove to me that you'll not waylay others and perhaps I will show mercy, perhaps even let you go free—under watchful eyes."

Adelard started to protest, but Wulfgar cut him short.

"Trying to trick me into returning your sword does not help you," he said.

"Trick?" Adelard acted as if he were truly wounded, but Wulfgar merely snorted, or started to, until Regis said sharply, "Silence!"

All eyes turned to the halfling.

"What?" Wulfgar whispered, seeing his diminutive friend's faraway look.

Regis motioned to Afafrenfere, who was on the road behind the wagon, kneeling with his ear to the ground.

Wulfgar stopped the wagon, all eyes on the monk.

"Horses," Afafrenfere explained. "Coming fast from behind."

All eight others of the party held silent then, straining to hear. Sure enough, a slight shift of the breeze brought the sounds of several horses galloping down the road from behind them.

Wulfgar looked around. They had just come through a copse of trees, but there was no time to get back around the bend and into cover.

"Arm us," Adelard whispered.

Wulfgar eyed him dangerously, warning him to silence. The barbarian tied off the reins and hopped down from the bench, motioning Regis to his side at the back corner of the wagon, where Afafrenfere stood waiting.

"Bandits?" the monk asked.

"Likely," Regis replied.

"If there are many, do we arm our companions?" Wulfgar asked, looking around at the ragtag band of six they had taken prisoner.

"Only the swordsman is a worthy fighter," Regis reminded him. "And we gamble that he will know the group approaching and join in with them."

"Then I kill him first."

Regis shrugged.

The sound of the approaching riders was clear then, nearing the copse of trees that was still in sight down at the bend in the road.

"Go and hide, all of you," Wulfgar told the bandits. "To the tall grass."

The six began to scurry, but not quickly enough. The posse—a dozen riders kicking up dust and thundering along the Trade Way—came around the bend. They drew their fine swords as soon as they pulled in sight of the wagon. Steel gleamed in the morning sunlight almost as brilliantly as Regis's wide smile.

"Is it . . . ?" Wulfgar started to ask.

The dozen approaching riders seemed quite easy in the saddle, as if they had ridden many, many miles over many, many months—and they were all quite short.

The barbarian put a hand on Brother Afafrenfere's shoulder, coaxing him out of his battle stance.

Wulfgar heard more than one bandit groan.

The Grinning Ponies had come.

"Hold, wagon, hold!" cried the rider in the center of the leading line, a finely dressed fellow with a wide-brimmed leather hat, one side pinned up and plumed.

"If we held any more, Master Doregardo, we would be rolling back at you!" Regis yelled in answer. He moved forward out of Wulfgar's shadow, drew his fine rapier, and dipped a low bow.

"Spider!" shouted the halfling at Doregardo's side.

Up the troupe thundered, kicking dirt and rearing their ponies. Even as his mount's forelegs touched back down, Doregardo lifted a leg over his saddle and dropped skillfully to the ground.

"Why, Master Topolino, it has been far too long!" Doregardo exclaimed, and he rushed up and exchanged a grand hug with Regis.

"But, good sir," he added, pushing Regis back to arms' length, "you seem to have lost your mount!"

"It has been a long and eventful few years, my old friend," Regis replied. "Years of war and adventure."

"And you will tell us all about it, then, aye," said Showithal Terdidy, the halfling who had first shouted Regis's name. He, too, slipped from his saddle and rushed over to embrace Regis.

"We were pursuing a band of highwaymen known to be in the area," Doregardo explained.

"Highwaymen and women," Wulfgar replied, gesturing at the six bandits, none of whom had managed to get off the road and out of sight.

"By the gods," they heard Adelard grumble, and he added quietly to the disheveled driver, "You gave a ride to a Grinning Pony?"

"They found us," Regis explained.

Doregardo glanced around curiously, waving his hand as he did so. The mounted halflings flanked left and right and began encircling the troupe.

"They are quite caught," Regis assured Doregardo. "We were allowing them the time to the Boareskyr Bridge to convince us they would mend their ways."

"Or kill you in your sleep," muttered Showithal.

"I do not sleep," said Afafrenfere, drawing a hard stare from Showithal.

"I give you Brother Afafrenfere of the Monastery of the Yellow Rose," Regis quickly explained. "Brother Afafrenfere, dragonslayer.

"And this is my long-time friend, Wulfgar of Icewind Dale," Regis pressed on, thinking it prudent to clarify the situation a bit, given the still-threatening look on Showithal's face. That one had always been eager for a fight, eager to elevate the stature of the Grinning Ponies above that of his old vigilante band from Damara, the Kneebreakers. Regis could well imagine Showithal drawing his sword on Wulfgar, and then the rest of them trying to figure out how to get poor Showithal down from the top branches of the tallest nearby tree after Wulfgar threw him up there.

Doregardo gave a little laugh, and graciously bowed to Wulfgar. "We are honored, good sir," he said politely, then turned to Regis. "And pray tell what you planned to do in the case that these ruffians could not convince you of their mended ways?"

"Then they would no longer be our problem," Wulfgar grimly replied, his meaning all too clear.

Doregardo looked up at him for a long moment. "Consider them your problem no longer, then." He motioned to his riders, who began rounding up the group.

"Well, that depends on your intentions," Wulfgar replied.

"You think them redeemable?"

"If we didn't, they would all be dead back on the road."

"Then our intentions are to escort you to the Boareskyr Bridge," Doregardo assured him, "and offer our help in managing your prisoners. And there at the bridge, we will hear your verdict."

"And honor it?" Wulfgar pressed.

Doregardo gave a noncommittal shrug. "I've associates who are gathering more information regarding this band. If there is blood on their hands . . ."

Wulfgar held up his hand to show that he understood and agreed. He nodded, satisfied.

The Trade Way was very much a wild land, with precious cargo constantly flowing and highwaymen constantly lurking. There were few jails available, and fewer guardians, like the Grinning Ponies, to patrol the long road. For all who traversed this region, safety often balanced on the edge of a fine sword. The same had been true in Icewind Dale, of course, where justice, out of necessity, was usually swift and almost always brutal.

Doregardo motioned to a nearby halfling rider, a wide-eyed young lass Regis did not know. She expertly swung her pony around and galloped back up the road, returning some time later after the wagon was rolling once more, with a pair of riderless ponies in tow.

"Will you ride with us again, my old friend?" Doregardo asked Regis when the spare ponies neared.

Regis grinned, as much at the curious reference—for how "old" a friend was Doregardo, after all, in comparison to the hulking barbarian who sat on the bench beside Regis?—as at the appealing prospect. He accepted the offer, and rode easily in a line between Doregardo and Showithal, and teased them with the tales he would tell them that night around the campfire.

And what grand tales those were!

Regis recounted the War of the Silver Marches all the way to the momentous battle at Dark Arrow Keep, and the great victory of King Bruenor and his allies. Many cheers went up from the Grinning Ponies—and even a few from the captured bandits.

Regis told them of the dragons above the mountain, and coaxed Afafrenfere into detailing his battle with the white wyrm on the side of the mountain, and even though the monk downplayed the event with proper humility, a multitude of gasps accompanied his every sentence.

It was long into the night when Regis finished, but none were asleep, not even Adelard and his band, all whispering and laughing at the grand story, all cheering for King Bruenor and King Harnoth and King Emerus Warcrown.

"And now you are bound for Boareskyr Bridge," Doregardo said when the whispers died away, halflings and bandits and barbarian alike moving to their bedrolls.

"Suzail, actually," Regis replied.

Doregardo and Showithal exchanged curious looks.

"Morada Topolino?" Showithal asked, and Regis's smile confirmed the guess.

"I promised Lady Donnola that I would return. It is not a promise I intend to break!"

Showithal Terdidy, who remembered well the lovely Donnola, nodded and returned the grin.

"And you?" Doregardo asked Wulfgar.

"My eager little friend is often in need of protection," Wulfgar replied.

"As is Wulfgar, who smashed his face into rocks in the dark tunnels," Regis quipped back.

"Another tale?" asked Doregardo, and Regis laughed, more than willing to comply.

But Showithal moved off to the side of the other three then, to a lone figure crouched on a flat stone, peering off into the darkness. Regis paused, all three straining to hear the exchange.

"The Monastery of the Yellow Rose, so said Spider. Damara?" Showithal asked, obviously intrigued. Showithal was from that faraway land and had begun his career there with a halfling vigilante band known as the Kneebreakers.

The monk nodded. "And there, I return."

"Ah, but we've got words to exchange, then, good monk! I've friends in that faraway land, too long estranged!"

He scrambled up on the rock beside the monk and took up a conversation.

"It is a good thing your friend insisted that he does not sleep," Doregardo said to Wulfgar and Regis, "for Showithal Terdidy is not known for his brevity in recounting his adventures."

Regis nodded, more than aware of that very fact.

"Now," Doregardo said, clapping his hands. "Tell me this new tale. One of my stature is always thrilled to hear of tall humans running into low-hanging rocks in the dark."

He stopped and flashed a wide smile, but it dissipated as he considered Regis and Wulfgar, the halfling offering a questioning stare, and Wulfgar eventually nodding his agreement.

"I do have another tale to tell you," Regis told Doregardo, in a voice much softer and more somber. "But one you will hardly believe, I fear, and one that travels back to a time before you were born."

Doregardo looked curiously at this halfling—who seemed no more than half his age—then at Wulfgar.

By the time the wagon began its roll down the Trade Way early the next morning, neither Regis, Doregardo, nor Wulfgar had slept. Doregardo most of all seemed as if his mind still whirled from the most fantastical tale he had ever heard, one of rebirth and a second chance at life, and one, he found to his own surprise, that he believed wholeheartedly.

A tenday later, the troupe settled comfortably at the Boareskyr Bridge. There, another group of Grinning Ponies found them, Doregardo's scouts seeking information on the highwaymen. That proved to be good news for five of the six captives, who would be granted leniency. But for the sixth, the bulky axeman, there came information of blood on his hands.

He was hanged that same day from a tree just west of the bridge.

Justice in the wild lands was swift and brutal.

To the surprise of the companions from the Silver Marches, Doregardo informed them that he and some others of his band would escort them all the way to Suzail.

"I know many of the ship captains, of course, and so can help you secure passage to Aglarond," he explained.

"Suzail is a journey of several hundred miles!" Regis reminded him.

"A ride I have not made in far too long," said Doregardo. "Showithal and I were discussing this very journey soon before we found you. Since the events of the Sundering and the great changes that have swept over the Realms, it is far past time for us to show the banner of the Grinning Ponies once more in Cormyr."

"We will be glad for the company," Regis replied.

"And we, too! But first we must secure for your friends two fine horses," said Doregardo.

Wulfgar nodded, but Afafrenfere shook his head. "I require no mount."

"Our pace will be swift," Doregardo warned, but Afafrenfere reiterated his stance. Soon after they departed, no one questioned him again. Afafrenfere ran easily beside the group and had no trouble keeping pace in the tendays following.

They had hoped to make Suzail by the beginning of summer, but the Western Heartlands remained quite unsettled following the many wars and upheavals of the tumultuous events of the previous years, and so that journey found many side streets, and small adventures, and goodly folk in need of assistance. It was well past midsummer when at last the troupe spotted the tall masts gently rocking in the harbor of Suzail.

There they said goodbye to Brother Afafrenfere, who sailed out for Mulmaster on the Moonsea, the swiftest route to his monastery home.

Ships to Aglarond were harder to find at that time, though, and so it wasn't until the very last day of Eleasis that Wulfgar and Regis at last boarded a squat merchant vessel, serving as deck hands and hired swords, bound for Aglarond's port city of Delthuntle.

"Fare you well, my friend Doregardo," Regis said at the dock. "I tell you now to keep your eyes and ears open to the Crags, north of Neverwinter. There will King Bruenor Battlehammer claim once more the most ancient homeland of the Delzoun dwarves."

"Fare you well, my friend Regis . . ." Doregardo replied.

"Spider Topolino," Showithal said with a wink behind the halfling, and all got a laugh at that.

"Regis," Doregardo corrected, "hero of the north. And you, as well, Master Wulfgar. I wish that I could cut you into three pieces and make of you three additions to the Grinning Ponies!"

"Until we meet again, then," said Regis.

"On the doorstep of Gauntlgrym, perhaps," Doregardo replied. "And from there, you can take us to meet this dwarf king you name as friend."

Regis bowed, Wulfgar nodded respectfully, and the pair boarded the caravel.

None of them could know it at the time, but on that very day, Bruenor, Drizzt, Catti-brie, and the vast army that had marched from the Silver Marches set its camp before the northern gates of the city of Neverwinter.

# PART 1

# As You Will

I LOOK UPON THE STARS AGAIN AND THEY SEEM AS FOREIGN TO ME as they did when first I climbed out of the Underdark.

By every logic and measure of reason, my journey to Menzoberranzan should seem to me to be a great triumph.

Demogorgon was destroyed. The threat to Menzoberranzan, and perhaps to the wider world, was thus lifted. I survived, as did my companions, and Dahlia is back among us, rescued from the spidery web of Matron Mother Baenre. Tiago is dead, and I need not fear that he will rally allies to come after me and my friends ever again. Even were the drow to resurrect him, the issue is settled, I am sure. Not Tiago, and likely no other drow, will come hunting for the trophy of Drizzt Do'Urden ever again.

And so, by every measure of reason, my journey to the Underdark met with the greatest success that we could have hoped, with two unexpected and welcomed developments.

I should be overjoyed, and more so to see again the stars.

But now I know, and once known, it is a truth that cannot be unrealized.

Perhaps, given the revelation, it is the only truth.

And that, I find abhorrent.

The only truth is that there is no truth? This existence, all existence, is just a game, a cheat, meaningless beyond the reality we place in our own eyes?

Wulfgar was deceived by Errtu in the pits of the Abyss. His entire existence was recreated, fabricated, and so his perception of reality moved toward his deepest desires—only to be pulled away by the great demon.

How far does that lie go? How deep into everything we see, everything we know, everything we believe, is the fabrication of demons, or gods?

Or are those beings, too, mere manifestations of my own internal imagination? Am I a god, the only god? Is everything around me no more than my creation, my eyes giving it shape, my nose giving it smell, my ears giving it sound, my moods giving it story?

Aye, I fear, and I do not want to be the god of my universe! Could there be a greater curse?

But yes, aye, indeed! Worse would be to learn that I am not the maestro, but that I am a victim of the maestro, who teases me with his own sinister designs.

Nay, not worse! No, for if I am the god-thing, if I create reality with my own perception, then am I not truly alone?

I cannot find the footing to sort this out. I look at the stars, the same stars that have brightened my nights for decades, and they seem foreign.

Because I fear that it is all a lie.

And so every victory rings hollow. Every truth to which I would have dearly clung slips easily through my weak hands.

That strange priestess, Yvonnel, called me the Champion of Lolth, but in my heart I understand her grand misrepresentation. I fought for Menzoberranzan, true, but in a righteous cause against a demonic horror—and not for Lolth in any way, but for those dark elves who have a chance to see the truth and live a worthy life.

Or did I?

In my journey, I walked the halls of House Do'Urden—as it was, and not as it is. I saw the death of Zaknafein, so I am led to believe, but that, too, I cannot know.

The only truth is that there is no truth . . . no reality, just perception.

Because if perception is reality, then what matters? If this is all a dream, then this is all simply me.

Alone.

Without purpose beyond amusement.

Without morality beyond whim.

Without meaning beyond entertainment.

Alone.

I lift my blades, Twinkle and Icingdeath, and see them now as paddles in a game. What conviction might I put behind the strikes of such weapons when I know now that there is no point beyond the amusement of a demon, or of a god, or of my own imagination?

And so I journey for Luskan this clear, starlit night.

Without purpose.

Without morality.

Without meaning.

Alone.

—Drizzt Do'Urden

# Chapter 1 ◈

# Foul Winds and Fronting Seas

AM NOT MUCH ENJOYING THIS," A GREEN-GILLED REGIS SAID to Wulfgar. The square-masted caravel *Puddy's Skipper* roughly rolled over the twenty-foot seas. The crew worked furiously to keep the lumbering vessel square to the waves, fearing that a sidelong roll would tip her right over.

"Too much in the hold," explained Wulfgar, who was not nearly as seasick as his little friend. "And it's not tied down well enough. Every roll sends the crates sliding."

Up they went again over a high wave, this one so steep on the backside that the pair, standing on the stern castle, found themselves staring straight down over the prow to the dark water. Both grabbed on tighter, and a good thing for that, as water rushed right over the bow, sweeping across the main deck.

Wulfgar laughed.

Regis threw up.

It went on throughout the afternoon, but mercifully the sea calmed a bit as night fell. The starless sky, though, promised more of the rain and wind the next day.

"Ha ha! I thought ye had yer sea legs, then!" the first mate laughed when Wulfgar escorted Regis down the ladder to the main deck.

"We've sailed often," Wulfgar answered.

"With Deudermont, on *Sea Sprite*!" Regis added, as if that should carry some weight. But the first mate and Mallabie Pudwinker, the captain, both simply shrugged.

"We're not on the Sword Coast," Wulfgar quietly reminded his little friend as they walked away. "We're on a lake."

"Some lake," the green-gilled Regis sarcastically replied.

"Aye, and that's why the waves can be nastier," answered Mallabie Pudwinker, who had overheard the conversation. The woman, sturdy and handsome, moved up to the pair, and it wasn't hard for Regis to notice the sparkle in Wulfgar's eye as he looked upon her. Regis certainly understood the sentiment. Captain Mallabie—in her looks, her build, and just the way she handled herself—evinced competence and strength. The woman who could out spit you, outfight you, and outlove you all at once. She was possessed of piercing dark brown eyes that seemed to look through a person as much as at him. Her black hair bobbed freely around her shoulders, the only aspect of the woman that seemed loose in any way. Her clothes fit perfectly, neat and straight, her vest tight around her, under a bandolier of medals and harbor pins. She wore a cutlass on her left hip, and though Regis hadn't seen her draw it, he had little doubt that she could do so with great proficiency.

"Not as deep, you see, in the sheltered run between Sembia and the Dragon Coast, and so the rolling water can gather a bit of a frothy head as it lifts over the reefs and shoals."

"Frothy head?" the halfling answered incredulously.

"I thought you said you were from Aglarond and had sailed the Sea of Fallen Stars?"

"I am, and did . . . but just once."

"Delthuntle, you said!" Mallabie protested. "A life on the water, you said!"

"In a rowboat, or a skiff. No bigger," Regis explained.

The captain sighed. "Might that I should have charged you more for the trouble of taking you back then, eh?"

Regis started to answer, but Wulfgar brought his arm across the halfling's shoulders, quieting him.

"What?" both Regis and Mallabie asked together.

"Listing," Wulfgar said.

"Rolling," Regis corrected, but Wulfgar shook his head.

"Listing, to port," he said, standing perfectly still and staring forward, lining up the mainmast and the prow.

"Below decks, now!" Captain Mallabie yelled at a nearby crewman. "Search the lower hold!"

Before that man even disappeared down the ladder, a cry came up that they were indeed taking on water. The bouncing had driven down the mainmast, cracking the timbers below her. And now, with so much of the cargo shifted to port, the water coming in rushed to that side, further unbalancing the caravel.

"Drop the sails!" Captain Mallabie shouted as soon as she realized the problem. The sails, straining under the weight of the wind, were only causing more stress at the damage point and thus exacerbating the problem below.

"A bucket team below!" she bellowed, and her crew jumped into action. Wulfgar started for the ladder, too, but Mallabie caught him by the arm. "Are you as strong as you look?"

"Stronger," Regis assured her.

"Good. Then to the tiller with you, both of you," Mallabie ordered. "The wheel won't be nimble enough without the sails, so we'll go direct to the rudder." She motioned to the man at the wheel, who locked it in place and nodded. "Bricker there will get the tiller up and free for you, then it's on you, barbarian. You keep us straight into the waves, or sure that we're to be rolled."

Wulfgar nodded. He had done such dramatic tiller duty before, turning ships bigger than this with his brute strength in the midst of a pirate battle.

"Once the seas calm and my crew has the bailing in order and have started the patching, you go below and get the cargo balanced," the captain added. "I'll not lose a pound of it!"

"If we're sinking . . ." Regis started.

"I'll throw the crew over, one by one, until I've got few as I need to get my goods to the east," Captain Mallabie interrupted. "And might that I'll start with you."

Regis's green face drained to white and Mallabie turned just enough to offer a playful wink at Wulfgar, who couldn't help but grin.

"She was joking, right?" Regis asked as he followed Wulfgar astern, hustling after Bricker.

"Why would you care?" Wulfgar asked. "I thought you were full of genasi blood and could swim the length of the sea if needed."

Regis shrugged. "Well, there are other things in there, you know. Big things . . . hungry things . . ."

"Bah, but you'd not be much of a meal, so fear not!" Wulfgar replied.

They worked through the night, with Wulfgar following the directions of Bricker and Regis to properly angle the ship for each incoming wave. Mercifully, those waves began to diminish in size, and above them the clouds broke apart and the stars shone down upon them.

The deck bustled with a line of crewmen hauling buckets, a cadence offered by the rapping of mallets down below as the ship's carpenters tried to brace and secure the mast and get some tar and wood over the cracks.

Still some hours before dawn, the crew slowed and Wulfgar's work was all but finished. With the sea calm once more, he and Regis tied the tiller down. After helping Bricker reattach the wheel, they slumped beside it, all three trying to find some sleep.

"No time for that!" came Captain Mallabie's voice soon after—so soon that Regis wasn't really sure if he'd fallen asleep or not. He looked up into the bright sky with bleary eyes, and it was wonderfully bright, the sun shining. Wulfgar yawned and Bricker jumped to his feet.

"Back to buckets," Mallabie explained.

"I thought her patched," said Bricker.

"A bit, aye, but the damage is under, by the keel. We'll slow it. Might be enough, might not." She shook her head and none of the three were given a sense of confidence .

Wulfgar climbed to his feet, and Mallabie looked him over carefully as he rose.

"You a swimmer?" she asked.

The big man shrugged.

"Ye're thinking o' putting boys under *Puddy's Skipper?*" Bricker asked with a gasp.

Again Mallabie shrugged. "Might."

"Why not?" Wulfgar asked Bricker. *Puddy's Skipper* wasn't that large a craft, after all, and he was pretty certain he could get to the keel.

"One up, one down, back down, back up," Bricker explained. "Ye'd not be down there long enough to get anything done. Not down there in the dark. Not nothing worth doing! Ye'd have to whittle the pegs and all, not just slap a board atop it and hope!"

"Better than nothing," Captain Mallabie said.

"Ye can't tar it," Bricker replied.

"And I can't dry dock her out in the middle of the damned sea, now can I?" the captain retorted, her tone reminding Bricker of the order of things out here on the water.

"Beggin' yer pardon," the man said respectfully, and he slunk back.

"It may take many dives," Mallabie said to Wulfgar. "But I might need you to try."

"So, he'd have to go down there and shape pegs to set them in the cracks?" Regis asked.

Mallabie shrugged again. "There's no easy answer, and no certain fix," she admitted. "But anything we can do to slow the leak will help to get us to shore . . ."

She stopped because Regis was already stripping off his vest and shirt. He removed his rapier, too, but kept the dagger. With a nod, he dropped his fabulous blue beret atop the pile then hopped up on the rail and dropped from sight.

"Look for him!" a shocked Captain Mallabie ordered, rushing to the rail.

"You'll be waiting for a long time," Wulfgar said, and when the other two glanced back at him, they saw a knowing grin.

◆ ◆ ◆

REGIS KNEW, OF COURSE, that he should be afraid. He was underwater in the open sea, the Sea of Fallen Stars, a place known for monsters and sea devils—all sorts of dangerous creatures. In this very sea, the halfling had found the most terrifying moment of his life—either of his lives!—when he had opened the coffin of Ebonsoul and faced the specter in the watery depths.

And still he was not afraid. There was something freeing about being in the water, something natural and wholesome, something calling him back to his ancestors, to the very inception of life that led to his own.

Even though it was mid-Eleint, the ninth month, with summer still holding on along the Dragon Coast and Gulthander and the other southern reaches of the sea, autumn was fast approaching. Cold wind was beginning to blow down from the Bloodstone Lands, and so the water out here was not so warm. But it didn't matter. One of the benefits of his distant genasi heritage was that the chilly water didn't really bother Regis, not as it would have in his previous life. He remembered the time he had slipped and fallen into Maer Dualdon in Icewind Dale, around this same time of the year. Had a fisherman not caught him in a net, he would have quietly and helplessly surrendered to death. The water up there was much colder than here, of course, but Regis understood that he could swim that Icewind Dale lake now. The cold water wouldn't bite at him as it had before his renewal, wouldn't take his life heat from his small body and slow him, slow him, until he expired.

He had been given a great gift through the bloodlines of his mother.

And so he was not afraid.

His body moved instinctively, every sway, every limb working in harmony to propel him along. In his previous existence, he had been able to swim, of course—when he had to—but not like this. Now he was more akin to a true creature of the sea, graceful in his movements, swift in his underwater flight.

Even his eyesight was stronger in the water now. Perhaps it was because of the many hours of his childhood he had spent far below the surface in the oyster beds, but Regis believed that his halfling lowlight vision was a bit different now, more accommodating and useful under the water.

He didn't understand the specifics of it, though, and he didn't need to. He only needed to use those eyes and those wonderful lungs, and his fingers, so sensitive to currents, as he came up on the keel and inspected the hull beneath the mainmast.

In short order he found the seam that was letting in the water. He could hear the song of the rushing water and so feel the flow of the sea reaching up into the boat.

He came up for breath amidships, to find Wulfgar and Captain Mallabie staring down at him from the rail. From Mallabie's relieved expression and Wulfgar's grin, he could fathom the conversation they had shared during his too-long absence under the water.

"A rope!" Mallabie called behind her, but Wulfgar grabbed her by the shoulder and shook his head, turning her back to regard the halfling.

Spider Parrafin didn't need any ropes. He scrambled easily up the side of the *Puddy's Skipper.*

"You were down there—"

"Too long. Yes, I know," Regis interrupted.

"You are a priest, then, with magic to breathe underwater."

"No," Wulfgar said, at the same time as Regis answered, "Something like that."

Captain Mallabie looked from one to the other, and both laughed.

"I found the crease in your hull and believe I can do some good," Regis explained. "A wedge, more a shim, this long." He held his hands up, about a forearm's length apart. "And a mallet. Then I'll come back for a ball of tar."

Mallabie looked at him doubtfully.

"A cooled ball," Regis said. "I'll just pound it in about the shim." He shrugged. "Every bit of a plug I can get in there will help, I expect."

Captain Mallabie seemed out of questions, or perhaps she just recognized that this whole sequence of unexpected and apparently inexplicable events was better left unanswered at that particular time, and so she nodded and moved off to fetch the mallet and shim.

"You are a shipbuilder now?" Wulfgar asked when he was alone with the halfling.

"I have no idea," Regis answered with an honest and helpless shrug. "I'm just going to stuff as much as I can up into the seam and hope it slows the leak."

"And if it doesn't?"

"It will. The water will instruct me."

Wulfgar stared at him skeptically. "And if the water lies to you?"

"Then I'll swim," Regis answered. "And I'll give you a rope and tow you to shore."

Wulfgar grinned, but Regis, who had felt the strength of the flow into that crack firsthand, wasn't smiling. He understood enough about the open waters to realize that *Puddy's Skipper* was in dire trouble, that the wound under the ship was profound, and that the force of the water would only pry apart that seam more as time went on. The crew could never bail enough to keep the boat moving all the way to Delthuntle. They had barely passed the city of Urmlaspyr, with three-quarters of their journey still ahead of them, and in far more difficult seas than the protected stretch that ran from Suzail to this point.

And probably with pirates yet ahead of them.

Captain Mallabie anchored *Puddy's Skipper* and Regis spent the rest of the day trying to hammer the shim into the seam he had found. He worked until the daylight began to fade, then went back to it the next morning. By midday, he had the shim hammered in, and a block of tar pressed in beside it.

As soon as the halfling was aboard to report, Mallabie raised anchor and ordered the sails trimmed. *Puddy's Skipper* once more glided across the waves, her sails full of wind.

By the next morning, though, they had sailed out beyond the protective stretch and into more open waters, and the wind shifted to the northeast. For all their tacking and pulling, *Puddy's Skipper* crawled along.

"Too early in the season for this shift in the wind," Captain Mallabie said to Wulfgar and Regis. She shook her head and blew a long sigh. "The gales of Uktar are a month too soon."

Wulfgar and Regis exchanged concerned looks. They didn't need to know the specifics to understand Mallabie's tone.

"But that's sometimes the way of it," Mallabie explained. "Were that it wasn't this trip, with the sea scratching hard to get in our hold, eh?"

The statement was true enough, a point accentuated by a crewman crawling out of the hold and hauling a bucket of water up beside him. He looked to the captain resignedly, then tossed a slight scowl the halfling's way.

"I did as much as I could," Regis heard himself whispering.

"No one's blaming you," Captain Mallabie said. "But we're needing a dry dock. I thought we could run it, but not in these headwinds and with the currents turning. We'll be a month to Delthuntle, and we've not a month left afloat."

"We can't," said Bricker, coming up to join the three. "Water's coming in faster. We'll be low in the water and crawlin' at best when we cross Pirate Isle, and there's none there we'll be outrunning."

"Where, then?" Wulfgar asked, holding his hand out to keep his clearly excited little friend in check.

Mallabie shook her head, but glanced back to the north-west, the southern coast of Sembia. Two cities, Urmlaspyr and Saerloon, with dry docks and shipyards lay behind them. If they turned back that way, back to the west, with the wind filling her jib, *Puddy's Skipper* could make either of them within two days.

That wasn't the problem, though, for those cities didn't have extensive yards, and the waiting list would be long—months or even a year.

Almost directly north of their current position lay Selgaunt, the capital of Sembia, with more extensive shipyards and perhaps a quicker access to a dry dock for repair.

"Selgaunt'd be quickest in and out," Bricker offered, following the same line of thought.

"Aye, but then we'd be running the Sembian Straights, and we might not find ourselves alone, eh?"

Bricker nodded.

"Back to Urmlaspyr would be our safest route," Captain Mallabie explained.

"Day and more o' sailing, straight back from where we come," said Bricker, and Mallabie nodded. "And they'll have no docks for us before next summer, to be sure."

"If then," said Mallabie. "And sure that it will take every piece of gold we have."

"How long will we be in Selgaunt, then?" Regis asked, his voice growing desperate, and he surely wasn't fond of where this conversation was going. If Uktar's gales were already blowing, he feared that even if they could find an available dry dock, he would find himself stuck across the sea from Aglarond until the spring. He was acquainted enough with the trade routes and the merchant runs to understand that few tried the waters of the Sea of Fallen Stars in winter.

"Better part of a tenday if we get right into a dock for repair," said Bricker. "Likely, more like a pair o' tendays."

"Then we're into Marpenoth," said Wulfgar.

"With the cold winds of Uktar ready to bite us," Bricker agreed.

Captain Mallabie took it all in and nodded, her expression showing that she was beginning to sort things out. "You said you'd prove your worth if we found pirates," she reminded the pair of passengers, and both Regis and Wulfgar nodded. "Or, should I say, if they found us. And they might well do just that in the straights."

"Selgaunt, then," Regis reasoned, but Mallabie shook her head.

"If we're to run the straights, then we're straight for Prespur Isle," she decided, turning her gaze right back to the east. "She's under the command of Cormyr, and I've a friend in the city of Palaggar who's owing me a favor."

"Aye, Palaggar's got the shipyard . . ." Bricker began.

"And a garrison to protect it," Mallabie reminded.

"Fifty miles o' open water," Bricker warned. "Full o' sharks, for they're knowing that the pirates're more than ready to feed 'em, eh?"

"Prespur," Mallabie said evenly. "And the town of Palaggar, and let's hope that we can get *Skipper* sealed and seaworthy before the gales of Uktar come calling."

"And if not?" Regis dared to ask.

"We'll find you work in the town through the winter," Mallabie explained, "and you'll step into Delthuntle by the end of Ches."

Regis sucked in his breath and tried not to cry out in dismay. Captain Mallabie was talking about a delay of more than half a year! The halfling didn't think he could survive another six months without holding Donnola in his arms . . .

But he couldn't argue. He knew enough of the sea to understand that the dark waters didn't much care for the schedules of humans or halflings or any other race, and those who disagreed and tried to force their timetables on the Sea of Fallen Stars were likely still here, forever far, far below.

◆ ◆ ◆

Regis pulled his furry cloak tighter across his shoulders and ducked his head under the side of his cowl, protecting himself from the cold northern wind as he paced the battlements at the top of the lone tower that stood on the highest point of the northern stretch of the island of Prespur. Snowflakes spun and danced in the crosswinds, and the halfling kept muttering his hopes that this wasn't the beginning of another large storm—the last one had filled the bowl between this small mountain and the rest of the island, effectively cutting off the few inhabitants of the Tower of Stars from the town of Palaggar for nearly a tenday.

He was lonely and miserable enough out here without losing the ruckus of the two taverns of Palaggar!

"You'll not find any attackers hiding under your cowl," came Wulfgar's voice behind him.

Regis turned and peeked out from under the hood to see his huge friend's approach. Wulfgar wore his typical garb: a cloak of winter fox hide and no more than a small helm upon his head. His arms were bare and often exposed, but if the cold wind bothered him at all, the Icewind Dale barbarian didn't show it.

"You've been too long away from the cold winds off the Sea of Moving Ice," Wulfgar remarked, coming up beside Regis and leaning on the parapet, looking out over the dark land and the sea beyond, facing right into the wind and caring not at all.

"Too long in the warm halls of King Bruenor," Regis replied, and walked up beside his friend to similarly look out across the dark winter night.

Wulfgar looked at him. "Do you miss them?" he asked, and Regis nodded.

"More than I thought I would. I've always loved them—all of them—but I knew my heart to be across this sea, out in the east and Aglarond."

Wulfgar nodded and patted Regis on the shoulder, reassuring him, "We'll see them again."

"I do not regret coming," the halfling replied, "though I didn't expect to still be out here, in the middle of the Sea of Fallen Stars, with less than two tendays to the turn of the year." He gave a little resigned laugh, again reminding himself that the timetable of the sea overruled the desires of wise men and rudely thwarted the desires of fools.

"The diversion has shown us a new land and given us a season of peace. That is not a bad thing," said Wulfgar.

"I've been here before," Regis replied. "Past this place, at least, on my journey west to meet upon Kelvin's Cairn. It's different now, though, I admit. When last I passed this way, Prespur was two islands. The water has receded greatly since the Sundering, joining the main island with this long rock we're standing on. Traitor Isle, this one was called, if my memory is correct, and none lived here, though the tower was, of course, in place." He blew a forlorn whistle into the wind. "So much has changed."

"Donnola Topolino is still there," Wulfgar replied, obviously realizing the source of the halfling's lament. "And the month of Ches is not so far away."

Regis grinned and nodded for the support.

He looked past Wulfgar to the south and saw a line of torches coming their way. With a chuckle, he pointed, turning the barbarian around.

"Captain Mallabie coming to your bed?" Regis asked.

"You say that as if it is a bad thing," Wulfgar replied.

"How many?" Regis asked. "In this new life you have found, how many women have graced the bed of Wulfgar?"

Wulfgar shrugged as if it didn't matter, and to Wulfgar, Regis knew, it did not. He had returned a very different man, as if he had paid all of his tributes and done everything correctly in his previous existence and so was on this second journey through life on a lark.

"Heartbreaker," the halfling chided.

"Not so. I do not lie to any of them. They know I won't be there with the sunrise."

"You make no promises?"

"I speak the truth of it. Then the choice is theirs."

"Why?" Regis asked sincerely, and that turned Wulfgar to face him directly. "Do you not wish to find love?"

"I find it all the time."

"Not just physical love!"

"I know," said Wulfgar. "I seek pleasure in this life, wherever I might find it. I've no desire for a hearth or home, or any family in the expected manner. There's too much to see and too much—and too many!—to know."

Regis stared at him for a long while, grinning and shaking his head. "Why Wulfgar," he said, "I do believe that your one regret will be in declining the dragon's romantic advances."

"We'll see both of them again," the barbarian said with a wink. He took his leave then, moving back into the tower to greet Captain Mallabie and the revelers who had come out beside her this cold and dark night.

Regis remained outside, staring off into the winter's dark, thinking of Donnola, imagining her warm arms around him once more, her soft lips against his. Wulfgar was wrong, and Ches was indeed a long, long time away. Far too long!

He blew into his hands and began his sentry circuit of the tower's battlement once more. It was the fifteenth of Nightal, the last month of the Year of the Nether Mountain Scrolls, and at that very moment, Gromph Baenre was casting a most mighty spell, one that would summon Demogorgon to his side and dangerously weaken the barrier of the magical Faerzress, allowing hordes of demons, even demon lords, to cross into Faerûn's Underdark.

# CHAPTER 2 ◈

# *Bloodstone Lands*

THEY THOUGHT HIM TOO OLD TO CONTINUE HIS BOWLEGGED patrol, for his beard was more gray than yellow now. Thus they had assigned him to the court of the King of Damara. He had served kings before, and so was not unaccustomed to the tedious trials of such a duty. But those had been dwarf kings, and never before had Ivan Bouldershoulder witnessed such a sheer display of inanity and foolishness as was a daily event here in the court of King Yarin Frostmantle.

Ivan had never been fond of King Yarin, and truly, in looking upon the man—balding and rat-faced, ever sniveling and hunched in a defensive crouch—it astounded Ivan to think that such a sinister and uncharismatic specimen could have claimed a throne.

But this was Helgabal, a city of merchants, and among the nobles here, wealth outshined all other qualities. Yarin Frostmantle had been the richest man in Damara before taking the throne—a throne left vacant some twenty-two years earlier when King Murtil Dragonsbane had died, quite suspiciously. Murtil's untimely death had ended the Dragonsbane line, the paladin kings who had ruled Damara in peace and prosperity for nearly a century—perhaps too much prosperity for too few individuals, Ivan often thought.

Yarin Frostmantle, the richest man in the region, one with a vast network of spies and private soldiers, had stepped into the void left by the demise of the childless bachelor

Murtil. Wealth had won the day, and Yarin Frostmantle had claimed the throne.

And through less-than-savory actions, Ivan assumed. Though he had come to this land after Yarin's ascent, he had, of course, heard the whispers.

Rumors that Yarin had murdered Murtil were nothing new in Helgabal, and the passage of time had done little to tamp down the whispers. Ivan didn't put too much stock in them, though he didn't doubt the possibility. He wasn't really invested in this land. It was true that he and his brother called Damara home now, but that was more because by the time they arrived here, after decades of wandering, the place seemed as good as any other.

He'd been rethinking that notion these past few tendays, though, as the hours dragged along in this court of ultimate pettiness.

King Yarin and his queen were holding open court, where anyone desiring the king's ear or judgment could, if time allowed, gain an audience with the noble couple. As usual, a crowd had gathered at the palace steps before dawn that morning, peasants falling all over each other in their desperate hopes to be heard.

The grievances were all too familiar to Ivan, for always did they follow the same course, or the same few storylines, at least.

King Yarin didn't even pretend to be interested as one poor farmer pointed a crooked finger at a neighbor and accused the man of stealing his chickens, which the other man denied, of course, or excused as "finders keepers," since the other farmer couldn't keep the birds on his own land.

"Split the eggs betwixt you!" Ivan mouthed even as King Yarin proclaimed it. The old dwarf had heard this verdict too many times to count, and of course, as soon as Yarin offered this wise solution, the nobles looking on broke into cheers and overwhelmed gasps at the king's infinite and divinely inspired wisdom. And so it went through the hours of tedium.

Ivan did perk up when a man and woman came forward, arm-in-arm, pushing a pretty young woman in front of them.

Their daughter, they explained, and she was with child by a rascal who had promised to marry her. That accused man, who was clearly not nearly as young as the daughter, protested with great animation and insult, and to many in the audience hall, it grew quite entertaining.

But Ivan kept his attention on King Yarin, and on the woman, many years Yarin's junior, who sat at his side. In the gossip of Helgabal, Queen Concettina was always described as beautiful, or pretty, or lithe, or other complimentary words, though she wasn't much for Ivan's tastes. The word "willowy," too, was often used in describing her, but Ivan was more of an "oaky" kind of dwarf—"a thick oak's trunk" might well describe the dwarf ladies that caught his fancy!

Willowy certainly seemed an apt description of Queen Concettina, though, the dwarf noted. She was very slender, looking much younger than her whispered age of twenty-five years. Her wrists and neck and fingers were all so long and so thin they gave rise to rumors that this one had a bit of elf blood in her, and though Ivan knew the queen denied those whispers, those features, along with blond hair that hung practically to her waist, certainly seemed wispy and fairy-like.

Perhaps she had a bit of wood nymph in her, the dwarf mused, grinning, then coughed to cover up a very inappropriate giggle. He tightened his halberd up close to his side, stood a bit straighter, and tried not to imagine Queen Concettina floating naked over the trees on dragonfly wings.

Ivan had perfected the art of sleeping on his feet, and it often got him through these interminably boring sessions. He'd never want to be a king, and doubted the citizens would ever want him there, for he'd get so bored with their nonsensical drama that he'd be tempted to execute them all just to shut them up!

That notion chased the dwarf's thoughts to the wicked device King Yarin kept in one of the gardens behind the palace, an instrument that the brutal man put to use quite often. It consisted of two rails with a crossbeam at the top, and a thick piece of wood at the base, notched with a curve that would fit a neck. Ivan had heard it called a "guillotine," and the dwarf thought it something far more appropriate for the hole of an orc king than for anyone leading a civilized race. He simply could not imagine a dwarf king, like his old companion Bruenor, ever using such a device.

To Ivan Bouldershoulder, if you couldn't look a man in the eye when ending his life, then you couldn't admit to yourself that the life needed to be ended.

It seemed even worse with King Yarin, who reportedly put this wicked guillotine to use quite arbitrarily, so it was whispered—and so Ivan believed.

Ivan had made it perfectly clear to Captain Andrus that he wanted no part of duty in that particular garden, going so far as to hint to the garrison commander that he'd not let an innocent man feel the pinch of that falling blade. Andrus respected the warrior dwarf enough to let that smattering of treason lie buried between them—and with good reason, for Ivan Bouldershoulder had proven himself repeatedly as one of the best soldiers in Helgabal. Whenever a new recruit entered the garrison, he or she was sent straight to Ivan for training.

No doubt, Captain Andrus thought he was doing Ivan a good turn by giving him this easy duty. Perhaps he should disavow the man of that, Ivan thought.

Indeed, that line of thought led him to an imaginary battlefield, where dwarven brigades clashed with ugly orcs while dragons screeched overhead . . .

The sound of Dwarvish voices brought the old dwarf from his contemplation, to see a gaggle of scraggly bearded, truly dirty little creatures standing before the king and queen. The lot of them looked as if they had just crawled out of a hole in the ground, and not a structured dwarven hole at that. And were they really dwarves at all, Ivan wondered. A couple of the fellows looked more like gnomes, or some strange crossbreed in between? They all had beards, though—scraggly, but full enough.

"Toofless!" insisted one hunched and crooked fellow.

"Toothless?" King Yarin asked, clearly at a loss.

"Toofless!" lisped the fellow, who wasn't quite toothless, but nearly so—and those choppers that remained were quite jagged and rotted, and every color but white.

"Aye, Toothless," said the king.

"Toofless! Toofless Tonguelasher!" the hunched dwarf insisted, and Ivan noted that the fellow's tongue did indeed remain outside of his toothless mouth, hanging off to the left and giving him very much the aspect of an old, panting dog. The other dwarves weren't any cleaner, either, or toothed, for that matter, and Ivan scrunched up his face with curiosity.

"Toofless, then," King Yarin conceded. He glanced to the side, to Captain Dreylin Andrus, and the man shrugged and shook his head, obviously trying to hold back a laugh. "And from what region of Helgabal, Master Tonguelasher?"

"Not fwom Heliogab . . .err, Helgabal," the dwarf replied, catching himself from using the old name of Damara's capital city, which had been banned by Yarin's decree. Toofless did chuckle a bit, though, at the sudden horrified look that came over King Yarin.

"Then where in Damara?" the impatient king demanded.

"Not really fwom Damara," said Toofless. "Not till just now, at least, when me clan burrowed right thwough the Galenas to put a new door to our home. A door in Damara."

"You dug through the mountains? From Vaasa?"

"Aye, though we's more undegwound than in Vaasa, and not sure which side o' the line down there in them tunnels, eh? Might that we been yer citizens fer all time and not knowing it!"

"Undegwound . . . what?" an exasperated King Yarin asked. He looked around, his gaze at last settling on Ivan, the only dwarf sentry in attendance. "What is he talking about?"

Ivan had never heard a dialect quite akin to this one's, even discounting the obvious lisp. "This clan . . . Tonguelasher?" Ivan asked of the dwarf.

"Bigger!" Toofless proclaimed.

"Bigger'n Tonguelasher?" Ivan asked, not understanding.

"Just Bigger!" Toofless insisted, and all the dwarves behind him shouted "Bigger!" and pumped their fists in the air.

"Clan Bigger?"

The dirty dwarf flashed what passed for a smile and nodded.

Ivan snorted to steady himself. "The Clan Bigger," he explained to King Yarin, "they been living mostly in their caves—likely a mine, and seems a big one if they come through the Galenas—for a long, long time's me guess. Now they come out, and in Damara."

"In a land of which they know nothing?" King Yarin asked, looking from Ivan to Toofless and back again.

"That one knowed the old name for Helgabal," Ivan reminded the king. "So they be knowin' something o' the place afore they climbed out."

"Aye, we're knowin' the pwace, or what was, and wantin' to be again," Toofless said.

King Yarin fixed him with a stern look.

"If ye're havin' us, I'm sayin'," Toofless went on, nodding, which made his tongue flap out the side of his mouth. "And not to worry, kingie, for we're knowin' our pwace. At yer pweasure, good sir."

"And if it is not my pweas . . . my pleasure?"

Toofless flashed his ridiculous grin and glanced back at his boys, two of whom hustled up, bearing a small chest. They put it down on the floor in front of Toofless, bobbed several bows the king's way, then rushed back to their fellows.

"We ain't comin' as beggars, King," Toofless explained. "But as good subjects." He bent low and flipped the catch on the chest, rolling back the lid as he stood once more.

Gold and jewels glittered, and Queen Concettina gasped and brought a hand to her lips so that any who could not directly view the chest merely had to look at the reflection in Concettina's eyes.

"We're knowin' our pwace, good king sir," Toofless said. 'And we're hopin' ye'll let that pwace be yer kingdom o' Damara."

King Yarin tried to remain calm, but Ivan could see that the scruffy little creatures of Clan Bigger had bought their way in. Yarin motioned for a couple of guards to retrieve the chest and shuffle it off to the side.

"There is more where that came from, I am sure?" King Yarin asked.

"Course. Good mine."

"Then I look forward to your next visit, my new subjects of Clan . . . Bigger?"

"Aye, bigger'n ye're thinking!" Toofless replied with a laugh. He bowed and began backing away. When he reached his friends they too began to bob and back up, until the whole lot of them exited the palace.

King Yarin looked to Ivan, as if seeking some explanation, but the yellow-bearded dwarf could only shrug and shake his head

◆ ◆ ◆

IVAN SWISHED HIS spoon around in the bowl of stew, trying to identify the vegetables and roots that popped up through the thick green base.

"Ain't natural," he muttered, as he did almost every night. He lifted one large spoonful to his lips and slurped it in. "Bah, ain't natural," he said again.

"Hee hee hee," came the reply from the green-bearded, one-armed dwarf moving around in the cramped kitchen.

It had become a ritual in the Bouldershoulder house, a squat stone building on the southern edge of Helgabal. The place was windowless, and dark in this section late in the day, the way Ivan liked it. It reminded him of the dwarven kingdoms he had called home in his earlier days. The entire back of the house was open, though. His brother, Pikel, had broken out the stones to construct a walled garden to the place.

And what a garden it was! Full, leafy stalks climbed the stone walls and fruits and vegetables and nuts and beans weighed down the vines, offering a variety of aromas not found anywhere else in this part of the world. The garden was part green thumb and part druidic magic—mostly magic—and so every night, Ivan was treated to a new mish-mash of beans and nuts and fruits and vegetables and roots and whatever else Pikel decided to create on that particular day.

It wasn't natural, as the dwarf often complained, but for all his grumping, Ivan couldn't deny that the meals were delicious!

"Strange bunch o' buggers," Ivan remarked, going back to the previous conversation. "Dirtier than a Gutbuster, most without teeth, and not a bit o' mail or armor or jewels on 'em—and that when they come to court a king!"

"Hmm," answered Pikel, who wasn't much for words.

"And Clan Bigger," Ivan huffed. "Clan *Bigger*! Who'd be callin' themselves Clan Bigger?"

"Dugers?" Pikel asked, his way of referencing "duergar," the gray dwarves known to haunt the Underdark—no kin or friends of Delzoun dwarves like Ivan and Pikel.

"Nah," Ivan said, and he slurped a few spoons of the marvelous stew. "Not grays, nor derro. Dwarfs, but a strange-lookin' bunch. First I thinked 'em gnomes, but too much a beard for gnomes. Aye, strange-soundin' bunch."

A loaf of bread came flying from across the room. Ivan caught it and nearly fell off his chair in the process.

"Hee hee hee."

Ivan huffed and blew on the bread, which had come right out of the oven. He tossed it from hand to hand, puffing on the loaf and his fingers alternately, much to the amusement of Pikel.

Finally he controlled it and got it down beside his plate, then tore off a hunk and plopped it into the stew. It came up on his spoon covered in beans. Ivan stuffed the whole monstrous bite into his mouth.

His lips were still smacking when there came a loud rap on the door.

"Hmm," said Pikel.

"Master Ivan!" sounded a familiar voice, followed by a more insistent rapping on the door.

Ivan belched and pulled himself from his chair, nearly tripping on it as he swung around for the door, and in that stumble he let fly a tremendous fart.

"Hee hee hee," said Pikel, the Prince of Bean Stew, who took that as the highest of compliments.

Ivan pulled open the door, and there stood Captain Dreylin Andrus, commander of Helgabal's garrison.

"Aye, Captain," Ivan said.

"May I?" Andrus asked, motioning for the room.

"Aye." Ivan moved aside. "Pikel, another bowl, what!"

"What!" said a happy Pikel, hustling for a third bowl.

"Ye're knowin' me brother, eh?" Ivan asked the captain.

"Me brudder!" yelled Pikel, and that brought a grin to the captain's face.

"Aye, soldier," he said. "He's been working the palace gardens."

"Hee hee, kingie!" Pikel cried.

"Well, we've plenty o' good gruel for ye, so sit and burp with us a bit," said Ivan.

To Ivan's surprise, Andrus accepted, and as the sun set on Helgabal, the three of them sat around the small table in the Bouldershoulder home, enjoying the fine bounty of Pikel's extraordinary garden.

"And to what're we owin' this honor?" Ivan asked soon after. "If ye've come for good food and better tales, know that ye're in the right house! But aye, there's more, I'm guessin'."

"I cannot deny the fine food and hospitality," Andrus agreed. "Perhaps I'm far too long in coming to see you here, good dwarf."

"Me brudder!" Pikel said happily, and Andrus smiled widely.

"But it's them dwarfs, aye?" Ivan asked.

Andrus's face went somber. "You didn't know them, it seemed."

"Ne'er heared o' them," Ivan confirmed. "Clan Bigger?"

"Hee hee hee."

"No one has, as far as I can tell," Andrus explained, casting a sidelong glance at the green-bearded dwarf.

Pikel, used to such looks, beamed more brightly.

"They have promised to return," Andrus explained.

"I seen the chest o' jewels and gold."

"Oooo," said Pikel.

"I'm guessin' King Yarin's not for tellin' them no," Ivan finished.

Captain Andrus shrugged, not about to disagree. "We will get more warning next time they come in," he explained. "They will be held out by the wall, and there, you will go to them, and escort them."

"And get 'em talkin'," Ivan replied, catching on.

"Anything we can learn," said Andrus. "King Yarin will be pleased indeed to add a clan of rugged dwarves to his subjects."

"And to his army," Ivan reasoned.

"Boom!" said Pikel.

"Do you find their story believable?" Andrus asked with another sidelong glance at the curious one-armed dwarf.

"What, that they been walking in circles underground and only now come up for air? Aye, heared many a tale akin to that afore. Mirabar's half dwarfs, and half o' them ain't been aboveground in a hunnerd years. Many's the clan just not wantin' such things."

"We're guessing they took to the depths in the time of Zhengyi," Captain Andrus explained, referring to the witch-king who had long ago ruled the neighboring kingdom of Vaasa and who had ravaged the land with his army of monsters and flights of dragons.

"Aye, good time to hide under a mountain, I'm thinkin'," said Ivan, who knew well the tale.

"Did they not impress you as a bit strange?" Andrus asked.

"More'n a bit!"

"Hee hee hee," said Pikel.

"Aye, and I know strange," an exasperated Ivan said.

"So we should watch them closely," said Andrus. "And we understand each other?"

"Aye."

"And do see if you can clean them up a bit before they are presented to the king."

"Aye . . . what? Nay!" said Ivan, and a puzzled Andrus stared at him.

"Worse thing ye can do," Ivan explained, "is to be offerin' a tunnel rat dwarf a bath."

"Oooo," said Pikel.

"And that clan's tunnel rats, to be sure," Ivan explained.

Captain Andrus grinned. "Well, do what you can. Make of them friends, and learn what they have to say. Then report to me."

"Aye," Ivan started to reply, but he was cut short.

"Uh-uh," Pikel said, waggling his finger and shaking his head.

Captain Andrus scrunched up his face and looked from Pikel to Ivan, at a loss.

"He's tellin' ye that ye're comin' to me for me report," Ivan explained. "Back here for a pot o' stew." He ended with a tremendous burp.

"Boom!" said Pikel, and Captain Andrus laughed, agreed, and Pikel farted.

"Hee hee hee."

◆ ◆ ◆

FIVE DAYS' MARCH west-northwest of Helgabal, Toofless Tonguelasher and his band of dirty dwarves came to the rocky passes into the wall of mountains called the Galenas, which separated Damara from the wilder lands of Vaasa.

The troupe climbed late into the night of that fifth day, following small trails they had carefully and secretly marked on their earlier descent.

Under a full moon, they came to a flat, wide stone, and Toofless went out onto it holding a torch and waving his arms. In the multitude of rocky bluffs above loomed sentries wielding crossbows that would launch him halfway back to Helgabal in his current diminutive state.

"Aye, Toofless," a voice boomed down at him. "Ye been to see the fancy king, then?"

"Aye, and what a pretty pair o' things he and his queen be," Toofless replied.

"No troubles?"

"None."

"So we be Damarans now, do we? Loyal dwarflings fer the fancy king," the loud voice answered.

"Aye, and he'll prolly put us in his army—might to roll o'er Vaasa, eh?" said another resonating voice, and the comment brought an explosion of laughter from the high places around the flat stone and from Toofless and his band, who came forth to join him in the open.

"Ye gots a vis'tor comin'," the first unseen sentry called.

"Her again?"

"Aye, I'm guessin'."

Toofless looked at his companions and shrugged, and they did likewise. They weren't happy about having that type in their home, of course, but she had brought them fine payment of gold and jewels for the last load of bloodstone, after all, and said she'd be back with more precious pieces this time.

"Well, push the stone out and let me in," Toofless called up, and barely had the words left his mouth before a massive boulder began to shudder and shift, revealing the dark entrance to a deep passageway, the entrance to a place called Smeltergard.

In went Toofless, the others close behind. Before they had gone twenty paces down the corridor, the massive stone shifted back into place behind them, sealing the cave.

"Taller halls!" one of the band complained many steps later. "Feel like I'm to bust through me head 'ere!"

"Aye, been too long," said another. "Too long!"

"We stay small for the drow, eh?" Toofless ordered to a chorus of groans. The dwarf leader sighed in reply. He, too, felt the itching. It had been a full tenday and more, after all.

"Come on, then, but fer this night alone!" he said, turning down a side corridor. The others cheered.

The band soon came into the first of a series of chambers, wide and spacious and with high ceilings. There they began to shed their clothing and armor, and their boots—these weren't the magical suits they usually wore. They wouldn't bring that trove into Helgabal with them.

Toofless was the first to get naked. He fell back against the wall and sighed again, and fell deep within himself to call upon his familiar magic.

He began to shudder, to jolt and gurgle, his bones crackling, tendons popping—and every one eliciting a groan of pain. But it was sweet pain, because he knew where it would end.

Finally, he sighed again, this one a sigh of relief. He pulled himself off the wall to consider his companions, many of whom were very near the completion of their own transformations.

Toofless, now more than twelve feet tall and looking very much like a tall and thin hill giant, nodded to each of his fellow spriggans as they came back to their more comfortable forms.

"Feelin' good to stretch," said Komtoddy, perhaps the best fighter in the clan.

"Aye," Grommbollus agreed. "How long we gots?"

"Wouldn't mind a nap in this skin," Komtoddy said.

"No nap," said Toofless. "Put up a beat and we'll dance a few jigs, then down to the meetin' woom with the wot o' us."

"Bah and snorts," Grommbollus said.

"Well, any not wantin' in on the talk can go take watch back outside," Toofless conceded, and that brought some claps and cheers. Komtoddy picked up a couple of heavy stones and began drumming on the heavy wooden door at the back of the chamber. The spriggan giants began to dance, kicking up their heels and leaping around, a ghastly sight for any cultured onlooker, particularly since the hairy and dirty creatures still wore no clothes.

◆ ◆ ◆

"MOST DISAGREEABLE LITTLE creatures, even for dwarves," Queen Concettina said to King Yarin when the two retired to their private quarters that same starlit night.

"Them again?" Yarin asked with obvious exasperation, and he added some response that sounded more like a dismissive "harrumph" than anything else, and waved his arm in the air, never looking back at the queen.

"But the jewels were well-cut, I am told, and one can never have enough gold, I suppose," she said, again with a slight titter in her voice. She didn't really care much for gold, they both knew, and they already had all the luxuries they could enjoy, and more.

King Yarin swung around and fixed her with a cold stare.

"And soldiers!" she blurted, misreading his obvious disdain. "Dwarves do make fine soldiers, from all that I have heard . . ."

"I care nothing for that which you might have heard, good lady," Yarin replied.

Concettina swallowed hard and bit back any impulsive response. So they were back to this again? She looked around, feeling trapped at that moment, then sought the only escape she knew and shrugged off her queenly robe. Only the offer of hope could assuage Yarin when he was in one of these moods. She began untying her decorated gown.

"The chest of gems and jewels does so excite me," she lied.

Yarin snorted at her derisively.

"Perhaps this time . . ." Concettina started to say.

"This time?" Yarin roared back at her. "This time? Why would this time be any different than the hundred before? How many years has it been, foolish woman? Bah!"

He pulled the crown from his head and threw it across the room, then spun away from her, his hands going petulantly to his hips.

"Is every woman in this accursed land barren, then?" he lamented, and that wasn't his true frustration, of course, but one that hit him much more to the heart of the matter. Concettina was King Yarin's seventh queen. He had divorced his first four after they had failed to produce an heir, though two of them, at least, were later rumored to have borne children to new husbands.

All of which had further embarrassed King Yarin, of course, and so his last two wives before Concettina had not been so fortunate. One was found guilty of treason, the other of murdering a baby in her bed. Neither charge held any substance, so said the rumors of court.

Their true crimes had been the inability to give King Yarin his heir, and their punishment exacted to make certain the monarch would not be further embarrassed by their subsequent relationships . . . and children.

He had memorialized those last two queens in the form of headless statues in two of the palace gardens. Indeed, the guillotine had been built specifically for Driella, Concettina's predecessor, after the beheading of his fifth wife had been botched, the headsman's axe striking a bit too low and so getting stuck on the poor, screaming woman's spine.

When the wind blew through the gardens in just a certain way, Concettina thought she could still hear the echoes of those agonized, dying screams.

"I will never bear you a child if we do not try," Concettina said, fighting back tears. "And you enjoy the trials, I daresay, so is it such a terrible thing that we must work harder?"

She dared to move over and put her hand on her husband's shoulder. She felt him tense under her grip, but he didn't yell at her, or even swing around to glare at her again. She began to gently knead his old shoulders, and gradually, he relaxed.

Soon after, she was able to coax him into her bed. She held no illusions that they would conceive, of course, but she had to maintain in King Yarin some measure of hope, at least.

She tried to keep the image of the blood-stained guillotine out of her thoughts as he rode her.

And she dearly hoped that her father, Lord Corrado Delcasio of Aglarond, would receive her letter and would find some way to help her.

Even that thought gave her pause, though. Penning the letter was tantamount to treason, and could she really trust anyone to deliver it half a thousand miles away?

That image of the bloody guillotine filled her thoughts as King Yarin shuddered above her.

◆ ◆ ◆

MANY HOURS LATER, Komtoddy and Toofless, back in their diminutive dwarf forms, sat on blocks of stone in front of a slender drow priestess who wore a fitted garb of some translucent material that resembled the work of an industrious, lecherous spider. Indeed, very little was left to the imagination of the spriggans, but their imaginations, one and all, were more fixated on the small coffers their visitor had placed on the floor at her feet than on the obvious charms of the seductive drow.

"Lady Chawwi," Toofless greeted.

Charri Hunzrin, First Priestess of House Hunzrin, nodded and replied, "Good dwarf."

"What have you brought for us this time, dwow? Your chest looks smaller."

Charri laughed and considered the small coffer at her feet. "Just two pieces this time," she explained, "but ones of extraordinary value."

"Bah, a bauble's a bauble."

Charri Hunzrin bent low and lifted the coffer. She turned to the dark elves around her, all of them wearing knowing grins and nodding as if this was some important revelation.

"I will require two tons of bloodstone in return for these, good dwarf," she said.

"Two *tons*?" Toofless balked. "Ye best be showin' me a weapon full o' dwow murder magic fer that!"

"Oh, this is a weapon, do not doubt," Charri Hunzrin replied. She moved forward and slowly lifted the cover from the coffer, revealing a pair of gem-studded necklaces, one delicate and beautiful on a silver chain, the other heavy with large and varied gemstones held by an ostentatious chain of gold.

Toofless shrugged. Unlike dwarves, the spriggan weren't overly fascinated by gems and jewels. Of course, Toofless thought, Charri didn't really know the truth of Clan Bigger, though, did she?

"Looks like a pwetty thing," he said. "Should be on yer own neck, eh? Yerself likes pwetty things."

"I do, but there is nothing pretty about these," Charri said, snapping the coffer shut as Toofless reached for the gems. "The smaller of them, at least."

The spriggan dwarf looked from his nearly snapped fingers to the drow priestess. "Looks pwetty," he replied, confused.

"You went to greet the king?" Charri asked.

"Clan Bigger o' Damara," Toofless happily replied.

"And you wish to serve this human?"

Toofless spat on the floor at her feet, a long green wad of disgusting sputum.

"So your goal is not to be good citizens of Damara, then?"

"Ye might not be as stupid as ye wook," Toofless replied.

"Then what is your goal here, good dwarf?"

"To not get taken for a fool by a damned dwow!" said a suddenly animated Toofless.

"Not here," the drow replied, indicating the room. "What is your goal in Damara? Why did you and your people decide to tunnel out of the Galenas?"

"Bored," Komtoddy remarked, and others nodded.

"Looking for adventure and a bit of a fight?" Charri Hunzrin asked. "Looking for fun?"

"Said as much," said Toofless.

"Well these necklaces will give you all the fun you could ever desire," Charri replied. From her pocket, she pulled another gemstone and tossed it to Toofless. The spriggan dwarf held it up to his good eye and studied it carefully for a few moments before shrugging.

"Nuttin' special," he said.

"Oh, but it is."

"Bad cut."

"Doesn't matter."

"So says yerself."

"It is not the appearance of the gem that matters, good dwarf, but that which it might hold," Charri explained.

"Hold?" Toofless and Komtoddy asked together.

Charri brought forth the coffer again and opened it. She pointed to a gem on the more delicate necklace within, one that very much resembled the gemstone Toofless held in his hand. Noting that, the dwarf reached out, but again, Charri snapped the box shut.

"Oh, do not touch it, good dwarf," the drow priestess explained. "For the gem on the necklace is not empty, like the one you are holding."

"Empty? What?"

"Deliver these to the king, as gifts for him and his pretty queen," Charri instructed. "Then, my friend, you will find some fun. Grand fun!"

Toofless and Komtoddy exchanged looks and nods. "Okiedokes, then, dwow," said Toofless. "We'll see yer fun and then figger what it's worth in bloodstone, eh?"

"Two tons," Charri Hunzrin insisted.

"We'll be seein'."

"I already know, and that is the price."

"And if it's not that worth o' fun?" Komtoddy asked.

"Oh, it will be, but if not, then you can argue again when next I return," Charri Hunzrin replied.

"Sounds like ye'll be takin' our bloodstone and running off fer yer deep tunnels to me."

"Then you are a fool," the drow replied, and turned back to Toofless. "I expect a long and mutually beneficial relationship here in trade. It isn't in my interest to put off my best supplier of bloodstone, now is it? How many in the region mine the stuff these days? And nowhere else in Faerûn can it be found!"

"Others dig the stuff," said Toofless.

"Others who would bargain with drow?"

"She's got herself a point," said Komtoddy.

Toofless regarded him for a bit then nodded. "Two tons, dwow Chawwi," he told Charri Hunzrin. "For now. Ye got the haulers?"

"I do."

Toofless motioned for the coffer, but Charri held it back.

"Do not touch the necklaces," she warned.

"Bah," snorted Toofless, motioning again.

"I am serious, good dwarf," she said. "Deadly serious—and by that, I mean your own death."

"Are ye thweatenin' me?" Toofless demanded, coming forward.

"I am telling you that that which is pretty is also deadly, and in a most profound sense."

"Poison?"

Charri Hunzrin scoffed. "Only the person caught by the gem will know it," she explained. "To those around her . . . well, they will merely think their friend lost to a foul mood, if they suspect anything at all. They will never connect it to the necklace, and by the time they even realize the change, it will be too late—for her and for them."

The dwarves both frowned, and Toofless held up the empty gemstone again.

The empty phylactery, he realized, and a wicked smile began to spread over his face.

"Two tons does not seem so steep a price now, does it?" Charri Hunzrin asked.

# Chapter 3 ◈

# *Homecoming?*

DWARVEN HAMMERS RANG OUT IN BRILLIANT CADENCE, A team of industrious Mirabar boys chip-chipping carefully at the stone in the lava-sealed anteroom, taking great pains to not strike the lever controlling the flow of water elementals into the primordial pit.

Another team, this one of former Felbarran dwarves, worked on the bridge spanning the pit, turning the makeshift walkway into a permanent, solid structure once more.

Across the chasm and over by the embalming stone, where the drow altar had formerly sat, King Bruenor stood with hands on hips, watching the progress of the dwarven teams, but listening to the continuing argument raging around him among the principal wizards who were working on rebuilding the Hosttower of the Arcane.

"We'll need that spell, often and repeatedly!" the Shadovar woman named Lady Avelyere kept insisting, referring to some arcane enchantment to control elements, or some such.

Bruenor wasn't too concerned with the details, focusing more on the bigger picture, which meant that they, including—indeed, prompted by—Catti-brie, were planning to let the primordial out of its hole.

The dwarf king had argued against that strategy, of course. But in the end, he found that he had few other options, and none that would offer him any chance of long-term success here in Gauntlgrym. This plan involving the primordial was how they would, indeed the only way they could, rebuild—or regrow, as Catti-brie had put it—the Hosttower of the Arcane, and without that construction, everything else became a moot point. Without the magic of the Hosttower, the primordial would soon enough break free, without hindrance, and without any power in the world able to stop it.

Bruenor glanced over at the pit and could see the waves of heat radiating up with the steam as the swirling cadre of water elementals gave their all to contain the monster volcano. The wizards and priests wanted to stunt that safeguard, wanted Bruenor to pull the lever when the room was clear and all set in place up in Luskan. They would let the primordial escape, but just a bit, sending its power and heat and magical energy into the long underground tendrils and through them to the waiting trunk of the great structure of the Hosttower.

It sounded crazy to Bruenor, suicidal even. He wondered how long his fledgling kingdom would last if the primordial found a way around their designs.

"Directional barriers!" he heard Gromph declare. "Walls of magical force will corral the vomit of the primordial beast."

It sounded coherent to Bruenor, at least—until, of course, he considered the speaker, the Archmage of Menzoberranzan.

What could possibly go wrong?

"Hail and well met!" came a call from the room's door, and Bruenor turned to see Jarlaxle rushing in, his smile as wide as any Bruenor had ever seen.

"Truly?" an exasperated Catti-brie asked the mercenary, giving words to the expressions on all around the stone, for how could anyone interrupt this most important meeting in such a cavalier manner?

"Drizzt Do'Urden is returned!" Jarlaxle announced, and that dour and serious mood changed instantly to hearty cheers from the dwarves and from many of the wizards and priests—even the Shadovar contingent and the cloud giant.

But not from Gromph Baenre, Bruenor noted.

No sooner had Jarlaxle announced him than the drow ranger entered the chamber. He looked around curiously, and seemed about to scratch his head, when Catti-brie hit him with a flying hug. Drizzt dropped the bag he was carrying to the ground at his side, and slowly lifted his arms up to reciprocate.

"Do not ever leave me again," she whispered, and she squeezed him tighter with all of her considerable strength, and plastered him with a wet kiss. Others came up then, all patting the drow on the back. Bruenor was there, of course, pushing to the front.

"Me friend!" he said. "Ah, me friend! When Jarlaxle and them other two good-for-nothings came back without ye, well . . ." Bruenor stopped and shook his head, then he, too, launched himself into the hug with his adopted daughter and beloved companion.

Drizzt nodded at him and offered a weak smile.

"Elf?" Bruenor asked curiously. "Ye all right?"

"I am tired, my friend. So very tired."

"Well, we got a bed for ye, don't ye doubt!"

A chorus of huzzahs went up, or started to, but then faded fast when another, less-known drow walked into the room.

Gromph chewed his lip at the sight of Kimmuriel, but nodded his acceptance.

"I accompanied Drizzt up from Menzoberranzan," Kimmuriel explained to Bruenor and Catti-brie, both eyeing him suspiciously.

"He did," Drizzt confirmed. "And he brought me here with his . . . magic." As he finished Drizzt cast a glance Kimmuriel's way, and he couldn't hide all of the suspicion in that look. If he was being deceived—about everything!—as he feared, then he fully expected that Kimmuriel Oblodra, the renowned psionicist, was likely playing a role.

But what could he do?

He bent and grabbed his bag, just at the time Bruenor was going for it.

"Spoils of war," Drizzt explained, and rolled it up over his shoulder. He took Catti-brie's arm and she led him away, out of the chamber and to the complex's higher levels, where their hearth and bed awaited.

Bruenor watched them go, hands on hips, not even bothering to glance at Kimmuriel as the drow walked past him to join Jarlaxle and Gromph. The three whispered for a few moments while others returned to their work, but Bruenor just stood there, staring at the open doorway and the corridor that led to the Forge Room.

"He has been through a great trial," Jarlaxle said to the red-bearded dwarf, walking up to stand beside Bruenor, his own gaze following Bruenor's to the open doorway and beyond.

Bruenor didn't even turn his head to regard the clever mercenary.

"Good dwarf, what is it?" Jarlaxle asked.

Bruenor shook his head.

"Bruenor?" Jarlaxle asked, more insistently dropping a hand on the dwarf's shoulder, and finally, Bruenor did turn away from the empty wake of his dear friends to look the mercenary in the eye.

"Something's not right," he said.

"Drizzt has been . . ."

"Yeah, ye telled me as much already," the dwarf answered. "All about yer journey." And he turned back to the empty corridor.

"Not all," said Jarlaxle. He gave a little laugh. "Not nearly all, I fear." He, too, looked once more to the path the reunited couple had taken.

A moment later, Jarlaxle put his hand back on Bruenor's shoulder—neither was sure exactly why.

"There's something ye ain't tellin' me, elf," Bruenor said.

"He will be fine," Jarlaxle replied. "He is surrounded by friends now."

Bruenor looked up at the drow then, and couldn't miss the look of concern on Jarlaxle's face.

• • •

CATTI-BRIE ROLLED OVER to consider the dark elf sleeping beside her. They had not made love, surprisingly, for Drizzt had shown little interest. Or at least, he had not been eagerly receptive to her kisses and teasing touches.

She reached over and brushed the long white hair from off his face. Then she returned her fingers to his cheek and delicately ran her fingers about the angles of his delicate features. He didn't stir at all, and Catti-brie realized that this was probably the first true rest her husband had found in many days.

Though she knew that she had much work to do back in the primordial chamber, where momentous decisions had to be made, she spent a long, long time just lying there, staring at Drizzt, certain that she could not love another person more.

She was afraid for him. Like Bruenor, she had seen the trouble simmering in his lavender eyes. Something had come back with him from the Underdark, from Menzoberranzan.

At last, she rolled over and looked across the dimly lit room, to the bag Drizzt had placed by the sword rack. He had shown her the contents—the shield, sword, and armor of Tiago Baenre—and had told her that he didn't want them, that he had only taken them because they were mightily enchanted, and if he had left them behind, some other drow, likely some other Baenre, would take them up and cause even greater mischief.

Drizzt had assured her that there was no revenge planned against him for killing Tiago. The fight had been honorable and sanctioned by the highest priestesses of the city, and he had won, and so had then been chosen for some other task, one he promised to relate to her at a later time. Completion of that quest had bought freedom for Drizzt and his friends, and the priestess—Catti-brie wrongly assumed it to be the matron mother—had given to Drizzt these spoils, fairly won.

But Drizzt didn't want them. Of that, he was adamant.

Catti-brie slowly rolled out of the bed and padded on bare feet across the floor to the bag. She lifted a small shield from it. "Orbbcress," she whispered. Drizzt had told her of the remarkable item.

She slid it over her bare arm, and cast a minor dweomer to identify the types of magic contained within the mightily enchanted shield. And she could tell that it was a marvelous thing, crafted with great care and tactile perfection. She would need to study another spell that night to better identify the item, she thought, but barely had she considered the possibility when she unexpectedly came to understand much more. She closed her eyes. With a thought, she made the shield wrap itself tighter, and it became a small buckler.

She reversed the silent command and the shield spiraled outward, growing larger and larger.

The woman laughed—she couldn't help it—and glanced back to the bed with concern, not wanting to wake her beloved.

Catti-brie slid the shield off her arm and brought forth Vidrinath, the beautiful sword the master drow craftsman Gol'fanin had created in the Great Forge of Gauntlgrym.

And it was a beautiful creation, as fine as any weapon Catti-brie had ever held. She could feel the balance, the easy swing, the fine edge of the glassteel blade, translucent and full of tiny stars and with an edge that would never dull.

She shook her head. This sword should be in Drizzt's hands!

She felt no malice from it, as with the malignant blades Khazid'hea and Charon's Claw, but the magic here was at least equally strong, and the balance of the blade, the lightness, the edge, were all even finer. She looked back at Drizzt and shook her head.

He had won this sword, and as much as she loved Icingdeath and the damaged Twinkle, as much as those two blades had carried Drizzt through so many trials, this one was finer—indeed, this was the very blade that had so damaged Twinkle here in these very halls, when Drizzt had battled Tiago. This, Vidrinath, was the blade that had so weakened the integrity of Twinkle that Doum'wielle's subsequent strike with Khazid'hea had sheared the scimitar and passed right through Drizzt's block, cutting him brutally across his chest.

Catti-brie looked at her hand, at the ring Drizzt had given her, and her face twisted with puzzlement and she chewed her lip, trying to sort out a confusing epiphany.

Then she smiled. She had an idea, a perfectly clever and wonderful idea.

She replaced the sword in the sack, but removed it right away and set it instead on the weapon rack beside Drizzt's blades. Then she dressed and returned to the sack, and took from it the magnificent shield.

She looked at Drizzt one last time then headed back to the primordial chamber.

◆ ◆ ◆

"ARE YE SURE, girl?" Bruenor asked for the fiftieth time when he and Catti-brie crossed the Forge Room, heading for the Great Forge of Gauntlgrym, the one oven most completely and directly tied to the fire primordial. The hammers were silent now in the workroom, so early in the morning. The two yawning guards at the door had been ordered outside by the king, leaving him and his daughter alone in the place.

There were no torches in here, and no illuminating lichen or glow worms. There didn't need to be, for even when not in use, the furnaces offered an orange glow. This room was an extension of the primordial itself, a masterwork of dwarven engineering and powerful magic, an outlet for the hot breath of the primordial settled into the pit in the adjoining room.

"If I was no' sure, then I would no've bringed ye here," Catti-brie answered, so easily reverting to her Dwarvish brogue—and more so in this place, where the ancient language of Delzoun was becoming more commonplace every day. She moved up to the tray of the Great Forge and placed the shield called Orbbcress, or Spiderweb, upon it.

"Bah! But every mage's thinkin' that," Bruenor replied. "Not for doubtin' that Gromph was surer than yerself when he blowed up the Underdark!"

"I'm not Gromph, and to be sure, I'm not bein' tricked by a demon queen!"

"Aye, but by a fire god?" Bruenor asked slyly.

That gave Catti-brie pause, but only momentarily. It shocked her when she considered the truth of her denial, but the plain fact was that she had come to trust the fire primordial. It sounded crazy as she admitted that to herself—this was a beast, a volcano, that had not so long ago blown the top off the mountain above them and sent its fires and ash far to the south to destroy the city of Neverwinter. How might the burned and melted souls of that city respond to Catti-brie's professed trust in the beast, she wondered?

Even those realities didn't cast much doubt upon the woman, though. She trusted, not in the beast, but in her understanding of it, in what it wanted and what it could not have.

She held her hand out to Bruenor, but he gave her a smirk and reflexively dropped his left shoulder back.

"Ye're trustin' me to have ye pull the lever and let the primordial out, bit by bit, to rebuild the tower, but not for this?" she asked incredulously.

"This be personal," said Bruenor.

"Who made the shield?"

The simple question had Bruenor flustered. His prized shield, with the foaming mug standard of Clan Battlehammer emblazoned on the front, had been with him for most of his life. But Catti-brie, with this very forge, had made the buckler so much more. No sword, not even Khazid'hea's fine edge, could gash the shield. Bruenor was certain—and Catti-brie agreed with him—that it would hold back dragon's breath!

And the foaming mug shield offered one other thing that was not so small a deal for the dwarf king. To remind his daughter of that, he pulled it around in front of him, closed his eyes for a moment, then reached behind the buckler and produced a mug of ale, a gift from the shield. He looked at Catti-brie and let his own expression show her that he feared this might be the last time his shield could bestow such a gift to him!

This conjuring magic had supplied all the drink for the solemn Rite of Kith'n'Kin that had bound the various dwarven communities under this one roof. To Bruenor, this magical facet of the shield was much more than a way to get a bit of mead, or ale, or beer foam on his beard.

He began to slide the shield from his arm, but hesitated. "I'm not for understanding," he said, shaking his head.

"It's the best gift o' the Forge, I tell ye," Catti-brie insisted.

"But which're ye givin' to which?"

Catti-brie considered the question for a moment, looking from Orbbcress to Bruenor's foaming mug shield. It was an important question, but it had no definitive answer that she could relate. Each of the items was imbued with several magical properties, and so choices might have to be made as to which to keep and which to expel. But were those to be her choices, or would the beast that fed the Forge's firepot decide?

And what if the primordial picked wrong? The notion that Bruenor's shield might lose its ability to produce the "dwarven holy water" was not a comforting thought to Catti-brie, either, after all.

Catti-brie took the shield from Bruenor and tentatively placed it on the tray beside Orbbcress. She took a deep breath and closed her eyes—she wasn't sure how to begin.

She let her thoughts flow into the magical ring on her finger, and wound them through the ring, glancing into the white hot flame in the shielded firepot, hotter than any peat fire, or coal, or even coke fire, or a wizard's fireball. Hotter than anything that was not of the Elemental Plane of Fire.

Her spirit began drifting toward those flames, that finger of the primordial.

She felt a strong hand on her forearm and she opened her eyes to see a horrified Bruenor staring at her.

"Ye gone bats, girl?" he asked.

Catti-brie looked at him curiously.

"Ye were puttin' yer hand into the damn oven!" Bruenor shook his head, his expression one of disgust. He mumbled, "Whole durn world's gone crazy," and reached for his shield.

Catti-brie grabbed him by the arm and pulled him back, and waved him aside.

"If ye see me in pain, then pull me out," she said, scolding him. "But if not, then ye know yer place, me Da, and yer place is to the side and with yer big mouth shut!"

"Bah!" Bruenor snorted, stepping back as if he had been slapped. "Fine way ye be talkin' to yer king."

"Bah!" Catti-brie echoed.

"And better way ye be talkin' to yer Da!" Bruenor retorted.

"And only way to be talkin' to a durned fool!" Catti-brie shot back. "Are we doin' this or ain't we doin' this? Ye said ye wanted it, but if ye do no', then I'll find me another, don't ye doubt!"

"I'm wantin' what ye said I'd be gettin', but I'm not wantin' me girl to stick her hand into the mouth o' the damned fire beast!"

"I been down in the pit with the thing," Catti-brie admitted, and Bruenor's mouth fell open.

"What?" Bruenor managed to whisper.

"Me Da, trust me," Catti-brie implored him.

"Ye didn't reach in last time ye worked on me shield and axe. Aye, but ye used a poker, like any smart smithy, eh? And ye had on the fire gloves, didn't ye?"

"This is . . . different," Catti-brie said, looking back to the enticing, alluring white fires within the oven of the Great Forge of Gauntlgrym.

"Ye're goin' to melt yer durn hand off!"

Catti-brie shook her head, never taking her eyes from the flames, and the confidence that came over her was reflected so clearly in her expression that Bruenor did indeed back off.

Catti-brie's spirit moved back for the white hot fires again. She felt the magic of the Forge, heard the voice of the primordial. She opened her hand wide just in front of the flames, and echoing through the ring, she heard more clearly.

Into the oven went Orbbcress, the magnificent shield forged by the drow master craftsman Gol'fanin in this very place.

Catti-brie paused for a long while, and in her mind, she saw the shield in an entirely new way. Images of its various components—the spiraling bars, the webs, the soft but impossibly strong material floated in her mind's eye like separate magic spells waiting to be cast.

Without opening her eyes, without releasing the images of Orbbcress's enchantments, Catti-brie worked her other hand back to the tray and found Bruenor's shield. No longer did she harbor any doubts, and so she brought the shield forward and into the oven without hesitation.

The enchantments of Bruenor's shield, too, came clear to her, swirling with Orbbcress's. Many floated separately, distinct.

"And . . ." Catti-brie whispered.

The material of Bruenor's shield faded in and out of her mind's eye with the softer webbing of Orbbcress, and Catti-brie understood a choice that needed to be made—a choice that she, not the primordial, would make.

"Or . . ." she whispered. She smiled and cast a powerful spell, one the primordial had shown to her.

She waved her fingers, still just outside the white flames that now engulfed the two shields. She could feel the heat, so intense, but it did not hurt her and instead warmed her to her very heart. There was a beauty here almost beyond her comprehension, another form of existence all together, as eternal as the gods . . . nay, as the stars.

She found herself grateful to the primordial, humbled that this immortal being of near unimaginable power, and of such universal intelligence, was welcoming her. She knew again that this godlike being could have so easily consumed her in the pit when she had gone to retrieve Charon's Claw for Jarlaxle. And it could melt her now, with hardly an effort. Her hand was so close, was inside the protective magical barrier of the Forge, exposed to the bite of the primordial if the beast so chose.

She was naked in front of the godlike creature, and was not consumed only because it did not want to consume her.

Instead it wanted to use her, to teach her, to find some sort of magical release through her.

A long time later, Catti-brie opened her eyes and stepped back from the Forge. She was covered in sweat, and fully exhausted, and had to lean on the tray for support and breathe deeply to keep herself from falling into darkness.

And Bruenor was there beside her, holding her, calling to her. "Girl? Girl?"

After a few steadying breaths, Catti-brie managed to open her eyes, and open her lips into a wide smile.

"What'd ye do?" Bruenor asked solemnly.

Catti-brie shrugged and shook her head, and that was an honest answer. It had all been beyond her understanding, beyond her mortal comprehension. It was a beautiful thing, an amazing glimpse into immortality that had touched her so profoundly that it was all she could manage to keep from giggling like a charmed child.

She motioned to the tongs hanging on the side of the table, an instrument as heavily enchanted as the greatest weapons in Faerûn. Any normal metal going to this fire pit would be consumed almost immediately, but these tongs had been constructed and enchanted at the time of the creation of this place.

Bruenor put on the heavy gloves hanging beside the tool and took up the tongs. Squinting against the white glare, he poked the tongs into the flames and felt around. His surprise became quite clear when he found not two shields but one.

"What'd ye do, girl?" he asked again, hesitantly, and he slowly began to pull back the tongs.

There on the tray lay his shield, but not his shield. The foaming mug standard remained, shining like silvery mithral now, with the foam milky white. It wasn't just an image now, but a bas relief. The shield upon which it sat seemed familiar, and yet different, for now Bruenor could see within the metal and ironwood, the etchings of filaments, a beautiful, symmetrical spider web.

He dared touch it with his gloved hand, then looked at it curiously and pulled off his gloves.

"Ain't hot?" he asked as much as stated.

Catti-brie simply smiled. She couldn't yet find the strength to speak.

Bruenor picked up his new shield. "So light," he said. Then, his face alarmed, he slid it over his shield arm then fumbled about only to breathe a great sigh of relief as he produced a foaming mug of dark golden ale with a smooth and frothy head spilling over the side.

Bruenor stared through the translucent glass, his smile widening with every bubble that floated up to reinforce the head.

He brought the glass to his lips and took a hearty swig, covering half his beard with the white foam. His nod affirmed his approval.

"Feels the same, makes the same, looks . . ." Bruenor paused and took a closer look at the shield, tracing the spidery lines with his finger. "Looks a bit different," he said, nodding and not wearing any sour expression of disapproval. "What else did ye do then, girl?"

"Perhaps we will learn together," Catti-brie replied, somewhat absently, for her thoughts remained with the Art of the crafting, for it was a level of magical manipulation she had never before experienced, not even when crafting a buckle-bow out of Taulmaril for Drizzt.

And she was looking ahead, for another challenge was strong in her thoughts, and she very much intended to return to the Great Forge that very night.

◆ ◆ ◆

WITH THE HELP of Kimmuriel, it didn't take Jarlaxle long to get back to his tavern, One-Eyed Jax, back in Luskan, and the mercenary leader set Kimmuriel to work immediately on this most important task. Outside the room where Kimmuriel was busily entering Dahlia's thoughts, Jarlaxle and Artemis Entreri waited, the assassin pacing anxiously.

"I have never seen you like this, my friend," Jarlaxle said.

Entreri turned to him, glowering.

"What?" the mercenary drow asked innocently. "Have I not done as you asked? And at great personal risk?"

Entreri stopped his pacing and stared at the drow. "I would say that it is the least you could do."

"Are we back to that?"

"Were we ever not?"

"I had no choice," Jarlaxle said quietly.

"I spent decades as a slave to Lord Alegni!"

"You would have been murdered, likely, had I not . . ."

"I would have preferred that!"

"Truly?" Jarlaxle asked him. "After all you've been through, after rescuing Dahlia, you wish that I had let you die a century ago?"

"I wish that a man I considered a friend had not so betrayed me," Entreri replied.

"I made you a king!" Jarlaxle said with flourish. "Artemis Entreri, King of Vaasa!" He smiled as he finished the pronouncement—the same pronouncement that had nearly gotten the pair slain by the legendary Gareth Dragonsbane, the King of Damara, a long, long time before.

But Entreri was not joining in with that mirth.

"I tried to help you," Jarlaxle said more somberly.

"You saved yourself," Entreri accused.

"Of course! So that I could continue to work for your release."

"You saved yourself. You betrayed me to save yourself."

"I saved Calihye," Jarlaxle replied, and that set Entreri back on his heels. Calihye had been the first woman to steal Entreri's heart, a fellow rogue from the Bloodstone Lands, and she was stolen from him by the dark elves.

By Jarlaxle's dark elves.

Entreri, angry, stuttered, trying to find a response.

"She would have killed you," Jarlaxle reminded him, for indeed, the half-elf had attacked Entreri in a fit of rage. And in that dangerous encounter Entreri had thrown her through the window of their room, into an alley, where he had left her for dead.

But the action, the entire tragic encounter, had broken Entreri's heart. This black-haired, blue-eyed half-elf had stolen his heart—she was the first woman he had ever loved. He could hear her voice, then, in his thoughts, that lisp he had found so endearing the result of a battle scar.

"Kimmuriel saved her—we saved her," Jarlaxle explained. "We gave her back her hope and her life. Indeed, Kimmuriel worked with her in much the same way he now works with Dahlia in the adjoining room. And she lived a long life, my friend."

Entreri looked at him curiously, and Jarlaxle nodded.

"She is still alive, I expect," Jarlaxle admitted. "She is not so old for a half-elf."

Entreri's knees went weak. "You only now tell me this?" he asked, spitting every word with incredulity and outrage.

"I cannot be certain."

"Bregan D'aerthe had her! A slave!"

"No!" Jarlaxle shot back. "We had her not for long, and never a slave."

"I witnessed it! I killed those Bregan D'aerthe drow who brought her to Memnon."

"I gave you those drow—they were simply orcs transformed for the event—so that you would find some time with Calihye," Jarlaxle explained.

Entreri's expression showed that he was hardly convinced.

"And then she left," Jarlaxle said. Entreri had freed her and he and Calihye had spent several tendays together in the Calishite city of Memnon, but then, one morning, Entreri had awakened to find himself once more alone.

"You took her, you mean, when you guided the Netherese to me."

"I took her," Jarlaxle admitted. "As was her desire. She cared not to stay with you. With the help of Kimmuriel, she had rid herself of her anger, and the life you—the life we lived at that time was not appealing to her. She asked me for some time with you so she could say farewell . . ."

"This is not the truth!" Entreri insisted. "This is not the tale that was told to me at the time. Do you think the years have blurred my recollections? Do you think me old, my brain feeble?"

"You were told a tale to keep you in line," Jarlaxle said. "And that, too, I allowed, because otherwise, they were going to kill you, do not doubt."

"Better that than you giving me to Alegni."

"That is a separate matter."

"It was the day after Calihye was taken from me!"

"For her sake, of course. The Netherese had found you, through no help of Bregan D'aerthe, I assure you, but because of that sword you now carry once more. It is a Netherese blade—we knew that, and they came for it, with overwhelming forces. I saved your beloved by granting her wish and issuing her away."

"You saved yourself by giving me to them."

Jarlaxle shrugged. "They had you in any case, and had me, too, had I not cooperated."

Entreri started to growl a bit at that, even came forward a step, but Jarlaxle held up his hands and pressed on.

"I thought I could get back to you, and quickly, and with sufficient force to break you free—indeed, I had made many plans with Matron Mother Zeerith for just that event," he explained. "But I did not know the whole of it at that time.

I did not foresee the fall of the Weave and the Spellplague. Matron Mother Zeerith was in no position to help me. Few were! We were all scrambling to secure our own positions and lives. And so yes, my friend, I did betray you, and for that I am ever sorry. But I tell you in all honesty that it was never my intent to leave you with those fiends, certainly not with Herzgo Alegni—and I pray that some foul devil has taken his soul as a plaything . . .

"But now I have tried to pay you back. Retrieving Dahlia was no small—"

He stopped as the door handle to the adjoining room turned, and right before Kimmuriel walked in, Entreri offered Jarlaxle a forgiving nod, though the man seemed a tattered mess. The details Jarlaxle had at last included in the old story had Entreri's thoughts swirling.

"What have you learned?" Jarlaxle asked Kimmuriel as soon as he appeared.

"The illithid Methil's work was quite impressive," Kimmuriel replied. "So many cues would throw her back to madness. Her moments of sanity were few."

"Were? Then you have corrected . . ." Entreri began to reason.

"No, of course not," Kimmuriel replied. "Not yet. It will take some time, but the hive mind will aid in my efforts—they remain grateful that Archmage Gromph invited them to the reconstruction of the Hosttower of the Arcane." He looked past Jarlaxle to Entreri. "You should go and see her while her brief hold of clarity remains."

Artemis Entreri didn't have to be asked twice. He rushed past the two dark elves and through the door, shutting it behind him.

"You heard?" Jarlaxle quietly asked.

"I thought you might need my assistance."

"He believed what I told him, and what I told him was true enough," said Jarlaxle. He shifted from foot to foot, clearly uncomfortable.

"Incomplete, but true enough," Kimmuriel agreed.

"The agreements signed between Bregan D'aerthe and the Netherese need not be revealed," Jarlaxle reminded him. "That was long ago, and they are no more, for the Sundering has sundered more than the worlds of Toril and Abeir!"

He left it at that, satisfied by Kimmuriel's unconcerned shrug, but Jarlaxle understood that it all might not be as clear-cut as he had pretended.

With Artemis Entreri, nothing ever was.

◆ ◆ ◆

Drizzt wanted to enjoy the celebration in the Throne Room that night—it was in his honor, after all.

He entered to a rousing song, every dwarf in the place with foam on his or her beard and lips, and every one hoisted a drink to the roar of "Elf!"

Bruenor was there, of course, and in fine spirits, with Athrogate, Ambergris, and Ragged Dain sitting beside him at the grand table they had brought in for the celebration. Notably, the two seats to Bruenor's right remained empty—for Drizzt and Catti-brie, of course.

Drizzt found himself wishing that two more were empty, and he thought of Wulfgar and Regis. The scene in front of him threw him back across time and space, to the celebration after the reclamation of Mithral Hall.

"Where's me girl, then, elf?" Bruenor asked as Drizzt approached.

"She said she would be along later," the ranger replied. "She has much to do, it would seem."

"All of 'em," said Bruenor. "Never stoppin'. They're meaning to put that durned tower back in place."

"Aye, and save Gauntlgrym in doing it," Ragged Dain added. That proclamation brought lifted mugs and a chorus of cheers.

Drizzt took his seat and accepted a mug of ale from Bruenor. The conversation and song continued around him in full force, but the drow ranger felt strangely detached.

Was he conjuring this perceived reality from memory? Transposing those real times in Mithral Hall to this place and time, wherever he might actually be?

Or were even those memories nothing more than the creation of his perception, or the intrusion of whatever being was now playing the puppeteer to his fragile sensibilities?

He looked across the room, taking some comfort in the statues, the sarcophagi, that flanked Bruenor's throne. There stood King Emerus Warcrown of Felbarr and King Connerad Brawnanvil, who had succeeded Bruenor to the throne of Mithral Hall.

A third sarcophagus drew his attention more fully, though, and despite his troubled state, Drizzt couldn't help but smile when he looked upon that one, set up on the wall some dozen long strides from the throne.

Thibbledorf Pwent, ever vigilant, ever loyal, ever fierce, ever crazy.

It surprised Drizzt how much he missed that wild fellow. Pwent had been a very old dwarf when Drizzt and Bruenor had left him in Icewind Dale, and yet, when the call came, Pwent had come roaring back to Bruenor's side, fighting like a young warrior.

Then had come a second existence for Pwent, but surely not a second life. The undead battlerager had haunted these very halls, where he had fallen, as a vampire.

Now he was at rest, and Drizzt couldn't think of a better sentry than that statue, looking down at Bruenor's throne, looking down at all who would stand beside and behind Bruenor, reminding them ever of true and selfless loyalty.

Drizzt winced again when it occurred to him that Pwent, too, might be nothing more than his own deluded creation. Either he was being horribly and forever deceived, the most cruel taunt of all, or he was god, an insane god, creating out of desire and fear and whim—and that possibility, Drizzt believed, would be the biggest lie of all.

He tried not to sneer, tried not to wail, and buried his voice in a deep swallow of frothy beer.

But why hide it? It was his game, or one being perpetrated upon him. But just a game nonetheless. Why hide his sneer?

He turned an angry glance on Bruenor, but before the dwarf even noted the inappropriate scowl, Drizzt's expression melted to curiosity. For only then did Drizzt notice that Bruenor wore a curious item strapped to his forearm, a tiny buckler or a badge, perhaps, that very much resembled his foaming mug shield.

"Bwahaha! A beautiful thing, eh, elf?" the dwarf said when he noted the stare. He lifted the arm so that Drizzt could better see.

"What?" Drizzt started to ask, but his word was stolen along with his breath as the buckler began to wind outward, growing into a small shield.

Drizzt had seen that trick before.

"What?" he asked again, shaking his head.

"Me girl," Bruenor explained with a wink. "She taked me shield and the one ye bringed back with ye and put 'em together in the forge. Ha! It's still givin' me brew, too!"

"Aye, but too bad it's not throwin' ye shots when it's so small on yer arm," Athrogate said, drawing laughter.

"She put them together?" Drizzt asked soberly, more closely inspecting the wondrous item. He saw the traces of Tiago's spiderweb shield in there, and could not doubt Bruenor's claim.

"By the gods," he said as he fell back.

"What?" Bruenor asked.

Drizzt shook his head, trying to sort it out, and suspecting now why Catti-brie had asked him to leave his weapon belt behind when he had come to the room, and also suspecting the real reason she might be late.

Drizzt slid his chair back and started to stand, but Bruenor grabbed him by the arm and looked at him curiously.

"Where ye off to?"

"She's at the Great Forge," Drizzt replied.

◆  ◆  ◆

"ETERNAL," DAHLIA SAID to Entreri when he knelt on the bed beside her. "Forever am I grateful. You cannot know . . ."

Her voice broke apart and she began to sob. Entreri grabbed her and pulled her close. He needed her support as much as she needed his. After a long while, he pulled her back to arms' length and stared into her beautiful eyes.

"I was as lost as you," he said.

Dahlia managed a laugh and a shake of her head. "You cannot begin to know . . ."

"I was once a prisoner of House Baenre," he assured her. "For many tendays. I know. And the thought of you there . . ."

His words, too, fell apart, and he just pulled her close and hugged her, and kissed her, and felt warmth he had rarely known in his many, many years of life.

"You and Jarlaxle and Drizzt, I am told," Dahlia said a bit later.

"There were others as well, but yes."

"You came for me, all three. I cannot ever forget that."

Entreri looked at her with some concern, particularly since she had mentioned Drizzt, who had been her lover for years. However much he had come to see Drizzt as an ally, if not a friend, he couldn't stand to lose Dahlia to the ranger—he couldn't stand to lose her at all.

"But it was you, most of all?" Dahlia asked. "You made them go with you to come and get me."

"I would have come alone."

Dahlia nodded, not doubting a word, and the upturned edges of her smile caught the tears that streamed down her cheeks. "I know little," she said. "My mind swirls and my thoughts are lost . . ."

"Kimmuriel will fix that," Entreri said.

"But one thing I know." She reached up and stroked the man's cheek, and it, too, was moist with tears. "I know that I love you, Artemis Entreri. Only you and always you."

"I love you," Entreri replied and fell into her arms.

Those were the rarest of words for him. He had not said that to another person since the earliest days of his childhood, to his mother before his mother had so awfully betrayed him. He didn't think he could ever proclaim such a thing again.

But there it was, laid out there, naked and unafraid—so amazingly unafraid.

Artemis Entreri was sure that he had never known such peace.

◆ ◆ ◆

Sweating and exhausted, and ultimately satisfied, Catti-brie held up the magnificent scimitar in front of her huge blue eyes, which reflected the stars in Twinkle's new glassteel blade.

The scimitar had the shape of Twinkle, making it a better match with Icingdeath, and Catti-brie had also recovered a bit of Twinkle's powerful defensive magic. But now the weapon had Vidrinath's blade, glassteel and full of tiny stars, as strong and fine as any blade ever forged. It would never again be broken. The scimitar could live up to Vidrinath's name, Lullaby, by producing the drow sleeping poison at its wielder's call.

A fitting addition for Drizzt, she thought, who did not want to kill unless no other choice could be found.

She silently thanked the primordial for giving her these insights, for showing her the true power of the Great Forge of Gauntlgrym. These were gifts far beyond what any mere fire, even one this hot, could ever produce. This was more than the flaming tendril of the primordial, it was a most ancient magic, a gift of a godlike being, and so Catti-brie was properly humble and truly grateful.

And more convinced than ever that her efforts would regrow the Hosttower of the Arcane in Luskan, and so save Gauntlgrym.

The door banged open and Drizzt rushed in, followed by Bruenor and a gaggle of rolling, drunken dwarves.

"What're ye about?" Bruenor demanded.

Drizzt ran up to her, his eyes locked on the scimitar.

"Vidrinath and Twinkle," Catti-brie explained, and Drizzt nodded with every word, exactly what he had expected when he had bolted from the Throne Room.

He said not a word, but took the weapon from her, holding it aloft, feeling its balance, feeling its strength—strength as he had never before known in a weapon. Holding this blade, feeling the power of Vidrinath, Drizzt found himself amazed that he had defeated its wielder, Tiago Baenre.

He looked from the tiny stars to the beautiful woman who had given him this gift, and he was overcome. He pulled her close.

And he was terrified, then, that this was all an illusion, a deception, perhaps a self-deception, and he felt as if he stood on shifting sands, and that all the world would never, ever be right again.

Was he hugging a demon queen?

# Chapter 4 ◈

## *Morada Topolino*

A PAIR OF—RELATIVELY—BURLY HALFLING GUARDS STOOD at the end of a hedged walkway, emptying onto the main boulevard of the wealthier section of Delthuntle. The two tried to appear nonchalant—though everyone in the city knew better, of course—pretending to talk to each other, with their eyes scanning, continually scanning.

Regis grinned at the sight as he and his companion crouched behind the corner of a tavern down the lane.

"That is the place?" Wulfgar asked him.

"Morada Topolino," Regis replied.

"It's been five years," Wulfgar reminded him. "Much has changed, perhaps."

Regis cast him an unappreciative glance, not emotionally ready to entertain such grim notions.

"Donnola Topolino is as wily as Jarlaxle," he replied rather sourly. "If Morada Topolino is there—and it is—then so is she."

Wulfgar started to respond, "The Delthuntle night is lonely, no doubt . . ." before catching himself, but he did say enough for Regis to see he wondered if Donnola had been as faithful to Regis's memory as he had been to her.

"What we had was real," Regis said, turning his longing gaze back to the distant house.

"I once thought the same," said Wulfgar, surprising him with the reference to Catti-brie, who had been Wulfgar's love before he had been taken to the Abyss in the clutches of a yochlol.

"Donnola knows I will return," Regis countered. "And so it is a different situation here. We all thought you dead, Wulfgar, and with good reason . . ."

"I know, I know," Wulfgar said, patting his hand in the air, and offering a sincere smile of contrition.

"All these years and you are still bitter," Regis said, and then he gasped. "Is that why you came with me? Because you could not trust yourself around Catti-brie and Drizzt?"

Wulfgar's laugh seemed sincere enough. "No, of course not. I came with you for adventure, and one that did not involve dwarven mines!" He put his hand on Regis's shoulder and looked into the halfling's gray eyes. "No, my friend. I only hinted those things about your beloved—foolishly, I am sure—because I am afraid for you at this moment. A few years really is a long time, after all."

"You said nothing I do not fear," he admitted. "Every day since I was chased out of this place by the specter of Ebonsoul, I have cherished the thought of this moment, of finding her again and holding her again." Regis turned his attention back to the house. "Donnola rode with me in spirit with the Grinning Ponies while I waited for the appointed day, she followed me in my thoughts to Kelvin's Cairn and then across the northland to Mithral Hall, and she is what sustained me when we were lost in the Underdark."

He took a deep breath and winced. "I cherished this moment and I was terrified of it at the same time," he said. "If she is not there . . ."

"She is there," Wulfgar stated flatly, surprising Regis. "She is there, waiting for your return."

"You just said . . ."

"Perhaps I did not understand. I have not before heard you speak of her like this, but if your love for her runs that deep, then I can only believe that her feelings are no more shallow. You would have waited for her for the rest of your days, wouldn't you?"

Regis smiled and nodded. "On my deathbed, I would have looked to the door, expecting the handle to turn."

"Well, good fortune and powerful friends have made certain that it will not come to that," said Wulfgar. "Let us go, Regi—Spider Parrafin, and find your long-lost love."

Wulfgar started around the corner, towing Regis by the shoulder, but the big man paused and stared at the house more closely. "Will I even fit in that place?" the nearly-seven-foot-tall barbarian asked.

"Crouch," Regis offered. "And do not sit in any chairs with arms, for I fear we'll not extract your ample haunches from their stubborn grasp."

Laughing, the seemingly unlikely companions, one more than twice the height and thrice the weight of the other, started out into the street to Morada Topolino. By the time they'd covered half the ground, they'd caught the attention of the guards, who regarded them curiously.

The guards stood to block them, and several more appeared from the hedgerows, including more than a few with leveled crossbows. Morada Topolino was clearly on alert, and that brought a concerned look to Regis's face.

"Who are you?" one of the burly guards started to ask.

"Your business?" the other asked at the same time, but barely had the words come out when more than one of the halflings with crossbows shouted "Spider!" and that sparked recognition in the two blocking the walkway, their expressions going to wide and happy smiles.

"Spider?" they both echoed, coming forward.

Regis greeted them, one by the name Donfellow, and the three shared friendly handshakes and hugs.

"My friend, Wulfgar," Regis introduced his companion. His eyes weren't on Wulfgar, though, but on the many guards who had sprung from concealment and on the others still hiding in the bushes that he only then noticed.

"We are careful," Donfellow answered Regis's questioning gaze.

"The new truth of Morada Topolino," the other burly guard added. "Since that night when you left, Grandmother Donnola will never allow us to be caught by surprise again."

"Never!" Donfellow said with grim determination.

"Donnola," Regis whispered and seemed about to burst into tears of joy. She was alive!

"Grandmother?" Wulfgar asked, prodding Regis and clearly confused.

"It is a title of leadership, not a badge of progeny," Regis replied. To Donfellow he added, "Pray, do not announce me?"

The guard looked at him suspiciously.

"Is she betrothed?" Wulfgar asked, surprising all, but certainly clarifying Regis's request.

"Spider?"

"You can take all of my weapons, of course, and keep my friend here, but pray give me this surprise entrance upon Lady Donnola."

Now Donfellow was smiling and nodding. "And no," he answered Wulfgar. "She has shown no interest in anyone these last years." He looked directly at Regis. "Perhaps now I understand why."

Wulfgar agreed to remain outside with the guards, while Donfellow led Regis into Morada Topolino. They were greeted by yet another guard in the foyer, and there waited for a few moments while that guard ran off to fetch the house wizard, Wigglefingers.

"I told you I would return," Regis said with a wide smile when the clever halfling prestidigitator appeared at the top of the stairs. A blink spell put Wigglefingers right in front of Regis, and before he realized what had happened he was being hugged yet again.

"I am so thrilled that you have!" the wizard replied with unexpected exuberance. Wigglefingers had never been overly fond of Spider, and certainly never warm to him—no enemy, though, and he had helped Regis escape on that most dreadful night when the specter of Ebonsoul had come looking for him.

Still, this greeting clearly had Regis caught by surprise, and it showed on his face.

"She has not recovered from that dark night," Wigglefingers said solemnly.

"The loss of Pericolo," Regis reasoned, but Wigglefingers shook his head.

"We grieved appropriately for Grandfather Pericolo, of course. And we buried him, and such losses are terrible, but expected and accepted. Now, my old friend, Donnola's pain is more one of anticipation and unrequited emotion than of grief."

Regis locked stares with the wizard for a long moment. "Take me to her," he said evenly, and Wigglefingers nodded.

◆　◆　◆

"HAHA, BUT A grand day it is!" the chubby old halfling named Brister-Biggus said to Wulfgar, handing him yet another glass of whiskey.

As soon as Regis had disappeared into the mansion, the guards had escorted Wulfgar through the maze of the hedgerow, though it really wasn't a maze to the tall barbarian since he stood about two feet taller than the least-trimmed hedges. Somewhere near the center of the hedge, and past several guard stations, they came to a clearing where a tapped keg stood waiting. Several other halflings joined them almost immediately, and the drinks began to flow. The halflings moved their drinks around, but with each passing hand, less was left in the glass due to less-than-accidental spills. They clanked their glasses in toasts repeatedly, and even took up an impromptu song:

> Any friend of Spider
> Has to be a blighter,
> Friendly to the whiskey,
> Laughing and so frisky
> And worthy of a flight . . . err . . .

"Err?" Wulfgar asked Brister-Biggus after one refrain, as the halfling lifted his glass to clank it against Wulfgar's—and slyly spilled a bit more of his own drink in the process.

"Well, it's off the sleeve, you know," Brister-Biggus replied. "We'll mend the right words when a few more're in ush."

"Ush!" Wulfgar repeated the slurred reference, and lifted his glass for another clink—and he noted that Brister Biggus spilled a bit more yet again, and surely more than the drunk-acting halfling was actually imbibing.

Wulfgar grinned knowingly, then laughed as a buxom halfling lass appeared as if from nowhere and plopped herself down on his lap—and of course she was carrying another full glass for him.

"To ush!" Wulfgar roared, properly slurring, and he belted back the drink Brister-Biggus had provided.

"To Spider!" he yelled louder, and he belted back the drink the lovely halfling lass had brought. "More!"

And more was promptly delivered. The lass began to bounce on his lap, taking up the song, and a grand party it seemed.

It seemed.

Wulfgar noted, too, that the halflings were rather cleverly shifting Aegis-fang farther and farther from his reach, dragging it inch by inch along the hedgerow.

"So how long've you known good shir Shpider?" Brister-Biggus asked, and he seemed ready to fall over.

He seemed.

"A hunnerd years'n'more!" Wulfgar declared, and that brought laughter all around, for to these Topolinos, Spider was barely into his twenties, and they had known the little fellow, or of him at least, for most of that time.

"Two hunnerd!" Wulfgar cried, and drained his drink once more. "Aye, an' we figh . . . err . . .fough . . . err, fighted?" he paused and shook his head, trying to look perplexed. "Aye, we fighted drow'n'dragons, orcs'n'chipmunks together!"

That brought exaggerated howls of laughter, and how amusing Wulfgar thought it when others pretended to be drunk.

"No, truly," he said earnestly, and he stood up quickly, plopping the buxom halfling lass onto her bum on the ground, and thus drawing more howls of hilarity. "Giant chipmunks with big teeth!"

Brister-Biggus howled with laughter.

"And shh!" Wulfgar said, stumbling and twisting his lips with his finger as he made the sign for silence. "Shh, for there's a secret I know."

"Ah, a secret," Brister-Biggus echoed, and he, too, brought his finger to his lips, and all the halflings closed in eagerly.

"I've a secret," Wulfgar said, nodding exaggeratingly. "When I was a young man—nay, not even yet a man—I was taken captive on the battlefield, me legs swept out beneath me." He slipped into a bit of Dwarvish brogue for effect. "Aye, and down to me arse I went, me standard pole flyin'."

He glanced around and brought his finger to his lips again. "Shh! For suren meself was a dead boy then, with a most ferocious beastie atop me."

"And Spider saved you?" Brister-Biggus asked breathlessly.

"Ha!" Wulfgar yelped, and all the halflings fell back, gasping.

"Spider?" Wulfgar asked incredulously. "Bah, but that one, he was on th'other side, don't ye know? Was his own friend that knocked me down!"

He stood up to his full height and crossed his massive arms over his chest.

"His friend," he declared, his voice clear and strong, any hint of drunkenness flown. "A most noble dwarf, a king indeed, and instead of executing me, as he surely could have done, he took me in as his son. And he made this for me."

He whispered, "Tempus," and the warhammer appeared in his hand, and the halflings gasped again.

"For aye, I name my father as King Bruenor Battlehammer of Mithral Hall, and never a finer dwarf have I known!" Guessing that a dozen crossbows were probably trained upon him from concealment in the hedgerow, Wulfgar eased Aegis-fang down and handed it to Brister-Biggus. "A magnificent weapon, eh?"

The halfling took it, and nearly fell over from the weight of it.

"And, Mr. Brister-Biggus," Wulfgar went on, "do you know what else King Bruenor gave to me?"

"What else might that be?" the curious and off-balance—in more ways than just physical!—halfling asked. He turned a bit aside so that Wulfgar couldn't easily grab the warhammer from him—though of course, Wulfgar didn't need to do any such thing.

"Gutbuster," Wulfgar replied. "Aye, plenty of Gutbuster." He noted some knowing nods at his mention of the famous dwarven brew. "And so you should know that your whiskey, fine as it is, won't be pushing me loopy, and won't be getting my tongue to wag."

The party seemed to stop then, and a dozen sets of eyes regarded him suspiciously.

"But you'll need no libations for such an event, for I've a thousand grand tales to tell you, and so I will, happily so. I am a friend of Spider—of Regis, though my father, King Bruenor, always called him Rumblebelly."

"Are you saying that the one who came with you is not our Spider?" Brister-Biggus asked suspiciously, and Wulfgar heard the hedgerows rustling as halfling guards ran for the mansion, to warn Donnola, no doubt.

"Of course he is, but there's so much more. So much more. We've traveled half of Faerûn to find you, to find Spider's love, and so do not ever fear that my warhammer—" he paused and summoned the weapon to his grasp again—"will ever be lifted in anger against any fellow or lady of Morada Topolino."

He sat back down, grabbed the halfling lass, and lifted her back onto his lap. Then he began to sing the halfling song, "Any friend of Spider . . ." but then fell to humming, having already forgotten the words. He kept humming as the others took up the tune, and only paused to belt back another glass of whiskey, and another after that.

"So tell us a tale, then!" one of the other halflings cried.

"For a kiss!" Wulfgar said to the lass on his lap, and when she obliged, he said more seriously, his crystal blue eyes flashing dangerously, "Have any of you ever met a white dragon in its lair? I have, and I killed it, too!"

"You've killed a dragon?" one asked skeptically.

"A young man like you?" another agreed with the doubter.

"I was younger when I did, too," Wulfgar said, leaving out the part that it was in another life. "And oh, but Icingdeath of Icewind Dale wasn't glad to see me and Drizzt Do'Urden, my ranger companion."

Now he had their full attention, and he noted that several nodded at the mention of the rather famous ranger.

"Aye, my drow companion," Wulfgar declared. That description of his friend brought a gasp from the halfling on his lap and several others, who had apparently never heard of Drizzt.

"Do you want to know how I killed the dragon?" he asked, leaning forward, his voice barely a whisper.

All the heads bobbed, and a chorus of "aye" came from the hedgerows.

Wulfgar smiled, for he had a tale to tell, indeed and one that should score him a few more gulps of that fine whiskey, at least.

◆ ◆ ◆

REGIS PACED IN the small but handsome drawing room where Wigglefingers had left him. He had no doubt that the wizard hadn't gone far, and was likely magically spying upon him even then, casting one divination spell after another to fully grasp the truth of Spider returned.

Finally, after what seemed like enough time to drop the midday sun behind the western horizon, a side door swung magically open. Regis hesitated, not sure if he was being invited into another room or . . .

There she was. Donnola Topolino appeared at the opened door. She stood there, frozen, and seemed to wobble, as if her legs would fail her, and that prompted Regis to rush for her.

"Spider," she whispered, and tears welled in her beautiful eyes, and Regis, too, sniffled more than once over the dozen steps it took him to get to her, to at long last, get to her!

He wanted to leap against her, but he wasn't sure if he should, and so he slowed in those last steps.

Donnola flew at him, burying him in a hug, smothering him in a hundred fast kisses. Regis didn't resist and let himself fall to the ground with his beloved atop him.

"Spider," she said between kisses. "Spider, I knew it! I knew! You would not stay away, you would never stay away!"

"I promised you," he whispered. "I will never break my promises to you."

His last words came out muffled, smothered by the long and lasting kiss Donnola put upon him, and it seemed to Regis, all at once, that he had never been gone from her arms, and also that he had been away forever and too long!

"I waited for you," she whispered. "I knew you would return."

Regis grinned and nodded, but a look of panic came over Donnola's face.

"How long?" she asked. "How long will you stay?"

Regis put his face very near to hers and stared deeply into her eyes. "Forever," he promised. "Forever."

# CHAPTER 5 ◈

# *Sava Pieces*

HERE ARE MANY TRUTHS AT THIS TIME," THE YOUNG DROW woman told her much-older aunts.

"And many are rooted in heresy," Sos'Umptu Baenre replied, her tone very near to scolding the young but mighty Yvonnel. Beside her, Quenthel Baenre, still Matron Mother of Menzoberranzan in title if not in actuality, shifted nervously, and even glanced at her devout sister with a look of warning.

They had just witnessed Yvonnel orchestrate one of the most incredible displays of power any drow in Menzoberranzan had ever seen, even those like Quenthel and Sos'Umptu, who had watched their mother tear the entire structure of House Oblodra from the roots of the cavern and dump it and the apostate drow family into the Clawrift. But this release of pure might both magical and mundane, this spear of all the combined power of Menzoberranzan, transferred through the living form of Drizzt Do'Urden, had exceeded even that tremendous feat by Matron Mother Yvonnel Baenre, an explosion so mighty and focused that it had reduced Demogorgon, a near god, the Prince of Demons, to a swirling puddle of bubbling goo.

"Who is to decide such a judgment?" Yvonnel asked Sos'Umptu. "You?"

"There is a Ruling Council . . ."

Yvonnel's mocking laughter cut her short. "You would convene a council now, after House Melarn just openly attacked another ruling House, and did so with the obvious blessing and encouragement of House Barrison Del'Armgo, among others? What good do you expect will come of that?"

"It is protocol."

Yvonnel laughed again and shook her head and looked directly at Matron Mother Quenthel. "Do not convene a council," she commanded.

"You wish for Archmage Gromph to be forgiven," Sos'Umptu said before Quenthel could respond.

Yvonnel flashed her a dangerous look—a look that Quenthel had seen before, and indeed, had seen right before Yvonnel had shown Quenthel the truth of her powers, in a most profound and painful way. But Sos'Umptu, ever the stubborn and assured priestess, pressed on.

"Gromph brought Demogorgon to this place."

"He was deceived," Yvonnel replied.

"There is no excuse—"

"Deceived by Lady Lolth," Yvonnel finished, and that, at last, seemed to silence Sos'Umptu, and Quenthel was glad of that.

"I know this," Yvonnel explained, "from my commune with the witch K'yorl. In the smoke of the Abyss, Lady Lolth took K'yorl's corporeal form and impressed upon Kimmuriel, K'yorl's son, the secrets for weakening the Faerzress and summoning Demogorgon. On the Spider Queen's instructions, Kimmuriel was then tasked with deceiving Archmage Gromph, and so he did, and so Gromph, in summoning Demogorgon, fulfilled Lady Lolth's will. Nothing less, nothing more. Are we to punish him for that?"

The Baenre sisters exchanged glances, both appearing quite uncomfortable at that troubling moment.

"Lady Lolth wished Demogorgon upon us?" Sos'Umptu asked, her voice halting.

"With faith that we would win, then," Quenthel stated as if she needed her words to be true. "We served her in defeating the beast!"

"Who can know Lolth's desires or designs?" Yvonnel asked. "Truly?"

"It is not our place," Sos'Umptu agreed.

"You would have me reinstate Gromph as Archmage of Menzoberranzan?" Quenthel asked.

Yvonnel laughed. "Of course not! Having Tsabrak Xorlarrin there better serves House Baenre at this time, particularly with the request of Matron Mother Zeerith to be returned to the city in full. Zeerith Xorlarrin will owe us a great deal, and her son is easily manipulated." She shrugged and snorted. "Is Gromph even controllable?"

Quenthel wanted to, and indeed almost did, shout out, "Are *you*?" but she bit it back, knowing the answer and fearing the consequences of even asking the question.

She didn't bite it back quickly enough, apparently. Yvonnel flashed her a crooked, knowing smile.

"I hold an interest in keeping House Baenre at the top of Menzoberranzan's hierarchy," Yvonnel then stated, and that caught both older Baenres as a most curious remark.

"That is the only reason I tell you this about Gromph, and counsel you to welcome him back," the young upstart went on. "He is a powerful ally, and would prove a ferocious enemy, of course. So that is a tendril best secured."

Despite her too-obvious disgust with Yvonnel, Sos'Umptu couldn't help but nod in agreement, but to Quenthel, the issue with Gromph suddenly seemed secondary to another revelation in Yvonnel's remarks.

"You counsel?" she dared to ask.

Yvonnel offered her a nod. "You are the matron mother, are you not?"

Quenthel stared at Yvonnel long and hard, fully expecting a sudden reversal.

"And what are you then, Yvonnel, daughter of Gromph?" Sos'Umptu asked, rather carefully.

"A fine question," Yvonnel replied. "And one I must inquire of myself."

With a shrug, she turned and left the audience chamber, and left her two aunts staring ahead, confused and afraid.

"Her power lies in keeping us off our balance," Quenthel quietly remarked, to which her sister had no response.

* * *

YVONNEL WALKED ALONE with her thoughts into the scrying room of House Baenre. She moved up to the cistern and ran her hand along its smooth rim, recalling the feeling of bliss she had known when she had sunk her hands into the stone, to find K'yorl Odran's hands waiting.

She missed K'yorl, and had felt regret when K'yorl had been consumed by the power of the kinetic barrier she had transmitted from the hive mind of the illithids onto the body of Drizzt Do'Urden.

In many ways, Yvonnel had come to conclude that K'yorl Odran, this apostate psionicist, was in truth a greater being than the priestesses of the Spider Queen, that her thoughts and actions served a higher purpose and potential than a life of offering crude and cruel satisfaction and amusement to the Demon Queen of Spiders. Yvonnel had found a place of freedom in the tortured mind of K'yorl that no matron mother would ever know.

She thought of Jarlaxle then, her uncle, and of that most unusual drow ranger, whom she had named as Lolth's Champion—indeed, she laughed at the mere notion of that absurd title bestowed upon Drizzt Do'Urden.

"Who are you, Drizzt Do'Urden?" she asked aloud, looking into the still water.

If K'yorl was there, Yvonnel might have forced a divination, flying to the surface to spy once more on the rogue.

Menzoberranzan was hers to take. She would be legend, a feared demigod among the dark elves, her every whim served.

She thought of Jarlaxle, of his assertions regarding Drizzt Do'Urden. How ridiculous they had seemed! That last conversation with the mercenary leader replayed in her thoughts, when Jarlaxle had simply accused her of something she had not consciously considered.

So how, then, was Jarlaxle right?

So why, then, did Yvonnel actually envy Drizzt Do'Urden?

◆ ◆ ◆

YVONNEL'S DEEP REVERIE was interrupted the next morning by the pathetic Minolin Fey, a creature Yvonnel was coming to despise more and more with each sighting. If Minolin Fey hadn't been her mother, Yvonnel would surely have murdered her long ago.

"Matron Mother Zeerith has come to meet with First Priestess Sos'Umptu and Matron Mother Quenthel," Minolin Fey explained carefully, reciting all the titles—which seemed to be shifting—with apparent trepidation.

Yvonnel responded with a puzzled look, as if to ask why she should care.

"Saribel and Ravel Xorlarrin have also been summoned," Minolin Fey went on quickly, as if she realized she needed to intrigue, or at least amuse, the volatile Yvonnel. "It is said that Matron Mother Zeerith will claim the throne of House Do'Urden, after all, and with her children serving as her court, along with many soldiers from House Baenre."

"Why are you telling me this?" Yvonnel bluntly asked.

"I was instructed—"

"You are always instructed!" Yvonnel snapped at her. "Your entire existence is one long journey of following instruction, one long demand, one long service to duty, one long movement out of fear. How can you awaken each day content in the knowledge that you are so pathetic?"

The woman didn't even bristle.

She didn't dare bristle!

Yvonnel laughed and shook her head.

"What would you have me do?" Minolin Fey asked quietly, almost reverently, and she lowered her eyes.

Yvonnel grabbed her roughly by the chin and forced her head up, forced her mother to look her in the eye.

"You are my mother," Yvonnel stated. "I have not forgotten that, nor do I discount it, as so many seem so eager to do in the curious drow definition of family."

Despite her fear, Minolin Fey's eyes widened at those most unexpected words.

"What would I have you do?" Yvonnel echoed, shaking her head in disbelief. "I would have you do what you would do of your own desires, for once in your miserable life." She let go of Minolin Fey's chin and stepped back abruptly, her stare seizing the woman as surely as her hand had. "It is always what the matron mother demands, or what Priestess Sos'Umptu—were I to kill one dark elf, it would be her—demands. And before that, of course, it was whatever Matron Mother Byrtyn would demand. Even Gromph, my—"

"Archmage Gromph," Minolin Fey reflexively corrected, and Yvonnel wanted to scream at the woman's complete conditioning to protocol.

"Even *Gromph*," she said pointedly. "Whatever he demanded of you, yes?"

The older priestess couldn't help herself, apparently, and she looked away.

"Is there ever anything you might demand?" Yvonnel asked in a softer tone. "Ever?"

Minolin Fey looked back at her, and now Yvonnel saw resolve there, and anger—clearly she had struck upon something to which Minolin Fey was quite sensitive.

"I have underlings," the priestess said. "Many. And they perform as they are told, or they are punished."

"In service to the Spider Queen?"

"That is the way of Lolth."

A disgusted Yvonnel shook her head, turned, and walked away. "You have delivered your message," she said. "So be gone."

The obedient Minolin Fey left the room.

Yvonnel flopped down into her chair, one leg up over the side, her head thrown back as she digested the information. Matron Mother Zeerith returning to the city and perhaps to the head of a house was no small thing. If she were placed on the Ruling Council as the replacement of Dahlia as Matron Mother of House Do'Urden, then House Baenre would have secured a powerful ally indeed.

The Second House of Menzoberranzan wouldn't like that. Nor would the Melarni zealots. They hated House Xorlarrin, with its sacrilegious elevation of males to positions of high responsibility. Matron Mother Zeerith was often quietly derided as a *baridame*, a derogatory term bandied by dark elf women against others who seemed too deferential to the males.

"Ah!" Yvonnel cried out, and she tugged the pillow out from under her and threw it across the room, simply because she needed to throw something across the room.

Scolding herself for reflexively deluding herself into caring about these developments, which were neither monumental nor particularly worth a moment of her time, Yvonnel pulled on her grand ceremonial gown and left her chambers. She didn't go straight to the audience chamber, though, but paused once more in the scrying room.

Again she ran her hand across the smooth stoup. Again, she found herself thinking of K'yorl Odran. She was surprised to admit that she missed the woman. Oh, truly, K'yorl was a wretch who would have had to be destroyed sooner or later, but in their time together, in this room particularly, K'yorl's strange powers had shown Yvonnel a lot of the world outside Menzoberranzan.

Yvonnel couldn't help but smile at the irony. This was the City of Spiders, the city devoted to the Lady of Chaos, yet it was arguably the most ordered and stable place in the Underdark. Oh yes, the drow created intrigue and upset the edges often, but most often in places outside the city, as with the War of the Silver

Marches. Here, there was the constant preening and scheming for power, the occasional assassination, the occasional House war.

But when the blood dried, it was just Menzoberranzan again, with House Baenre sitting at the head of the Ruling Council—a gaggle of nine now, counting Sos'Umptu—which had remained remarkably stable over the decades.

Yvonnel thought of K'yorl, then of Jarlaxle, and the mental image of her flamboyant uncle brought a grin to her face.

She thought of Drizzt Do'Urden, and fantasized about the life he must live. The contrast to Minolin Fey was too stark for her to ignore. Who demanded anything of Drizzt Do'Urden, other than his own heart?

Yvonnel set out for the audience chamber. She found Sos'Umptu huddled with Quenthel at the throne. Both glanced at her as she approached, and neither seemed happy to see her. She took special note of Quenthel, and it occurred to her that Quenthel was gaining back her footing, might even be plotting with Sos'Umptu and others to secure her hold on the title of matron mother.

A thought flashed in Yvonnel's mind that she might have to again properly—and painfully—instruct Quenthel on the order of things in House Baenre.

But she brushed the notion aside.

"It would seem that I have interrupted you," she said.

"We would have expected you much earlier this morning," Sos'Umptu replied. "There are many troubling events in the wake of the fall of Demogorgon."

"There are always 'troubling events.' It is our way. It is how we get up each day and find meaning, such as it is, in our existence."

A curious expression did not prevent Sos'Umptu from continuing, "We were discussing House Melarn."

"Why?"

That simple question brought curious looks at Yvonnel, then Sos'Umptu asked, "What would you counsel regarding Matron Mother Zhindia Melarn?"

"I would counsel that she is not worth your counsel."

"She sits on the Ruling Council!" Quenthel stated, rather excitedly.

"You sit on the Ruling Council," Yvonnel retorted. "Both of you! And Zeerith, too, when you name her as Matron Mother of House Do'Urden."

"They will move to demote House Do'Urden and allow House Duskryn to ascend to the Eighth Rank and a seat at the Ruling Council," Sos'Umptu explained.

"Then tell them no."

"It is not so simple a matter—" Quenthel started to reply.

"Zhindia Melarn just lost a war against the very House you expect her to try to demote. Demote her House instead and move Do'Urden above her."

"You would have us try to humble Matron Mother Zhindia Melarn?" Sos'Umptu asked.

"It is already done," Yvonnel replied, secretly recalling the delicious fight where Jarlaxle, Drizzt, and the human named Entreri had decimated the ranks of Zhindia's priestesses, and had nearly killed Zhindia as well. "In the fight with House Do'Urden, she and I spoke at length," was all she bothered to tell the two older Baenres at that time. "Zhindia's anger festers, as it always will, but she knows now her error. I showed her."

"What did you do?" Sos'Umptu asked, as if fearing to hear the answer, and Quenthel also wore a nervous expression.

Yvonnel laughed yet again, only this time, she ended with a most heartfelt and primal scream. "You are toys!" she scolded. "All of you. You are pieces on a sava board, willingly walking from square to square."

Her entire demeanor and expression shifted then, insultingly, mockingly, to one of apparent bemusement.

"Pet rats," she said to them, "placed upon an upright and turning wheel to exercise, running up, up, up, but never really climbing."

"We are servants of the Spider Queen," Sos'Umptu protested, finding her voice more clearly in defense of her station, obviously determined that her devotion would not be mocked.

"And so?"

"How can you ask such a thing?" Quenthel asked before she could stop herself, while beside her, Sos'Umptu quietly mumbled, "Blasphemy."

"More akin to boredom," Yvonnel corrected. "And incredulity at your blindness. Lolth just sent Demogorgon into your midst! Lolth instructed you, Quenthel, to fill the streets with demons. The War of the Silver Marches . . . who gave Tsabrak the power to darken the skies?"

"You know the answer," Sos'Umptu said, even as Quenthel mouthed "Lolth."

"And now you connive in a desperate try for order," Yvonnel replied with open disdain. "Tell Matron Mother Zhindia her place—tell her and do not ask her. And that place is below House Do'Urden, which now becomes, under Matron Mother Zeerith's command, the Seventh House of Menzoberranzan."

"Is that what Matron Mother Yvonnel will, or would, do?" Quenthel asked.

"Matron Mother Yvonnel would surely kill herself if she had to listen to the gossiping nonsense of you two," Yvonnel replied, and she waved her hand as she spun and departed the audience chamber.

"There is more!" Sos'Umptu called after her, but Yvonnel just lifted her hand and waved dismissively again.

For them, there was more. For her, there was nothing more—nothing, here in Menzoberranzan.

# Chapter 6 ◈

# The Magnificent
# Heretic

I N A QUIET CORNER OF THE HEAVILY FORTIFIED ENTRY CAVERN
of Gauntlgrym, Drizzt Do'Urden danced.

He had stripped off most of his clothing, all but a
loincloth, and he enjoyed the complete freedom of movement, encumbered only by the magical anklets he wore
and the weight of his scimitars in his hands, Icingdeath
and the newly created starlit blade, part Twinkle and part
Vidrinath. Typically, he had carried Icingdeath in his right
hand, his dominant fighting hand, but that had lasted barely
five steps into his practice dance this day. He couldn't deny
it: this new weapon, the one Catti-brie had forged, was the
superior blade, its cut smoother, its blade stronger, its edge
keener. Surely if he was fighting a creature of fire or the lower
planes, he would favor Icingdeath, but in most fights, this
starlit scimitar would lead the way.

"Vidrinath," he decided, bringing it in close to study the
tiny flecks of starlight contained within the curving glassteel
blade. "Lullaby."

He ran his finger across the fine edge, almost daring it to cut
him, to inject into him the sleeping poison that gave the drow-
made weapon its name.

Drizzt went back into his dance, the scimitars flowing
one over the other, then cutting half-circles in front of him
as he turned with perfect balance and performed a sweeping
defense against an imaginary foe. He closed his eyes,

conjuring a mind's-eye swarm of enemies coming before him, playing out the fight, moving to counter every strike, to block, to parry, to riposte.

He was into the dance fully then, and free at last from the nagging doubts he held about . . . everything.

Here, in this practice, the only thing that mattered to Drizzt was his perception, his imagination, the muscle memory of his physical movements. Here, he need not worry about the reality around him, or the grand delusion he feared. This was honest and straightforward—there were no lies to be told, no false images to trouble. Here, it was just physical and emotional escape.

And so he danced, sweeping the blades in perfect synchrony and harmony, leaving no openings, taking every offensive opportunity to slay an imaginary foe.

Not far away, a trio of dwarf sentries, Mirabarran boys, watched him, nodding admiringly. They had heard the many tales of Drizzt's battle prowess, and one of the group had even witnessed it in the lower chambers, when Drizzt had taken on the demon Marilith and won.

"Bah, but me axe'd push them blades aside and cut him low," one red-bearded fellow boasted.

"Ha, but no," said a second, a dwarf woman, eyeing the sinewy and muscular Drizzt with more admiration than for just his fighting movements.

"He'd turn ye into bits small enough for the spit," agreed a third.

The first was about to respond, but he gasped instead when the distant drow turned suddenly, double-stabbing his blades then kicking up between them, his leg fully extended as if he had just driven his heel into the face of a nearby opponent.

Down went the leg, then back up again, but this time continuing, leading the drow in a backward flip and turn that had him stabbing his blades out the opposite way in the blink of an astonished dwarf's eye.

"We'd all be on the spit," the female dwarf remarked breathlessly.

"Ain't no wonder why King Bruenor kept him along, now, is it?" the third agreed.

"I hear there's a flock o' giants sneaking into the north passage," came another voice, a woman's voice, and the three dwarves nearly jumped out of their boots, spinning around to see a grinning Catti-brie.

"What?" they all said together, and the newcomer grinned wider.

"Beggin' yer pardon, Missus Drizzt," said the female sentry, and she blushed to be caught spying on the nearly naked drow.

Catti-brie winked and the dwarves hustled away, leaving the woman to watch her husband's continuing battle dance.

Catti-brie's entertainment turned to a bit of concern as she came to understand the intensity of Drizzt's practice. Sweat glistened across his nearly naked body in the low light of the cavern lichen and glow worms, and his breathing was heavier than she normally noted in these morning sessions.

She could see the troubled cloud on his face. Even from this distance, Catti-brie could feel the uneasiness in her husband.

It had been this way since his return from Menzoberranzan

◆　◆　◆

HE WAS FREE now, fully into the play, his arms working furiously, his legs ever turning, keeping his weight continually on the balls of his feet, his balance perfect. He rushed out to the side and dispatched an imaginary enemy, then leaped and spun a circle kick above the defense of an orc in his mind's eye, landing in a run back to the original spot, where he re-engaged the duo he had left before they even realized he wasn't there.

He launched a dozen sudden stabs—high, low, low, high, blade-to-blade—and there was only one remaining, and out of that fourth stab came a turn back around, Icingdeath leading at the perfect angle to decapitate the solitary orc enemy.

The orc blocked, but it didn't matter. The lead scimitar had been the ruse and the trailing Vidrinath took the beast in the lungs and laid it low.

Drizzt saluted and spun the blades to his sides, points down to the cavern floor.

He heard the slow clapping before he opened his eyes to see Catti-brie standing in front of him, respectfully and cautiously distant, smiling warmly.

"What monsters have ye slain this day, me love?" she asked.

Drizzt winced, caught off guard by a sudden, angry thought, but then he shrugged.

Catti-brie approached, her smile—that lying smile!—leading her to him.

"I didn't think ye'd leave the bed so early this morn," she said as her hands came up to rub his sweaty arms.

"Where is your staff?" he asked. "You should not be out here unarmed."

"The place is thick with dwarves," she replied. "And I have me Drizzt to protect me." She brought the back of her hand up to stroke his cheek, but he pulled away before her knuckles touched his flesh.

"And why're ye thinking I'm needing protection?" Catti-brie asked, a bit more sharply, and he should have known that his recoil wounded her.

But Drizzt was too concerned with his own swirling thoughts.

Catti-brie stepped back and held her arms out wide.

Drizzt couldn't really answer her expression, be it one of deception or an honest response to his own vivid delusions. He collected his clothes, donning them swiftly and sheathing his weapons.

"I did not mean to interrupt you," Catti-brie said when he started off across the cavern. She hustled to pace him. "I do like to watch you at your dance. Once we danced together."

Drizzt swallowed hard. Of course he remembered those long-ago days when the two of them had learned to fight side-by-side in perfect harmony. Such fine days.

Or just another lie?

"I should have waited—" she started to say.

"No," Drizzt interrupted. "No, I was finished in any case. I should have told you where I was going, but I did not wish to wake you."

Catti-brie watched him closely but said no more. They were well back into the complex proper, across the Throne Room and into the passageway leading to their private chambers, when Drizzt added, "I should not have sneaked away."

The woman's sidelong glance, so full of incredulity, showed him the hollowness of his apology—and in truth, he didn't even know what he was apologizing for, nor had she asked for any such thing. She could see his unease, and it occurred to him that such a revelation as the competing emotions in his mind might then prove dangerous.

They went in silence to their room Drizzt moved right to the weapon rack but hesitated, his hand hovering over his belt buckle, yet another item Catti-brie had crafted for him.

It would fail him now if he needed it, he thought.

"I must go back to Luskan," the woman behind him said.

He turned and regarded her curiously.

"We're almost set to free the primordial, just a bit," Catti-brie explained. "And so I'll need go to Luskan and make sure that the dwarves there are filling the hollow trunk with the correct stone."

Drizzt shrugged, clearly at a loss.

"Bruenor told ye what we were doing, eh?"

"Growing a tower," Drizzt replied, thinking the whole thing preposterous.

"Aye, we pack the material and let the primordial into the connecting tendrils. The beast'll turn it to magma and so it'll grow and harden anew."

"A tower?" the drow asked, not even trying to conceal his doubts.

"A bit, no more, for we'll be doing this a year or ten."

"Adding stone and bidding the primordial to shape it."

Catti-brie nodded and Drizzt shook his head.

"It's how they did it," the woman said.

"Millennia ago?"

"Aye."

Drizzt's snort was clearly derisive, and he noted the woman's wince. She came over to him, though, and draped her arms over his shoulders. "It will be wondrous," she whispered. "And beautiful. Primal creation, like the gods'—"

"We are not gods," he said sternly. "Do you think yourself a god? Are you Mielikki now, shaping the world to your purpose?"

"What?" Catti-brie's face screwed up a bit at that, but she held on and painted on a look that seemed more sympathetic than anything else.

"To tell me that all orcs are evil and that I should slaughter babies to satiate your bloodlust?" Drizzt asked, and he honestly had no idea where that accusation had come from.

"Are we back to that?" Catti-brie asked, stepping back, but only for a moment. "Please, not now," she said, coming forward yet again.

He shied from her touch, but she persisted and cornered him, cupping his chin with one hand, stroking his cheek with the other. "Not now," she quietly repeated. "We have found a time of peace, for the first time in many tendays. The road of adventure before us is of our choosing now, and not to a dark place and not to a war. Come with me to Luskan."

Drizzt didn't answer. Something was wrong here. He just knew it, just knew somehow that something was very wrong.

"It's time for us, me love," she said softly. "Not for Jarlaxle and not for Bruenor. For us, meself and yerself. And all we e'er wanted. We can create beauty now."

"The tower?" Drizzt asked doubtfully.

"Aye, and more beautiful still." Her crooked grin gave it away. She was talking about children, about the two of them finally starting a family. And why not? It did seem as if the conflicts around them were still, for now at least. Why wouldn't she want and suggest such a thing?

Except that Drizzt then understood the truth.

The floor shifted under his feet.

This was eerily similar to Errtu's plot designed to destroy Wulfgar. This was the diabolical lie to drive Drizzt to madness, the prelude to watching some great fiend devour everything he treasured in front of his helpless eyes.

She would make love with him and she would bear a child, and that child would be eaten—a demon's feast!

And everything that was Drizzt Do'Urden would die—everything that was Drizzt Do'Urden except for the physical shell left behind to forever feel the agony!

◆ ◆ ◆

IN THE SCRYING room in House Baenre, Yvonnel watched the scene unfold. This was her trigger, the suggestion that she had placed upon Drizzt Do'Urden.

She had felt the tingle of magical warning when Catti-brie hinted of a family to Drizzt, and that sensation had sent her running to this place, to bring forth the image of the ranger.

And now she saw Vidrinath drawn, so expertly, so smoothly, so swiftly, that Catti-brie clearly hadn't even noticed!

Yvonnel held her breath and shook her head, so suddenly unsure, so suddenly full of regret.

◆ ◆ ◆

"IS IT ERRTU?" Drizzt demanded.

Catti-brie stepped back, her eyes widening as she finally noted Vidrinath in Drizzt's hand.

"Errtu?" Drizzt asked again. "Tell me!"

"Drizzt?"

"Or Demogorgon, come to repay me?" the drow asked, advancing as Catti-brie retreated.

"Drizzt . . ."

"Or you, foul Lolth?"

Up came the blade, level and sliding for Catti-brie's throat.

"Do you think to fool me? Do you think—" he shouted as he struck.

Catti-brie gasped and dived away as the blade nicked her neck, drawing blood, and it was only that bright blood that saved her, that at last stayed Drizzt's hand.

He couldn't bear it. He knew this wasn't Catti-brie, that it was some demonic deception, likely some demon itself in most diabolical disguise.

But he couldn't stab her. He could not bring harm to this image, this deception, this beautiful, wonderful creature he had come to love more dearly than his own life itself.

He couldn't.

"Damn you, Lolth!" Drizzt cried, spinning away. "Be done! Be done!"

He turned completely around to face Catti-brie once more, and the sight of her halted his spinning thoughts, her blue eyes opened wide in shock, her nostrils flared in anger, her arms waving.

Drizzt leaped at her, but she had the lead then and her spell caught him in mid-stride and sent him flying back against the wall, a great wind pressing him there.

He covered himself in magical darkness. He didn't want the woman to see him in his shame and defeat.

But the darkness was dispelled and there hovered Catti-brie, floating off the ground now, and there crouched Guenhwyvar beside her, ears flattened, eyes locked upon Drizzt, telling him that if he moved against Catti-brie, he'd catch the panther first.

"What is wrong with you?" Catti-brie demanded, reaching up to her throat, and retracting bloody fingers. "How dare . . ."

"Just be done with it," Drizzt replied. He slumped against the wall in total despair.

"Done with what?"

Drizzt spat on the floor. He knew now that this was all a deception. All of it! The magical forest, the resurrection of lost friends, the return of Entreri, even—all of it! A demonic trick to utterly break him.

Catti-brie backed to the door, Guenhwyvar in front of her, protecting her.

Drizzt dropped his scimitar and reached for her plaintively.

But then he got hit by a gigantic, magically summoned disembodied hand, which appeared in the air beside him and punched him in the side, sending him flying to the floor.

Catti-brie chanted and the rug beneath Drizzt came alive and enwrapped him, rolling him around with ease, coiling over him.

He didn't resist. He didn't try to wriggle out before the fabric tightened around him. He wanted to simply die.

And Guenhwyvar was there in front of him. Guen! Beautiful Guen, his oldest friend, her ears back, her fangs revealed in a long and angry growl.

Drizzt couldn't move, couldn't even shift his face against the press of the animated carpet. He saw Catti-brie come into view behind the panther. He saw the blood on her neck.

He saw the tears glistening on her cheeks.

"Know me love, and aye, but I do love ye—or might that I did!—that if ye e'er lift yer blade or yer hand against me again . . ."

She seemed as if she could barely speak and was trembling so badly that Drizzt thought she might simply fall over. She slapped her hand to her neck again and Drizzt thought of the poison.

"If e'er," she said through gritted teeth. "Aye, but I'll be th'end o' ye. Don't ye doubt . . ."

She gasped and stumbled out of the room, Guenhwyvar following.

Perhaps Drizzt could have extracted himself from the carpet then, but he didn't even try. He hoped it would squeeze tighter, hoped it would squeeze the life out of him.

• • •

BACK IN HOUSE Baenre, Yvonnel sweated and gasped for breath, overcome with . . .

She fell back, astonished by her own feelings.

She had sent Drizzt to this place, had placed a suggestion that would play upon the Abyssal madness in his mind to launch him into a murderous rage against Catti-brie—not for the reasons Yvonnel had told her idiot aunts, though. Not completely at least. With Catti-brie dead and Drizzt broken, Yvonnel would find him and take him away.

And he would be hers, and what a plaything he would prove!

But now, with this scene playing in front of her, Yvonnel was surprised to discover that she could feel no disappointment at the unexpected outcome.

Indeed, she was overcome with relief.

Despite the devious Yvonnel's mighty enchantment, despite the Abyssal madness swirling in his broken mind, Drizzt couldn't bring himself to do it.

Was it possible that he loved something more than he loved his own life?

Was that possible for anyone?

If Drizzt had killed Catti-brie in that moment, Yvonnel only then realized to her utter astonishment, she wouldn't really want him as anything more than a temporary distraction. But now . . . There was more to this than any desire she might have for the unconventional rogue. The implications reached deeper than anything Drizzt might or might not ever do. But how?

She wasn't sure. She searched her memories, the seemingly endless memories of Matron Mother Yvonnel the Eternal, and could find no suitable answer to the puzzle that was Drizzt Do'Urden.

The mighty witch of Menzoberranzan waved the image out of the scrying pool, turning the water still and dark.

She leaned on her folded arms on the edge of the stoup and closed her eyes, reaching back into her thoughts and deeper into the memories of her namesake to find an answer, some answer, any answer.

But she only knew what she felt.

A long while later, she lifted her head to stare into the empty water. She brought her hand forth to stir it, to see the ripples.

"You didn't kill her," the confused and intrigued and thrilled Yvonnel whispered to the empty room. "You magnificent heretic, you didn't kill her."

# CHAPTER 7 ◆

# *A Pirate's Life*

RELIEF FLOODED THROUGH REGIS. THE SPARKLE HE HAD seen was not the flicker of a silver scale in the moonlight but the magical beacon, thin though it was, that Wigglefingers had placed on the bottom of the small rowboat before Regis and Wulfgar had rowed out.

The halfling was still a hundred feet down, rising slowly, his bag full of oysters, and he had to continually remind himself to keep his patience on the ascent, to let his body properly adjust as he drifted up through the dark water. He didn't like these night dives. Big things swam in the Sea of Fallen Stars, with big teeth and bigger appetites than a tiny halfling might sate.

Still, common sense told him that the assertions of Morada Topolino's waterborne soldiers were surely correct, and the sea would be much worse in daylight hours, when the little boat could be spotted from far away. Pirates had been thick about the region of late, and even absent the arrival of those who specifically sailed these waters to plunder, any larger boat might see this craft, obviously the base for a deep-diver, as too lucrative and easy a hit to pass up. Regis was diving for a particular type of deepwater oyster, a small shelled mollusk from which pearls could be coaxed, and in this case, a certain near-perfect grade of pink pearl that was greatly prized by spellcasters for its lack of impurities, making it a fine receptacle for a particularly useful dweomer.

The pink pearls had always been somewhat rare, but in recent years, new supplies had become almost nonexistent, save the occasional lucky find by the more conventional divers of Delthuntle, if those happening upon such a treasure even understood its value! As soon as Regis had returned to Morada Topolino, Wigglefingers had wasted little time in convincing Donnola that this fine fellow, with his partial genasi heritage, should get right back into the water.

Truly, Regis didn't mind, except for the uneasiness of the night diving. He felt free in the water, even with the memories of Ebonsoul's specter, which he had uncovered in these very waters, still fresh in his mind. All Regis had to do was remind himself that he was helping Donnola and Morada Topolino, and he would willingly return to the deep.

He broke water right beside the boat and called out to Wulfgar, who appeared at the side almost immediately, hushing him.

"What do you know?" Regis whispered, handing up his bag of oysters.

Wulfgar took them then reached down, grasped Regis's hand, and easily hoisted him into the boat. His barbarian friend remained in a crouch, pointing to starboard.

"Pirates?" Regis asked, noting the single lantern and more worryingly, the lack of running lanterns, on some vessel out there on the open water, not too far away. The silhouette showed it to be a sloop, and a small one at that. Regis nodded—though he couldn't be certain from this distance and in the night, he had seen this type of vessel before, one designed for speed and agility, tucking in tight to the rocky coast in shallow, shoal-filled waters.

"Running dark if not," Wulfgar replied. "Might be a merchant caught out later than expected, and as fearful of pirates as are we. Might be a Delthuntle patrol out hunting."

Regis shook his head at that last suggestion. Any patrol from Delthuntle, a heavily armed warship and likely with several wizards on board, would burn bright her lanterns, both to offer help to anyone caught out this far and also to send any pirates scurrying away.

Regis spent a long while staring at the distant lantern, then up at the stars to mark its bearing. "She'll be passing close by," he whispered.

Wulfgar nodded. "We can move aside far enough and quietly enough so they'll not notice us."

Regis noted that the big man wasn't making any move for the oars.

"Unless, of course," Wulfgar added, and Regis could see his wide smile in the moonlight, "we want them to notice us."

❖ ❖ ❖

DONNOLA LOOKED AT the timepiece in the parlor of Morada Topolino and grimaced, an expression not unnoticed by the other halfling in the room.

"They were bound for a reef far out," Wigglefingers reminded her. "They'll not likely return until dawn is near."

Donnola turned and glared at him.

"Are you to be like this every time Spider goes out?" the mage asked. "He knows the coast as well as any."

"He has been gone years!"

"And he spent many years in those waters. Grandfather Pericolo discovered his talents and brought him into the family precisely because he could deep dive for pearls." The wizard gave a little chuckle. "It was Pericolo who named him Spider—he once confided in me that he should have called that one Fish instead."

"The coast has changed since last he was here," Donnola reminded him, referring to the great floods that had occurred during the time of the Sundering.

"It isn't like you to lack such faith in one of your soldiers," Wigglefingers pointed out, and Donnola gave him a help-less, guilty shrug.

"Because you still love him, of course," the mage said.

She shrugged again. There was no denying it.

"Grandmother . . . Donnola," he said, his tone changing as he went from the formal title to her given name. He came close and offered a hug, which Donnola accepted. "Spider is a most resourceful water rat. Did he not steal Ebonsoul's dagger? Would anyone else have survived that encounter with the specter in the deep ocean trench?"

"His name is Regis," the Grandmother of Morada Topolino corrected.

"Not to me," said Wigglefingers. "To me, he'll always be that annoying little Spider, chased by danger and bearing great treasures."

Donnola pushed the mage back to arms' length and studied him carefully, surprised to learn how much this grumbling wizard actually cared for Regis.

"He'll be back, trouble in tow," Wigglefingers said with a grin and a shrug.

"And treasures in hand," Donnola agreed.

◆ ◆ ◆

REGIS STAYED LOW under the water, swimming fast. Back on the small rowboat, Wulfgar had lit a lantern and now, predictably, the pirate sloop was gliding in and running dark, speeding for the kill.

From its sails, Regis figured there would be no more than a dozen pirates on the small sloop. He had estimated the boat's size at no more than twenty feet.

He hoped he was right, and only now, under the water, about to engage, did it occur to him how disastrous this whole thing would turn out if he was wrong. A thirty-foot sloop could carry thirty armed men, easily. The speedy coast-runners he had known, on the other hand, with a small hold and minimal cabin, were usually crewed by no more than twelve, and more often half that number.

The halfling came up for air, peering into the darkness, trying to reassure himself. He spotted the silhouette directly ahead of him, and saw the sparkles of water splashing up from its prow as its closed fast.

Regis maneuvered to glance at Wulfgar's light. The timing had to be perfect, with the barbarian dousing the beacon to slow the pirate—if it was a pirate!—so that it didn't simply speed past the bobbing Regis. Were that to happen, Wulfgar might be shot dead off the deck of the rowboat before he had a chance to fight back.

Back under the water Regis went, his whole body working gracefully to propel him along.

He came up again soon after, glancing at Wulfgar just in time to see the light go out, then back at the sloop, so much closer now. And the halfling breathed a sigh of relief. It was a small coast-runner, a twenty-footer, if that. But Regis grimaced as well. This one wasn't interested in taking prisoners, it seemed. In the moonlight, Regis noted a pair of archers at the forward rails, bows already leveled and bent.

Regis chewed his lip. Wulfgar had trusted him.

Was that trust misplaced, after all?

The halfling shook the dark thought away and scolded himself for his weakness. He and Wulfgar could do this.

He could do this.

He went lower in the water, drawing his dagger and setting it firmly between his clamped teeth while he adjusted his position just to the side. With the light extinguished, the sloop had indeed slowed, and more pirates appeared at the forward rails, peering and pointing, while others worked furiously to turn the sails and keep her steady and slow.

The boat glided past, and Regis was fast to her side, coming out of the water like a leaping dolphin, high enough to catch the port rail halfway between the tiller and the mast. Now he earned his nickname as he pulled himself up slowly, peering over. A pair of crewmen worked the tiller, a third standing at the stern and peering out left, right, and behind the boat. To Regis's left, a trio leaned out from the rail beside the jib. A fourth, the archer on the port side, visible up front, held his bow at the ready.

The halfling realized his error. Because of the sails, he couldn't see let alone get to both archers. He carefully lowered himself back along the side. He could not. Wulfgar would have to find a way.

"Here now!" he heard a cry, and before any more doubts could give him pause, the halfling went up fast, throwing himself up onto the rail and drawing his hand crossbow in one fluid motion.

Away went the dart. The archer on the forward port rail jerked, gave a small cry of pain, and looked back at his fellows curiously, just as the men at the tiller gave a howl.

The archer, poisoned with drow-styled venom, simply tumbled over the rail to be run over by the boat. But Regis heard the other one let fly, and heard, too, a cry of pain from farther ahead.

From Wulfgar.

Regis almost went back over the side and dived deep, staying down for a long, long time. But instead he whispered, "Trust him."

Regis spit the three-bladed dagger back into his hand. He dropped his hand crossbow, which fell to the length of the chain on his vest. Then he drew out his fine rapier just in time to parry the sword from the nearest man to his left.

Regis rolled his blade over that weapon fast, and riposted with a straight thrust that brought a grunt and stumbling retreat, and he nodded as the man tangled with the next two pirates in line. The halfling couldn't pursue, though, knowing there were three behind him—and then a fourth, leaping at him from between the jib and the mainsail.

Purely on instinct, a simple reaction out of stark terror, Regis yelped, ducked, and released one of the side blades of his magical dagger into his hand. Hardly aiming, hardly thinking, he threw the living serpent at the man. Just as the pirate reached for him, the serpent caught around his neck and the specter appeared. If he thought about it, Regis might have known great relief, but all he could do was gasp in horror as the pirate was yanked back the way he had come, through the gap in the sails and more. His feet never touched the deck as he back-flipped over the starboard rail and splashed into the water where the specter of the dagger would surely finish him.

"Shoot him again!" came a cry from behind the jib, but it was followed by a profound grunt—which drew a sigh of relief from the halfling—and the sounds of three men stumbling and tumbling, the heavy weight of Wulfgar's hammer throw blasting the archer from the rail and hurling him back into his companions.

With pirates coming at him from both sides, Regis skipped across and used his diminutive size to scramble fast under the mainsail. He found three pirates there, all in a jumble, including the broken archer who had felt the weight of Aegis-fang. He couldn't discern one target from the other in the mess of torsos and limbs, but it didn't much matter as he stabbed down repeatedly with his rapier.

The sloop tilted as the large barbarian leaped from the rowboat, and the shocked and terrified calls of the remaining trio Regis had left on the other side of the sails told the halfling that his mighty friend had come aboard ready to fight.

◆ ◆ ◆

THE BROKEN ARROW in his left shoulder sent waves of pain coursing through Wulfgar, but that only angered him as the pirate ship glided in closer. He let fly Aegis-fang, taking out the archer and the men behind him. Then he gathered his strength in a crouch and launched himself from the small boat to the rail of the approaching vessel. He caught hold of the rail and stubbornly held on as he collided with the sloop. Wasting no time he heaved himself up over that rail, and with such tremendous strength it brought him upright to the deck before the pirates in front of him could begin to react.

He caught the first by the shirt with his right hand and flung the man far overboard, then called to Tempus and brought his warhammer back to his grasp. The next pirate in line, turning with a gaff hook, opened wide his eyes in surprise, sucked in his breath, and dropped his arms low as if in surrender.

But too late, and Aegis-fang swept across from Wulfgar's left to right, spinning the man over the rail.

The sloop lurched and Wulfgar nearly lost his footing. The remaining pirate on the port side fell back. Another pirate was down against the taffrail, hands clawing at his own throat, a ghostly apparition leering over his shoulder as it pulled on the magical garrote of Regis's cruel dagger.

"Surrender, I say!" Regis yelled from the other side, where he battled the remaining two who had been aft. The pirate in front of Wulfgar dropped his weapon and fell to his knees, pleading for mercy.

Wulfgar laid him low with a heavy slug in the face as he rushed past, scrambling all the way to the tiller and over it, crossing behind the mainsail.

"Surrender!" he heard Regis yell again, and now he could see his friend, or at least, he could locate the halfling behind the man and woman who had rushed up to confront him.

"Yes, do!" Wulfgar agreed.

When the startled woman spun around, Wulfgar met her with a tremendous uppercut that lifted her right from the deck and into the mainsail, where she slumped, quite unconscious, into the slack canvas.

The remaining pirate dropped his weapon.

"Do you have them?" a frantic Regis asked.

Before Wulfgar could even respond, the halfling leaped past him and stuck his rapier at the apparition that was choking the life out of the man at the taffrail, destroying it and leaving the man gasping and limp below the rail. Then he leaped out into the night, disappearing into the sea.

Only two left on the deck were standing, or kneeling, and Wulfgar ordered them to tend the wounded. One went to the pair tangled with the archer who had taken the hit from Aegis-fang—that man was certainly beyond any help—and began tearing his shirt to make some quick bandages, while the other went to extract the unconscious woman from the mainsail.

Wulfgar kept a close eye on them as he moved to the taffrail and the man back there, who had been choked to unconsciousness. The pirate was still alive, but didn't seem to be much of a threat.

"A hand, please," he heard from behind, and he glanced over to see Regis, already back and with a sleeping, half-drowned pirate in tow. Wulfgar reached down and grabbed the pirate by the shoulder, easily hoisting her aboard. He noted the hand crossbow dart in the back of her neck as he brought her in. He nodded to Regis and said, "Fine aim."

"Of course," Regis replied with a shrug, as if nothing less should be expected, which tipped Wulfgar off to the truth that the shot had probably been more luck than skill. Wulfgar couldn't deny his friend's valor, though, and was impressed by Regis's willingness to board a boat full of enemies alone.

The two heard a splash, then, and recognized the sound of an oar hitting the water.

"Our boat!" Wulfgar said, rising and turning, but he paused when he noted the grin on Regis's face.

The halfling drew forth his hand crossbow. Holding the rail with one hand, he deftly set a quarrel and cocked the weapon with his other.

"I will be right back," he promised, then he dropped into the water.

He soon swam up alongside the sloop with the rowboat, rowed by the pirate Wulfgar had swept from the deck with Aegis-fang. Another pirate, the man Wulfgar had thrown from the deck, slept peacefully under the effect of drow poison.

So in the end, only two of the eleven-pirate crew were lost. The archer Wulfgar had hit with Aegis-fang, the same one who had put an arrow through Wulfgar's shoulder, was too broken for any of the healing potions Regis produced from his magical belt pouch, and the man who had been violently yanked overboard by Regis's first garrote was never to be seen again.

The other nine, Regis determined, would live or die on the word of Donnola Topolino.

◆ ◆ ◆

"YOU SHOULD NOT have brought them here," Wigglefingers scolded Wulfgar and Regis.

The three of them, along with Donnola and another halfling woman who went by the name of Parvaneh, were gathered in a secret chamber far below Morada Topolino. From there tunnels stretched all the way to a small seaside cave, which now contained both the rowboat Wulfgar and Regis had taken out to gather oysters and the small pirate sloop—though that one had to be slipped into a side berth where the cave roof remained high enough to accommodate the mast, and that only at low tide.

"Where would you have us bring them?" Regis asked, not hiding his surprise at the scowling tone of this meeting. In his previous life at Morada Topolino, acquiring goods like boats and treasure, and even potential recruits in these scalawags he and Wulfgar had taken prisoner, was considered a grand achievement.

"You should have just left them at sea, or killed them all and sank their damned boat on top of them," the wizard replied.

Regis's eyes widened, and Wulfgar laughed out loud.

"Just sail them to the harbormaster and be done with them," Parvaneh explained. "And offer no hint of any tie to Morada Topolino, either for you or them."

"So do it now," Regis offered. "The tide will come in soon after midday and the sloop has to be put out before then, in any case."

"They've been here now," Wigglefingers reminded them all. "We are known to them."

"You're not killing them," Regis bluntly replied, a clear threat that brought a scowl from the wizard.

124

"Enough, both of you," said Donnola. "This is my fault, and mine alone. Regis cannot be blamed for not understanding the changes that have come over Morada Topolino in the years of his absence. His—and his large friend's—actions were commendable and heroic in the old ways of Grandfather Pericolo."

"They should have rowed off into the dark to avoid the fight," Wigglefingers had to put in.

"Of course," Donnola answered. "But in the days of Grandfather Pericolo, we would be lifting glasses of fine wine in toast to this great victory and gathered treasure."

"My friend has spoken of you every day since we were rejoined," Wulfgar said to Donnola. "And always with the highest of praise, both in his love for you and in his belief that you would take House Topolino to greater heights even than the great Pericolo had achieved."

"And she has," Parvaneh quickly replied, before Donnola could respond. "Only in a different direction."

"I do miss the old days," Wigglefingers mumbled, and Donnola looked his way sympathetically.

"What has changed?" Regis asked soberly, rising and moving to stand right in front of Donnola. "What has happened here?"

"Chaos," the woman replied. "The floods, the rise of enemies, the rise of heroes . . ."

"So many damned heroes," Wigglefingers remarked, drawing a grin from Donnola.

"I cannot deny the aggravation of that," she said.

"Vigilante bands?" Regis asked.

"Too many to buy off," Donnola explained. "And too many eyes watching too many . . . unsavory transactions."

"What does that mean?" Wulfgar asked.

"It means that killing people is dangerous in Delthuntle now," Regis replied.

"We have become more of an errand house," Donnola explained, "and a merchant of information."

Regis nodded, not really surprised when he considered it more deeply. Donnola's value to Morada Topolino during the reign of Grandfather Pericolo had been mostly as an infiltrator. The woman was a social butterfly, always invited, always welcomed, and revered by the aristocracy of the city. She could do the dirty work when necessary, of course, but Grandfather Pericolo had always tried to keep her somewhat removed from that nasty reality of life along the wild streets of Delthuntle, and of Aglarond in general.

"So, errand boys," Regis said.

"And girls," Parvaneh was quick to add, and Regis nodded.

"I do miss the old days," Wigglefingers mumbled again.

"So you've taken Morada Topolino to a safer place," Regis said, and he cast a sly sidelong glance at the wizard. "Safer, if a bit less exciting."

"Boom," said Wigglefingers, and he brought his hands up and out, fingers waggling as if in some magical explosion.

Regis laughed, and nodded. "I understand. So what do we do with the nine and their boat?"

"I will take care of that," Donnola assured him.

Regis looked at her skeptically.

"I'll not kill them," she answered that look. "But please, I pray you, bring home no more strays."

"But more pearls!" the wizard said, and it seemed as if Wigglefingers's mood had greatly improved. "The market is bare."

"Yes, more pearls," Donnola agreed, and, in a very un-grandmother-of-assassins way, she went up on her tiptoes and leaned in to give Regis a quick kiss on the lips.

"Any gem you want, my love," the beaming Regis replied.

## Chapter 8 ◈

# *Kimmuriel's Sigh*

L ET DOWN YOUR GUARD," KIMMURIEL SAID TO DRIZZT.

"I didn't know it was up," the broken drow said, his voice showing his resignation. He had attacked Catti-brie! He had almost killed the person he most loved in all the world.

But no, it wasn't her, he reminded himself. It was a demon, a trick of Lolth—all of this was a grand deception, played out to break him.

And so it had, even before the inevitable reveal.

"Surely you feel my quiet intrusions, and your own revulsion to them."

"Perhaps everything about . . . you, revolts me," the defiant Drizzt retorted with as much conviction as he could muster. He focused on his larger issues and tried not to make it personal, reminding himself continually that this was all a ruse, all a lie.

If Kimmuriel was insulted in any way, he certainly didn't show it, but then Drizzt couldn't remember ever seeing any emotion from this one, positive or negative. His dealings with Kimmuriel Oblodra had been few, though, and fewer still when he only counted those he knew—or believed so, for what did he know, after all?—had occurred before the great deception of Lolth had been put into effect.

"What do you fear?" Kimmuriel asked, or maybe he wasn't even talking—so delicate and smooth were the communications of the master psionicist that Drizzt couldn't be sure. "Tell me your fears, Drizzt Do'Urden and let down your guard that I can help you."

"Help me?" Drizzt scoffed, and when he felt Kimmuriel's thoughts penetrating his mind once more, he threw a wall of anger up in instinctive defiance. "How do you know that you won't be the one needing help?"

Kimmuriel chuckled, but it was a mirthless thing, and more designed, Drizzt understood, to convey his pity for the petty insect that was Drizzt than out of any honest amusement. "That is why there are no weapons in this room, of course. And why Jarlaxle and Gromph are just outside. Perhaps you are powerful with your bare hands—you do spend your days in close combat, fool that you are. But I am in no danger here, so please, dismiss your threats and let us both be done with this insipid exercise so that Jarlaxle will grant me my time alone."

Drizzt made a sudden move, just to see if he could elicit a reaction from Kimmuriel.

He did, but it wasn't what he was expecting. A wave of discombobulating energy blasted into his mind, mixing up every signal coming in from his senses and twisting every command going back out from his thoughts to his limbs. What was supposed to be a sudden and short movement became an awkward mix of mismatched moves that had Drizzt stuttering and swaying, and quickly tumbling to the floor.

He fought it off, bit by bit, forcing Kimmuriel's mental blast away and eventually rolling back to his knees. But by that time, Kimmuriel was across the room, staring at him hard.

"I am not some weak-minded human woman who will be caught off guard by your charms," Kimmuriel assured him.

"What do you want from me?" Drizzt demanded.

"I already told you," the calm psionicist replied.

"Go to the Nine Hells—nay, back to the Abyss where you belong!" Drizzt told him. "Back to the foul Spider Queen and tell her that I know. Oh, how I know!"

"Know? What do you know?"

"Liar!" Drizzt accused. "All of it. Everything! You, my friends—aha, my long dead friends, miraculously restored to me! Lolth's plan is flawed, for I have been warned of this diabolical game before!"

Kimmuriel came forward and sat once more in his chair facing Drizzt, who managed to get back to his feet and was leaning on his own seat, directly across and not far away.

"Your friends are liars?"

"My friends are dead," Drizzt insisted.

"They are down the hall—"

"No!" the ranger shouted. "No! Your doppelgangers are known to me. Your trap will not break me."

Kimmuriel paused and cocked his head. "Drizzt Do'Urden," he stated calmly, and with a hint of amusement, "you are already broken."

Drizzt shook his head.

"You attacked Catti-brie, but then stopped yourself," Kimmuriel reminded him. "You could have killed her with that unexpected strike—and quite easily, by her own words—and yet you did not. Because you do not know—"

"Liar!"

"Perhaps I am. Perhaps not. You do not know."

"And you will enter my thoughts to tell me, and convince me that all is aright," Drizzt reasoned, and he laughed because it all came clear to him then. "I see now." His laughter had Kimmuriel looking at him ever more closely, he noted. "It's not working—Lolth knows that it's not working."

"What?"

"Shut up," said Drizzt. "She cannot break me because I know, and so you will come into my thoughts and make it so that I don't know, and so when the blow falls, the great and terrible revelation, I will break. Aye! But nay! You'll not find your way to my thoughts, fool drow!"

"Amazing," said Kimmuriel. "You think this whole thing is a deception? All of it? The return of your friends, of your wife? What of your battle with Demogorgon? Was that, too, but an illusion?"

Drizzt stared at him hard and hatefully.

"Amazing," Kimmuriel said. "Such trouble the Demon Queen of Spiders would go to over . . . you. Your arrogance is beyond even my low opinion of you. Your friends have been back for years. You fought a war—"

"I believe we fought a war."

"How many memories become reality, then?" the psionicist asked. "If life is merely a delusion, then at what point is such delusion simply a reality?"

Drizzt started to respond, but just fell back and glared.

"Then why not let me in?" Kimmuriel asked. "If this is your fear, then to what end and to what point do you keep me at bay?"

"Because you will convince me that I am not convinced!"

Kimmuriel laughed at him. It caught Drizzt off guard because it was an actual laugh, even if one obvious of pity.

"So you will be stubborn and strong in your misery because you fear greater misery?" Kimmuriel said, and he paused and chuckled. "And if you are wrong?"

Drizzt didn't have an answer.

"How long, Drizzt Do'Urden?" Kimmuriel asked. "And if you strike down Catti-brie and you are wrong, then what for you? Or if you force this woman, who so greatly professes her love for you, to kill you? What would that do to her, or to Mielikki, who has chosen her?

"And if you are right, and this is the grandest lie, then where is your goddess to intervene?" Kimmuriel said when no response was forthcoming. "Why has Mielikki abandoned you?"

"Because I will not kill the babies!" Drizzt growled, and he was back then, mentally replaying that awful conversation with Catti-brie soon after she had returned from the place she called Iruladoon. They were all evil, she had said, all the goblinkin, and so he must kill them all when he found them, including the babies. That thought assaulted his sensibilities—he had known a goblin who did not seem evil at all. He and Bruenor had found the ruins of a city where orcs and dwarves had lived in unison and apparent harmony The town of Palishchuck in Vaasa was full of half-orcs and was not at war with any of the goodly folk of the region—far from it!

And the Treaty of Garumn's Gorge had failed, but that did not dismiss the good work done by many orcs, the true followers of Obould, who strove for decades to hold the peace.

Or was all of that, too, nothing more than a grand deception, this long plan, laid out and worked brilliantly to seem like the passage of centuries in the broken mind of Drizzt?

Had he ever even actually gotten out of Menzoberranzan in what he perceived to be a century and more before, when Zaknafein had died that he could be free?

"How far back?" he asked, tears flowing down his cheeks. He fell into his chair, more lying down than sitting, feeling as if all the strength had been sucked out of his body.

"You tell me," Kimmuriel replied.

"You tell me!" Drizzt demanded, and he was sobbing then, feeling as if he had walked not out of Menzoberranzan but into the lair of Lolth, who had punished him with all of these false memories, a life never actually lived, and all done by the wretched Spider Queen for the single point of tormenting him beyond anything he could ever imagine.

He heard Kimmuriel clearly then, and had no response to offer, for indeed, he had hit the lowest point of all.

"Let us find out together," the psionicist offered, and Drizzt could only cry, and offered no resistance as Kimmuriel's fingers came lightly against his forehead.

And into Drizzt's mind went Kimmuriel, into the twisted dreams and burgeoning fears and the shifting sands of perception of a broken drow who had lost all sense of where reality stopped and deceit began.

The psionicist searched deeper, guiding Drizzt's thoughts and holding fast to them on their speeding and winding journey.

Kimmuriel looked for an anchor to reality, a solid raft of reality that he could bring to the forefront, a not-subtle demarcation between perception and truth upon which the drifting Drizzt could cling.

Kimmuriel's confidence waned as the moments slipped past, as each reality he discovered became, to Drizzt, a lie, as each truth became, to Drizzt, demonic deception.

And how could he disagree, Kimmuriel came to wonder? Perhaps he was the one in the wrong here, and Drizzt had found, after all, the awful truth of existence. Kimmuriel, above all others, should of course recognize the power of mental deception.

The shape of reality was molded in no small part by the conniving of godly figures.

Kimmuriel Oblodra cried out and fell back. He sat staring at the sobbing Drizzt with an expression of abject horror. He heard the door bang open behind him, but he didn't react, couldn't react, and instead sat staring at his counterpart with confusion and fear—fear inspired by a near break from all that he once held as truth.

"What is it?" Jarlaxle demanded, rushing up beside his Bregan D'aerthe comrade.

"Did he strike at you?" Gromph demanded, his voice dripping with his hopes that Kimmuriel would answer in the affirmative and thus give Gromph an excuse to obliterate Drizzt, just because he thought it would be a pleasing experience.

They both knew the truth before Kimmuriel began to answer, though, for it was obvious that this broken creature sitting in front of them, immersed in pathetic sobs and with his violet eyes looking nowhere but inward, had done no such thing.

"Come," Kimmuriel told them both, and he hustled from the room, dragging them along, and was quick to close and secure the door behind them.

"What have you learned?" Jarlaxle demanded.

"Demarcation," said Kimmuriel in a very somber voice.

"A boundary?" a confused Gromph asked.

Kimmuriel shook his head. "The mind flayers have among them a reference to a sickness," he explained. "They name it demarcation, but they mean it as quite the opposite of the word as we have come to know it—a de-demarcation, if you will. In our tongue, it means a boundary, yes, the marking of a distinction between realms or farmholds or the Houses of Menzoberranzan, but in this sense, the word refers to a specific sickness in which the sufferer loses the lines of distinction between truth and perception."

"I know a few matron—" Jarlaxle started to quip, but a very serious Kimmuriel cut him short with a cold look.

"We all suffer it, to some degree," the psionicist explained. "And many, like you, seek to inflict it upon others, with speech so persuasive that they lose their grounding and come to believe as you would have them believe."

Jarlaxle tipped his wide-brimmed hat at the compliment.

"Illithids are vulnerable," Kimmuriel explained.

"They prey upon others with just such tactics," Gromph argued.

"I would expect them to be the least vulnerable," Jarlaxle agreed. "I would never deign to practice my Art upon a mind flayer."

"They are invulnerable to your soothing words, yes," Kimmuriel replied. "And indeed to most, if not all, external suggestions and persuasions. But for them, the sickness comes from within, where they create reality in the thoughts of others and so can easily lose the proper distinction between that illusion and the truth they try to hide or warp."

"Self-deceit?" Gromph asked.

Kimmuriel nodded.

"So they come to believe their own lies," said Jarlaxle. "As I said, I have known many matron mothers so afflicted."

"That is different," Gromph told him.

"Not so much so," Kimmuriel corrected, which surprised Gromph and Jarlaxle, who, after all, had only been joking. "In both cases, the sickness is contracted through an overblown sense of pride, the deadliest of faults."

"Then Gromph should be dead," Jarlaxle said.

"Then Jarlaxle should be dead," Gromph said at the same time.

Kimmuriel just paused and tightened his face in disapproval. The brothers looked at each other and scoffed—mirror images, they seemed.

"I have never known pride to be a fault of Drizzt Do'Urden," Jarlaxle said at length, bringing the conversation back to the matter at hand. "His wont is humility, often to the point of supreme aggravation."

"The sickness in his mind was conceived externally," Kimmuriel said.

"The Faerzress," Gromph reasoned.

"An Abyssal sickness," Kimmuriel went on, nodding. "Magically rooted." He looked at Gromph, a budding and curious psionicist, and added a warning: "Beware your intrusions and explorations upon Drizzt Do'Urden, Archmage, for this malady is infectious. Hence my cry, for even I found myself falling under the Abyssal spell of doom and utter despair. To attempt to draw a clear line of reality against perception in the mind of Drizzt Do'Urden is to erase that same line in your own understanding, and to no benefit to Drizzt."

"What are you saying?" Jarlaxle demanded, and now his voice took on a bit of a nervous edge, as if it had never occurred to him that the great Kimmuriel couldn't fix the swirling confusion in Drizzt's mind.

Kimmuriel's responding shrug, so helpless, was as definitive an answer as Jarlaxle had ever known.

"You are mending Dahlia!" the mercenary protested. "She is far more lost than Drizzt . . ."

"It is different," Kimmuriel tried to explain, but Jarlaxle spoke right over him.

"Or are you just afraid that you will be infected?" he accused. "Is that it? Well then take Drizzt to the hive mind! Promise them whatever they need to mend—"

"No!" Kimmuriel shouted, and the uncharacteristically vehement outburst rocked both Jarlaxle and Gromph back on their heels.

"No," Kimmuriel said more calmly. "To do so would invoke a great risk. Would you have a colony of mind flayers lose the distinction between their perceptions and reality? Between their wishes and the truth of the world? The destruction they could wreak . . ." He stopped and took a deep breath, even patted his hands in the air to physically stabilize himself.

"They could do nothing to help Drizzt," he said at length, and calmly.

"But Dahlia . . ." Jarlaxle protested.

"Dahlia's sickness was implanted by Methil," Kimmuriel explained. "The mind flayer inflicted her with a series of tangential and confusing thoughts, luring her with powerful suggestions triggered by a multitude of cues that Methil set in her mind like a rogue's clever traps. Perhaps a word, perhaps a movement, will break the flow of Dahlia's present thoughts and wind her down an unrelated side corridor and so she is lost, winding back upon herself. And that supreme frustration, in turn, leads to dismay and sows further confusion. It was quite brilliant of Methil."

"But you can fix it?"

"Yes, though it will prove a painstaking and long process. I must seek out each cue and erase the suggestion Methil attached to it. But what Methil wrought, I can undo."

"But Drizzt?"

"It is a magical erasure and not simple misguiding suggestions," Gromph answered before Kimmuriel could. Kimmuriel looked at him and nodded approvingly at his comprehension.

"What your friend is experiencing is a complete break, a complete blurring of the demarcation of the relationship of his perception against the simple truth and reality that plays out before him," Gromph explained. "His very senses deceive him, so he believes, and there is no truth."

"Worse, that perception is rooted in doubt and terror," Kimmuriel added. "Not fear, but pure terror. Drizzt has come to believe that all that he once held as true, all that he took for granted as reality, was and so is indeed nothing more than a grand deception played upon him by a malignant force, some demon—likely Lolth—as some form of unending torment."

"He does think highly of himself after all," Gromph said with a chuckle, and Jarlaxle's look showed that he didn't much appreciate the levity at that grim moment.

"He has nothing to hold onto," Kimmuriel explained.

"And so his beloved Catti-brie is a demon in disguise," Jarlaxle said quietly, nodding as he finally caught on to the depth of this sickness, why Drizzt had nearly killed Catti-brie, and why he would likely do just that the next time.

"We cannot redraw the line," Kimmuriel warned. "Only Drizzt can. Any outside attempt to persuade him will be viewed with the same damning terror, that if it is meant to soothe and reassure him . . ."

"Then it is done to strengthen the deception," Jarlaxle finished.

Kimmuriel nodded.

"He is lost, then," said Gromph, with a tone of finality that stabbed at Jarlaxle's heart. "And will not be found. And as he is doomed to make tragic and deadly mistakes, he will never find his way."

Jarlaxle wanted to argue, wanted to scream into Gromph's face to silence him. But when he looked at Kimmuriel, whom he did trust, he found the psionicist in full agreement.

"My eye patch!" he blurted, looking for something, anything.

"The delusion is not external," Kimmuriel said. "Your eye patch will not protect him or cure him."

A defeated Jarlaxle blew a sigh of resignation.

"I could kill him painlessly and swiftly," Gromph offered.

Jarlaxle almost agreed.

◆ ◆ ◆

"I HAVE NEVER seen you so . . . wobbly," Tazmikella teased, sitting on the divan beside Jarlaxle. She wore lace and sheer veils, so beautiful and tempting in her human form, but the mercenary simply couldn't bring his focus to that matter.

"This is about the ranger again, isn't it?" the copper dragon asked.

Jarlaxle ran his fingers over his bald pate. "It is a horrible descent to witness."

"Helplessly," Tazmikella added, and the drow nodded.

The dragon shrugged. "If there is nothing you can do, then why waste your thoughts fretting over it? You have so few years of life as it is."

Jarlaxle pulled back from her touch and looked at her hard. "Would you say the same if it was your sister so afflicted?"

"Of course," came the answer from the door, and in walked Ilnezhara, no less alluring, and no more clad, than Tazmikella.

"Oh, you think us beasts!" Tazmikella said. "He does, sister!"

"Should we be insulted?" Ilnezhara asked breathlessly. "I thought Jarlaxle wiser than to insult dragons."

"Please," the drow surrendered, holding up his hands. "I cannot find mirth in your taunts. Not now."

"Your friend who loves the mind flayers could do nothing?" Tazmikella asked with just a hint of concern in her voice.

"It is magical, and nothing he can affect."

"Then what of Drizzt's wife?" Tazmikella asked.

"Aye," her sister agreed. "That one is quite powerful with her magic, both arcane and divine."

But Jarlaxle was shaking his head. "She has tried, of course, as has Gromph. But to no avail. And I have to believe that if Gromph cannot find a countering dweomer, there is no magical answer."

"Indeed, there aren't many mortals more powerful," said Ilnezhara.

"Mielikki, then?" Tazmikella asked. "Is Drizzt not a Chosen?"

"Catti-brie has prayed . . ." Jarlaxle said, but again ended by shaking his head.

"Good, truthfully," Ilnezhara said.

Tazmikella nodded, and Jarlaxle sat up straight with confusion and anger.

"The less the gods meddle, the better for all," said Ilnezhara.

"They view their mortals as toys," Tazmikella said, her voice dripping with contempt. "And I loathe to call them gods. More like accomplished wizards playing as gods to soothe their own sense of personal vanity."

"Oh indeed, sister."

"Except for Bahamut," Tazmikella was quick to add.

"Of course," Ilnezhara replied.

"Then go to Bahamut!" Jarlaxle shouted.

The two stared at him incredulously, then laughed at him.

"Well, what then?" the exasperated drow asked. "What am I to do?"

"Kill him quickly," said Tazmikella. "I could—"

"Stop it!" Jarlaxle demanded. "Is that your only answer to anything? First Gromph, now you . . ."

He jumped up from the divan and paced back and forth across the room.

"If magic neither arcane nor divine can cure it, and if psionicists are helpless, indeed afraid, then how?" he asked. "What is my answer?"

"What do you know?" Tazmikella prompted. "Kimmuriel went into his mind, you said, so what do you know?"

"Kimmuriel said that Drizzt must find his own way out of the tangle, that his cure must come from within," Jarlaxle explained. "That seems unlikely, impossible even."

"Drizzt is a disciplined warrior," Tazmikella offered.

"Yes, sister," Ilnezhara agreed, and something in her tone made both Jarlaxle and Tazmikella look to her with intrigue.

Ilnezhara was smiling.

"What do you know?" Jarlaxle demanded.

"Perhaps he is not disciplined enough," Ilnezhara said with a knowing grin.

"You would be hard-pressed to find one more so," Jarlaxle argued. "He is near perfect in his training, as fine a warrior—"

"*Near* perfect," Tazmikella interrupted, her tone and grin showing that she, too, was beginning to catch on to her sister's thinking.

"What?" Jarlaxle asked.

"But he has not ascended," Ilnezhara explained.

"Really, sister, has any drow ever?"

"If a human can . . ."

"What are you talking about?" Jarlaxle demanded.

But the cryptic dragon sisters just smiled.

# PART 2

# The Bloodstone Lands

I CANNOT WASH THE BLOOD OFF MY HANDS.

The wound was minimal, the actual bloodletting almost nonexistent, but my blade was there, against Catti-brie's neck, and my intent was there, undeniably, to slash Vidrinath across and brutally cut out her throat and bathe in her spurting blood. To exact revenge!

Oh, how I wanted to do that!

Because she was a demon in disguise, I knew, and know, and do not know, tormenting me by taking the physical appearance and aspect of my lost beloved.

When did she intend the revelation? In the midst of lovemaking perhaps, when a leering monstrous face would stare down at me, a grotesque and misshapen demon form swaying above me, perhaps taking my seed to conceive a horrid half-breed?

Or not. Or none of it.

Or, I put my blade against Catti-brie's throat—Catti-brie—and came a single breath from murdering her.

In that case, were I to sail the Sword Coast and drag my hand in the water, then surely I would leave the entire sea red in my wake! So little blood did spill, and yet to me it is all the blood of the world, washing upon me, marking me a great scarlet badge of shame.

Murderer!

Because I did kill her, in my mind. I did doubt her, in my heart. My arm failed me. My courage fled.

Because the demon should have died!

The imposter should have died, and killing it would give me one last act of defiance against Lolth. One simple act, one clean kill, to tell the Spider Queen that in the end, she did not score her craven victory. She would obliterate me at her whim—I could do nothing to prevent that act if she so desired—but nay, in the end, she would not break me.

I am not her plaything!

Unless it was really Catti-brie who felt the edge of my scimitar against her soft neck—how am I to know?

And that is the conundrum, that is the deeper curse, that is why I have already lost.

I rouse from my Reverie every morning and declare to myself that this day, I will be happy, that this day, I will look upon the sunrise and know hope. Perhaps it is all a ruse, all a great deception by a demon queen to inflict the ultimate torment.

So be it, I say each morn. So be it!

And each morning, I ask myself, "What choice have I?"

What other course? What other road might I walk? If it is all perception, then at what point must perception, even delusion, simply be accepted as reality? And if that reality is pleasant, then should I not find happiness in it, for whatever time the illusion, or delusion, remains? Is it worthwhile or even sensible to refuse to enjoy years of perceived calm among friends and loved ones, to not simply be happy, out of fear for what may or may not come?

Is the sunrise any less beautiful? Is Catti-brie's smile any less enchanting? Is Bruenor's laughter any less infectious? Is Guenhwyvar's purr any less comforting?

Every day, I tell myself that. Every day, I initially reason my way to a state of happiness and contentedness. Every day, I repeat this litany against madness, this armor against ultimate despair.

Every day.

And every day, I fail.

I cannot create meaning in the midst of a dream. I cannot create purpose when I am alone in a fancy design of my own creation. I cannot create freedom to smile with the ever-present thought that my enemies await the deepest smile they can elicit before tearing the pretty facade away.

And worse, now I am stained with the blood of Catti-brie or of an imposter demonic creature, and if the former, then I struck out at the woman I love, and so wallow in shame and blood. And if the latter, then I had not the courage to complete the kill, and so there, too, I have failed.

They have taken my weapons, and for that I am glad. Would that they would take my life and end this misery.

They pretend to care. They feign spells and mind intrusions to heal my malady, but I see the sinister eyes and smell the Abyssal fog and hear the quiet cackles behind the sighs of their supposed concern.

Let me rot with the blood of Catti-brie on my hands or let me rot in the shame of my cowardice.

Either way, it is a fate I surely deserve.

—Drizzt Do'Urden

# CHAPTER 9 ◈

# The Client

REGIS WAS GLAD TO ACCOMPANY DONNOLA TO THE BALL that fine summer evening in Delthuntle, and gladder still when she came down the stairs in her lavender silk gown, trimmed in white lace and cut low, offering a generous glimpse of her curvaceous bosom. She wore a brilliant set of pink deepwater oyster pearls, perhaps collected by Regis himself.

And more than a few of those were likely magical. Donnola, though no true wizard, did have a bit of training in the Art.

Regis could hardly draw breath as she glided down the main stairs of Morada Topolino, her smile outshining both the pearls and the silver and gold tiara that shaped her thick hair.

"I have your approval, good sir Spider?" she asked when she swept up before him.

"Madam, there is nothing you could ever do to evoke my disapproval," Regis replied. He performed a low bow, gracefully sweeping off his blue beret as he dipped. He, too, was dressed in finery, with a new gray waistcoat, gold stitched, and a wonderful black cape with a high, stiff collar to complement both his fabulous beret and the brilliant basket of the precious rapier that hung at his hip. His boots, too, were new, black and shiny, high and hard-soled so he could click them imperiously when making a dramatic entrance.

"Are you ready, my charming suitor?" Donnola asked.

"Milady, in seeing you . . . let us stay here . . ." He ended with a wicked smile and an exaggerated wink, and Donnola tittered appropriately—they were playing the part of the empty-headed courtiers, of course, all batting eyelashes and moustache-twirling.

"Let's make it an early evening," Regis said in all seriousness, turning and offering his arm for his lady.

"It will take as long as it takes," Donnola replied, reminding him that this wasn't pleasure—though they might find some entertainment, or amusement at least—but rather business. These social gatherings allowed Donnola to keep in touch with her secret contacts and to cultivate new business suitors. Her product was, among other things, information. And with the Zzar and Rashemi firewine flowing, there was no better place than a court ball to gather her wares.

"But they so bore me when I am done making fun of them," Regis said as they went out the front door, and Donnola laughed.

And Wigglefingers, who was outside waiting for them, rolled his eyes.

"Do try to make it a profitable evening," the wizard reminded them both.

Donnola replied, but Regis didn't hear it, so entranced was he by Wigglefingers's strange robe, which was covered in garish representations of a quarter moon and gigantic stars, making the grumpy mage look very much the part of a neophyte wizard hired to garner "ooohs," "aaahs," and laughs at a noble child's birthday party.

"Whatever are you wearing?" Regis asked incredulously.

"Our good friend plays the role of jester this night," Donnola explained, and Wigglefingers snapped his fingers and produced from nowhere a single rose with petals of assorted colors, the hues shifting as they fell, one by one, each fluttering almost to the floor before turning into a butterfly and flittering away.

"Well played," said Regis.

The wizard rolled his eyes again and walked briskly to the waiting coach.

"You will let them mock him in such a manner?" Regis asked Donnola.

"Wigglefingers knows his role and plays it wonderfully," Donnola replied.

"He looks the part of the fool."

"And so he is always underestimated." Donnola stopped and tugged Regis's arm as he continued down the walk, turning him around. "Isn't that always the way with our people?" she asked in all seriousness. "We are fools, children, playthings, the accepted object of mockery."

"I fail to see how any could look upon you and not think you most impress—"

"Oh, stop it," Donnola said, but she did offer a conciliatory smile to accept the compliment. "In truth, you must admit, we understand the reality of living amongst the larger folk of Faerûn. The wiser halflings can turn this condescension to an advantage, yes?"

"Of course, my beautiful lady," Regis replied, offering his arm to her once more. When she took it and they resumed their walk to the coach, Regis added, "Wulfgar, you know, would never harbor such thoughts."

"You were, and are, blessed with unusual and exceptional friends," Donnola replied.

He knew that Donnola didn't even begin to understand how true that statement rang. He merely nodded in reply, but could have gone on for hours about the Companions of the Hall, of which he had always been a valued member, even when his own actions should have limited his role, and sometimes even invited their scorn.

"Your barbarian friend is too unusual to be formally associated with Morada Topolino, you understand," Donnola said, bringing the conversation back to Wulfgar alone. "Though that, too, will play to our advantage."

"You would deny him a warm bed?"

"I have already arranged for one, indefinitely, at a most lovely inn," Donnola replied. "From there, he will journey to the home of Lord Toulouse."

"Wulfgar will attend the ball?"

"He agreed, yes," Donnola answered.

Regis laughed, trying to picture his enormous friend dressed in foppish Delthuntle finery. "How did you even find him a waistcoat large enough?" he stuttered to ask.

"A waistcoat? But Master Spider Parrafin, what a silly thing to say!"

Regis couldn't help but smile into his dimples when Donnola called him that, particularly with her impressed tone.

"Why, the barbarian beast, Wulfgar, is a proper ambassador from a faraway land called Icewind Dale, on a mission to secure the very best libations for the dwarves of Kelvin's Cairn," Donnola explained.

Regis looked at her curiously. "The dwarves of Icewind Dale? They have been displaced . . ."

"The ruse was Wulfgar's idea, and a fine one," Donnola explained. She let Regis help her up into the coach, not out of any feminine sense of decorum, certainly, but simply because her gown was not a practical item for ladder climbing—though it surely sufficed for hiding daggers and the like. "You met this Wulfgar creature on the crossing of the Sea of Fallen Stars, of course, and introduced him to me, but though I secured an invitation for him to attend the ball, he is unconnected to Morada Topolino, except perhaps as a client buyer."

Regis nodded at the cover story, and was still grinning widely at the thought of Wulfgar in fine clothing when he, too, ascended into the coach, but he said no more. Nor was he about to question Donnola on her wider decision to lower the profile of Morada Topolino, or to play upon the natural inclinations of the larger folk to look down upon the halflings in ways more than physical. Her observations about the realities of being the smallest of the races could not be denied. To be a halfling in many of Faerûn's cities was to be overlooked, chided, often mocked. Grandfather Pericolo had done much to convince many in Delthuntle that such attitudes were dangerously misplaced, but even the previous successes of Morada Topolino had only dissuaded the persistent trope and prejudices so far.

Indeed, from what Regis was beginning to glean from Donnola and Wigglefingers—with the drama of the captured pirates and boat, with this evening's plan, and with the quieter general aspect of Morada Topolino—that much of the previous gains of the powerful halfling house had faded. The Sea of Fallen Stars had seen rough times during the Sundering—even to altering the landscape—and powerful vigilante and mercenary bands had come into play all around the coastal cities.

For better or worse, Donnola had decided to lower the profile of Morada Topolino. Perhaps it was an admission of failure, perhaps an acceptance of reality, perhaps an act of timidity when an aggressive posture might have salvaged more of the previous glories. It was not Regis's place to argue, surely, but to be ready to help her in any way she saw fit. He could only hope, though, that she would choose to step forth once more when things had better settled, if that ever happened, and return Morada Topolino to the heights Grandfather Pericolo had achieved.

◆ ◆ ◆

AFTER A CONSPICUOUS absence—at least to Regis—of nearly an hour, Wulfgar reappeared in the grand ballroom of Lord Toulouse, one of the richest and most influential men in all of Delthuntle—indeed, in all of Aglarond. The barbarian appeared to be pulled together, though his hair was a bit more messed than usual and his winter wolf cloak hung a bit askew.

Less composed was a Lady of Court who entered soon after Wulfgar, her hair sticking weirdly from a comb on one side, several buttons on her gown undone.

Regis just lowered his head and shook it, reminding himself that he shouldn't be surprised. He lifted his fine glass of Zzar, the most famous sherry wine from Waterdeep, considered its beautiful orange hue, and inhaled its almond scent before taking a tiny sip.

By the time he looked up again, Wulfgar was arm-in-arm with a woman, moving to the dance floor, and it was not the same woman who had just returned disheveled.

Regis could only sigh.

He watched his barbarian friend unabashedly bumble around the floor for a bit. Wulfgar appeared graceless compared to the sophisticated lords of Delthuntle who did nothing but prepare for or attend various balls and who practiced dancing more than swordplay. But Wulfgar clearly didn't care, nor did the wide-eyed—truly, it seemed as if she was panting—woman moving across the floor in his arms. And certainly none of these fancy lads in the room would find the courage to insult the imposing ambassador from Icewind Dale.

Indeed, it seemed a fine play to the amused halfling.

Another dancing couple, though, quickly garnered Regis's attention. Donnola was dancing with a man Regis didn't know, an older gentleman with silver hair, expensive robes and jewelry, and a fine bearing. She moved about up on his toes, as was convention when a halfling danced with a human in Delthuntle. He was stooped over low so his face was buried in Donnola's pretty hair.

"It is business," a voice beside him startled Regis.

He turned to see Wigglefingers holding a stemware glass of Zzar.

"Lord Delcasio," the mage explained, motioning to the man who hovered over Donnola. "When first we arrived, he begged Donnola for a dance, or more precisely, for an audience."

"Must he paw her so intimately?"

"And whisper into her ear, I would expect," said Wigglefingers. "Tell me about him."

"A merchant lord, mostly with business outside of Aglarond," the mage answered. "Usually his queries have to do with the goings-on at the docks, with one shipment or another, and he is known to often complain about the pirates—though half of them are probably working for him, at least in part."

"He is looking for business with Icewind Dale, perhaps?"

"No," the mage said. "Lord Delcasio quietly related word of his desire for an audience before your smelly hill giant friend was ever announced to the courts." The wizard looked past Regis then and snorted, and Regis turned to see Wulfgar slipping out of the room, and a cursory scan showed Regis that the woman Wulfgar had just been dancing with was nowhere to be seen.

"I do expect that the next generation of Delthuntle nobles might be considerably larger in stature than the present," the mage quipped. "Truly, is that all he does, eat and cavort?"

"If he could, I expect," Regis replied with a shrug and a smile—one that turned fast into a frown when he swung his head back around, surveying the dance floor as he did, and just in time to see this nobleman, Lord Delcasio, disappearing through a different door.

"Business," Wigglefingers assured him quietly. "Just business. Put away your petty jealousies, Master Parrafin, and remember the role of Lady Donnola."

Regis looked at him, about to argue, but the mage just shrugged and started away.

◆ ◆ ◆

"THE STAINS ARE her tears!" Lord Corrado Delcasio said, his own eyes showing gathering moisture as if he would soon add his own stains to the small parchment.

Donnola again examined the letter he had handed her.

"Oh, my dearest little daughter! What have I done?" The man stepped aside in the small anteroom off the main ballroom, dramatically throwing his arm across his face as if to hide his shame.

Donnola reread Queen Concettina Delcasio Frostmantle's letter and excused the overwrought lord for his emotional outburst. What father would not be concerned with such a note, after all?

Dearest Papa,

King Yarin grows angrier by the day. Each time I am visited by the cycle of blood, bloody too are his eyes and the face he wears seems not his own, but that of some demon come to Helgabal. He will have his heir, no matter how many wives he must discard to get it.

I have seen the statues in the garden, my Lord and Father. They are headless, the way the last queens left this life. I see no way out of my prison here, for I cannot run away and I am a virtuous queen.

In trust and love,
Concy

"Concy?" Donnola asked.

"My name for her when she was a child," Lord Delcasio replied, and the question seemed to work in drawing the man from his overwhelming grief.

"You raised a fine woman, it would seem."

"Who plots to cuckold her husband?"

You should hope so, Donnola thought but did not say. The halfling smiled and nodded, not ready to argue the point, though she figured that if she were in Concettina's position, she would have long before thrown this ridiculous notion of virtue to the dung heaps of the court stable!

Virtue? What matter virtue? The King of Damara was clearly going to execute her if she could not bear him a child, and given the renowned history of the troubled tyrant Yarin Frostmantle, it seemed quite clear to Donnola and to everyone else that the Damaran king needed his finger of blame to be twisted back around.

"If Yarin . . ." Lord Delcasio started, but had to pause and take a deep breath. "I know King Yarin well. He is not a merciful man. If he became aware of this letter, my Concy . . ."

"Why are you showing me this?" Donnola asked.

The lord's expression turned incredulous and desperate. "I knew Grandfather Pericolo well," he said.

"Grandfather Pericolo is dead."

"But Morada Topolino . . ."

"Why is your daughter in the Bloodstone Lands?" Donnola asked, and the lord's wince told her all she needed to know. Corrado had arranged his dear Concy's marriage to this King Yarin Frostmantle, and now his mounting fears were being compounded by his guilt.

"Please, Lady Donnola, I have few options."

"You would have me arrange a return letter to your lovely daughter?" she asked, and the man moaned.

"An emissary, then?" she asked. "Do you desire a dowry paid for a proper and reasonable divorce?"

"No, no . . ."

"Have you tried?"

"King Yarin cares more about his legacy than any wealth I could offer," Lord Delcasio explained. "He properly divorced his earlier wives—with great sums collected from their merchant families—and more than one then proceeded to produce children. His embarrassment was great, I assure you."

"But Damara is a long way from Delthuntle."

"And whispers travel faster than speeding dragons."

Donnola nodded, unable to refute that truth—indeed, it was one upon which Donnola was trying to build her fortune and power.

"Please, lady."

"I do not understand what you would expect that I could do, Lord Delcasio. I am merely a socialite of Delthuntle . . ."

"I knew Grandfather Pericolo!" Lord Delcasio cried.

"Grandfather Pericolo is dead. And I implore you to keep your voice down."

"Lady!" He came forward a step with an intimidating posture, almost threatening.

But Donnola fixed him with such a stare as to freeze the blood in his veins, a not-subtle reminder that she had been trained by the very halfling, Grandfather of Assassins Pericolo, whom Delcasio kept telling her he knew so well.

"I . . . I . . ." he stammered, easing back a bit.

"And, wait, but you knew, too, of King Yarin's history, of course," Donnola reasoned. She held up Concettina's note as an accusation. "You knew of the headless statues in Yarin's gardens? Surely this is not news to a man as impeccable and prepared as Lord Corrado Delcasio."

"I had faith in my daughter."

"You had greed in your heart," Donnola accused. She didn't want to emotionally bludgeon the already-battered man, but she needed to back him off here and calm him down. Delcasio was about one step from feeling the bite of Donnola's poisoned dagger, after all, and that would have done neither of them any good.

"Lady, I implore you," he said, clearly back under control—and Donnola silently congratulated herself. "I have no other moves to play. Concettina is no child, and no overly emotional fool. Her tears are on that note."

"Rain, more likely, or spray from the journey across the sea."

"The risk she took in penning it . . ."

Donnola conceded the point with a nod. "But still I do not understand what you would wish from me, or from Morada Topolino. We are merchants, nothing more."

"I want you to kill him," Lord Delcasio said bluntly.

"Kill him? Who? King Yarin?" she asked with obvious skepticism.

"Grandfather Pericolo would do so, and did so, many times," Lord Delcasio insisted, not backing down. "He was a halfling of severe justice, and is this which I beg of you not just?"

"Pericolo Topolino was a wealthy halfling," Donnola said.

"I have great coin to offer."

"You are asking me to murder a king," she said. "Perhaps there is not enough coin in all of Faerûn."

"Well . . . then I care not if you kill Yarin," the desperate man improvised. "I do not even hold him in contempt."

Donnola did well to hide her sneer at that remark. This man, this father, was willing to accept another man whom he thought about to murder his own daughter? To Donnola's thinking, Lord Delcasio's last admission had just erased any sympathy she might hold for him, and so the lord had just unwittingly raised the price, considerably.

"Just rescue her," Lord Delcasio pleaded.

Donnola spent a long while staring at the downcast lord, formulating a plan and weighing the consequences. "I will see if I can fathom a way," she said.

"The reward will be great!" Lord Delcasio blurted, and in his great relief, he came forward with his arms out wide for a hug. "A hundred pieces of gold!"

Donnola ducked the hug and skipped around behind him. "That very amount in each of the ten shipments to Morada Topolino," she said as a surprised Delcasio swung about, his mouth falling open.

"And *The Aardvark*," Donnola added, referring to one of the finest caravels of Delthuntle, one under the flag of Lord Delcasio, and the man's eyes popped open wide.

"L-lady . . ." he stuttered.

"And her crew," Donnola insisted. "You ask me to anger a king, after all."

"But . . ."

"Oh, I know of Yarin Frostmantle, Lord Delcasio," explained Donnola, who indeed knew many details of all the nobles of the eastern and northern reaches of the Sea of Fallen Stars. "I knew of him when you handed over your beautiful daughter, you fool."

"I-I had faith in her," he stammered.

"So claimed several fathers before you," she retorted. "I am sure that your daughter is quite fertile. Do you think that matters?"

A clearly defeated Lord Delcasio visibly slumped.

"Do we have a deal?" Donnola asked. "A thousand pieces of gold and *The Aardvark*."

"You can get her out of Damara? You can bring my beautiful Concy home?"

"If I cannot, then I will arrange for a proxy to make her with child," Donnola said. "Let King Yarin believe the child is his own—he will shower her with jewels and your fears will be assuaged. In that event, half the gold, and still I take *The Aardvark*."

Lord Delcasio's eyes lit up at that, and Donnola wanted to stab him, for surely he was then thinking this latter foolery the better course, as it would prove cheaper and might be one where he could further profit down the line.

"A deal, Lord Delcasio?" she asked sharply.

He nodded, and Donnola left the room, pointedly closing the door behind her. She moved down the short corridor, her mind whirling as she considered what roads might be open to her here. Despite her threats and cold-hearted attitude with Lord Delcasio, Donnola wanted to find some way to help Lady Concettina. She knew Lord Delcasio's daughter personally from her earliest days in the social circles, when Grandfather Pericolo had first put Donnola out among the lords and ladies of Delthuntle as the quiet representative of Morada Topolino.

Concettina was about Donnola's age, and along with her noble friends had welcomed Donnola to the court celebrations. Donnola had never been overly fond of any of them—the gatherings were simply business to her, her acquaintances were needed contacts, and rarely resembled anything like true friendship—but neither had Donnola disliked this member of the young noble coterie, and surely she understood poor Concettina's current desperate plight.

No woman deserved that.

Lord Delcasio could have made a better bargain, given Donnola's personal feelings, and Donnola actually felt a bit guilty about pressing him for such an extravagant payment.

Just a bit, though.

She came back into the ballroom and noticed Regis dancing quite gracefully with one of the ladies of court. Donnola couldn't help but giggle when the couple came together, for Regis got a faceful of bosom.

Donnola continued her scan, nodding to Wigglefingers who was preparing his next performance, some inane trick involving a rabbit. She didn't linger on the wizard, though, moving her gaze past him to find one for whom she might have just found some value.

Yes, she thought, when she spotted Wulfgar, surrounded by a bevy of flapping fans and batting eyelashes. That large northern human would hardly be out of place in the Bloodstone Lands, and wouldn't King Yarin be thrilled at the thought of such a strapping young heir?

# Chapter 10 ◈

# *Queen Infecund VII*

THE GREEN-BEARDED DWARF WANDERED THROUGH THE palace gardens, pausing often to offer his greetings to each lush plant. Summer was short in Damara, but Pikel made sure to bring it to its shining brilliance in the palace grounds of King Yarin, with colors upon colors of roses, orchids, tulips, and daylilies—so many daylilies!

Still, the hedgerows and not the flowers were the centerpieces of these magnificent gardens, natural walls creating as many and as varied "rooms" out here as in the palace beyond. And never had they been lusher or more neatly groomed than this summer.

Each year, Pikel built on the successes of the previous summer, tightening his friendship with the plants, talking to them, helping them to find their greatest potential.

And they talked back, and in conversations spoke of things that few in the world beyond Pikel Bouldershoulder could ever begin to imagine. For with a quiet spell, the druidic dwarf could coax from the flowers the echoes of the garden conversations of the people who congregated here. It was almost always nonsensical stuff, trivial gossip and sexual innuendo that seemed to be the lifeblood of the self-absorbed and somewhat pathetic nobles of Helgabal.

All in all, Pikel found his greenery gossip quite amusing, a guilty pleasure, but since everyone at court thought him a simpleton anyway, his giggles when he recognized some of the more ridiculous gossipers or gossipees were usually met with nothing more than a condescending nod.

Sometimes, though, Pikel did garner useful information for his soldier brother—one time he had uncovered a clandestine operation and so had whispered to Ivan a plot to steal the king's own scepter.

When the youngster, the teenaged son of a Vaasan merchant, opened the great King's Receptacle in the palace audience chamber, he had found not a scepter and robe and assortment of jewels but a yellow-bearded Ivan Bouldershoulder crouched within the box, a smile on his hairy face and a brass wrap around his knuckles.

Then the youngster saw those brass knuckles much more closely, for a moment.

And so, a diligent and easily amused Pikel Bouldershoulder always took the time to listen to the echoes of the garden flowers. He cast a spell to speak with the flora and crawled on his knees, whispering niceties and flashing his sincere loving smile.

He found a cooperative tulip just inside the Sunset Garden, a chamber the gossiping nobles had nicknamed "Driella's Mausoleum," since the headless representation of Yarin's sixth queen was tucked into the waterfall display below the southern hedgerow, the one place in this particular garden chamber that was always in shadow.

Echoes of the titters of several young women caught the dwarf druid's attention. With his right hand, his only hand, he gently stroked the flower as he chanted a special song, coaxing the memories from it.

Gradually, the recent voices began to whisper in the air around him. He recognized one, a young, black-haired woman nicknamed "Pretty Feet," for the special attention she received, with very special gifts, from one of the older noblemen of Yarin's Court.

Pikel giggled at the thought. "Pretty Feet, hee hee hee," he said quietly and crouched lower, leaning on the stump of his left arm and putting his ear right to the confluence of petals.

Pretty Feet was talking about the current queen, he realized, and of the whispers that King Yarin was fairly finished with her. Other voices chimed in, then, but mostly inaudibly in the background. Pikel sensed their fears, for clearly none wanted to be chosen as a replacement.

"Oh, but to be Queen of Damara!" one said.

"Until death, so not for long!" another reminded, followed by nervous laughter. The grim inevitability of such a fate seemed hard to dismiss, particularly in this place so near to the headless statue.

"Unless you just outlived King Yarin," Pretty Feet responded. "He is no young man, nor a very satisfied one, it would seem."

More laughter followed.

"Alas for poor Queen Concettina," one said, and Pikel couldn't tell if she was being serious or mocking.

"Queen Infecund the Seventh," Pretty Feet agreed, and there was honest regret in her voice, the green-bearded dwarf realized.

Pikel rolled back into a kneel and kneaded at the grass with his bare toes, as he always did when he was down about the ground—that was why he wore sandals all the time, after all.

"Hmm," he said a few times, bothered by this development, though it was not unexpected. King Yarin wanted an heir. The aging man spoke of little else. And in this garden, of all places, it was not hard to remember the consequences to any queen who did not give him one.

The dwarf stroked his beard and considered all the elixirs he might concoct to help with this problem. There were some for virility, perhaps, though those seemed more concerned with willingness and not necessarily ability . . .

The dwarf sighed, trying to decide if he should tell Ivan.

But what good would it do?

He sighed again and crawled away, then spotted a squirrel and invited it to join him for some lunch.

The rodent accepted.

◆ ◆ ◆

THERE WOULD BE no cuddling when the lovemaking finished. Concettina knew that, and was glad of it, for she could barely stand the touch of Yarin now that she was convinced he was going to behead her.

She lay in the rumpled sheets of the bed, watching him as he quickly dressed, this pitiful old man who could now barely perform his husbandly duties and who had long ago given up on cleanliness. He was growing increasingly agitated, she could tell from his movements and from the way he had attacked her, a style of lovemaking more desperate than passionate.

"I have duties to attend," he grumbled, or something like that—Concettina couldn't be sure.

And out he went, and the queen sighed and dropped her face into the bedclothes.

The slamming door startled her, but also brought her great relief. She wanted to remain in bed throughout the rest of the day and night, to just lie there and hide in her covers and pretend she was a little girl in Delthuntle.

She thought of her mother, long dead. Concettina had not yet been a woman when Chianca Delcasio died in childbirth, along with the brother Concettina would never know.

That day had changed her father, Corrado. Before that darkest of days Corrado had been a loving father, but the tragedy broke him. He had become more concerned with his business interests than with her, and thus had young Concettina been sold off to this King of Damara as part of a lucrative trade deal.

Surely it was Corrado Delcasio's grief that had driven him to this point. It had to have been.

The woman pulled herself from the bed and began to collect her clothing. She noted then that the left eye of the painting of King Yarin was not identical to the right—again.

Acelya, the king's sister, was in the secret passageway that ran behind the interior wall of the room, crouched there, watching.

King Yarin knew Concettina was becoming aware of her predicament, and so he suspected that perhaps his queen would find some secret lover to make her fat with child.

The thought had indeed crossed Concettina's mind.

In truth, it echoed there whenever she walked through certain areas of the palace gardens, where the last two "barren" queens had been immortalized.

She knew what the coterie were saying about her now, about the name, Queen Infecund the Seventh, they whispered behind her back.

She tried hard to not let the thoroughly wretched Acelya know that she was aware of her presence.

She dressed and went out to resume her day.

◆ ◆ ◆

"Ah, but you should be more relaxed, my King," Rafer Ingot said when King Yarin reappeared at the fountain patio behind the castle.

King Yarin snorted and motioned for one of the servants to fetch him a glass of Impiltur whiskey. Few men would dare to address Yarin in such a manner, but Rafer, the huge and powerful murderer who headed one of the king's spy networks—the one King Yarin was beginning to lean on more and more heavily of late—was one of them.

Rafer Ingot had done a lot of very dirty work for King Yarin, and had been just a young and promising apprentice when Murtil Dragonsbane had unexpectedly met his demise more than twenty years before—unexpectedly, at least, to all but a few close associates of Yarin Frostmantle. And those close associates were gone now as well, except for Rafer, by whose hand the line of Dragonsbane had ended.

Yes, he had been a promising apprentice, and was now the master assassin of Yarin's court.

King Yarin took the whiskey and swirled it around, letting the aroma preface the drink. He looked off across the garden field and nodded, spotting Captain Dreylil Andrus riding along the far hedgerow.

"I become less sure of that one," Yarin remarked off-handedly.

"Likely with cause," said Rafer, and that drew a curious glance from Yarin. It was one thing for the king to disparage the Captain of the Guard, but something quite different for someone else to agree.

"What do you know?" Yarin prompted.

"Bah, but it's just the way he looks around in court," Rafer explained. "Seems always sour, and I'm never for trusting one with a forever scowl."

"I have heard the same said of you."

"Bah, but you see me laughing all the time, my lord!"

"Yes, like when I go to bed my wife," Yarin remarked.

"But that's a cheer for your good fortune, for you've a pretty one to ride!"

King Yarin took another drink and silently reminded himself of Rafer's unique value. And so silently reminded himself not to have the crude man murdered.

❖ ❖ ❖

SHE HATED THAT the ladies-in-waiting followed her like a trio of obedient dogs, and every time she came out to the gardens, Concettina found herself longing for her home in Delthuntle. She used to go for longs walks there, usually along the docks to watch the sun set over the Sea of Fallen Stars. When she imagined it now and closed her eyes, she could almost smell the seaweed on the shoreline—just enough to give a slight taste to the air but not enough to make it unpleasant.

Still, it was nothing like the aroma in those gardens. Every flower bed had been placed and nurtured to give each of the hedged-off chambers its own unique smell, and Concettina more often chose her course for the anticipated aromas as the views, particularly now, with Damara's short summer in full bloom.

Lilacs drew her to the long walk down the right hand side of the castle grounds. Bees buzzed around, too engaged with the flowers to even notice the queen and her entourage.

Another creature, too, seemed not to notice, but Concettina grinned when she spotted him and made her way up to him directly after turning to motion for her attendants to be silent.

The queen crept over to the hunched-over fellow, taking great pleasure in the little ditty he was singing to the flowers, a light-hearted melody that seemed more grunts than words, which, knowing Pikel, didn't surprise Concettina at all. She moved right up behind the dwarf, whose face was fairly buried in the lilacs, and smiled wider. There were long pauses, as if Pikel was asking the lilacs to sing back at him.

And they probably were.

These gardens were the envy of any in the Bloodstone Lands precisely because of this green-bearded, green-thumbed gardener. They bloomed first and held their petals longest, a summertime blast of color and aroma beyond even those meticulous rows along the grounds of the Monastery of the Yellow Rose or the Lord's Palace in Impiltur. And all because of Pikel.

The little dwarf finally finished his song, then giggled and turned. He nearly jumped out of his open-toed sandals to find Queen Concettina standing right behind him.

"Good day, Master Pikel," she said politely. "The air is full of the sounds of happy bees."

"Queenie!" Pikel greeted and bowed so low that his green beard tickled the ground—and though that beard was long, such was no small feat. Unlike most dwarves, who let their beard hang low as a source of pride, braided or not, Pikel had braided his beard back and up over his ears, tying it in with his shaggy hair. That affect also pulled the hair from Pikel's ample lips, so that when he smiled, he showed his teeth, full and straight and surprisingly white given his advanced age.

He came up from the bow bobbing, grinning, and giggling, obviously overjoyed to see Queen Concettina out this fine summer morning.

And that in turn delighted Concettina, though she was taken aback then as a cloud seemed to pass over Pikel's cherubic face, and he even mumbled, "Oooo," unintentionally, it seemed.

"What is it, good sir dwarf?" Concettina asked.

Pikel just smiled again and shook his head, but the cloud remained. The dwarf's grin kept shifting to a grimace and he was moving from foot to foot, as if nervous. Concettina had met up with Pikel scores of times in these gardens, and never had she seen that behavior before.

"Pray tell me," she whispered, moving closer.

Pikel continued to bob and started to whistle. He looked past Concettina to acknowledge the other ladies, who were all bunched together, whispering and giggling, no doubt at Pikel's expense. Concettina shooed them away, doing so until they were far off, back by the entrance to this long side garden.

When she finally turned back to Pikel, Concettina found that he had dropped all pretense of lightheartedness.

"Oooo," he moaned again.

"Master Pikel, I do not think I've ever seen you like this," the queen remarked. "What is the matter?"

"Me friend, Queenie?" the dwarf asked.

"Of course I am your friend."

"Me friend Queenie," the dwarf answered somberly.

It took Concettina a moment to realize that Pikel was answering her first question, that what was wrong had to do with her.

"Me?" she asked and Pikel nodded. "Something is wrong with me?"

He nodded more emphatically.

"Pray tell me what you know."

He shrugged, indicating that he really didn't know anything.

"Then tell me what you think might be wrong," she prompted.

Pikel glanced left and right and chewed his lip, as if looking for a way to explain—which was always the way with this strange little gardener. Finally, he put his hand on his ample belly, then moved it forward and pointed his stubbed arm at Concettina's rather flat belly.

The queen was taken aback by that. None were allowed such intimacy as that with her. The negative thought didn't hold, though. This was Pikel, gentle and simple.

"No, Pikel, I am not with child," she quietly replied, glancing back at her attendants to make sure they were nowhere near enough to hear.

"Oooo," Pikel said, then he hopped suddenly, his face brightening, and he pointed his finger at the sky as if he had just thought of something. He motioned for Concettina to follow and led her along the left-hand hedgerow, down near the far end of the long run. There, he stepped aside and motioned for Concettina to look more closely at the hedge.

She did, briefly, but came right back to the dwarf curiously. It was just a thicket of lilac bushes, after all.

Pikel pointed more emphatically, motioning for Concettina to lean in closer.

She gave him a curious look but obliged, putting her face very near the wide leaves, and still Pikel coaxed her on. She moved a tiny bit closer, and the dwarf whistled, and the leaves began to shift in front of her, shifting aside so that she could move in even closer.

The hedgerow parted in front of her inquisitive face, revealing the garden adjacent.

And more pointedly, revealing the statue in that adjacent garden, one of a headless woman.

Concettina stood up straight, shocked, and on Pikel's request the lilac bushes moved back into place, stealing the view. The queen turned to look down at Pikel, her face a mask of coldness and disappointment, her mind screaming to her: How dare he?

She almost yelled that very thought at the dwarf, but when she noted his apologetic and sad aspect she couldn't help but recognize the sincere concern upon his face.

"Oooo," he said, emphasizing the point.

"Master Pikel, what do you know?" she demanded.

Pikel pointed to her belly, then ran a finger across his neck and said, "Oooo" once more.

Queen Concettina swallowed hard and spent a long moment composing herself. "This is important, Master Pikel," she said evenly. "Is this something you heard from Captain Andrus? Or your soldier brother?"

"Uh uh," he replied, shaking his shaggy head.

"Gossip, then?"

"Ayup."

Again Queen Concettina swallowed hard, trying to find her patience with this poor little fellow. So it was gossip—he had heard the titters and whispers of the nattering socialites, almost surely.

"Ladies of court?" she asked, and he nodded enthusiastically, and Concettina saw where this was going. "Young ladies?"

Pikel nodded. "Pretty Feet!"

Concettina didn't know the particular reference, but it didn't matter, for even if she figured out who this "Pretty Feet" person might be, there was nothing she could do that wouldn't simply compound her problems. She wasn't surprised by the revelations and gossip—of course not! The pattern in Helgabal had become predictable: a queen would fail, the gossip would begin, and something would push King Yarin to take drastic, even murderous action. And often, she understood from the confidences of her ladies-in-waiting, that precipitating event would begin with those young ladies hoping to be next in line.

Very predictable, except it boggled Queen Concettina's mind why anyone would want to be next in line. It was bad enough that she had to share her bed with an old and smelly man, so self-absorbed that he cared about nothing but his own pleasure and power, but was anyone foolish enough to believe at this point that the fatal failures to deliver an heir to Yarin lay on the shoulders of the queens?

In moments like this, young Concettina Delcasio had to work hard to not curse her father for putting her into this untenable and likely fatal situation. But he couldn't have known—she had to believe that.

She looked back at Pikel, who was nervously hopping from one foot to the other, seeming very small then, and very upset.

"Thank you, good dwarf," she said, trying to sound upbeat, certainly not wanting to tip her hand that she had already sent out a call to Delthuntle for help. "It does seem as if everyone is becoming anxious because the king grows older and still has no heir." She gave a great sigh, very dramatically. "I lied earlier, good dwarf," she admitted, or, rather, lied again. "So fear not, for that situation will soon be remedied."

Pikel's smile exploded across his face, and he hopped up and down, clapping excitedly and verily shouting, "Baby!"

"No, no, hush, Master Pikel, I beseech you!" said Concettina. "It is our little secret, yes?"

"Ayup," Pikel said, nodding furiously. He settled then and began quietly casting a spell, but Concettina didn't notice, her gaze going back to the lilac bushes, where they had parted to reveal the headless statue of the previous "barren" queen.

When she turned back to Pikel, she did note a cloud pass over his face, though Concettina didn't think much of it.

She bent and kissed the gardener dwarf on the forehead, eliciting a giggle. Then she bid him farewell, gathered up her ladies-in-waiting, and moved along.

Pikel watched her go, nodding until she had turned the corner of the hedgerow and thus moved out of sight. Only then did he mutter, "Oooo," yet again. He had cast a spell that would detect life, and focusing the magical divination on Concettina had revealed to him one living heartbeat, not two.

To Pikel's thinking, if Queen Concettina believed that she was with child, then she was sadly—likely fatally—mistaken.

◆ ◆ ◆

BACK IN HER room later that morning, Concettina paced around in circles. The whispers were all around her, and so King Yarin must have been hearing them, too, and that man did not take well to anyone mocking him.

"Help me, father," the poor young woman whispered desperately.

But was that even possible? Could Lord Delcasio get to her and wrest her away from King Yarin in time, or even at all?

Likely not, she understood, and she nodded and found strength.

"Anamarin!" she called, and her favorite attendant appeared in her doorway. "Go and fetch King Yarin and bring him to my bedroom."

"My lady?" the young woman asked.

"Tell him that I am feeling rather fertile this day, and quite amorous."

Anamarin giggled, embarrassed, and nodded. She repeated, "My lady!" but with a very different tone.

"Go, go, girl," Concettina ordered, and Anamarin rushed away.

Concettina nodded, trying to sort out some plan in her mind. She would counter the whispered insults with great affection to begin with. Yes, and she would convince King Yarin that this time would be different, that her body was now ready for a child, and so she would work him to his limits every day.

Each and every day.

She would fornicate him to death, hopefully.

Or if not, then she would exhaust him so fully that a pillow over his face would put an end to her terror.

Concettina gasped aloud as the murderous plan came clear to her. She had never thought herself capable of murder. Even with this man, whom she had grown to loath, could she do such a thing?

Perhaps he would just die in the midst of their lovemaking—she had to play on that hope for now, at least, as she bought herself some time.

But if that didn't work . . .

"My statue will not be headless," she vowed.

◆  ◆  ◆

"HEE HEE HEE," the green-bearded dwarf giggled as he dropped a pinch of powder into a foggy concoction in the vial on the table in front of him. The new ingredient brought forth a puff of greenish smoke that filled Pikel's nostrils and elicited a profound and satisfied sigh.

"A love potion?" Ivan said skeptically from across the kitchen.

"Hee hee hee."

"For the queen?"

Pikel wagged his head and searched for other ingredients. "Queenie!" he declared.

"Queen ain't the problem," Ivan reminded him. "Even if yer potion'll make her more fertile, there don't be any bees in that flower."

"Oooo."

"King's the problem, and ye're knowin' it," Ivan said. "Can ye make a potion for the king?"

"Harder," Pikel admitted.

"Exactly," said Ivan, crossing his arms and tapping his foot, waiting.

It took Pikel a while, but in due course, he giggled, "Hee hee hee."

"And how're ye to get King Yarin to take it? That one's a bit particular about what he's lettin' into his mouth, bein' king and all."

"Oooo," Pikel admitted, and then he flashed a brilliant smile and said, "Me brudder!"

"Not me! Not for nothing!" Ivan balked, holding one hand out as if to hold Pikel back from that ridiculous notion.

"Kingie," Pikel declared, thumping his chest with his hand and puffing out his chest in a show of virility. More mischievously, he added, "Sha-la-la."

"King's wanting a shillelagh, eh?" Ivan said with a snort. "Might be true, but that ain't the point or the problem. And more'n that, to get him to drink it, ye'd have to tell him why, which means yerself or meself'd be implying that it ain't his queens who been barren, eh? I'm guessin' that anyone telling that to King Yarin'll be stainin' his guillotine same day."

Pikel's face dropped and his shoulders slumped, and Ivan huffed a resigned sigh and went over to him to pat him on the back. "Ye just keep working at it. Yer heart's right, and might that we'll find a way to make something that'll help."

A still-despondent Pikel looked up and nodded.

"Ye got yerself a good heart, me bro—me *brudder*!" Ivan clapped Pikel hard on the back.

"Me brudder!" a beaming Pikel replied, and he went back to his work.

Ivan said no more, just went to the table and finished his dinner. Then he gathered up his gear and moved to the door. "Don't ye be mixing yer concoctions when ye get tired," he warned. "Last time, ye durn near blew up the neighborhood!"

"Hee hee hee," said Pikel, and he dropped in another pinch of the green herb and waved his hand to direct as much responding smoke into his nose as possible.

Ivan just shook his head and smiled, and went to his patrol along the city's eastern wall.

# Chapter 11 ◈

# The Road
# to Helgabal

OUR WAGONS," KOMTODDY TOLD TOOFLESS AND THE OTHERS. The spriggan gang was less than a day out of Smeltergard, bound for Helgabal with their special gifts for King Yarin. "Twice that number o' guards, and all on horseback."

"Tasty!" said Brekerbak, flashing a broken-toothed smile that was mirrored by his half-dozen companions.

"Armor up!" Brekerbak added, apparently thinking he had the ear of all.

"Nah, don't ye," Toofless Tonguelasher ordered.

"Eight soldiers!" Brekerbak protested. "Just a hand-and-a-half!"

"And eight drivers," Komtoddy added. "Travelin' merchants they be, and so in these parts, men-at-arms."

"Ready for a fight," said Brekerbak.

"Aye, and I'm weady for whate'er fight they got," Toofless assured the others.

"We don't have our best gear," Komtoddy said. As with their first visit to Helgabal, the band hadn't brought their magical arms and armor, which would grow with them when they expanded to their giant size. That gear would be too easily detected by the king's wizards, its properties too easily discerned, by even a minor spellcaster.

"Just men," said Toofless. "And we be just dwawfs, eh?" He flashed that toothless grin at his close friend.

Komtoddy couldn't resist it. "Aye, dwarfs until we're needin' to not be dwarfs."

"I telled ye when we leaved Smeltergard." Toofless motioned for Komtoddy to lead the way.

◆   ◆   ◆

"A LOT OF whistling," Guard Commander Balleyho said, walking his horse up to the drivers on the lead wagon.

Aksel, the burly man holding the reins, the chief enforcer and lead hunter for an enterprising merchant guild in the Vaasan town of Darmshall, looked past the hired soldier and turned to the woman sitting beside him. He found her deep in spellcasting, eyes closed, lips moving slowly in an arcane chant.

"Dwarves," the wizard Amiasunta said after finishing her divination. She winced and shook her head as she made the claim. These bearded folk struck her as a bit odd. "Dirty dwarves, indeed, carrying sacks and pulling a cart."

"Merchants?" asked Aksel as he tightened up the reins, stopping his team. He lifted his right hand to halt the other three wagons behind him.

The woman started to shake her head, but stopped and shrugged. "They carry few goods that I can discern."

"Might be trouble, then," Aksel said.

"Doubt it, with dwarves," Balleyho replied.

Aksel cracked his knuckles and flexed his big, meaty hands, punching one hard into the other. "We can hope, though," he said with a wink.

Balleyho, despite his grand reputation and years of fighting in the Vaasan wilds, reflexively leaned away. Aksel wasn't as tall as the rider, but he was as thick as an oak, with no neck to speak of and hard, muscled arms that could deliver crushing blows. His nose was flat, having been broken dozens of times, and one of his eyes was perpetually bloodshot, ruptured repeatedly in his nightly brawls. Those facial blemishes seemed not to bother him at all, though. Indeed, those who knew the man understood that Aksel took great pride in such obvious battle scars. He was known for leading with his face, smiling through a barrage of blows, then twisting his opponent's head off.

"Put your men at the ready," Aksel ordered Balleyho. "Might be time to earn your gold. Aye, and let's hope! Forward line."

Balleyho sat tall in his saddle. He was an impressive sight, balanced and strong—so much so that Aksel was thinking of bringing him into his circle of commanders when they got back to dangerous Darmshall. With a nod and a whistle to his charges, Balleyho and the other seven riders rode out ahead of the wagons, with Balleyho and his second in front and the other six forming a line of horseflesh and armor across the width of the road behind them.

"Don't look like much trouble," Aksel said to Amiasunta when the dwarven band came into view, climbing over the ridge. They walked lightly, laughing and whistling.

Aksel counted half a dozen, with the trailing duo tugging an uncooperative cart that was little more than a large wheelbarrow with a bent axel.

"Why are you shaking your head?" the dangerous man said to the wizard sitting beside him.

She didn't answer, just wore a curious expression and shook her head. Clearly, something about this dwarven band wasn't sitting right with Amiasunta, and Aksel knew the wizard well enough to understand that she was usually right about such things.

"Sit ready!" he called up to Balleyho. The dwarves had moved very near the riders by then.

"Clear the road!" Balleyho ordered the approaching troupe. "Get that cart off to the side."

"But where ye goin' then?" asked the lead dwarf. "We might be wantin' a ride, what."

"Clear the road," Balleyho said again.

Aksel stood up, trying to get a better view. He could barely see the diminutive folk behind the wall of riders, but he could hear them. They were whistling some silly song in unison. And then they started wildly dancing, arms flailing.

"You will be run down!" Balleyho shouted at them. "Move aside!"

A dwarf moved off to the right of the rider line. "Hey driver," he called, "might we be buyin' passage to Helgabal, if that's where ye're bound?"

"You were told to move, so move!" Aksel shouted back, poking his finger ahead. He wanted to punch the impertinent little fellow. It didn't take much to get Aksel's fighting hackles up.

"Hit him with a stinging missile of magic," he snarled to Amiasunta, never looking her way. Then he shouted back ahead at the dwarf, "Move!"

From the side, he heard a thump and a gulp of air from his companion. He turned then to see Amiasunta sitting perfectly straight and unblinking, her eyes wide with surprise. Without a word, without a movement to ease the blow, she rolled over to the side and tumbled from her seat.

"Hope the wady ain't dead. She's purty," said a voice behind him. A shocked Aksel swung around to see a filthy-looking dwarf standing in the bed of his wagon, just behind the bench.

Up ahead on the road, Aksel heard Balleyho cry out "Giants!" followed by the snorting of excited horses and a commotion of hoof beats.

The burly driver couldn't even look back, though, and didn't want to, focusing his rage on the dwarf, who was in range of his devastating punches. Aksel was quite famous throughout the stretches of southern Vaasa for his short jab, a fast punch that had broken too many faces to count. He got that blow off then, and with perfect accuracy. His powerful fist slammed into the dwarf's face and rocked its ugly head back in a vicious snap.

But the dwarf only smiled with blackened gums and a tongue eagerly licking at the blood on his lip. "Toofless!" he proclaimed, as if to tell the man that there weren't any teeth to knock out, after all.

Aksel growled and moved over the bench to tackle the fellow, but then he wasn't moving at all, stopped by an impossibly strong thrust of the dwarf's hand, one that hit him in the leading shoulder and sent him spinning back around to sit in his seat. He started forward immediately, to gain some distance and get square to the fight, but the dwarf's other hand caught him by the hair and yanked him backward half over the bench back, stretching him down to the wagon bed.

"Toofless!" the dwarf yelled.

Before Aksel could find his footing enough to propel himself into a back roll over the bench and thus out of his awkward position, the dwarf helped him along, tugging down against Aksel's hair with his right hand and turning and driving down with his left elbow, slamming Aksel in the chest with unbelievable force.

So much force that it splintered the heavy wood of the bench back.

So much force that Aksel's spine cracked under the blow.

So much force that Aksel jolted down, then bounced.

But the dwarf still held him fast by the hair, and guided him as he came up into the air, tugging him over the seat and into the wagon bed. And there he lay, broken and unable to move, but still awake, the drivers behind him shouting, the riders up ahead engaged in heavy melee, the toothless dwarf snickering at him as if the whole thing was one fine joke.

◆ ◆ ◆

"HOLD THE LINE! Hold the line!" Balleyho screamed when the dancing dwarves on the path in front of him became giants right in front of his astonished eyes. The seasoned veteran had been ready for some trick or other when the filthy dwarves began their dancing.

Or at least, he thought he was properly prepared.

When the creatures twirled, they enlarged, and it wasn't until they were much larger that Balleyho or any of the other riders even realized the transition had happened. And when the commander did realize he wasn't facing six filthy dwarven peasants but rather half a dozen giants, all twice—some thrice—his height . . . he didn't react in time.

If there even was an "in time."

He did get his sword out, even managed a stab into a fleshy giant arm before he was yanked straight up in the air, right out of his saddle as his horse reared, then thrown aside some twenty feet to crash down into the grass.

Broken, near unconsciousness, the man stubbornly pulled himself up to his elbows to try to call out to his men.

Three horses were already down, their riders with them. Balleyho's horse galloped away, which gave the doomed man some measure of satisfaction. It proved short-lived, though, as a giant fist pounded down atop the head of another of his soldiers, denting the helmet under its tremendous weight and driving the poor man's head right down between his shoulders. He slumped forward on his mount, the terrified horse kicking and leaping wildly as it scrambled to get away.

Balleyho, his senses leaving him, followed the horse's run, saw his soldier, his friend, slumping off to the side, and finally tumbling from the saddle.

He didn't see the man hit the dirt, though, as a giant foot came stomping down upon Balleyho, squashing him into the ground.

◆ ◆ ◆

TOOFLESS LEAPED OVER the wagon bench and dropped to the ground in front of the carriage and behind the horse team just as the first arrows from the drivers began to sail in at him. He looked ahead between the horses and saw that his boys had things well in hand. Only a trio of riders were still fighting, with four down and one trying to ride away—though three of Toofless's best artillerymen had their chain bolos up and spinning. A few of the spriggans were bleeding, but they'd heal fast. One or two dead would give him a bigger share of the treasure and more turns torturing the prisoners.

With that thought in mind, the spriggan glanced over at the wizard, who lay moaning on the ground. He hoped he hadn't hit her too hard. They weren't much fun when they couldn't even wiggle and scream, after all.

Another rider went down, two giants yanking his horse down atop him. Behind that line, the flying chain bolos took down the fleeing man, though his horse kept going.

Toofless sighed. One less meal.

Off to the side of the action, Toofless spotted Komtoddy. The giant had an arrow in his chest, and another had obviously clipped him across the face, drawing a line of blood.

"Get 'em," Toofless quietly coaxed. He winced as his bones began to crackle and extend. His clothing tightened around him—no time to peel it off—and he wished he had his magical spriggan armor.

Komtoddy's chain bolo went soaring past him. The horse team on the next wagon whinnied and stomped in protest. Peering out from under the wagon, Toofless saw that second wagon in line lurch and rush off the road and onto the uneven, rough ground. The growing spriggan managed a smile when he saw the female drivers frantically—and futilely—trying to control the team. The ground was simply too uneven. The wagon lurched and turned fast, one wheel digging into the mud. The back of the wagon went up in the air. The two drivers desperately tried to leap aside, but the wagon crashed down upon them, then bounced and rolled away leaving the two women shattered in its wake.

"Oh, wadies," Toofless lamented, and out he crept. He sprinted from the side of the wagon, rushing in on the next drivers in line just as they let fly arrows at Komtoddy.

Toofless had them dead, certainly, but he just ran past, grabbing one man and yanking him from the seat, taking him along as he went after the last wagon. The drivers there were desperately trying to turn it and gallop away.

A human missile interrupted their work and took one from the seat, slamming him forward between the horses. The team stomped both of them to death in short order.

They were the lucky ones.

# CHAPTER 12 ◈

# *Tactical Surrender*

D O YOU RECALL THE DRAGON FIGHT IN THE SILVER Marches?" Ilnezhara asked Jarlaxle. The two of them stood out near the blasted Hosttower of the Arcane, with Tazmikella nearby. It was a blustery day, with a chill wind swirling off the water that felt refreshing. Summer was on in full and the sun was quite warm. "The one where the son of Arauthator was slain?"

Jarlaxle tentatively nodded.

"Slain by a monk," said Ilnezhara.

"A monk possessed by a monk," Tazmikella agreed.

"A monk possessed by a monk who long ago transcended his mortal coil," said Ilnezhara.

"Godlessly," Tazmikella added. "And the man should have died of old age before the onset of the Spellplague, even."

Jarlaxle stared at them blankly, at a loss as to what this conversation might mean. He knew it involved Drizzt, of course. The sisters had hinted that this concept of ascendance might be the elixir they needed to save the lost drow ranger. He also knew they were speaking of Kane, of the Monastery of the Yellow Rose, and of Brother Afafrenfere, who had returned to that temple of aesthetics.

"Imagine!" Ilnezhara exclaimed. "A human who found transcendence without the need of a phony god, and entirely from within. Do you think a drow might be so insightful, sister?"

"I don't know, sister," Tazmikella replied, casting a sly look Jarlaxle's way. "Sometimes these drow appear very dull witted to me."

Jarlaxle winked back at her and smiled at the taunt, but his grin disappeared and he began tapping his fingers together pensively as he digested the hints from these two lovely creatures.

The healing had to come from within Drizzt, Kimmuriel had insisted. And here was an example, an old, old human who was once known well to Jarlaxle—a skilled warrior who had found the kind of inner strength that might serve Drizzt now. Jarlaxle wasn't deeply schooled in the manners and ways of the monks, though, and had always assumed their mystical powers, if not their almost superhuman fighting techniques, to be the result of some divinity or various arcane enchantments. Was that not the case?

"The winds are warm again," he said to the sisters. "How do you feel about a rather long flight?"

"Not so long," Tazmikella replied.

"We were considering a jaunt home to Heliogabalus," Ilnezhara added.

"Helgabal," Tazmikella sourly corrected, and Ilnezhara laughed.

"To Helgabal, yes, of course," Ilnezhara explained, "to retrieve some of the things we left behind in our rather hurried exit."

"Hurried because of a curious little girl," Tazmikella said, aiming the remark straight at Jarlaxle, who had, of course, been that very child imposter.

"Such a gossipy creature," Ilnezhara said. "We should have dined on her flesh."

"Indeed," the other agreed.

Jarlaxle took it all in stride. "You will deliver Drizzt to Brother Afafrenfere and the monks at the monastery?"

"We will deliver you and Drizzt to the forest near the monastery," Ilnezhara corrected. "From there, the introductions fall to you. We have little desire to go and bargain with the monks, and less to reveal ourselves to the Grandmaster of Flowers, who served a king named Dragonsbane."

"A name well-earned, and in no small part, because of that very monk," Tazmikella elaborated.

Jarlaxle wasn't about to quibble. He knew enough about the ways of monks to realize that it had taken Grandmaster Kane, a very special human, the bulk of his life in deep and dedicated training, to reach this level of ascension of which the dragons spoke. He also knew that Kane was the exception, and even the most devout and dedicated practitioners could never approach his level of skill and discipline, whether it came from within or from a god. Drizzt had many years left of life, obviously, perhaps enough to dedicate himself and find his way.

But wouldn't it take a human lifetime, the mercenary wondered? In delivering Drizzt to the Monastery of the Yellow Rose, he was doing Drizzt a good deed, perhaps, but to Jarlaxle personally, and certainly to Catti-brie, would it really be any different than if Drizzt had just died? Oh, certainly they could feel better about his fate, and hold on to a thread of hope, but in practicality, he would be lost to them, likely forever as far as Catti-brie was concerned.

But then again, the mercenary mused, given Drizzt's continuing descent into this most frustrating and impenetrable madness, wasn't it as if the ranger had already passed on?

◆ ◆ ◆

"YOU ARE SAD to see him go," Dahlia said. She stood in the tent behind Artemis Entreri, who peered under the flap to watch the goings-on out by the Hosttower.

The question surprised Entreri, but he couldn't deny the truth of it. "I . . . we owe him a great deal," he reminded her. "Drizzt got us out of Menzoberranzan. He went down there, left everything behind, to find you."

"So did you," Dahlia replied. She walked up against the man's back and looped her arm around him, offering a gentle kiss on the back of the assassin's neck.

"Because I had nothing to lose," Entreri admitted. He turned and returned the hug. "I had nothing in my life. Perhaps, at long last, I saw a way to what I wanted."

"Me?"

Entreri smiled at her and nodded. "You were more than worth the risk for me. But what gain for Drizzt? He had everything he wanted right here in front of him. His friends and his wife returned, and Bruenor on the throne of Gauntlgrym. And yet he went for you, willingly and without hesitation."

"And for you?" Dahlia asked, and after a moment of digesting that, Entreri nodded.

"And he lost himself while saving me," Dahlia added.

Entreri glanced back over his shoulder, out of the tent, to see Jarlaxle and some others leading Drizzt to the waiting dragons. He nodded again, his face as tight as his heart.

◆ ◆ ◆

"IT'S A DANGEROUS journey," Jarlaxle explained as Drizzt stared doubtfully at the weapon belt. "Take it."

"Even Taulmaril?" Drizzt asked when he took the item. "Do you not fear that I'll shoot you off Ilnezhara's back?"

"You might try," the mercenary said with a wink, and walked away.

Drizzt strapped on the belt, adjusted his scimitars, and turned to his mount. But he stopped halfway around. King Bruenor stood, hands on hips, with Catti-brie beside him.

It was a typically blustery and gray Luskan day, the clouds rolling above at a great clip, the brilliant summer sun finding enough of an opening now and then to shoot beams of heavenly light upon the cold city. But even in that gloominess, Catti-brie shined bright. She wore her white robes, opened low enough in front to reveal the brilliant, multicolored blouse that had once been the magical garment of Jack the Gnome. She had her black lace shawl up over her head, holding her thick hair in place only somewhat against the sea breeze, and she carried her silver bark staff, the blue sapphire retaining its rich hue even against the dim reflections of the cloudy sky.

And that rich blue accentuated those eyes that had haunted Drizzt Do'Urden for most of his life, and that would surely follow him into whatever existence came after this mortal realm.

He saw profound sadness there now, and it wounded him even though he knew the truth, that this was not really Catti-brie standing there watching him.

So caught was he by the image of the woman that he hadn't even noticed Bruenor's approach.

"Ye go and do what needs doin', elf," the dwarf said.

Drizzt looked down at him, at the hand Bruenor had extended.

"Be knowin' forever that ye've e'er a home in Gauntlgrym, even when meself's no more," Bruenor added, his voice quaking. When Drizzt took his hand Bruenor yanked him low and wrapped him in a tight hug.

"E'er a friend," the dwarf was barely able to whisper. He held on for a long, long time, and Drizzt could tell that Bruenor was trying hard, if futilely, to compose himself.

And in that moment, Drizzt knew the truth. And what a fool he felt himself to be. How could he have ever doubted this, or any of them? This was no deception of Lolth. It was Bruenor, just Bruenor. And that was Catti-brie, forever his beloved.

How could he be so stupid as to think otherwise?

He shoved Bruenor back to arms' length, smiling widely.

Then scowling when he realized that he had been deceived yet again. Was that a flicker of Abyssal fire in the back of Bruenor's eye?

He nodded curtly and spun around, rushing for the waiting dragon, taking with him that last image of Catti-brie standing resolutely, arms in tight to her sides, auburn hair escaping the edge of the shawl in wisps to wave in the breeze, and her eyes . . . those eyes . . .

The drow paused at the dragon's side, determined not to look back, determined not to give in to his futile and foolish hopes, for doing so would give Lolth the victory, and that, in turn, would utterly destroy him.

He climbed up to the saddle, but she was there beside him then, and he couldn't ignore it.

"I know you'll come back to me," she said.

Drizzt looked down at her from Tazmikella's back, but then closed his eyes, trying to shake away the reality he knew to be lurking there, behind the surface of those deceptively wonderful eyes. This wasn't Catti-brie, he reminded himself. It was the greatest ruse of all, the grand deception designed to utterly destroy him.

When he opened his eyes again, he found Catti-brie staring at him still, and now holding out a familiar figurine.

"Guen belongs to you," she said quietly. "With you."

Drizzt recoiled and shook his head. None of this made any sense to him.

"Take her!" Catti-brie implored him. "She's your constant, my love, the friend you ever knew, and ever shall. Perhaps she'll help you find your way through the maze."

Despite the warning screams inside his thoughts, the drow wasn't strong enough to refuse. He reached down and accepted the onyx panther figurine. But as he came up straight once more, it occurred to him that perhaps he was wrong about the nature and expected course of the grand deception. Perhaps it wasn't ultimately Catti-brie who would be revealed as a lie, but Guenhwyvar.

"Oh, clever . . ." he whispered, trying to follow through with the notion.

But no, that made no sense. Guen had been with him the whole time, all of his adult life. The lie was the resurrection—the woman, the dwarf, Wulfgar, and Regis.

Or did it go back longer than that?

In that case, what matter?

"Jarlaxle told you not to wait for me," he said coldly. "This is farewell."

"How would I do anything but wait for you?" Catti-brie asked with a sad smile that tugged at Drizzt's heart and tore it asunder all at once. "I've no choice in such a matter."

"No . . ." Drizzt started, but Catti-brie cut him short.

"You, above all, understand that," she told him. "When I was gone . . ."

Drizzt had no answer to that. In this moment of clarity, he wanted her to be Catti-brie, exactly as he thought of her. Catti-brie, that girl standing on the side of Kelvin's Cairn who had welcomed him to Icewind Dale; that young woman who had served as his conscience, his guide, his friend, through all those difficult early years when he had been trying to make better sense of a daunting world; that lover with whom he had found his way.

"Who are you?" he asked, and Catti-brie could only stare at him blankly.

"You waited for me," she whispered.

Drizzt wanted to argue further, but the reminder hit him hard, brought his thoughts cascading through the last century, and all the journeys and adventures and companions he had known, and the underlying emptiness of it all throughout that time, even in Bruenor's triumph in Gauntlgrym, even in his own experiences with Dahlia and the others.

Because she, this woman, hadn't been there with him.

He winced and silently cursed that he had ever known the love of Catti-brie, for what was life itself without her? What joy might Drizzt Do'Urden ever know to match the sweetness of that experience, to fall asleep inside her, to wake up in her arms, to the warmth of her smile, to the knowing love of her wondrous eyes?

It took all of his resolve not to draw out his new sword, the very weapon forged and given to him by this imposter, and strike the damned illusion down, then and there.

Indeed, his resolve would not prove to be enough to stop him, he realized, nodding and going for the blade, determined to be done with it all. But then Jarlaxle called out, and before Drizzt even touched the hilt of Vidrinath, his dragon mount leaped away and into the air, climbing high beside her sister, who bore Jarlaxle.

"Perhaps we will find a fool riding a white wyrm that we can engage, my friend," Tazmikella said when they were among the clouds, the dragon turning her head back to regard him. "Have you your bow ready?"

Drizzt nodded, even managed to fake a smile. But only so that the copper dragon would turn around and leave him alone.

He rested back in the saddle and watched the world opening wide below him. He glanced back to see Luskan receding, the dark waters of the Sword Coast spreading wide beyond the City of Sails. Turning north, he saw the Spine of the World, a mountain range he knew so very well, though mostly from the other side, from the north, from Icewind Dale that had been his home for so long.

His first home.

The world had seemed so simple then, even to this drow who had walked out of Menzoberranzan and into the tumultuous wilds of the Underdark, even to this young man who had felt the agony of grief when Zaknafein had been murdered, and who had watched friends die in battle, and who had known and lost Montolio. Everything had made sense, even when so profoundly painful. His life had followed a logical path, guided by conscience, through the Underdark and to Mooshie's Grove, and to Kelvin's Cairn in Icewind Dale.

To Catti-brie and to Bruenor.

And to the banks of Maer Dualdon and Regis.

He caught a flash of silver through a pass in the mountains to the north, and thought it might be one of the lakes—Redwaters, perhaps, or Lac Dinneshire

And he remembered when young Wulfgar had come into his life, captured on the battlefield by a merciful Bruenor.

His life's journey rolled out in his thoughts as the world rolled out below him, to the lairs of dragons, to Bruenor's homeland, to the far south and his fierce struggles with Artemis Entreri. All of it, all the way to that fateful day when the Weave had unwoven, when Catti-brie had been struck in the blue fire of the Spellplague, when the whole world had stopped making sense.

He felt as if he had wasted the subsequent century of his life, but He felt as if he'd wasted the last century of his life?

It was all an illusion, a deception. Or if not all, then somewhere within that time, reality had become unbound, and perception had become reality, and the passing of time had become meaningless because it was no more than a deception.

Had he even really found Gauntlgrym with Bruenor, when and where he had watched Bruenor die?

"I found it, elf," he whispered, echoing the dwarf's final declaration, and those quiet words were lost in the wind.

Indeed, had it even been a century? Or had all these experiences, all of these impossible things, most notably the return of so many lost, been injected into his memory by the merciless Lolth, as Errtu had done to Wulfgar in those years when the balor had tormented the poor man?

Aye, that was the truth of it, Drizzt knew.

In that realization, he thought to simply slide off of Tazmikella's back—though he feared he would just find himself on the floor of Lolth's Abyssal palace.

He pulled the onyx figurine from his belt pouch, barely glanced at the panther carving, and moved to hurl it into the sky.

*"She's your constant, my love . . ."*

Catti-brie's words echoed in his mind and he hugged the panther figurine close, and was ashamed that he had ever thought to so be rid of it.

Gently, carefully, he replaced the figurine in his belt pouch, taking care to secure it, and in that moment, a great change swept over Drizzt.

Yes, he decided, it was all a dream, a deception, and one to utterly destroy him. And for any preparation he might vainly try to do, this deception surely would. When the revelation was unmasked, when he saw the image of Catti-brie to be a grotesque lie, when Bruenor and Regis and Wulfgar and all the others were shown to be demon manes dressed up as his friends, then indeed would Drizzt Do'Urden shatter.

But that wouldn't be the end of it, he resolved. No, in that moment of his enemy's greatest triumph, he would attack, relentlessly, until his body was more broken than his heart.

He pictured it, throwing himself, likely naked and unarmed, at the Spider Queen. Clawing at her, biting at her, forcing her to fight back and put an end to it all.

And he would laugh at her.

In the end, yes, Drizzt would laugh at her.

"And then I will know eternal peace," he whispered.

And he didn't believe a word.

# CHAPTER 13 ◈

# *Damaran Friends*

**A** FAR BETTER JOURNEY THAN OUR VOYAGE FROM SUZAIL TO Delthuntle," Regis said to Wulfgar when the docks of New Sarshel, the northernmost port city of the Kingdom of Impiltur, came into view that midsummer morning. He looked up at the barbarian, but Wulfgar just shrugged and even shook his head a bit in apparent disagreement.

"We did not encounter a single storm!" Regis protested.

"I did not mind our winter diversion to the Tower of Stars on Prespur," Wulfgar slyly replied. He leaned on *The Aardvark*'s rail and grinned.

The halfling sighed and fell silent, and Wulfgar laughed boisterously.

The ship anchored far out in the harbor. The water had become quite shallow here during the Sundering. Indeed, a few years earlier, they could have sailed another hundred miles to the north, to the Damaran port of Uthmere, but that port was now just a village surrounded by a flood plain.

"First boat in to the docks," Boyko, the first mate, said to the pair, motioning for Wulfgar and Regis to get to the netting so they could climb down into the small craft that was even then being lowered.

The pair looked at him curiously, Regis even pointing to himself to confirm. "First?"

"Aye, be on your way," Boyko replied, moving over to them. "Well met and fare you well." And in a lower voice, the gruff little man added, "Put up for the night in the Rolling Pig."

"The Rolling Pig?" Regis asked.

Boyko nodded and moved away, barking orders at someone else.

"We are expected, it would seem," said Wulfgar.

Soon after, the pair found the tavern in question, a small building within the wall of New Sarshel and not far from the docks. The place was nearly deserted when they entered, but by the time they sat at the bar and finished their first drink, other patrons had begun to congregate, including more than a few from *The Aardvark*.

"Another round of Zzar for me and my friend, please," Regis called to the bartender, hoping to catch him before the lines began forming.

The barkeep nodded to indicate that he had heard, but went to serve another patron first, and indeed, it was none other than Boyko of *The Aardvark*. That struck Regis as curious, but the halfling reached into his purse and produced some silver coins.

"Your silver's no good here," the bartender said with a wink, refilling their glasses. He turned back from the bar to glance at a board of notices he'd posted. He pulled a sheet of parchment from the board and slid it over to the pair. "Helgabal caravan looking for some guards."

"Helgabal?" Wulfgar asked innocently. "Why would you presume that we . . . ?"

But the barkeep just turned away to tend to some others and Regis grabbed Wulfgar's arm. He motioned with his chin at the exit, and both glanced that way just in time to see Boyko depart.

"To Donnola," Regis said quietly, lifting his glass in toast.

◆ ◆ ◆

A TRANSFIXED DRIZZT watched the transformation of Ilnezhara and Tazmikella, the sisters polymorphing from their graceful serpentine dragon bodies to those of willowy human women, equally graceful and with a beauty different, but no less magnificent, than the glorious copper dragons.

Could he possibly create such a thing within his own imagination?

"Come," Jarlaxle called to him, motioning the other way, to the edge of the forest and the long, clear hill beyond.

"Fare you well, Drizzt Do'Urden," Tazmikella said.

"We hope that here you will find peace and enlightenment," added Ilnezhara. "Do understand that we would not have offered such insight, nor our wings, to simply any mortal creature. Nay, and to whom so much is given, much is expected."

Drizzt stared at the tall, copper-haired woman curiously, trying to sort out any hidden meaning behind her curious remark. What might any dragon ever want from him?

Jarlaxle grabbed Drizzt's arm then and pulled him away.

"They are wondrous creatures, yes?" he asked.

"I do not understand them."

"That doesn't mean you cannot appreciate them," Jarlaxle replied. "They did much for you, my friend. I hope that you will come to fully appreciate that."

"Why?" Drizzt asked. He stopped and pulled from Jarlaxle's grasp. The mercenary took another step and turned to regard him, but Drizzt didn't meet that gaze. Instead, he looked over Jarlaxle's shoulder, through the remaining trees, and up the long hill to a magnificent structure set atop it. The massive stone building looked as if it had been built over the course of many generations, with different stones and different architectural styles all blending together like an enormous tapestry. Turrets, balconies, and grand windows of all shapes and sizes were capped by a crenelated tower.

"Why do I hope you will appreciate them?" Jarlaxle asked.

"Why did they do so much for me?" Drizzt clarified.

"Because they are my friends, and I am your friend. Is that not what friends do for each other? Is that not the entire reason Drizzt Do'Urden was forced by his own conscience to leave Menzoberranzan those many decades ago?"

Drizzt's face tightened, and he couldn't suppress his wince. To him, Jarlaxle's words sounded like the greatest taunt he could imagine.

"Everything, yes?" Jarlaxle asked, nodding at the expression. "Everything that is said is taken in your thoughts as a deception? A trap?"

Drizzt didn't soften his look.

"Come," Jarlaxle bade him. "I give you great credit that you have found the courage to agree to this, even though you surely have nothing left to lose."

"Only because I have nothing left to lose," Drizzt emphasized. He followed the mercenary out of the forest and to the base of the grassy hill.

"My dear friend, there is always more to lose."

"A threat?"

"Hardly," said Jarlaxle. "You fear your footing lost, that all beneath your feet is the shifting sands of a grand deception. Yet now you come to face that fear openly, forcing the truth, however horrible it might prove. It is, perhaps, a concession to desperation, like going to a cleric to confirm that you are afflicted with a malady that you privately know cannot be cured. But even then, I applaud your bravery."

Drizzt cast his gaze downward, then closed his eyes to steady himself, and to convince himself not to draw blades and leap upon Jarlaxle—that would force the truth, after all.

Up the hill they went, but before they ever neared the Monastery of the Yellow Rose, a bevy of monks dressed in simple brown robes appeared on every balcony, staring down intently, and many with crossbows held at the ready.

"Pray tell Brother Afafrenfere that his friends have arrived for a visit," Jarlaxle shouted to them.

"There is no Brother Afafrenfere anymore," one woman shouted back a few moments later.

That brought a concerned look from Jarlaxle, but one that shifted to curiosity when that very man Jarlaxle had known came out from the monastery's grand central doorway, bounding down the steps to stand in front of the two drow.

"Well met, again!" Afafrenfere said, bowing low and smiling widely.

"But she just said . . ." Jarlaxle started to protest.

"Master Afafrenfere!" the woman called back. "Afafrenfere, Master of the South Wind!"

"Are they known to you, and trusted, Master?" another monk called out.

Master Afafrenfere turned and nodded to the man. "I give you Drizzt Do'Urden, hero of the north!" He swept his arm out to Drizzt and many on the balconies nodded, some cheered, and others clapped.

"I feel so small," Jarlaxle quipped to Drizzt.

Drizzt could only shake his head.

"Master Afafrenfere, may we speak privately?" Jarlaxle asked. "Or better still, will you take me inside that I can address the leaders of this wondrous place?"

"Master Perrywinkle Shin?"

Jarlaxle nodded. "This is not merely a visit, but a desperate request."

"The two of you follow," Afafrenfere said, turning for the door.

"Just me," Jarlaxle said, looking to Drizzt and nodding.

Both drow turned to see Afafrenfere wearing a curious and skeptical expression. He motioned for Jarlaxle to head for the door, then called out, "Take him to Master Shin at once!" and then he turned back to Drizzt.

"We will talk," the monk said to Drizzt in an inviting and pleasant manner. It has been far too long! I wish to hear of our old companions, and your new ones!"

"Take great care," Jarlaxle quietly warned him, walking past and heading swiftly for the door.

A clearly surprised Afafrenfere swung around to watch the mercenary go, then turned back to Drizzt with a most puzzled expression.

"What has happened?" he asked Drizzt.

"Nothing or everything," the emotionally defeated ranger replied.

"With nothing in between?"

"Nothing worth talking about," the surly Drizzt replied.

"Truly?" asked Afafrenfere, and he grew a wide smile and boisterous nod. "Not even a battle between four dragons and their riders? Not even of the shot that sundered the saddle of Tiago Baenre, or the rush that sent the white wyrm Aurbangras crashing to the side of Fourthpeak?"

Despite himself, Drizzt couldn't help but flash a grin at that reminder. It had indeed been a remarkable fight, as thrilling as any battle Drizzt had ever known. He could almost feel the wind upon his face in simply recalling it.

"I am not too proud to admit that I was terrified on the side of that mountain, facing a dragon," Afafrenfere said.

"But you held your calm and won."

"Not alone," the monk said. "Not alone."

Drizzt stared at him curiously then, but only for a moment. Jarlaxle was already back out the door, now followed by a high-ranking female monk.

"Mistress of the East Wind Savahn," Afafrenfere said, nodding his chin that way.

"You have met with Master Shin already?" a confused Afafrenfere addressed Jarlaxle when the pair approached.

"In time," Savahn answered. "This visit was anticipated, the gist of Jarlaxle's request known, and accepted, before they arrived."

"Anticipated?" Afafrenfere asked, clearly at a loss. "Master Shin?"

"At least," Savahn replied, and she turned to Drizzt. "You are welcome inside, ranger. There are many eager to meet you."

Drizzt looked to Jarlaxle, who nodded. "Fare you well, my friend," the mercenary leader answered that expression. "I may soon return to this place, though perhaps you will, even then, be too deep in your new studies to take note. I do hope that we will meet again in this lifetime, but if that is not to be, then please always know that my thoughts to you are good ones, full of hope that you will find your way."

"Wait," Afafrenfere said as Jarlaxle clasped Drizzt's hand briefly, then hugged him, then started back down the hill. "You are leaving?"

"The world turns swiftly beyond the walls of your home, Master Afafrenfere," Jarlaxle replied. "I would be remiss if I was not there to steer it, eh?"

He laughed, tipped his hat, and added, "I will return soon enough." Then he started away, and Mistress Savahn took Drizzt by the hand and led him into the Monastery of the Yellow Rose.

Master Afafrenfere stood in place for a long while, looking from Jarlaxle back to Drizzt, and when both disappeared from view—one into the monastery, the other into the forest— he continued to stand there, trying to sort out this most curious turn of events.

More curious, he thought, when he saw the copper dragons emerge from the forest, flying into the summer sky, heading to the east with Jarlaxle astride Ilnezhara, the same mount Afafrenfere had ridden in the fight with the white wyrms above Mithral Hall.

◆ ◆ ◆

"HERE'S WHERE YOU GET OFF," the caravan leader ordered Wulfgar and Regis.

"Here?" Regis asked as Wulfgar bristled. The halfling looked around at the empty road and rolling hills, still some distance south of the city of Helgabal. "Where is here?"

"Where I'm dropping you," replied the leader. These were the first words other than grunting commands the man had spoken to the pair since they'd signed on in New Sarshel a tenday before, ostensibly as guards to the five wagons rolling north to Helgabal. That duty, strangely, had involved nothing more than sitting on the back of a wagon, and one instance where one of the wagons had gotten bogged in some mud, where Wulfgar went out and lifted the thing clear to keep them moving.

"We were to go to Helgabal," Regis protested.

"Less than a day's march," the leader replied. "Half a day, more like."

"And a shorter ride than that!"

"Not to doubt."

"Then why . . . ?" Wulfgar began to ask.

'Because this is what I was told to do," the leader interrupted. "Now kindly get off my wagon."

The companions looked to each other, neither having the beginning of an answer. But this had been coordinated from the outside. Obviously under orders from Donnola, Boyko had arranged for the tavern keeper to direct Wulfgar and Regis to this caravan, and so it seemed a good bet indeed that this man was getting his orders from the same chain of command.

Regis shrugged and hopped off the back of the wagon. "Some food, at least?" he asked.

The man motioned for him to take what he wanted from the supply wagon, which was third in line.

Soon after, Wulfgar and Regis sat in the shade under a tree, eating a lunch of biscuits and potatoes, and watching the caravan disappear over a hill far to the north.

"To be fair, we haven't walked more than a few short strides all the way from Morada Topolino," Regis remarked between bites.

"You do not need to defend her," Wulfgar replied. "Your taste in women is superb, I must admit. Lady Donnola is a fine lass."

"Grandmother Donnola," Regis corrected, but Wulfgar shook his head.

"It seems a silly title for such a young beauty as that!"

"It is a title of respect, and a necessary one among—" he paused and looked around—"assassins."

"I will remember that if ever she is near to Artemis Entreri." There was no mistaking the tone of disapproval in Wulfgar's voice.

"She is not a killer," Regis protested, not catching on to the ruse until Wulfgar smiled wide. "Well, unless she has to be—but can any less be said of any of us?"

Wulfgar laughed. "Be at ease, my friend. I already told you that I find your Lady Donnola quite charming."

Regis nodded and smiled at that, until his face turned to a scowl once more. "Do not tempt her," he warned.

Wulfgar looked as if he had been slapped. "I?"

"You!" Regis said, poking a stubby finger Wulfgar's way.

They shared a laugh—interrupted by hoof beats—and sprang up from the grass, hands fast to weapons.

They relaxed when the rider came into sight, though. It was a halfling on a gray pony, moving in their direction with apparent purpose.

"Donnola," Wulfgar remarked, nodding.

The rider pulled up in front of them soon after. And a splendid fellow he appeared, dressed in fine chainmail and riding cloak, with a plumed leather hat, one side pinned up. He was quite a bit older than Regis and Wulfgar in physical appearance, probably in his sixties, which was still youthful for a halfling, and showed no gray in his long brown hair. He pulled his pony to an abrupt halt. Before the mount had even stopped moving, he threw his leg over the saddle and slipped down gracefully to the ground.

"Well met," he said, dipping a bow and extending a hand.

"And to you," said Regis, taking the offered hand, and then wincing with surprise at the little one's strength. He was actually shorter than Regis.

"Tecumseh Bracegirdle, at your service," said the newcomer, offering his hand to Wulfgar, who shook it—and so began a silent struggle of strength. It seemed ridiculous to witness, surely, but Tecumseh held his own against the barbarian, each squeezing powerfully and smiling knowingly, for many seconds.

Magic, Regis assumed, and he focused on the half-ling's gauntlets.

"And you are?" Tecumseh asked, turning to Regis after finally breaking the grip with Wulfgar.

"A traveler."

"From Aglarond, yes, I know," Tecumseh prompted. "I was more interested in your name."

"Spider."

"Master Spider Paraffin, then, and good," said Tecumseh. "And you must be Wulfgar of Icewind Dale," he added, looking up at the big man.

"You seem to know a lot about us," Wulfgar replied, "though we cannot say the same of you."

"Happy to tell you!" the halfling said. "Oh, more than happy. Would you like a bit of lunch before we travel to Helgabal?" He ended by pulling a large sack from off his pony, one whose contents smelled quite delicious.

"We just had some," Wulfgar said, at the same moment Regis insisted, "Of course!"

And so they sat down for another meal, this one of fine steak and with brilliant red wine to wash it down.

While the food settled and the belches sang out, Tecumseh went to his pony and from a saddlebag produced a curious glass globe. He settled on the grass between the two companions once more and held up the globe, giving it a good shake.

It seemed to be snowing inside the glass, and in that little storm, an image appeared, one of a halfling standing in a heroic pose. Regis and Wulfgar peered close. The fellow looked very much like Tecumseh, and wore the same gloves and carried the same sword.

"Hobart Bracegirdle," Tecumseh explained. "My great-great-grandfather." He nodded and smiled, seeming quite satisfied, as if that name should impress them.

Regis shrugged.

"Hobart Bracegirdle!" Tecumseh insisted. "Surely you have heard of him!"

The companions exchanged looks, but shook their heads.

"Well, all living in Damara know of him to be sure," Tecumseh said, seeming a bit off-balance. He moved the globe back a bit. "He founded the Kneebreakers . . ."

"I know of them!" Regis was happy to report, and Tecumseh smiled.

"Aye, a fine band of peace-keepers, and well-appreciated by the Great King Gareth Dragonsbane and Queen Christine, and all of the Order of the Golden Cup," Tecumseh explained. "Why, this magical globe of memory was crafted by Emelyn the Gray himself! And he'd not do that for any ordinary person, now would he?"

"I'm guessing he would not," Regis said with proper deference, though of the names Tecumseh had dropped, the only one he had heard before was King Gareth.

"So you have heard of my band, then?" Tecumseh asked.

"Your band? You lead the Kneebreakers?"

"Indeed, and of course. I carry Hobart's sword and gauntlets, and other . . . items."

"I rode with the Grinning Ponies of the Trade Way," Regis said, smiling, though the somewhat smug grin didn't last when no flicker of recognition crossed Tecumseh's face.

"A band akin to your Kneebreakers," Regis explained. "And started, in part, by one of your own, a fine gentlehalfling named Showithal Terdidy."

"Terdidy!" Tecumseh exclaimed, certainly recognizing the name. "Terdidy! Ah, a fine lad! He is well, then?"

"He is."

"I was saddened to see him leave. He had such promise."

"Then why did he leave?" Wulfgar asked.

Tecumseh glanced around, then leaned in and whispered, "In Damara, when one gets on the wrong side of King Yarin's scowl, one is wise to move along. For Terdidy, it was a messy affair involving the child of one of King Yarin's early queens—the second, I think, or perhaps the third. After parting marital ways with the king, she birthed a child, and that young girl would have been killed, I fear, except that Showithal Terdidy happened to be in town at the time, and so foiled the attack—if it was an attack, and most think it was."

"As assassination ordered by the King of Damara?" Wulfgar asked.

"I would never go so far as to say such a thing," Tecumseh whispered, waving his hands for Wulfgar to keep his voice down. "But let us agree that whoever was behind the events of that dark night in the small community of Helmsdale, they were not pleased with the heroic actions of your friend. And so, on the advice of many whispers, we sent Showithal Terdidy on a fast boat south."

Regis spent a long while digesting that information. Donnola had told him that King Yarin wasn't to be trusted, but would the man move with such callousness and boldness against the son of his former queen? And then against a member of the Kneebreakers?

"You do not have King Yarin's ear, I take it," Regis asked.

Tecumseh snorted as if the whole notion was preposterous, and that made it clearer to Regis why someone like this, representing a band notoriously vigilant and law-abiding, would now be doing business with Morada Topolino!

"I do not have his ear," Tecumseh admitted. "Indeed, the Kneebreakers do not have his graces. We are informal now, a scattering of glories lost and whispered hopes of a brighter future. King Yarin burned our charter before my very eyes! No need for us, he explained, since he had many of his own organizations. What he meant, of course, was that we would not put our code beneath his desires, and so perhaps he thought us a threat."

"You are that strong in number and influence?" Wulfgar asked.

"A dozen!" Tecumseh insisted. "Or, we were a dozen until Brouha retired to her farm, and Calumny Trailwalker got a saddle rash that still has him standing for dinner . . ."

"Ten?" Wulfgar said. "King Yarin feared ten halflings?"

Tecumseh straightened, taking exception, but Wulfgar quickly added, "Your reputation must greatly outstrip both your size and numbers!"

That brought a smile, and a toast of red wine.

"King Yarin's spy networks are everywhere, I warn you," Tecumseh said more solemnly a moment later. "And he'll suffer no rivals. His heart is ice and his fist is iron, and mercy is not a humor that runs abundant in his blood."

"Yet you dare to come and speak with us," Regis remarked. "Do you know why we have come to Damara?"

Tecumseh recoiled and held up his hands to silence Regis. He clearly didn't want to hear any more. "I do not have King Yarin's ear," he said again. "But I was asked to provide his ear for you, and that I can and will do, because Dono . . . your benefactors have been friends to the Kneebreakers in these dark times and have assured me that your cause here is just and good."

He reached into a pocket under his chainmail and produced a folded and sealed parchment. He tapped it against his fine hat, then handed it to Regis. "You now represent a consortium in Delthuntle and southern Aglarond that is interested in proffering libations to the Court of Helgabal, so says your Imprimatur Regal." He indicated the note.

"You will get the king's ear, surely," Tecumseh went on. "And he will listen keenly, I tell you, if you also express interest in buying. He has become quite proud of his garden in recent years, and that includes tangles of grapes far too sweet and juicy for the Damaran clime. The cellars of King Yarin should not be able to produce such wine. It is impossible in the cold and dark land of Damara, but yet, I must admit, it is a worthy vintage."

Regis nodded and pocketed the note.

"Now, let us be on our way before we lose the sun," Tecumseh suggested, and he hopped to his feet, seeming very sprightly for one his age. "I will explain where you should lodge and how to contact me as we walk. I will do what I can to help, of course, whatever your cause—so long as it is just and good—but only from afar, you understand."

"You have already been a great boon to us, good sir Kneebreaker," Regis assured him. "The great Hobart Bracegirdle is smiling from the Blessed Fields of Elysium, I am sure!"

Tecumseh couldn't contain his smile, and he bowed deeply.

❖ ❖ ❖

"And so we meet again," a voice from the shadows said to Jarlaxle a tenday later, catching him quite by surprise. "Have you come to name a new King of Vaasa?"

Kane, the Grandmaster of Flowers, walked out of the dimly lit room in the grand house, the manse of Ilnezhara and Tazmikella, located in a secret valley just outside of Helgabal. The dragon sisters weren't there at the moment, leaving Jarlaxle feeling vulnerable indeed before this very dangerous man.

"You have seen him?" Jarlaxle asked. "Drizzt, I mean, and no new king."

Kane smiled and moved to stand in front of Jarlaxle, who sat in front of the hearth. It wasn't a cold day, but Jarlaxle had stoked the fire, that he could stare into the flames and ponder.

Jarlaxle motioned to the other chair, but Kane eschewed the invitation and instead simply squatted down low in front of it.

"Drizzt is in the care of Perrywinkle Shin, Master of Summer, whom you met when you visited my home."

"I had hoped he would be with you."

"In time," Grandmaster Kane replied, "perhaps."

Jarlaxle cocked an eyebrow warily at that equivocation.

"He has much to prove," Kane explained. "To himself as well as to his benefactors at the monastery. Master Afafrenfere speaks highly of him."

"Master," Jarlaxle echoed. "It would seem as if my friend Afafrenfere has risen quickly through your ranks."

"Very quickly," Kane confirmed. "More so than any I have ever known."

"Because of you, I expect."

"In no small way," Kane agreed.

Jarlaxle eyed him closely, trying to sense some measure of pride in that remark. But there was none. Kane was simply speaking the truth, and not hiding behind some false measure of humility.

"Afafrenfere's journey with me allowed him to reach for his

potential quite efficiently," the grandmaster explained. "Soon he will do battle with Mistress Savahn, it seems, to see if he can elevate himself to her level."

"And you have given him an advantage."

"Hardly!" Kane replied. "I have helped accelerate him toward the truth of his journey, but if he is not the stronger, Savahn will defeat him."

"And if he wins?"

"Then he will become the Master of the East Wind, and she will revert to Mistress of the South Wind."

"And she will be resentful?"

Kane laughed at that absurd notion. "If that were a remote possibility, then Savahn would never have attained her present rank. We are not a drow House. Our competition lies within ourselves."

"And so you fight each other?"

"It is a test, not a fight, and for both combatants. The titles are given to a select few at each level."

"Even your own?"

Kane smiled, and Jarlaxle got the distinct impression that this particular character was unique.

"Enough of this talk about my order, for it does not concern you," the grandmaster said.

"It concerns my friend."

"Perhaps. Perhaps not. Now, I bid you, tell me everything you know about Drizzt Do'Urden, and about this malady that so afflicts him."

"It will be a long tale."

"Good!" said Kane. "Perhaps our dragon friends will join us before you are through."

Jarlaxle didn't quite know how to respond to that, though he didn't doubt that Grandmaster Kane considered the copper dragons as "friends," at least somewhat. Kane had ridden Ilnezhara, after all, though in the body of Afafrenfere, in the battle over Mithral Hall.

Still, it seemed strange. Grandmaster Kane had gained his reputation in the company of King Gareth, whose last name was well-earned by reputation. And the dragon sisters had not wanted to approach the monastery specifically because of this very man.

"Ah, Drizzt," the mercenary said. "I have known him for almost all of his life, and knew his father before him, perhaps better than any drow in Menzoberranzan. Much like Drizzt was Zaknafein, and I am sure that he is looking upon his son from whatever just reward he found in the afterlife, and is very, very pleased."

"And very, very concerned, I would guess," the monk said.

Jarlaxle nodded, and grimaced. At that moment, Drizzt's travails crystallized for him, and he came to appreciate how great a tragedy this insanity was, particularly in this time of supreme triumph for all that Drizzt had ever wanted.

And so Jarlaxle began his tale, from the earliest days, when a twist of good fate—and of a dagger—had spared Drizzt from a premature end at the hands of his own mother.

The dragon sisters did return soon after, and though they seemed a bit off-balance at first to find Grandmaster Kane in their house, once Jarlaxle continued his tale, they, too, became attentive and interested in the remarkable story of the rogue drow.

# CHAPTER 14 ◈

# *Damara's Fiend*

ROM A SECLUDED KNOLL SOME DISTANCE FROM THE northern gate of Helgabal, First Priestess Charri Hunzrin of House Hunzrin of Menzoberranzan watched the approach of the dirty spriggan band.

"When will we know?" asked Shak'kral, a young and eager noblewoman of that same House, one known as a powerful trafficker for trading beyond the drow city's borders, indeed, even here on the uninviting surface.

"Malcanthet is a queen of the lower planes," Charri scolded. "We will know when she wants us to know, or if she wants us to know."

"It seems a tragedy to invoke such chaos and not witness it," the young drow woman replied. "We have brought the consort of Demogorgon to this unwitting fool king. Surely there will be great pleasure in observing!"

Charri wanted to scold the other, particularly when the few other drow in the merchant party began nodding and smiling in agreement. But she, too, hoped they would have some view of the coming catastrophe. Malcanthet, Queen of the Succubi, was hidden in that necklace, ready to come forth in all her terrible splendor.

Truly, it would be grand . . .

"Beware your wishes," said Denderida, one of the more seasoned of House Hunzrin's surface traders. It was she who had arranged this rendezvous with the spriggans of Smeltergard.

Denderida was not a noble of House Hunzrin, but Charri offered her great deference and respect in this matter. She had centuries of experience and knew the World Above as well as any drow from Menzoberranzan, with the possible exception of Jarlaxle.

"You would not wish to witness the glory?" Shak'kral asked.

"You speak truly of Malcanthet," Denderida replied. "But Demogorgon was destroyed—banished from this plane of existence, at least."

"All the better, then!" Shak'kral argued, but Denderida was shaking her head at the clearly expected response.

"Malcanthet has made no shortage of enemies in the Abyss, and with Demogorgon removed . . ."

"There are rumors that Graz'zt has appeared in the Underdark," Charri warned. The war between Dark Prince Graz'zt and Malcanthet was no secret to the drow.

"We served Malcanthet in bringing her to this place," Denderida added. "Would you wish to explain that to the Dark Prince of the Abyss?"

Shak'kral shrank back from the older woman, shaking her head.

"We will watch from afar," Charri promised.

"Our filthy couriers are held up at the gate," Denderida remarked then, turning all eyes back to the distant city. "Do the victims suspect?"

Charri shook her head, for it seemed unlikely. She had no definitive answers, though, and so she said no more, and along with her sisters, simply watched.

◆　◆　◆

"'Ere but we don't wike waitin'!" the dirty fellow named Toofless complained when Ivan Bouldershoulder finally arrived at the gate to greet them.

"None do, but look like ye're comin' unannounced to see the king, aye, and so his guards were told to fetch me if ye did," Ivan countered, trying to be polite but having a very hard time of it.

The smell of this crew offended even his tough dwarf sensibilities. There was something simply not right about this "Clan Bigger," though Ivan couldn't put his fat finger on it.

"So ye're comin' to see me king?" he asked when none of the visitors moved to reply.

"Aye, and with pretties," said Toofless.

"We wouldn't be comin' in without proper tribute, what!" another added.

"And who ye be?" Ivan asked.

"Komtoddy," the more muscular fellow answered. "Champion o' Smeltergard."

"Champion?"

"Aye, Komtoddy's a fighter, and a good one," Toofless Tonguelasher explained. "He be givin' yerself a good beatin' if ye're wanting it!"

Ivan wanted nothing more than to take the dirty fellow up on that challenge, but he swallowed his pride and remembered his place. "Me King Yarin sent me out to bring ye in proper, with proper announcin' and all," he explained. "It's a compliment to ye, for the king's wantin' ye to be properly recognized by all observers as decent citizens of the realm."

"Decent?" Toofless asked with clear skepticism.

"Bah, but who ye callin' decent?" another of the troupe shouted, and he sounded properly insulted.

Ivan started to reply, but bit it back then huffed and shook his head, and focused on Toofless, who seemed the leader. "Are ye wantin' to see the king or ain't ye, and are ye Damarans now or ain't ye?" he asked bluntly. "If ye are to both, then ye come with me, and ye listen to me all the way, and I'll be tellin' ye how to do it proper. And if it ain't done proper, it ain't done at all, don't ye doubt."

"He's threatening us!" said the same loudmouth from the back.

"He ain't thweatening!" Toofless lashed back, and he reached behind and slapped Komtoddy, who slapped the next in line, and all the way back until the loudmouth got a backhand across the face.

Ivan sighed. He felt as if he were watching the worst stereotypical insults hurled at dwarves come to life before his eyes.

"Take me to yer weader," Toofless said with a wide and gummy grin.

"Aye, that's why I'm here to meet ye," Ivan replied. "And I'll tell ye how to behave when ye get there, too, and if ye're smart and lookin' to e'er get afore King Yarin again, ye'll hear me words and hold to them."

Toofless looked around at his kin, and for a moment, Ivan was uncertain as to how this might go. He even wondered if he was about to have a fight on his hands.

But Toofless turned back to him, offered a smile that signified nothing, and dipped a bow.

◆ ◆ ◆

CONCETTINA COVERED UP as soon as Yarin was finished with her. There was no sensitivity, no love, no connection at all between them. It was just an act for a purpose, and that purpose, Concettina feared, would never be fulfilled. Not by this man, at least.

She didn't, couldn't, even watch him dress, and couldn't suppress her whimper as she tried to hide her revulsion for this man who was her husband.

"Are you coming to court?" Yarin asked sharply. He was dressed and noted that his wife hadn't even left her bed. He sneered at her and snickered rudely.

"No," he decided, "you stay here. Better for me to be out of your sight so that I am not continually reminded of your failure."

He moved to the door and threw it wide. "You two!" he called to the guards in the hallway. "None in!" He turned back to regard Concettina and added hatefully, "And none out."

"But I would go to the gardens," the queen meekly argued, but King Yarin screamed before she had finished.

"You will stay in this room until you fulfill the purpose of a wife's bed!"

He slammed the door as he exited, and Concettina pulled the blankets up over her face, terrified and ashamed.

◆ ◆ ◆

SOON AFTER, IVAN handed a coffer over to King Yarin, who slowly opened it, never taking his eyes off the filthy dwarf visitors as he did.

Until it was open enough for him to see the necklaces, of course. Both beautiful and set with fabulous and expensive stones, they caught his greedy eye.

"A gift, me kingie, for yerself and yer queen," Toofless explained.

On a nod from Red Mazzie, the court wizard who had already cast spells upon the items to determine if they were magical and perhaps malevolent, and another nod from Junquis Dularemay, the court priest who had cast divine spells to detect any poison on the items, King Yarin lifted the larger of the two and eyed it carefully. He smiled, the weight of the ostentatious piece convincing him that the thick chain was indeed pure gold.

"Ye'll wook good," Toofless assured King Yarin, who wasn't even regarding him then but was instead looking to Dreylil Andrus. Andrus motioned to a guard to join him and rushed to the king, then took the necklace from King Yarin, hesitating not at all before slipping it over the head of the lower-ranking soldier.

"The king's bauble and not yer own!" Toofless protested.

Captain Andrus eyed him dangerously and unfastened the necklace then reached for the opened coffer. There were dangerous necklaces on Toril, of course, which defied spells of detection and divination, one in particular that appeared normal by every indication until it was put on the head of an unsuspecting victim. Then it would constrict and choke until the victim was properly dead, before returning to its "normal" state.

Such necklaces of strangulation were not discerning items, however, and since the soldier was still alive and the necklace had come off without incident, this particular necklace was clearly not trapped in that manner.

Nor was the other, they discovered, when Dreylil Andrus removed it from the soldier and dismissed the man back to his station. There were other cursed necklaces about the Realms, though, and some were not simply a trap to be sprung, offering more malevolence and more intelligence in their dastardly plans.

On orders, Andrus fastened the large gold chain around King Yarin's neck, and on a cue from the captain of the guard, all in attendance began clapping enthusiastically.

King Yarin adjusted the jewelry and nodded, seeming impressed.

"Clan Bigger Damarans now?" Toofless asked.

"Well on your way, I would say," King Yarin replied. "What else have you brought?"

Toofless looked around and seemed on the edge of panic. The other dwarves shrugged and scratched their heads.

And King Yarin laughed, and all joined in, even the dwarves, when they figured out that he was simply teasing them.

"Yes, my loyal subjects, you can consider yourselves in the good graces of the king," Yarin told them. "Return regularly, and with proper tithing, and you shall remain so."

"Bwoodstone?" Toofless asked hopefully.

"Yes, please!" King Yarin replied. He turned to Dreylil Andrus. "Give them a writ to stay in some inn on the south side—beyond the wall, if you please," he commanded. "And bid them a fair journey home, with their carts resupplied."

He waved the dwarves away, and they were all too happy to comply. Toofless dropped his hand in his pocket as he exited, rubbing it over the empty phylactery, the gem identical to the one set on the smaller silver-chained necklace.

He didn't know exactly what was going to happen, but he figured it would prove to be great fun.

◆ ◆ ◆

MALCANTHET HAD ALMOST used that brief moment when she was in contact with the soldier to break free—how she longed to be free of this wretched little prison she had helped the drow House Hunzrin concoct for her. The clever dark elves of Menzoberranzan, deceitful Lolth's wretched children all, had devised a way to banish the Abyssal demons even with the damaged barrier of the Faerzress.

No, not banish, but ensnare into gemstone phylacteries, which they were then trading all over Toril.

Worse, the clever dark elves had destroyed Demogorgon, who was one of her very few allies in the Abyss, and that against many powerful enemies including Graz'zt, whom she knew to be out and about in the Underdark.

But the succubus was not without her own considerable wiles and wit, and she had found unlikely allies in this House Hunzrin, a lower-ranking but very powerful mercantile House, and one that despised the current matron mother and her allies—those same allies who had destroyed Demogorgon.

And so Matron Mother Shakti Hunzrin had helped Malcanthet escape the Underdark, and now First Priestess Charri had delivered her to a place where Graz'zt would not find her—and where she could wreak some lovely chaos and lovelier murder.

"Patience," Malcanthet, the Queen of the Succubi, told herself. In her brief time around the soldier's neck, she had been able to scour his thoughts enough to know that he was a bit of a simpleton, and only a minor player, and also that he was testing the necklace at the behest of a king.

"Yes, a king," Malcanthet purred in her extra-dimensional prison. "A king with a queen?"

◆ ◆ ◆

HE DIDN'T KNOCK, and burst through the door suddenly and with great force, surprising poor Concettina so completely that she let out a scream before realizing it to be King Yarin come calling.

"You startled me!" she protested.

He moved right up to her and shoved her down on the bed and began stripping his clothing, revealing a gaudy necklace of gold and gems. "Not another word from you or you'll feel the sting of my hand," he warned, lisping slightly and so letting on that he had found his way to his liquor cabinet before venturing to her room.

She stared at the necklace, not daring to ask where he had come by it.

"You like it, yes?" Yarin asked, and Concettina simply nodded, lying with the motion, for surely she thought the ostentatious thing quite ugly.

"Fitting for a king, yes?"

She nodded again.

"And I am a king!" he declared. "The King of Damara! And do you know what else is fitting for a king, woman?"

Afraid, Concettina meekly shook her head. She noted some guards in the hall. Yarin, though he was quite naked and tearing at her clothes with licentious intent, hadn't even bothered to close the door behind him.

"An heir!" he yelled. "And you're to give me one. And soon! Know that my patience is at its end, foolish girl."

He threw himself on top of her, forcing her arms down by her side, and Concettina just closed her eyes and tried not to cry. She didn't know if the guards had shut the door, or if they were just out there, watching.

She couldn't even summon the strength to care.

# CHAPTER 15 ◈

# *Creation*

P ROCEED," THE WIZARD CALLED FROM ACROSS THE CHASM.
Bruenor looked back from the anteroom to Gromph
and the others, all gathered by the pit, most deep into
spellcasting. He wished that Catti-brie was among the
group—he wanted to hear the command from her so he
could have some confidence that it was indeed time for this
momentous occasion.

Bruenor closed his eyes and recalled his last visit to the Throne
of the Dwarven Gods. He had relayed these plans, though of
course he had no way of knowing if that call crossed the planes of
existence to the ears of Moradin, Dumathoin, and Clangeddin.

But the throne hadn't launched him across the room, to crash
into the wall, as it had at other times when its godly audience
wasn't happy with the dwarf king's heart.

"They cannot hold their dweomers forever, foolish dwarf!"
Gromph bellowed, and it occurred to Bruenor that there might
be a bit of magical suggestion in that command. Before he
even paused to consider it, he yanked the lever controlling the
water elementals.

Bruenor held his breath and the rush of water from the ceiling
halted. Almost immediately after that, the primordial rumbled
and the cavern floor trembled.

Bruenor couldn't see into the pit from his vantage point, and
he didn't dare leave the lever—indeed, he wouldn't let go of the
thing, ready to tug it back and release a renewed rain of water

elementals upon the fire primordial. He saw Gromph, though. The wizard was smiling widely, his eyes glowing in reflection of the bubbling orange lava far below.

The primordial belched, a burst of magma lifting from the pit and into the waiting tendril. Then it vomited, releasing mighty preternatural energy. A line of molten power shot up from the pit and into the opened tendril above.

Bruenor thought this whole thing foolish. He had let free the beast! All of Gauntlgrym would be consumed!

He grabbed the lever harder and started to tug.

"Not yet!" Gromph screamed, and the dwarf was shocked to find the archmage standing beside him.

"No, no," Gromph said more calmly. "Look, King Bruenor! Witness the power! Even a dwarf should appreciate the glory of this moment!"

He coaxed Bruenor forward, and the dwarf felt the blast of hot air keenly when he came to the edge of the anteroom. His eyes stung, his beard singed even, but he didn't care. He stood there transfixed, amazed by the bared power of this godlike being before him.

A line of lava sprayed up from the pit, hot and thick and rushing into the tendril, filling it and rushing to Luskan.

Many heartbeats later, he heard Gromph counting—a most poignant reminder. His trance broken, though still awestricken, Bruenor stumbled back to the lever.

Bruenor didn't know the drow language enough to follow the count, but finally Gromph looked up at him, held up all ten fingers, and began the last countdown. Bruenor readied the lever to flood in more elementals and trap the beast in its pit once more.

◆ ◆ ◆

CATTI-BRIE AND JARLAXLE stood beside the hole in the ground amidst the rubble of the old Hosttower, staring in at the mound of ruins and limestone and gemstones the dwarves had collected and dumped into the pit. Behind the pair, thousands looked on, many half-turned and stepping in place, setting their legs as if readying to flee.

And why wouldn't they be? Catti-brie was summoning a volcano here, a fire primordial, the same beast that had obliterated the city of Neverwinter a few decades earlier and killed thousands.

The tons of piled stone in the pit bounced then, ever so slightly, and Catti-brie jumped an equal amount.

Jarlaxle tightened his grip around her shoulders, and she glanced at him and could tell that he wasn't much more comfortable than she.

The rubble bounced again and a fountain of lava shot up from the hole, straight into the air to fall back down upon itself. And the pile in the pit began to roll and to rise, and the distinct edges of the stones and broken bits of the former Hosttower began to soften and blend then fold over each other. Bubbles of lava burst and sent a terrible stench into the air.

But Catti-brie just pulled her shawl over her face to lessen the smell, and neither she nor Jarlaxle, who seemed unbothered by the stench, turned away.

The whole ball of slag rose up from the hole and seemed to stretch and grow. It started thin, but then widened quickly, forming what looked like the base of a gigantic tree. It continued to grow upward from there, taller than the onlookers, ten feet and more. A large bubble appeared on the side facing Jarlaxle and Catti-brie, and they cautiously backed away a few steps.

It burst as they had feared, but didn't splatter. Instead, a massive branch began growing straight out from the hole in the trunk, then began to turn upward.

Then the eruption was over, and the new creation, fifteen feet of hollow trunk and a single massive hollow branch extending only a few feet out from the main trunk, poured smoke from both openings. The new material, this super-heated, primordial-infused limestone, glittered in the daylight almost as if it was a wet, polished stone.

On the field all around Jarlaxle and Catti-brie, the onlookers began to cheer and gasp. What they had just witnessed seemed almost holy, a preternatural creation, perfect and godlike. Stones growing as mountains must have grown, so many eons before.

Unlike the others, though, Catti-brie just pulled her shawl tighter around her and expressed no joy.

"It is a powerful beginning," Jarlaxle said, coming up and putting his arm around her. "It is all that we had hoped and more. Your insights have been proven correct."

Catti-brie nodded slightly, but her expression did not soften.

"This is your moment of greatest triumph," Jarlaxle said, "but he is not here to share it with you."

Catti-brie looked at him. She didn't answer, but she didn't have to. Her expression said all that was needed.

Everything in the world seemed to be going right, and toward a beautiful and peaceful goal, but Drizzt wasn't there with her, and might not return for years, or decades, or ever. Catti-brie had the desperate feeling that their story together was now, at last, fully told.

Jarlaxle wanted to comfort her, but he held silent, knowing that anything he said would reveal the truth that he couldn't disagree with her grim assessment.

◆　◆　◆

Yvonnel Baenre wasn't even aware of the fact that her jaw was hanging open. She stared into the water of the scrying pool, dumbfounded, overwhelmed by the beauty and power of what she witnessed within.

"Gromph . . . beautiful Gromph," she whispered

Her father led a team of mighty wizards and priests in the calculated and controlled release of the fire primordial.

When the water elementals fell from the channels in the ceiling once more, sealing the great beast back in its pit, Yvonnel waved her hand over the scrying pool and changed the image to the scene in Luskan where her uncle Jarlaxle and the human woman Catti-brie stood in front of their creation.

Her breath was stolen yet again, Yvonnel could only shake her head as she considered the scope of what these people were attempting. The trunk and first sprouting limb of a massive, wondrous tower, full of magic and full of . . . life . . .

Dare she think that?

Was it even possible?

That was exactly what Yvonnel's heart and mind were telling her, that this tower was more than a simple construction of unliving materials. It resembled the husk of a once-great tree, but she sensed something more, something alive. Whether that was rooted in the process of growing the tower or in the tower itself, or even in both, she could not tell.

All she knew was that her heart sang to her, its melodies certain that she was witnessing something . . . divine.

It took her a long while to tear herself away from the scrying stoup and stumble out of the room, and a long while after that to fully regain her sensibilities.

She called Minolin Fey to her side and together they went to see Matron Mother Quenthel.

"When is the last time you have spoken with Gromph?" Yvonnel demanded, dispensing with etiquette. "Or Jarlaxle? Have you heard from the rogue of late?"

"No, neither," Quenthel replied. "Not since you allowed Jarlaxle to leave the city with the rogue Do'Urden and the others. I thought it better to remain removed from them."

"From me, you mean," said Yvonnel, and Quenthel didn't deny it.

"What else do you know?" Yvonnel demanded. "Of the city and of that which is happening outside of Menzoberranzan?"

Quenthel held up her hands as if in surrender. That was quite a wide-reaching request, after all.

"Are any moving against us, or against House Do'Urden?" Yvonnel demanded.

Quenthel shook her head. "Matron Mother Zeerith is in place in House Do'Urden. She has brought in all of the former House Xorlarrin charges. She doesn't even need our soldiers in her compound any longer. Only Barrison Del'Armgo could threaten her alone, and Matron Mother Mez'Barris would not dare such a move at this tentative time."

"Allow Matron Mother Zeerith to regain her old House name—it is not fitting to have any entity named House Do'Urden, in any case," Yvonnel said. "They were properly obliterated, leave them so."

"But is not Drizzt the Champion of Menzoberranzan?" a confused Quenthel asked, eliciting a growl from Yvonnel.

"Better for all that he is simply forgotten," Yvonnel explained. Quenthel nodded.

"Move the reconstituted House Xorlarrin up the hierarchy," Yvonnel continued. "Demote House Melarn to Eighth House and elevate House Vandree above them, so that Vandree may retain its current rank as Seventh House. It is fitting that Matron Mother Zhindia Melarn be punished for her attempt on House Do'Urden, and this shuffling will stifle any protests forthcoming from House Vandree."

Quenthel considered the ordering for a moment, then nodded.

"And so that will leave Matron Mother Zeerith's as the Sixth House," Yvonnel went on. "Let that remain for ten tendays, and during that time, inform Matron Mother Byrtyn Fey that Matron Mother Zeerith will soon ascend above her. Byrtyn Fey's options are nil. She cannot argue, for she knows that the only reason she retains her seat on the Ruling Council is because of her allegiance to House Baenre. Without you, House Fey-Branche would be crushed by one or another, even with House Melarn so clearly weakened and chastised."

"Would you have me tell Houses Mizzrym and Faen Tlabbar that they, too, will be demoted to make room for the rising return of House Xorlarrin?" Quenthel asked, and though she seemed properly respectful, there was no missing the nervousness in her voice.

"Matron Mother Zeerith will be comfortable, for now, in place as the Fifth House," Yvonnel replied. "She cannot expect more from us after her failures with her fledgling city."

Matron Mother Quenthel considered the situation for a moment then nodded. "As you will."

"You and your sister asked me for counsel on the matter of Matron Mother Zhindia Melarn, and so you have it," said Yvonnel.

Quenthel nodded respectfully and repeated, "As you will."

"This is my advice, not my command," Yvonnel explained, and after a moment, that remark apparently sank into Quenthel's mind and had her staring at Yvonnel, wide-eyed.

"The choice is yours, in the end," Yvonnel said, "for you are the matron mother of Menzoberranzan, not I."

Quenthel's look turned suspicious, and she even shook her head a little bit as if denying any thought of heeding that unexpected ordering of things. She had battled Yvonnel that one time, of course, and so it was obvious to both—and to anyone else who had noted the struggle—that Quenthel had no desire to ever do so again.

Indeed, standing beside Yvonnel, her mother, Minolin Fey, seemed no less baffled.

"If the matron mother decides to promote House Xorlarrin above your former House, then you will help to persuade Matron Mother Byrtyn that this is a good thing," Yvonnel instructed her mother.

"This is a test," Quenthel stated bluntly.

"A test?" Yvonnel asked.

"You wish to determine if I will hold fast to your desires without you commanding me to do so," Quenthel explained, and she truly seemed to have nothing left to lose, like a rat caught in a corner.

"No."

"Do not play with me in such a manner, I beg," said Quenthel.

"You are the Matron Mother of Menzoberranzan!" Yvonnel scolded. "You do not beg anyone, other than Lady Lolth herself."

But Quenthel shook her head, clearly overwhelmed and more than a little afraid.

"This is no trick, and no test," Yvonnel said, her voice calm and even. "With Minolin Fey Baenre as my witness. I have rethought our arrangement, and recognized my place here in Menzoberranzan. I will not submit to you, Aunt Quenthel."

She said that last bit with a wry grin then added, "Indeed, if I do not show the proper reverence to you, in private, then you will simply have to suffer my insolence."

Quenthel's eyes narrowed, but she said nothing.

"But I am not to be matron mother," Yvonnel finished. "Not now, likely not ever. You need not fear that I will attempt to usurp your throne, and indeed, should any usurpers come against you, you can count me as one of your staunchest allies—and I will ensure that Sos'Umptu is likewise dependable."

"Why?" The suspicion remained clear in Quenthel's voice.

"Because it bores me," Yvonnel said. "And you bore me. I have no desire to play the little games of worthless intrigue that dominate your waking hours, and those in Reverie as well, no doubt. So call it a curse I place upon you and not a favor, and thus I curse you to suffer your fate."

Quenthel was shaking her head through it all, but now seemed to be growing bolder and more confident, with even her posture firming. "Lady Lolth foretold your arrival in the Festival of the Founding in House Fey-Branche. She said that you, Yvonnel, daughter of Gromph, would become the Matron Mother of Menzoberranzan. She said that to me directly, which is why I have not thought to, and could not begin to, conspire against your designs of ascension. You are sanctioned by Lolth, and so your claim on House Baenre, and thus of all Menzoberranzan, is guaranteed."

"Unless I do not want it," Yvonnel replied. "And I do not."

Quenthel's eyes widened and she even fell back a step in shock, shaking her head.

"I leave you to your curse, Matron Mother," Yvonnel said respectfully and with a bow. "And I leave you with Minolin Fey, my mother. I find that I do not much want her, either."

With that, she gave a curt laugh, spun, and strode from the room, leaving the other two women staring at her with helpless confusion.

◆　◆　◆

YVONNEL WASN'T REALLY surprised, but was still shaken a bit when Quenthel showed up at the door of her private quarters with a handmaiden of Lolth, in drow form, right beside her.

"Leave us, Quenthel Baenre," Yiccardaria said as soon as Yvonnel greeted them.

Yvonnel didn't miss the fact that the handmaiden hadn't used the title of matron mother when addressing Quenthel, and that was no minor thing.

"It is true, then?" Yiccardaria asked when they were alone.

"It?"

"Do you believe that you have garnered the favor of Lady Lolth?"

Yvonnel shrugged. "I can only do that which I think the best course, and hope that such a course pleases her. Unless you would have me summoning you or one of your sisters to my side for every decision I make."

The handmaiden scowled at the impertinence. "Do you think this a game, daughter of Gromph? Would you like to be taught that it is not?"

"The Spider Queen wished Demogorgon stopped," Yvonnel replied, somewhat hesitantly—as much for effect as because she was momentarily unsure in the face of the threat. "I arranged for Demogorgon to be stopped. Cleverly, I thought."

"By using the rogue apostate."

"A fitting touch," Yvonnel protested. "For now the aura of stench around House Do'Urden is lifted enough for Matron Mother Zeerith to occupy the physical house and the seat at the Ruling Council, which again strengthens the hand of the matron mother and firms the alliance of House Baenre."

"A matron mother who is not Yvonnel," Yiccardaria reminded her. "Even though the word of Lady Lolth was that Yvonnel would become matron mother. Would you make of Lolth a liar?"

Yvonnel's impulse was to argue that Lolth, the Queen of Chaos, should enjoy such a title, but she wisely held her thoughts private. "In the moment of crisis, I was viewed as matron mother, and all in the city understand the truth of that," she replied instead. "I led the response to Demogorgon and took no orders from Quenthel nor any other matron mother."

"Not formally."

"And perhaps I will again assume the title of matron mother, but in the future," Yvonnel quickly added. "There is much I must learn."

"You act as if it is your choice. It is not."

Yvonnel held up her hands, for what might she say?

"And you have failed the Spider Queen," the handmaiden added, and Yvonnel's expression changed abruptly, her eyes going wide both with confusion and a moment of fear. Failing the Spider Queen was not to be taken lightly.

"You were to destroy the apostate after exploiting him," Yiccardaria explained. "You could have turned him into a drider, as Matron Mother Quenthel advised. You could simply have tortured him until the pain became meaningless, and then dragged him to his death through the streets of Menzoberranzan, allowing every House, every drow, to spit upon him or kick him. But you did not. Nay, you chose to be clever, always clever."

"You cannot deny that my plan to have him murder the one he most loves would have broken the rogue more than anything physical might have ever—"

"I deny that your plan worked," the handmaiden interrupted. "Would you dispute my denial?"

Yvonnel stared hard at Yiccardaria. They knew! She couldn't believe how closely she and Drizzt had been watched. Didn't Lolth and her minions have enough to contend with in the swirling gray smoke of the Abyss, particularly when her grander plan of freeing the demon lords into the Prime Material Plane gave the Spider Queen such an opening for Abyssal dominance?

But they knew the details here, and Yvonnel licked her lips, waiting for judgment to fall.

"So you choose not to become matron mother at this time?" Yiccardaria asked.

"I will assume the mantle if that is the desire of Lady Lolth," Yvonnel replied, and she hated herself for her cowardice.

But there it was.

"Someday, perhaps," the handmaiden replied. "At this time, and even with the knowledge and memories of your namesake given to you as a great gift by the Spider Queen, you clearly are not prepared for such a task. So go. Leave this city. It is what you want."

Yvonnel stared at the handmaiden, and her expression was blank with shock.

"Go and right the error you made with the apostate," Yiccardaria added.

"You would have me kill Drizzt? Or drag him back to the city? Or to the Abyss, to present him before Lady—"

"I would have you go and do as you believe the correct path," Yiccardaria explained. "If you are to become matron mother, then Lady Lolth must come to see that you have the judgment for such a role."

"I . . ."

"Are you afraid?" Yiccardaria purred.

After a moment's hesitation, Yvonnel nodded.

And Yiccardaria laughed and left her alone.

# CHAPTER 16 ◈

# *Fire and Water*

"YOU SHOWED HIM THIS?" SAVAHN ASKED AFAFRENFERE.

The two stood on the balcony overlooking the circular fighting pit of the Monastery of the Yellow Rose, where the monks performed the bulk of their martial training and sparring. A multitude of doors led into that lower level, each flanked on both sides by elaborate weapons racks, with every weapon imaginable—and more than a few exotic instruments that few outside the order knew about—available at one or another. The central training area of the floor was raised a step, that step being orange in color, and the floor itself was ringed with symbols of fire. A mosaic of a springing tiger centered the floor, the newest addition to the room.

"Drizzt has been practicing in such a manner for longer than I have been alive," Afafrenfere replied. "Longer than my mother's mother's mother has been alive. It is his way, and so, Drizzt has told me, fairly common among the drow."

"No wonder, then, that they are feared warriors," Savahn said. She leaned on the railing and studied the movements of the drow ranger. If he noticed the onlookers at all, he made no outward sign of it. He turned and dipped so very slowly, precisely mimicking the movements he would make in an actual fight. His blades flowed like two streams of clear water, crossing, joining, separating once more, so fluid and perfect in their movements that it was hard to tell where the cut of one scimitar ended and where the swing of the other began.

"Hypnotic," Savahn said. She turned back to Afafrenfere and remarked without sarcasm, "Perhaps I should spend my energies training him instead of you."

Afafrenfere straightened at the unexpected remark. "Do you doubt my abilities?" he asked without a sneer, without any judgment at all. Savahn would never say such a thing as an insult, of course, and it would be remiss of Afafrenfere to take her words as such.

"Hardly."

"Then why?"

"Perhaps I fear that you will learn from Drizzt instead of the other way around," the woman said with a wry grin.

Only then did Afafrenfere catch on. Savahn and Afafrenfere would do battle soon, as Afafrenfere tried to ascend to become a Master of the East Wind, the rank currently held by Savahn. Within the order, there could only be one such master. If Afafrenfere came to meet all of the other qualifications, which, given his continued remarkable progress, he seemed destined to achieve shortly, he would rightly challenge Savahn to single combat in this very room below them. The winner would assume the title currently held by Savahn, the loser reverting to the rank now held by Afafrenfere.

"In training Drizzt, I slow my own personal studies," Afafrenfere replied. "Perhaps you would do well to accelerate your own training since Master of Winter, the rank above your present, is currently unoccupied in the order."

She nodded at his remark. It was true enough. The only members of the order higher in rank than Savahn were Perrywinkle Shin and Grandmaster Kane himself.

"Do you believe that I am afraid to fight you?" Savahn asked, again with a smile. Their fights would be vicious, of course, and without reserve, and often both combatants would spend many days or even tendays recuperating. But the outcomes were always accepted with grace and deference. Whomever lost such a fight did so because the other combatant was proven to be the better. The answer to such a defeat could never be anger or vengeance but an honest look inside of oneself and a renewal of training and discipline.

"Which of us, do you suppose, will one day challenge Grandmaster Kane?" Savahn asked, and Afafrenfere looked at her incredulously, shrugged, and shook his head.

"It will never be me," Savahn admitted. "I am already past my peak physical years, and passing the Trials of the Four Seasons is a greater task than all the ranks before combined."

Afafrenfere nodded then, understanding. There were seventeen ranks of achievement among the Order of the Yellow Rose. Afafrenfere had attained eleven, Savahn twelve, and Master Perrywinkle Shin was Master of Summer, the fifteenth level.

Shin was an old man now, and barely trained anymore, and had openly admitted that he had found the limit of his potential, and so would never achieve the subsequent rank of Master of Spring, let alone pass through those trials to challenge the great Grandmaster of Flowers.

Savahn's statement regarding her own ascent was also true, Afafrenfere believed. She might become the Mistress of Winter, the thirteenth rank, though the level of skill and inner power between those two ranks, East Wind and Winter, was perhaps the second most profound climb within the order, only behind the ascension to Grandmaster of Flowers.

But Afafrenfere was young—young enough to conquer those barriers if he could remain fully dedicated.

The monk shook those prideful thoughts out of his mind and silently chastised himself for even harboring them. The goal was—the goal had to be—self-improvement, not titles.

He knew the truth now from his time occupying the same body with Grandmaster Kane. The greatest barrier facing Master Afafrenfere in his ascent were these very lapses in focus and purpose, the distraction of a shiny object or a perceived ring of gold waiting to be plucked, only in Afafrenfere's specific and most-damaging case, the love of a man who was proven to be unworthy of his love.

Yes, that was Afafrenfere's great internal barrier. And it was not a blockage in terms of ascension through the ranks of the Order of the Yellow Rose—though it would certainly play out on that stage, as well. Indeed, to no small extent, those ranks were arbitrary, a measurement, but hardly a precise one, of the harmony a brother or sister had attained, either physically or in inner emotional peace.

Afafrenfere's lack of inner harmony would harm Afafrenfere alone, and in the most profound way, by never allowing him to achieve his highest order of contentment and understanding of the world around him, of his place in that world, of life itself. Before leaving the monastery and fleeing to the place called Shade with Parbid, his lover, Brother Afafrenfere had been nearing the rank of Master in the Order of the Yellow Rose. Since his return, and through the possession of Grandmaster Kane, Afafrenfere had soared through the next ranks in line, becoming a Master, a Superior Master, a Master of Dragons, and progressing through each of the Trials of the Four Winds to the point where he was nearing his challenge to Savahn. The most profound and helpful gift Kane had given to him in that time when they were joined as one was a matter of reminding Afafrenfere of who he was, and of why he had joined the order in the first place. Afafrenfere could never have achieved the level of success he had found before running off with Parbid if he hadn't come into the order with the goal of contentment.

Now he was back on that path, fully focused, but every now and again, he had to remind himself.

He moved beside Savahn, looked down upon Drizzt, and nodded. In this drow, Afafrenfere recognized a level of discipline he could only ever dream of attaining.

"What a pity that this magnificent warrior is so lost," Savahn said, as if reading Afafrenfere's thoughts.

"Then let us find him," Afafrenfere replied.

◆ ◆ ◆

"THERE IS NO difficulty and there is complete difficulty," Afafrenfere said to Drizzt. "Your pain and growth is entirely up to you as you instruct your body into the pose."

"To bring yourself to the very limit of the bend," Drizzt replied, and Afafrenfere smiled.

With a shrug, the drow went into the movement his monk friend had described. First standing perfectly straight, then falling into a crouch, Drizzt smoothly stood and lifted his arms over his head. Then he leaned so far back he could see the majority of the wall behind him. With a sudden and powerful swoop, Drizzt went forward, bending at the waist and putting his head right against his knees. He held there for some time, feeling a slight pull at the back of his legs, but nothing he couldn't maintain for a long, long while.

And so he did, as Afafrenfere had bade him, holding perfectly still as the candles burned and the sun moved low in the western sky.

"Find peace," the monk quietly whispered now and again.

Drizzt didn't. He remained still in body but not in his heart.

And so went their journey together over the next hours, with Master Afafrenfere showing Drizzt each of the movements the Order of the Yellow Rose called "Childish Grace," movements designed to free the mind and ease the heart as much as release the tensions and limitations of reach and stretch.

Drizzt performed every pose to near perfection on the first or second try, and with such amazing agility and stamina in sustaining the pose that Afafrenfere was left scratching his chin and wondering if there was any benefit at all for the drow with these practices.

Still, Master Perrywinkle Shin had ordered him to do this, and Master Shin had explained that he was simply relaying the orders of Grandmaster Kane, and so how could Afafrenfere refuse, or even question?

◆ ◆ ◆

DRIZZT WAS GROWING tired of this journey. He felt like a passenger aboard a ship he could not steer, and since that ship was his own life, this diversion to the Monastery of the Yellow Rose was, in those first few days, doing no more to him than increasing the level of his frustration.

Master Afafrenfere noted that, surely, as the days slipped past, and so did the other masters, and so on the seventh day, the monk did not come to Drizzt early in the morning to take him to Childish Grace.

Instead, a much older man, Master Perrywinkle Shin, appeared at the cloth flap blocking Drizzt's small room from the private chambers of many others. The elderly man's face was impassive, and he said nothing at first, just motioned for Drizzt to follow as he exited the chamber.

"You will not need those," he did remark to Drizzt when the drow moved for his gear. "Any of it. Just the robe we have given to you."

Drizzt hesitated a bit longer, and offered a quick glance at the older monk. In the end, he shrugged and complied, though he was certainly thinking that his passive obedience to this nonsense was nearing its end.

Master Shin led Drizzt into a small circular chamber, one of the few places Drizzt had seen inside this grand structure that had few markings, statues, or other illuminations. Drizzt hesitated before following Master Shin to the center of the room, though.

Set in the exact middle of the floor was a single large candle set on an ornate candlestick, giving Drizzt the notion that this might be a chamber of summoning. He spent a moment studying the floor, looking for some design or pentagram or runes, but as far as he could tell, it was bare and featureless.

"Come, stand opposite the candle from me," Master Shin requested, and he took a position directly across from the door and turned back to face Drizzt.

"What being will you summon?" Drizzt asked, moving up to take his place.

"Being? Summon?"

Drizzt motioned to the candle.

"Ah," said Master Shin. "No, my friend, I am no sorcerer. All that will be summoned here will be, I hope, a moment of emptiness."

Drizzt didn't know what that might mean, so he shrugged. To him, it did not matter.

Master Shin moved his feet a bit wider than shoulder-width, then turned his toes outward at a slight angle. He brought his palms together in front of his chest, as if in prayer, and slowly bent his legs, lowering himself straight down into a squat until his legs were bent slightly more than a right angle at the knee.

"Can you do this?" he asked, and closed his eyes.

Drizzt copied the movement with his legs.

"Your hands, too," Master Shin instructed, and Drizzt thought it curious that the man, who had not opened his eyes as far as Drizzt could tell, had noted that omission.

Drizzt brought his hands together.

"Does this position pain you?" Master Shin asked.

"No."

Perrywinkle Shin stood up, but held out his hand when Drizzt started to do likewise. The master produced a small item from the pocket of his robe, and with a flick of his fingers created a tiny flame atop it.

"Flint and steel with a wick," Master Shin explained, lighting the candle. "We call it a *fusee*." He brought the small item, the *fusee*, back in close, blew out its flame, and replaced it in his pocket.

"I leave you to your thoughts," Master Shin told the drow. "Remain in that pose for as long as you are able. For as long as you are capable. To the absolute end of your endurance."

"That could be a long time," Drizzt remarked, but Shin seemed not to notice, or at least, not to care.

"When you must release the stance, when you have failed, please simply extinguish the candle and sit here to await my return."

"How long?"

"That is not your concern. How long can you hold the pose? Until the candle is burned out?"

Drizzt looked at the burning candle skeptically. It was nothing one might carry through a darkened home in one hand.

"Days?" he asked.

Master Perrywinkle Shin gave a little laugh and walked out of the room.

Drizzt looked back at the candle. He pressed his palms together more solidly and strengthened his posture. He thought to softly blow on the candle—perhaps the breeze would make it burn hotter.

Or perhaps he would blow it out.

Though why would he care, after all?

He thought of Catti-brie and the great deception that had been perpetrated upon him. He thought of Menzoberranzan, his home yet never his home, and the sacrifice of Zaknafein that he had witnessed in his dream state in House Do'Urden.

Or was this a dream state, he wondered?

Who decided what was real and what an illusion, he wondered?

Who was the puppeteer, he wondered?

He thought and he wondered.

He wondered and he thought.

And his wondering was, in the end, a wandering of focus.

And so he winced often, and pressed his hands together as if trying to push the frustration right out of himself. And he tightened his legs until the muscles began to burn.

And his mind wandered and the room became a blur and the pose fell away as he fell away . . . into darkness.

◆  ◆  ◆

"COME NOW," HE heard Master Shin's voice.

Drizzt opened his eyes. He was lying on the floor in front of the candle—he vaguely remembered squeezing out the flame between his finger and thumb after he had collapsed onto the floor. He had remained there for a very long time—hours likely—but didn't remember falling asleep.

"You must be hungry," the monk added, and the mention of it did indeed clue Drizzt in to the fact that he very much was.

"How long?" he asked.

Master Shin bent low to examine the candle, which was notched to determine the length of a burn.

"I mean, how long have I been in here?" the drow clarified.

"It is morning."

Drizzt nodded, then noted the curious grin upon Master Shin's face.

"What do you know?"

"About?"

Drizzt nodded his chin to the candle. "You are amused?"

"Surprised, really, though it was predicted."

"What are you talking about?" the drow demanded.

"I have witnessed your morning practice routines and have heard of your great exploits in battle—from Master Afafrenfere; from the drow Jarlaxle, who brought you to this place; and from the more general rumors that sometimes whisper your name. I have no doubt that you could defeat many in this monastery in single combat, and that you have achieved such a level of skill honestly."

He turned to the candle. "And yet, in this challenge, there are many young monks here, some not even yet worthy of the title of brother or sister, who could defeat you."

Drizzt didn't let his pride bubble into anger. "Perhaps I did not see it as a challenge."

"Of course you did. You see everything in your life as a challenge." He moved for the door, motioning for Drizzt to follow, and making that last remark, be it insult or observation or warning, the final word.

Later that same day Drizzt was back with Afafrenfere, back to the exercises, and with little explanation beyond what he had already been given. A few days later, he was squatting in front of the candle once more, to be awakened by Master Shin again, hungry, the next morning.

And so it went, day after day, seemingly without purpose.

On the occasion of Drizzt's third visit to the candle room, when Master Shin bade him to assume his crouch, Drizzt didn't comply.

"Enough of this," he said. "I see no reason."

"Your second attempt was no better than your first," the master replied. "Worse, even."

"And so I have failed."

"That is not an option."

"By whose reckoning?" Drizzt demanded.

"By the reckoning of everyone who cares for you. And by your own, if you were wise enough to look more deeply into your heart."

"A grand claim." Drizzt made sure that his voice had a biting edge to it.

Master Shin's expression remained impassive—this one was very good at that particular effect, Drizzt thought, and it irked him more than it should have.

"Will you accept the challenge?" Master Shin asked.

"I am done with your challenges," the drow replied. "It is time for me to go."

Master Shin's shrug surprised him. Drizzt had expected to be told that he could not leave.

"There is only one who would stand in your way," the monk said instead. "Come, let us gather your things and I will show you the way out."

Drizzt paused, trying to decipher the riddle, and stared at the empty doorway and corridor beyond for a long while after Perrywinkle Shin left the chamber. He gathered up his possessions and hurried to catch up.

"Stand in the way?" he asked skeptically. "I am a prisoner now?"

"You were a prisoner before you came here, Master Do'Urden. Indeed, that is why you were brought here and why we agreed to allow you entrance."

He led Drizzt into a medium-sized room, comfortably deco-rated and with a wonderful hearth, though no fire was burning. Before that fireplace, only a single chair was set, but the room's occupant was not using it, and was, rather, squatting in front of the hearth, staring into the ashes.

"Your disposition, your prison," Master Shin cryptically explained, indicating the squatting man, and Shin turned and left, shutting the door behind him.

The squatting man made no move to stand, nor did he even glance back to see who had entered his chamber, and looking at him, so perfectly still, Drizzt wondered if he was even aware that he was no longer alone.

The drow let it play out, time passing without event or acknowledgement. Finally, Drizzt walked over to the chair and sat down, taking a longer look at the man's face as he did.

This one was older than Perrywinkle Shin, his face appearing as if he was in his seventh decade, at least, perhaps even his eighth, though his muscle tone, from what Drizzt could see of that which wasn't covered by his simple white robe, and his limberness, clearly, given that he was in a full squat, spoke of a man much younger, physically.

Drizzt understood then that this was the Grandmaster of Flowers, the legendary monk named Kane, who had fought with King Gareth in the previous century and now was somehow still alive.

Or was he? the drow wondered. He grinned, thinking he had it all sorted out. So many were still alive who should not be. It wasn't coincidence, it was deception.

Afafrenfere had spoken of this man many times, had even claimed that Kane was with him, sharing his body, in the War of the Silver Marches—and indeed, Afafrenfere's exploits in that war, particularly in slaying the white dragon on the side of Fourthpeak high above Mithral Hall, spoke of something quite beyond what any might expect.

Jarlaxle, too, had spoken of this man, Kane, confirming to Drizzt that he knew Kane, and that he and Entreri had met the man, even in combat, when they had come through the Bloodstone Lands that long, long time ago.

Kane made no move to acknowledge Drizzt. His eyes were open, but it didn't seem to Drizzt that the man was seeing anything in that room at all. Drizzt got the feeling that Kane was hollow, mentally, simply empty, in a state of complete relaxation despite the stressful pose.

In watching him, Drizzt wondered if there was any physical limit on how long the man could maintain that deep squat.

Maybe this, then, was also a test of Drizzt's patience. Would he interrupt Grandmaster Kane's meditation, or simply wait out the man?

He decided to wait, and the day passed. Drizzt got up several times and walked around, trying to be quiet about it, at least at first, for he found that he was growing increasingly agitated here, to say nothing of the growling in his belly.

The room darkened, daylight waning.

Drizzt sat back and closed his eyes. He'd find Reverie, at least.

The voice came so unobtrusively that it took the drow a while to even realize he was being spoken to, and then some more time to understand that it was an actual voice and not some mental impartation.

"You wish to leave us," Kane said.

"I waste my time," Drizzt answered after a long while.

"Your entire existence is a grand deception, so you have determined," Kane replied. "Is not time wasted no less valuable than time spent in futile and meaningless actions?"

The simple logic kept Drizzt from responding, but did nothing to lighten his irritable mood.

Kane turned his head and regarded the drow. "I would prefer that you stay. I believe that your answer is here, or at the very least, that you will find the road that leads to the answer you need."

"If you know the answer, then tell me."

"If I told you the answer, you would not believe me. In fact, you would likely trust me even less, yes?"

"Perhaps I trust you not at all right now."

"As you will," said Kane, and he turned back to the hearth. "Do you know the four elemental planes?"

Drizzt looked at him curiously. "Of course."

"We associate with them in our teachings and our practices in the Order of the Yellow Rose," Kane explained. "To advance the levels of the Order of the Yellow Rose, one must find peace within all four elements to the satisfaction of that rank."

"You have to swim and run over hot coals?" Drizzt asked flippantly, and quite disrespectfully. He knew it as soon as the words left his mouth. He wished he could take it back, but felt a bit better about his mocking when Kane managed a slight chuckle and a warm smile, clearly taking no offense.

"The element of earth is the material world around us," the Grandmaster explained. "It is our place in it and how we must manage that place, both in terms of nature and community. It is our outward morality."

Drizzt nodded. It seemed simple enough.

"Air is the spiritual," said Kane. "It is the hardest to define and the hardest to understand. Our place in the multiverse, our life energy contained within this mortal physical form. It is the matter of accepting limitations and understanding that we are part of something much grander all at the same time, and so, the paradox of rational existence, and the ability to find peace in the uncertainty beyond this apparent life."

The monk's words conjured in Drizzt one of his many nights atop of Kelvin's Cairn, with the stars all around and the feeling that he was lifting up into them to be one with them in some grand universal scheme that remained beyond his comprehension. He understand Kane's words quite profoundly, and his expression and nod reflected that—and that, too, drew a wide smile from Grandmaster Kane.

"Fire is the perfection of the body, the arts martial, the hardened core," said Kane. "In this, you are quite advanced, perhaps as greatly so as any now studying at the monastery.

Your skills and discipline in the realm of fire are quite remarkable."

"As advanced as yours?" Drizzt asked, and it occurred to him that perhaps that had sounded like a challenge, and so perhaps it was.

"It would not matter," the monk replied. "Fire is most entwined with water, and water is thought, both flowing and still. Whatever you may have attained in the manner of fire, Drizzt Do'Urden, is diminished by the dam of thought you have placed in front of your personal water. Neither stillness nor free flow are within you at this time, and so you are not nearly as formidable as you might believe. You are wounded and broken."

Drizzt stared at the man hard, and almost wanted to strike out at him.

"Your feeble count at a simple meditative pose belies all that you have trained in the realm of fire," Grandmaster Kane said.

There was no tone of insult in the man's voice, and yet Drizzt had to tell himself repeatedly that there was no insult intended. All of his frustrations began to creep up around him again, black wings in which he knew he would be forever lost, and he wanted nothing more than to give that frustration a focus. He grimaced repeatedly, and with each grimace, he noted that Kane, who was not even looking his way, nodded his chin knowingly, as if reading Drizzt's every thought.

The demon deceiving him would know. Lolth would know.

Drizzt's hand slid to his belted scimitar, but Kane stood up and turned to face him directly. "I do not wish for you to leave at this time. You contradict all that you have achieved and whatever memory or honor led you to that achievement in the first place. You have thrown aside your road—for whatever reason does not matter—and I wish to help you back to it."

"Then tell me!"

"It is not a lie," Kane said quietly. "None of this is a lie. Your life is as you perceive it to be."

Drizzt's expression hardly softened.

"And you cannot believe me, and indeed, now trust me less, if that was even possible. But it matters not. Stay. You have nowhere better to go."

"Unless I am certain that there is nothing worth learning from you," Drizzt replied.

"Then strike me dead in the arena, in single combat," Kane said. "I will arrange our duel this very hour."

Drizzt rocked back in his seat and stared at the monk incredulously.

"Use your blades and every trick you know," said Kane. "Your bow, even, if you so choose."

"In that event, I could simply stay away and shoot you dead."

"Then this should be easy for you."

Kane started out of the room, pausing to turn back and motion for Drizzt to follow. "Are you afraid to face me? Or are you afraid to face yourself?" the monk asked.

It all seemed so surreal to Drizzt, and he felt less grounded than ever in that terrible moment. But he settled his thoughts solidly, telling himself that perhaps he would find an answer here, one way or another, and reminding himself that anything he could do to precipitate the end of this delusion, whatever the final cost, had to be preferable the shifting sands upon which he now stood.

They went into the circular training room and Kane dismissed the few monks he found within, leaving the pair alone on the floor, though some others, including Perrywinkle Shin, Savahn, and Afafrenfere, remained up on the overlook. The grandmaster turned to face Drizzt and brought his palms together in front of his chest, then bowed low. He came up in a fighting stance that reminded Drizzt somewhat of Regis's new sword, fighting style, with his front foot forward and pointed at Drizzt, his back foot perpendicular and strongly grounded.

Kane, though, bent that back leg and slid the front foot forward, going low, almost as if he were coiling for a strike.

Drizzt hesitated, his hand shifting to draw his blades even though this seemed ridiculous to him. Kane was unarmed and unarmored, while Drizzt possessed weapons that could cut a man in half, that could slice through muscle and bone as easily as he could slide his own hand through water.

"You are uncertain," Kane said, coming only slightly out of his stance.

"I have no desire to kill you."

"Even if I am nothing more than a lie? That is your confusion, is it not?"

"If you are not a lie, and are indeed the man I have been told of in many heroic tales, then killing you would be a travesty and a waste," Drizzt said. "If you are yet another illusion and part of the deception, I gain nothing by fighting you, for in that . . ."

He ended with a great "oomph" as Kane charged in suddenly and brutally, somersaulting and double-kicking Drizzt to launch him backward. The drow fell into a roll and executed it three full times to absorb much of the shock, but came up near the wall, far from Kane, wincing from the sting and trying to catch his breath.

Kane laughed at him. "Perhaps not as much of a challenge as I had hoped," the Grandmaster of Flowers teased. "Draw your blades, Drizzt Do'Urden."

"And if I refuse?"

"Then there is nothing I can do for you," Kane answered matter-of-factly, "and in accordance with my agreement with Jarlaxle, I will simply kill you here and now. Is that what you desire?"

Drizzt stared at the monk incredulously, and shook his head as Kane approached, stalking like a determined murderer indeed.

Out came the scimitars, Icingdeath and Vidrinath, in a sudden movement, one that had Drizzt rushing forward with a sudden swing at the approaching monk. He should have had the win right there. His draw and strike was perfectly executed, and too quick for almost any opponent to even realize the attack had begun.

But this was the Grandmaster of Flowers, a legendary warrior, and so Kane's left hand came up and out as Vidrinath stabbed forward, the back of the hand slapping the flat of the blade and turning the strike harmlessly wide.

Drizzt's movement with Icingdeath anticipated exactly that, the slightest delay followed by a low sweep coming across left-to-right just below the monk's waist. With the sharp edge leading and coming in so powerfully, Kane surely couldn't use his own flesh to parry.

The blade went right across, and the monk seemed to simply disappear from its path, so fluidly did Kane leap and tuck his legs up and over, touching down and immediately launching forward.

Drizzt slowed that advance with an up-angled backhand of Icingdeath, and the drow dived out the other way, not wanting to get into close combat with the unarmed man. He had the reach advantage with his scimitars, and it was not an advantage he wanted to relinquish.

But Kane was close behind, moving as fast as Drizzt—faster even!—despite the magical boost of speed offered by Drizzt's enchanted anklets.

The monk leaped and spun to the left, his left foot executing a circle kick up high, and Drizzt leaned back just enough to avoid the blow. But Kane came around, right foot touching down, and snapped off a straight kick with that same left foot.

Drizzt crossed his blades to block, but the sheer power of the kick rocked him backward and almost took the scimitars from his hands. The ranger kept his wits enough to bring one scimitar in and around though, slashing at the monk's extended calf.

With stunning dexterity, Kane turned that leg and collapsed it before the cut, bending at the knee to wrap his leg over the slashing blade. He rolled his foot and extended the leg, twisting Drizzt's arm and threatening to dislodge the scimitar.

But Drizzt let go of Vidrinath so that he could retract his arm before Kane's leg could twist and break it, and the drow went low and caught the falling blade before Kane could counter the disengage.

Drizzt ran out to the right, Kane close behind, the drow wisely double-crossing his scimitars down over his head and behind him to block another strike. He veered right, then dived left, coming up and around several strides away from the monk.

"Brilliant!" Kane congratulated. "Oh please, warrior, do not disappoint. Do not make me kill you here."

Drizzt hardly heard the words, more concerned with Kane's left leg, particularly around the back of the monk's knee. There should have been blood there. His strike had been solid, even with the clever monk's brilliantly executed parry.

But there was no blood, leading Drizzt to wonder if the grandmaster's white tunic was somehow enchanted, lined with mithral, perhaps.

On came Kane, hands and feet punching and kicking in a furious flurry.

This was the type of fighting Drizzt knew well, though, and his blades worked with swiftness and surety, picking off strikes and countering repeatedly to be similarly blocked and countered by Kane. The drow couldn't help but remember his fights with Entreri, or with Marilith, perhaps, where the movements were too fast for conscious thought, were simply a reaction and flow of form.

It went on for many heartbeats, a breathtaking and dizzying array of punches, stabs, kicks, and slashes, repeated and simultaneous even, for both fighters were fully ambidextrous. It was a blur of motion—no onlooker could have separated the combatants, could have discerned where scimitar ended or arm or leg began. There was no ring of metal on metal, of course, just a constant *thud* and *whump* and *slap*.

Around down low and out to the right went Vidrinath, then up high, outside of Kane's left hand and forcing the arm across. Drizzt used the movement to free up his right foot and kicked up high and hard into the monk's side.

Only then, in the moment of impact, did Drizzt realize that Kane's corresponding left leg also went up behind the flow of arms, only much higher, indeed straight up in the air above the monk's head.

Drizzt couldn't even fathom the speed and dexterity of the movement, and wisely didn't dwell on his own shock. He had to move quickly, falling and leaping back as the monk's leg came sweeping straight down.

If the downward kick had hit him, it would have shattered his shoulder. As it was, the monk's foot did clip him, just a bit, but enough to send him staggering back even farther.

Separated again, Drizzt barely had time to set himself before the fury of Kane was upon him once more, this time with the monk's attacks coming more sidelong, sweeping and spinning kicks and hooks, accentuated by sudden jabs of tremendous power.

Drizzt matched and blocked, but his counterattacks came fewer now. It seemed as if Kane had increased the speed and fury beyond what Drizzt could reasonably match. The drow had never witnessed anything quite like this—even Marilith with her six blades could not strike as often or as precisely as Kane.

Drizzt backed up—he had no choice—and the monk paced him, never breaking his practiced assault, a series of movements so precise and so built into Kane's physical memory that he seemed to hardly be working at all.

He would not tire.

Drizzt backed some more. He sensed that he was approaching the wall.

He couldn't fight this opponent conventionally, so he improvised, daringly, desperately. He threw himself up high and into a backward somersault, coming around right near the wall, Kane following.

But Drizzt didn't hold the tuck and touch down but rather extended his legs to plant them against the wall. With tremendous strength, the drow caught the momentum of the leap, and with startling agility, he re-angled his torso upward as he crashed into and pushed away from the wall, going higher and launching a second somersault, this one a forward roll, that projected him right over Kane's head, and for the first time in the fight, the drow knew that he had actually surprised the grandmaster. He turned as he descended and came to his feet facing Kane, who had also turned.

Out slashed Icingdeath, and out came Kane's right arm to block the blade and stop it short.

Out slashed Vidrinath, and out came Kane's left arm to block the blade and stop it short.

And there the pair held, scimitars outside the monk's bare arms, and Drizzt couldn't believe his magical and mighty blades hadn't simply cut right through.

"First blood," Drizzt managed to say, falling back in disbelief. Indeed, there was a small line of blood on Kane's left arm where Vidrinath had struck.

Kane merely smiled wryly and countered, "Hardly."

Only then did Drizzt realize that he, too, was bleeding, and more than Kane, with a gash running from his lower neck and down over his collarbone from the downward cut of Kane's earlier, seemingly impossible kick.

On came Kane.

Drizzt created a globe of darkness on the spot and met the man inside, and so they resumed, no less furiously. Fighting blind didn't much hinder Drizzt, and, he quickly realized, did not seem to hinder Kane at all.

The drow's senses attuned to the moment, hearing the rustle of clothing, the slight smudge of a foot turning on the floor, feeling the rush of wind ahead of an incoming strike. Drizzt ducked a high kick and stabbed out, hitting nothing, then reflexively leaped and tucked as Kane tried to leg-sweep his feet out from under him.

On and on they battled, sometimes connecting, oftentimes not. Drizzt took a stinging blow in his left shoulder and for a moment he felt his arm go dead. He rolled around to drop that shoulder back, and kicked out hard, connecting solidly on . . .

some part of Kane. And with that recognition of his opponent's position, Drizzt launched Vidrinath into a furious series of short stabs, all the while stubbornly trying to hold onto Icingdeath as the feeling gradually returned to his left arm.

This time it was Kane who leaped away, and Drizzt didn't want the monk to come back into the globe of darkness from some unseen direction, so he, too, charged off, diving defensively, coming up with wild swings until he cleared the edge of his drow magic.

He saw Kane, but far back and off to the side. In that moment, Kane's eyes flared and he leaped into motion, bringing his left arm in close, grabbing at his tunic—or rather, Drizzt realized, grabbing something from a hidden pocket on his tunic. And when Kane extended the arm again, he launched a series of small, spinning, star-shaped discs at the ranger.

Drizzt threw his feet out from under him, sheathing his scimitars as he fell flat to his belly on the floor, the monk's missiles spinning past above him. He landed and popped up to his knees, and with Taulmaril the Heartseeker in hand.

Drizzt hated that it had come to this. He felt as if he were about to destroy a masterpiece, but off went his arrows, silver streaks of killing power, in a line at the monk.

Kane leaned back to the left, narrowly avoiding one, then farther to dodge a second. Then he swept forward and to the right as a third arrow flew harmlessly past. He leaped, he ducked, he flipped, he lay out flat, and he flipped again, and arrow after arrow went flying past him.

Finally, Drizzt stopped the barrage. He recognized that he simply could not hit the man. He blew a sigh of disbelief, flipping his hand over to return the magical bow to his enchanted belt buckle, then drew his scimitars resignedly, shaking his head.

"No, my friend, the fight is over," said Kane.

"Then I can leave?"

"No, to leave you must defeat me."

"You just—"

"Surrendered?" Kane asked with a chuckle. "Hardly."

"Then fight!"

"You have mastered fire, the art of the physical," Kane explained. "But not so the art of thought and calm. Water is your weakness now, Drizzt Do'Urden, and I, too, can strike from afar."

"The throwing stars . . ." Drizzt started to say, but his voice trailed off before he finished the thought. Kane clutched his fists against his chest and dragged his arms straight down as if pulling something from his torso. His hands went down to his abdomen before he thrust them forward and opened his palms, as if launching something Drizzt's way.

And indeed he had, but not stars and not anything that Drizzt could see, and not anything that Drizzt could block, and not anything that Drizzt could dodge.

A wave of stunning, stinging energy struck Drizzt and blew the wind out of him and turned his forthcoming question into a gasp of pain and shock. He staggered back and didn't even realize that his scimitars had fallen from his grasp, didn't even hear them hit the floor.

He felt the power that had entered his body, disorienting and purely numbing, and he felt as if some great talon had hooked over the line of his life energy and strummed it like a lute string.

And he felt that inner energy reverberating, singing a discordant tune within him, and his legs went weak and he continued to stagger and wasn't even sure how he was still standing.

He had a fleeting notion that he should retrieve his scimitars when he found Grandmaster Kane standing right in front of him.

The monk shrugged and gave a resigned sigh, then hit Drizzt with a right cross that launched him head over heels and dropped him unconscious to the floor.

"We have to save him," Kane said loudly, to the masters he knew were watching from the balcony above. "He has dedicated his entire existence to bettering himself and the world around him, and so he is a work of art, fine art, and we cannot let it be destroyed."

# CHAPTER 17 ◈

# *A New Outlook*

ONCETTINA KNEW THAT KING YARIN WOULD EXPECT HER to be extra attentive this night. He came to her bearing a beautiful necklace, with glittering gems on a silver chain. She didn't understand why, but Yarin was obviously quite proud of this gift, and of the very similar new necklace that he wore as well. He insisted that she keep it on during their lovemaking.

So she tried to feign delight, and tried to be attentive, though really, the necklaces did little to change the doldrums that inhabited their bed.

At least at first.

"Truly, you are not very good at this," she heard herself saying, and she couldn't believe it—and neither could Yarin, who was above her and who had been, in his mind at least, working furiously.

"What did you say?" he asked after a long hesitation, his face more full of incredulity than anything Concettina had ever before witnessed.

"Perhaps if you were more skilled, we would have a better chance at conceiving a child." Again, Concettina couldn't believe what she was saying, or where that courage—or stupidity—had come from.

Yarin pulled up from her a bit, stared at her, and trembled. Then he gathered up his fist and punched her right in the face.

Concettina wanted to yell out, but she heard herself . . . laughing.

"Better," she said.

King Yarin punched her again, and tried for a third, but this time, Concettina caught his hand in mid swing, and stopped it as surely as would a castle wall.

"Good, you can learn," she said, and with frightened strength, she lifted Yarin up from her and flipped him over onto his back, and was atop him before he could shout his protest.

King Yarin stumbled out of her chambers a short while later, half-dressed and thoroughly out of sorts. One of the guards in the hall said something to him, but he dismissed the man with a wave of his hand—and that wave sent him stumbling right into the opposite wall.

In the room behind him, Queen Concettina laughed, and that followed King Yarin down the hallway until one of the sentries shut the door.

On the bed, Concettina felt . . . empowered. She couldn't believe what she had done, or how she had done it. She had never been so adventurous or so forceful, not ever in her life. She wasn't sure where it had come from, her brave words and her physical power—to take the punches and to so easily stop them and turn the tables!—and her sexual abandonment . . .

Desperation, she thought. Perhaps she was past the point of good sense and decorum. She knew that she was going to die if she could not conceive.

Or if King Yarin lived.

Despite her shock and the wrongness of her thoughts and actions, the woman couldn't suppress a grin as she considered the disheveled old man limping out of her bedroom, or the fact that King Yarin wouldn't survive many encounters like the one they had just shared.

She removed the necklace to place it with the rest of her considerable jewelry collection, but hesitated, as if her hand simply would not let her put it down.

"You can't sleep in it, you fool," she whispered, scolding herself, and she tried to put it down again.

"Put it on," she heard, or thought she heard, in a soft whisper.

Concettina looked around, her gaze finally settling on the painting, and she wondered if Acelya was back at her spying post.

But no, she thought, Acelya's voice was nasally and stuck in a perpetual whine, but this whisper she had heard had come from a low and melodic voice, a beautiful voice.

"It is your only course, Concettina," the voice said. "Put it on."

Growing alarmed, Concettina moved to the door and put her ear to it, then even cracked it open just a tiny bit.

One sentry was out there now, half asleep and in a chair, leaning on his halberd.

She moved back into the room. "Who are you?" she whispered.

"Put it on," the voice replied more insistently. "You need the strength."

Concettina started to obey, but then, horrified, she moved to throw the necklace to the floor.

But she found that she didn't want to let go of it.

She had heard of magical items that conveyed strength, and considered again her actions that night, how easily she had lifted Yarin and tossed him over onto his back. She could not be the helpless victim here or she would surely die. She had to rely on herself, on her wits, and likely, on her strength.

She noted her reflection in her dressing mirror then, and moved closer to it, standing in front of the reflection. She dropped her nightgown, which she hadn't yet put on, and considered her image in the glass. She found herself strangely held by that image, and thought it quite beautiful, though she had never been an overly vain woman.

"He will finish you," the voice whispered.

"Who?" she demanded and she glanced around. "Who is this? Who is speaking?"

She found her breath coming in gasps. She thought that she should run out of the room, and of course, that she should throw aside this necklace.

But she was caught by the image in the mirror once more, and dark smoke rose as if within the glass, swirling up around her reflection, obscuring her fully.

The smoke continued to rise, and she saw her feet again, and her legs were slowly revealed, and all the way up her torso, to her breasts, her shoulder and neck . . .

"Put it on!" the voice insisted, and Concettina hardly heard it, her eyes widening with shock, for in the mirror was her reflection, the glass clear once more.

Except that her head was missing, blood pouring from her severed neck, and so convincing was that image that the gasping, breathless woman reached up to pat at her neck and chin, needing the reassurance that her head was still attached.

Hardly thinking of the movement, Concettina clasped the necklace around her neck and rushed to gather her bedclothes, then dived back into her bed and pulled the blankets up over her head, listening all the time for the whisper.

She finally convinced herself that there had been no whispering voice, nor any real deception in the mirror, and that it was all her own heart telling her that this necklace was a good thing for her, that it would remind her to take command of King Yarin's carnal advances.

She would become with child, or *he* would die trying.

◆　◆　◆

"I AM SPIDER Parrafin of Morada Topolino, good King Yarin," the smartly dressed halfling introduced himself to the King and Queen of Damara on a fine summer morning.

The mention of Morada Topolino piqued the interest of Ivan Bouldershoulder, who stood guard at the side of the great hall, half asleep. He knew of Morada Topolino—enough, at least, to know that it was a house of intrigue located in Queen Concettina's homeland of Aglarond, in the town of Delthuntle, he believed.

"I have come to deliver this great friend of Morada Topolino to your court, good king," the halfling went on.

There was something strangely familiar about this halfling, Ivan thought, but he dismissed the notion almost as soon as it entered his head. He had known many halflings in his life, and to him, they all somewhat sounded, and looked, alike.

"I give you Wulfgar of Icewind Dale," the halfling said.

That name, too, struck a chord in Ivan Bouldershoulder, reminiscent of a name he had heard so long ago, in another life it seemed.

Those memories brought a smile to the dwarf's face, but he thought no more about them and went back to his practiced, standing snooze.

◆ ◆ ◆

"AND TO WHAT end might I desire meeting this . . . man?" King Yarin asked.

Regis almost missed the question, caught by the eye of Queen Concettina. He managed to offer her a slight nod, almost daring to wink, to let her know that there was more to this tryst than an introduction to the king.

Her returned smile caught the halfling off guard with its intensity, and he stuttered a few times before managing to reply to the king, "Goods! Wines and drink of all sorts! Aye. Wulfgar of Icewind Dale is a merchant come from across Faerûn bearing some draughts and a promise of proper supply."

"And you have brought these samples?"

"Of course, King Yarin."

The king motioned for a nearby attendant, who rushed up to stand in front of Regis. "Give them over," King Yarin instructed. "Once they are properly tested, I will sample them, and if I am pleased, perhaps I will invite you back to stand before me. You are empowered to make a bargain, yes?"

"I am . . ." Wulfgar started to say.

"Not you," King Yarin cut him short. "What are you, Uthgardt?"

Wulfgar nodded, for that description seemed close enough, and he wasn't here to quibble, or even to trade. "The Tribe of the Elk of Icewind Dale," came his simple response.

"Well, good," said King Yarin. "But I know you not, nor any of your people. Perhaps if your wares are fine enough, I will allow you to speak in my presence. Perhaps not. It is this little one who has come to make a deal, and from a source I know well and have reason to trust. Were it not for your diminutive friend here, do you believe that I would have even allowed you into my court? You are not a subject of mine, nor friend to any kingdom I know."

Wulfgar started to respond, but Regis wisely punched him in the shin to silence him.

"Forgive his manners, I beg, King Yarin," Regis said. "In his land, Wulfgar is a great man and known all about the Sword Coast. He has stood before the Lords of Waterdeep as an equal."

King Yarin seemed less than impressed, but Regis did notice Queen Concettina's eyebrows rise at that, and her eyes sparkled more than a little.

Good enough, the halfling thought, in case they had to go to their backup plan.

"Perhaps someday he will have earned your trust enough," Regis said. He bowed, and slapped Wulfgar's leg to elicit a similar supplication from the big man. Regis kept bowing as he backed away, and Wulfgar, though looking thoroughly perplexed and even disgusted, did likewise.

"Oh, do stay," Queen Concettina said unexpectedly, catching Regis, and very clearly the king, off guard.

"We will garner a room at a proper inn in the city," Regis replied, not sure if that was his place or not, since he had already offered his farewell bows.

"Yes, do," King Yarin said, obviously a bit perturbed. But it only got worse, for at the very same moment, Queen Concettina added, "Oh no, that would be silly. We have guest houses all about the palace for luminaries such as yourselves."

King Yarin stared at her hard, his expression a mixture of anger and astonishment.

"I would be remiss in too many ways to disparage an emissary from Lady Donnola, who was my friend in Delthuntle," Concettina replied into that stern glare. "They will stay here, and I will hear no argument."

King Yarin's eyes widened, as did those of every soldier and attendant in the hall, Regis noted, and he held his breath. Clearly, Yarin wasn't a man used to being talked to in such a manner. For a moment, Regis almost expected that he and Wulfgar would find themselves in a fight right there in the audience chamber.

But Queen Concettina didn't back away from Yarin's dagger-throwing stare. Indeed, she put her hand on the king's forearm and gave a squeeze, and from the look on the man's face, it was something much more than a gentle press.

She also gave him a look, one that had Regis gulping—and again, he wasn't the only one—for it was so suggestive that it took the halfling's breath away.

"Yes, yes, go and find a room in a guest house," King Yarin said absently, not looking at the pair and waving them away, then waving for another attendant to come to the visitors and show them off.

Regis noted that the king and queen had left their seats before he and Wulfgar were even out of the hall, and that despite a line of peasants and merchants and tradesmen and the like waiting for their turn in front of the royal couple.

Regis spent the next little while trying to sort out his doubts and confusion as he and Wulfgar were escorted to a small cottage, one of several set near the vast gardens behind the palace.

"You are welcomed to join us for tea and biscuits at the garden tent as soon as you settle your belongings," said the attendant who escorted them to their accommodations.

Wulfgar beamed at the thought—they hadn't eaten that day, rushing to be first in line to gain an audience—and he was surprised indeed when Regis rather rudely declined.

"My stomach is growling at you," the barbarian warned when the attendant left them. "Take care that I do not eat you instead!"

"You saw her power," Regis replied, shaking his head.

Wulfgar looked perplexed.

"Queen Concettina . . ." the halfling explained. "She was in control in that audience hall, not King Yarin."

"So it is with many couples," Wulfgar replied. "Have I told you about the time when my wife in Icewind Dale insisted that I needed to go and get her a yeti fur rug? The scars didn't survive Iruladoon, but . . ."

"No, it was more than that!" Regis interrupted, shaking his head and moving to the cottage door, which was still open. "She handled him with ease and aplomb."

"Aplomb?" Wulfgar echoed with a laugh.

"Surety," the halfling explained. "Poise."

"I know what it means, but to hear you say it . . ." Wulfgar gave another laugh. "The cultured Spider Paraffin of Morada Topolino. Take care, my friend, for you have mud on your fine boots!"

Regis, still a step or two from the door, reflexively glanced down before shooting Wulfgar a glower.

"You saw it, didn't you?" Regis asked. "Queen Concettina was in command in that room—she even coaxed him out with many still waiting to be heard, and so obviously for carnal reasons."

"It's a weapon," Wulfgar admitted with a shrug and a sigh.

But Regis was shaking his head. "The letter written to Donnola did not reveal such confidence—quite the opposite!" He moved to the door. "I cannot reconcile . . ."

Regis paused then, hearing a bit of a commotion in the garden outside, and a "Hee hee hee," that struck him curiously and familiarly. He wasn't sure what that might be about, but instead of shutting the door, he stepped outside and glanced around.

Just a dozen strides away, a dwarf crouched in front of the hedgerow, chatting with a blooming flower—a green-bearded dwarf with one arm, and with his beard braided back over his ears to mix with his shaggy hair.

"By Moradin's own whiskers . . ." the halfling whispered.

• • •

CONCETTINA'S SLEEP WAS filled with fitful dreams. She tossed and turned and watched the guillotine descend. She thought of running away, took hope that Morada Topolino had come for her, and considered the other plan for a secret sire—was that why Donnola had sent the handsome Wulfgar?

So she found hopes, but they were all fleeting.

She thought of her newfound strength, magical likely, and of how she had toyed with King Yarin the previous night and again that morning. She was the stronger!

But he was in command everywhere but their bed, and her newfound power over him would wane. If she killed him she would be horribly executed—hung until nearly dead, then quartered in a public square.

Fleeting.

The guillotine blade dropped upon her.

She was running, then, but as if in mud and going nowhere that would bring her to safety. And terrible winged creatures flew all around her, swooped down at her and made her duck and cry out, and they kept badgering her, not just with threatening claws but with questions.

Demanding answers. Scaring her, diving at her, clawing at her.

Demanding answers.

And the mud was deep around her and she tried to run, but couldn't run, and plowed along, and the demonic things laughed at her.

She awakened with a scream, lathered in sweat, her eyes red, her bedclothes all tangled around her. Reflexively, she felt for the necklace, and found that it was still there.

Concettina pulled herself to the edge of the bed, and too wrapped and tangled to stand up, she just let herself fall out of it. She struggled to her feet and stumbled across the floor, settling in front of her large mirror.

Sniffling, wiping away tears, Concettina was shocked by the redness of her eyes. She reached up to rub them, but noticed then that she appeared larger somehow, more solid.

Before she could begin to sort that out, she noticed the horns sprouting from her head, and as she shied away in shock, a barb-tipped tail whipped around her.

"What? What?" she stuttered, thinking herself still asleep. Yes, that had to be it.

Still, she nearly fainted when great leathery wings spread out from her back.

And then she knew, from a voice inside of her that no, this was no illusion. The name "Malcanthet" rolled off her tongue, a name that meant nothing to her.

But it wasn't an illusion in the glass, or some conjured image, but her own reflection.

Her thoughts spun crazily. She had to get to Yarin and the priests. Yes, the priests! She turned for the door and even took a step.

Just one.

"No, you cannot leave, silly Concettina," she heard herself saying.

She looked back into the mirror, and the image of her in bat-winged, demonic form was smiling widely.

"You were quite chatty this night," the reflection said to her, or was it just the reflection showing that she was saying those words even though she didn't try to say those words?

She didn't know, and couldn't sort it out, and only then thought of her last two lovemaking sessions with Yarin and the things she had heard herself saying.

"The big one is handsome, I agree."

Her dreams, she realized.

"Already I know all I need to know about you, and about those around you," the reflection told her. "Do you know what that means?"

Concettina tried to scream, knew that she needed to rouse the guards immediately. But her mouth wouldn't cooperate. She couldn't begin to coordinate her movements to make a sound beyond a muted gurgle.

The image in the mirror became that of Concettina again, just Concettina, without the horns, without the tail, without even the bright red demonic eyes. The woman relaxed briefly and told herself that she was still in the midst of her nightmare.

She brought her hand up to the necklace and touched the large gemstone at its center. It was cool to the touch, like the others, but she could feel it warming, as if some energy was building inside it.

Only then did she realize that some other being, someone inside of her, had suggested the movement, and too late did Concettina try to pull her hand away.

The gemstone grabbed her spirit and drew it in, tearing it from her corporeal form. She didn't even realize it at first, and found herself confused as to why the image of the mirror in front of her had become so blurry . . .

She heard herself laughing.

She saw the reflection of Concettina admiring the gemstone . . . the phylactery!

This creature, Malcanthet, had stolen her body.

Desperately, in horror and utter revulsion, Concettina tried to break free, tried to get back into her own body.

"Oh, you intend to fight me?" her reflection, Malcanthet, taunted. "Relentlessly, I am sure, were you to remain here. But of course, I have too much to do and so I cannot allow that."

Concettina recoiled as a giant hand closed down over her, and it took her a moment to realize that it wasn't a giant hand at all but only her own hand, clasping the gemstone, controlled by this demon named Malcanthet.

She heard an incantation in her own voice, and felt a great wind come up around her, pushing her, driving her away. She fought, she clawed, but there was nothing to grasp, and she was flying far, far away along a swirling tunnel of dark mists and ending, so it seemed, right back in the gemstone prison.

But no, she realized soon after, for she was not in her room any longer, and there was no mirror to be seen.

Just a pair of ugly, misshapen dwarves, moving their jaundiced eyes close to the semi-translucent wall of her prison, peering in with their rotten, even toothless smiles.

"Two tons!" one of them exclaimed.

"I'd be givin' ten times that an' more for the fun!" the other replied. "But hey-ho, we should be far away!"

# CHAPTER 18 ◈

# *Broken Bone, Broken Mind*

VONNEL STARED AT THE MATRON MOTHER FOR A LONG while. To the side, Sos'Umptu was trying to get her attention—to distract her, so she pointedly ignored the Mistress of Arach-Tinilith.

Yvonnel wanted Quenthel to know with certainty that she understood the veiled threat, and that she was more than ready to answer it. Yvonnel had just announced her departure from Menzoberranzan to the matron mother, and Quenthel's response, that it would be wise for Yvonnel to offer ample warning before returning to the city, was simply not acceptable.

"The handmaiden was quick to my call," Quenthel replied, to Gromph's daughter's cold stare.

"Because the Spider Queen is concerned with my every decision," Yvonnel said without the slightest hesitation, and in a tone that made "concerned" sound very much a positive thing.

"Yes, concerned," Quenthel said, clearly trying to remain strong. But Yiccardaria had departed, after all, and even with Sos'Umptu and several other House Baenre priestesses in attendance, it was obvious that the matron mother wasn't excited about the prospect of a confrontation against the mighty Yvonnel. "The Spider Queen was concerned enough to send Yiccardaria to scold you."

"To seek clarification," Yvonnel corrected. To the side, Sos'Umptu moved as if to speak, but Yvonnel threw her hand up forcefully to warn away the words before they began.

"Let us understand each other, Matron Mother," Yvonnel went on. "It is to Lady Lolth's dismay that I have not assumed the throne of House Baenre, and thus, the primary seat at the Spider Table of the Ruling Council. I could please her greatly by fixing that situation immediately."

There was nothing veiled about that threat, obviously, and more than a few priestesses in the room gasped, and Quenthel looked as if she wanted to do so as well.

"But that is not to my liking," Yvonnel explained, "and Yiccardaria has accepted my preferred course. For now. I will return to Menzoberranzan when I so choose, and if I so choose, and if you are still, at that time, matron mother, then you and I will find agreement. For the good of House Baenre, for the good of Menzoberranzan, and for the blessing of the Spider Queen. You would be foolhardy, I assure you, to bet on that outcome prematurely."

She turned, gave a derisive snort to Sos'Umptu, a dismissive glance to Minolin Fey, and turned to leave, but paused just long enough to add, teasingly, "Perhaps you will be fortunate, Matron Mother Quenthel Baenre, my aunt, and I will choose to forever stay away."

And with those surprising parting words, Yvonnel Baenre walked out of the room.

She took a fine lizard mount from the stables of House Baenre and was soon out of the city, riding the tunnels of the Underdark, making swiftly for the lower halls of Gauntlgrym.

◆ ◆ ◆

"ALWAYS EAST," DAHLIA said.

Artemis Entreri, standing at the flap of their tent on the field around the growing Hosttower of the Arcane, glanced over at her with a curious expression.

"You are always staring to the east," Dahlia clarified.

Entreri shrugged as if he had no idea what she was hinting at.

"And thinking of him," said Dahlia, and then he understood.

"It concerns me," the assassin admitted. "I would not see it end this way for him."

Dahlia shrugged. "I wish better for Drizzt, too, but there is nothing we can do. Catti-brie is a powerful priestess, and she could not cure his malady. Gromph tried, and is there a more powerful wizard to be found? And Kimmuriel, too, and I know first-hand of the beauty of his methods in such things as a broken mind. I sit here healed and clear in my thoughts because of Kimmuriel's strange magic. And yet Drizzt's troubles were beyond him."

"And that is my frustration," Entreri said. He looked back out, and indeed, back to the east. "That I can do nothing."

He didn't even notice Dahlia's movements and was a bit startled when she draped her arm around him and put her chin on his shoulder.

"He is your friend," she said.

"He is one to whom I am indebted," Entreri corrected.

"It's more than that."

Entreri didn't answer, and he knew that spoke volumes. He wasn't sure if "friend" was the correct word for his complicated relationship with the drow ranger, but there was surely a camaraderie there, a kinship of blood.

And his claim, even if not wholly complete, was true enough: he was indebted to Drizzt Do'Urden both because of Drizzt's willingness to travel to Menzoberranzan on such a dangerous mission to rescue Dahlia and also because of Drizzt's raid on the drow in Gauntlgrym to rescue his former companions, including Entreri.

Even more than that, over the course of the events of the last two decades Drizzt, both with intent and simply by example, had shown to Artemis Entreri a different way of seeing the world. Drizzt had dragged Entreri halfway up the Sword Coast, teasing him with tangible rewards—his jeweled dagger—and also with rewards harder for Artemis Entreri to understand, or even appreciate, for a long, long while.

But yes, it had felt good to help the folk of Port Llast, Entreri had been forced to admit, and it was a revelation that he now embraced.

Artemis Entreri could look in the mirror again without loathing—nay, not "again," but for the first time in his memory.

"Yes, Drizzt," he whispered to the too-empty air, "saving Port Llast from the sea devils brought me some peace."

Dahlia hugged him closer.

◆ ◆ ◆

"Do'no what ye're thinking, drow lass, but ye stop yer hairless horsie now or we're to splat ye both in the middle o' the hall!" a dwarven voice boomed down the tunnel.

Yvonnel pulled up short and crossed her arms defiantly, all the while sorting a sequence of spells that would obliterate this lower corridor guard, if need be.

"Well, I have complied," she called out impatiently after a few moments. "I have come to see your King Bruenor, and you would do well not to make me wait."

"What business ye got with—?"

"That is none of *your* business, dwarf," Yvonnel interrupted to the unseen sentry. "Your king will see me, for I have heard that he is not a fool. Tell him that the daughter of Archmage Gromph has come."

Another few moments passed before a group of dwarf warriors, fully armored and with weapons brandished—and with a pair of battleragers in their spiked armor among them—came out from a cleverly designed side passage.

"Daughter o' Archmage Gromph, ye say? But how're we to know?"

"Ask Drizzt, or Jarlaxle if Drizzt is not about."

Her stated familiarity with that pair did give the dwarves pause, she noted, and she was quite content when they were moving soon after along the tunnels. They came to a stable area, set up with stalls for rothé and some surface creatures—sheep and cows and the like—and Yvonnel was bade to leave her mount.

"Well, what am I to be doing with this?" the dwarf farmer demanded when the lead sentry handed him the reigns of a drow lizard mount.

"Well, don't eat it and don't let it eat yerself," the sentry replied. "Anything else is yer own call."

A heavy guard, including a trio of dwarf clerics who cast spells all the way, escorted Yvonnel through the complex. Yvonnel laughed at the priests. They were trying to detect magic upon her, and likely with spells of magical silence ready at their lips in case she should try to cast anything of her own.

She almost cast her own silence dweomer first, just to show them she could. But the young drow woman's impulsiveness was tempered, as always, by the long memories within her, the memories of Yvonnel the Eternal, the greatest matron mother any drow city had ever known.

Those memories told her to be careful around this particular clan of dwarves, and reminded her that a little bit of respect would go a long way in achieving her ends.

So she suffered the constant barrage of divine spells and the smell of a dozen dwarves, and soon, but not soon enough, she was brought into a sizable room in the lower levels of the complex, somewhere near to the legendary Forge Room, she believed, for she could hear the hammers ringing.

A trio of dwarves, two male and one female, stood at the end of a carpeted walkway, a large throne behind them and two smaller thrones flanking that.

"Might that ye tell us yer name?" asked the apparent eldest of the group.

"Might," Yvonnel replied.

The dwarf clucked and chuckled. "Ah, me manners," he said. "Ragged Dain o' Gauntlgrym, at yer service, and I give ye Athrogate and Amber Gristle O'Maul o' the Adbar O'Mauls," he added, indicating the pair flanking him.

"We've heared ye're wantin' to see King Bruenor," the male, Athrogate, asked.

"Aye, and that ye're callin' yerself the daughter o' Gromph," Amber added.

"I am Yvonnel Baenre," she told them. "My business is not with you or your king, but as I am passing through his domain, I thought it polite that I grant him an audience."

The proud dwarves bristled and snorted.

"And accept his own graciousness in return," she added coyly.

"Ah, but this one's a bit filled with her own face, ain't she?" Amber remarked, but the dwarf on the right, Athrogate, hushed her quickly.

"I been with Jarlaxle a hunnerd years," Athrogate said. "Been to Menzoberranzan, too, on occasion. Why am I not knowin' ye?"

"I'm not as old as I look," Yvonnel replied, but didn't elaborate.

"But ye're Gromph's girl?"

"I am much more than the daughter of Archmage Gromph," she said. "And I am bored with this discussion. Fetch your king and announce me, or take me through this rather dowdy place and point me along the road to find my father, or Jarlaxle if that course would prove easier."

Amber snorted again, Ragged Dain's eyes opened wider, but Athrogate on the end again calmed the situation.

"No need for announcin', for I heared ye well enough," said another, a red-bearded dwarf coming in from a passage hidden by a curtain in the back of the room.

Yvonnel's eyes narrowed at the sight. She recognized this particular dwarf from the memories of her grandmother.

King Bruenor moved to sit in the grand chair, a pair of young dwarf women moving to sit in the smaller thrones flanking him. Yvonnel hardly looked at them, her unblinking gaze never leaving the king.

"Well met, King Bruenor," she said, moving past the trio to stand in front of him. "I have heard much about you."

"And meself nothing about yerself," Bruenor replied.

"That will change," Yvonnel promised.

"Ye come on business from Menzoberranzan, have ye?"

Yvonnel shook her head. "Nay, and likely never. I am here of my own accord and for my own reasons. I have come to find my father, or Jarlaxle, and this is the place I know, and so I ask of you only that you show me where to find them."

"They ain't here."

"Drizzt then," she said.

Bruenor snapped his fingers in the air. "That easy, eh?" he asked. He leaned to the side and threw a leg over one chair arm. "Ye come here, unknown to all, and ye're thinkin' I'm to walk ye up to me friend? Might be a prize ye're lookin' to claim, I'm thinkin'"

"Understand something, good dwarf," Yvonnel said, "were it not for me, your friend Drizzt would not have returned to you from Menzoberranzan. I am the one who allowed him to rescue Dahlia. I am the one who empowered him to serve as the spear to destroy Demogorgon. I am the one who interceded when he was taken to the dungeons of House Baenre, and there he, Jarlaxle, Dahlia, and the human named Artemis Entreri would have horribly perished were it not for that action. The only reason your friend has returned to your side stands before you, King Bruenor, and if you do not believe me, then perhaps you would do well to go and speak with Jarlaxle before you insult me. You do not want to insult me, King Bruenor."

"Ye're the one who let them go?"

"I am."

"All four?"

"All four."

"So now we're to be friends, are we?" Bruenor asked.

"Hardly," the drow woman replied, her expression purposely souring. "I can live my life fully and with complete satisfaction without ever naming one of your kind as friend."

"I might've once thought the same about yer kind," Bruenor replied as the five others bristled—and indeed, it seemed as if Queens Fist and Fury were about to leap up and attack the drow.

Yvonnel conceded the point with a smirk and a slight bow.

"Well, then," said Bruenor, "might that we'll be friends soon enough."

But Yvonnel shook her head and her expression hardened once more. "It is not a future I envision, Dwarf King, for I still remember when your axe split my skull wide open. I claim no friendship with King Bruenor Battlehammer."

That strange reference had all the dwarves looking around curiously, Athrogate shrugging when Ragged Dain and Amber looked to him for an answer, and Bruenor seeming equally at a loss to the questioning looks of the queens flanking him.

But Bruenor was beginning to sort it out, Yvonnel could tell. He had heard about her, at least tangentially, and her name was surely familiar enough to him, even if it had been held by another when they met that long ago day in Mithral Hall.

"Yer Da's not here, nor is Jarlaxle," Bruenor explained rather coldly. "They be in Luskan, a city to the north, and I'm not knowin' when they're meanin' to come back."

"You will show me the way?"

Bruenor considered it for a while and a host of concerns and arguments flashed across his expression. Yvonnel was wise enough, of course, to anticipate his understandable reservations.

"Aye, we'll get ye there if ye're who ye're sayin' ye are," he answered.

"You will send word?" she reasoned.

"Aye. Won't be takin' long. We got runners and callers set up all the way to Luskan. We'll get yerself a room where ye can rest, and none'll be botherin' ye if ye're not botherin' no one else."

Yvonnel bowed again, satisfied, and Ragged Dain called in the dozen who had escorted her to this room and led them all off, Yvonnel in tow.

"Split her head?" she heard one of the dwarf queens whisper to Bruenor.

"Might that ye'll be doin' it again," the dwarf named Athrogate added.

Yvonnel took note of it all, thinking that someday she might have to kill more than one of these dwarves.

Her entourage led her to a private, and no doubt very secure, chamber. There she was told to wait, and the hall outside of the room's only door was lined with dwarf warriors and clerics.

So Yvonnel settled in.

She didn't have to wait long, however, for before she had even slipped away into her first Reverie, the room's door opened and a familiar figure walked in.

"Well met again, father," she greeted.

Archmage Gromph did not appear amused.

◆ ◆ ◆

SHE WAS SURPRISED to see him, not overly happy about it, and she didn't hide it. Catti-brie had never been comfortable around Artemis Entreri, despite Drizzt's more recent assurances. They had met long ago, after all, when the assassin had kidnapped her.

"I am sorry this happened to Drizzt," Entreri told her.

"I haven't said that I blame you," the woman replied, but not in a comforting tone.

"You don't have to. I know why Drizzt was in the Underdark, and part of that reason was me."

"You didn't know about the Abyssal mind plague sweeping the tunnels," Catti-brie replied, but again, there was no softness in her tone. "In his life, Drizzt has traveled on scores of adventures that could have been the end of him, in many ways. If you wish to wallow in guilt, then do so about the innocents—"

"Enough!" Entreri snapped, but he caught himself and closed his eyes and held up a hand as if wanting to retract everything. "I did not come here to fight with you, quite the opposite."

"You have no business here, either way."

"But I do," the assassin insisted. "Because I have business with Drizzt. I owe him my life . . ."

"Many times," Catti-brie interrupted. "And yet that never stopped you from your mischief before."

Entreri accepted the barb with a resigned chuckle. "I owe him more than my life," he added. "You cannot begin to know the world through my eyes, and I don't expect you to try. I only came to tell you that if there were anything at all that I could do, even give my own life, to bring him back to you whole, I would."

Catti-brie's eyes narrowed and she seemed about to lash out, but she held back and instead just nodded.

"I hope that he returns to us—to you," Entreri finished. "And I hope that you both find that which you desire."

He gave a slight nod and departed, leaving Catti-brie flummoxed.

She tried to dismiss this surprising visit. She had too much to worry about with Drizzt to let the surprising words of Artemis Entreri concern her, and had too much responsibility with the reconstruction of the Hosttower of the Arcane to be sidetracked by the surprising humility of the assassin. If she failed in her task of making anew the magic of the Hosttower, then Gauntlgrym and more would be lost and many hundreds, even thousands, might perish.

What did she care for the conscience of a killer?

But she did.

◆　◆　◆

"UNBELIEVABLE," JARLAXLE MUTTERED when Yvonnel walked into his room in Illusk, where he was meeting with Gromph and Kimmuriel on some matters unrelated to the Hosttower.

"Ah, Jarlaxle, you seem as if you missed me dearly," Yvonnel replied.

"She simply walked in?" a surprised Kimmuriel asked. Bregan D'aerthe's defenses in the ancient Undercity were undeniably formidable and redundant. The psionicist was clearly at a loss, for he was quite sure that Yvonnel held no love for him and might well destroy him then and there.

"Should I expect the lackeys of House Baenre to turn me away?" Yvonnel replied. "That is the role of Bregan D'aerthe, is it not? And the reason why House Baenre affords you such freedom and protection."

"I am not surprised," Jarlaxle said, speaking to Kimmuriel more than to the visitor. "Or perhaps I should say that I am surprised that the rumors from House Baenre are proven true. In any case, our guards were alerted to the possibility that we would have a visitor from House Baenre."

"Then they were alerted wrongly," said Yvonnel. "For I have forsaken House Baenre."

That had the three drow looking at each other curiously, and with great concern. It pleased Yvonnel to learn how much her mere presence had unnerved these three formidable characters.

"I was not told of this," Gromph said—rather imperiously, Yvonnel thought.

"Why would you be?" came her smart answer. "Do you still fancy yourself to be the Archmage of Menzoberranzan? Why, Tsabrak Xorlarrin has settled in nicely—more so now that his Matron Mother Zeerith is reestablished on the Ruling Council as Matron Mother of House Do'Urden, though it will soon be renamed appropriately to her family. Why would Matron Mother Baenre inform you of anything more than you need to know, when the mere reminder of you brings her concern about the lessened stability of her rule?"

"Then she is a fool," Gromph replied.

"We already knew that," Yvonnel said.

"So, I was told that you had left, and you have left," Jarlaxle interrupted. "And now you have come here. Is there any reason in particular?"

"Do I make you uncomfortable, my uncle?"

"Truthfully?" Jarlaxle replied. "Yes."

"That brought a laugh from the woman. "Good. It will keep you from becoming too complacent, then—to your benefit as well as my own."

"You haven't answered my question," Jarlaxle said.

"I am here because I am curious."

"About?"

"All of this," Yvonnel admitted, glancing back at the growing Hosttower. "I have watched you from House Baenre, of course, and am amazed at the beauty of this creation."

"If Menzoberranzan has any designs on the Hosttower, or on Luskan, they should be made aware that it would mean full-scale war."

"Is that a threat?"

"Simply a truth," Jarlaxle replied. "King Bruenor—"

"You call him a king!" Yvonnel said mockingly.

"*Bruenor*," Jarlaxle began again, "will not interfere with Luskan in my hands, nor with the Hosttower under the purview of Gromph. It is a deal to which we have all agreed. But if Menzoberranzan were to come in force to take the city, then you would find all of the Delzoun dwarves allied against you, and likely with the Lords of Waterdeep standing beside them."

"Why do you include me in your threat?" Yvonnel asked innocently. "Have I not already told you that I have forsaken House Baenre and, thus, Menzoberranzan? Perhaps for all time? I am more interested in what you are doing here, and in your merry band of rogues. My dear uncle, am I not welcome?"

Jarlaxle glanced at the other two, and there was no missing the concern on each of their faces.

"The hierarchy established here would not please you," Gromph asserted.

"And no, I will not surrender my place, nor will Kimmuriel," Jarlaxle said.

"I would ask no such thing," Yvonnel replied. "I am a guest in your home, and eager to learn."

"You have more knowledge in your memories than all three of us combined," Gromph said, and he seemed more than a little upset.

Yvonnel shrugged. "About many things. But there is much I also wish to learn." She paused and adopted a coy look, focusing it on Jarlaxle. "And perhaps much I can teach."

He stared back at her, unblinking.

"You survived your journey through the Underdark unscathed?" she asked Jarlaxle.

He nodded. "I seem to be in fine mind and health, yes."

"Unlike Drizzt, who was . . . afflicted."

Jarlaxle's face grew tight.

"I should like to see him," Yvonnel said.

"He is not here."

The woman winced. "I should like to see him," she said again.

"You cannot."

She started to reply, but Jarlaxle seemed to gain his strength then, and shook his head against her forthcoming words. "Drizzt is in a place unreachable by any."

"In his own mind," she said.

"And in body, now, too. As it must be."

Yvonnel took a long moment to compose herself, and she was surprised to discover how much this revelation was bothering her.

"You cured him?" she asked.

"We cannot," Kimmuriel answered, and then added, "you cannot."

"Tell me!" Yvonnel insisted. "Tell me everything! I must know what you have learned of his affliction, and of how you know that you cannot cure him—and I cannot, either, as you insist."

"My spells did not work against the Abyssal Plague," Gromph said, jumping up from his chair. "That is my only contribution to this subject." He moved to the door. "I have far more important things to consider than the fate of a fool rogue, who should have long ago been destroyed."

"He doesn't understand," Yvonnel said, shaking her head, when the archmage had gone.

"What do you know?" Jarlaxle asked.

"You first," the woman said, taking Gromph's seat. "Tell me. Tell me everything you know about Drizzt's malady, and everything you have tried to help him. Both of you, I beg."

Kimmuriel and Jarlaxle exchanged confused glances again.

"Why?" Jarlaxle asked.

"You first," the woman insisted, and the look on her face reflected the urgency inside.

The mercenary leaders looked to each other again, and Jarlaxle shrugged.

"Please," Yvonnel said, "tell me."

And so they did. They explained to Yvonnel all the efforts of the priests, the wizards, and of Kimmuriel with his psionics, to bring peace to the beleaguered drow, ending with Kimmuriel's insistence that any cure for Drizzt had to come from within Drizzt.

"And now he is gone," she said when they had finished. "Why?"

Again, the pair looked to each other.

"I am not going to hunt him down and kill him!" Yvonnel shouted at Jarlaxle. "If I had wanted Drizzt dead, I could have done so, easily, and you above all others know that."

"True enough," Jarlaxle admitted. He sighed and looked over at Kimmuriel, who seemed less than thrilled with being in the same room with the namesake of the woman who had destroyed his House. After a few telling winces, Kimmuriel nodded his agreement, and so Jarlaxle told Yvonnel of their latest plan, of their fleeting hope that Drizzt might find some level of inner peace through the efforts of a great Grandmaster of Flowers and an order of trained and disciplined aesthetics.

She took it all in, considering every angle, searching the memories of Matron Mother Yvonnel the Eternal for some hints.

At long last, she smiled and stared at Jarlaxle.

"You are wrong about Drizzt," Yvonnel stated flatly.

A long while of uncomfortable silence passed.

"Are you not even curious of how you are wrong?" she asked.

"You had him in your dungeon," Jarlaxle reminded her. "If we are wrong about him, then why did you let him go?"

"Not in that way!" Yvonnel replied. "You are wrong . . ." She looked at Kimmuriel and corrected herself, "Or more to the point, you, Kimmuriel Oblodra, are wrong, about how Drizzt's malady might be repaired."

Again, and obviously despite his best intentions, Jarlaxle was leaning forward, tipping his hand about how much he really cared.

"You have insisted that Drizzt's cure must come from within, from him," Yvonnel explained.

"There is no magic, nor suggestion —" Kimmuriel started to answer.

"The magic of the Abyssal Plague is real and persistent," Yvonnel said. "Drizzt is ill, and he cannot simply will himself to not be ill, no matter how profound and enlightened these monks believe themselves to be."

"Grandmaster Kane has transcended his mortal coil all together," Jarlaxle told her.

"I do not know this man."

"He is the Grandmaster of Flowers of the Order of the Yellow Rose in Damara," Jarlaxle explained. "He is human, yet I battled him a century ago, long before the advent of the Spellplague. A century, perhaps two, and still he lives, and can, to this day, defeat almost any opponent in martial combat. His body is merely a conduit through which his spirit interacts with the material world, or so it is said. And having witnessed the great magic of his will, I cannot disagree with that assessment."

"He found a place of perfect thought?" Yvonnel asked.

"Perfect focus," Kimmuriel corrected. "He is no illithid."

"Still," the woman countered. "And this Kane, he did so because his mind was clear and his thoughts rational. To find the perfect focus, he needed to find the perfect harmony within. His achievement of that perfect harmony led him to this transcendence—but can you hope the same for Drizzt? Truly? When he is so lost?"

"Kane will help Drizzt find his way to that place," Jarlaxle insisted, an edge of desperation in his voice.

"How?" Yvonnel laughed at him and at the nodding Kimmuriel. "How?"

"Drizzt's malady is his inability to see the truth, and so he imagines falsity everywhere," Kimmuriel explained.

"You already said that."

"Then how am I to use my mind intrusions to unwind such a misconception of reality when there is no trust to be found? How, when my very healing attempts seem to Drizzt the most deceitful and vicious plays of all?"

Yvonnel folded her hands and assumed a pensive pose. "If I find the answer, will you help me to execute it?" she asked.

"He will," said Jarlaxle before Kimmuriel could even agree.

That wasn't enough for Yvonnel, though and she looked to Kimmuriel, who, after a quick sneer at Jarlaxle, nodded his agreement.

"I would speak with my uncle alone now," she said, and Kimmuriel was more than happy to leave, not even bothering to say goodbye before striding out of the room.

"This is an unexpected day," Jarlaxle said when Kimmuriel was gone.

"I put a curse on him," Yvonnel admitted.

"On Kimmuriel?"

"On Drizzt," Yvonnel replied, and Jarlaxle fell back in his seat, gripping the arms of his chair as though he meant to leap up and attack her.

She didn't blink.

"Not the Abyssal Plague," she clarified. "That is as you presume."

"Then what? When?"

"When he left House Baenre, my curse followed him. When he returned to and first looked upon Catti-brie, he saw her as a demon," Yvonnel explained. "It was not all my doing, of course. As you know, Drizzt has lost all sense of trust. So I teased his delusion to bring him to the point to which he was already inevitably heading. He was supposed to kill her, and in doing so, he would utterly destroy himself. A fitting finish for one who has so defied the Spider Queen, and a remedy approved by Lady Lolth herself."

Jarlaxle brought his hands up in front of him, and he was fighting hard not to twitch, Yvonnel recognized. He had just told her where to find Drizzt, after all.

"He didn't do it," Yvonnel said.

"Catti-brie fended—"

"No, he didn't do it," she said again. "The woman was caught by surprise and should have, could have, been summarily executed. But he didn't do it. There is no reasonable explanation for why he didn't do it, for how he avoided the trap I set for him, but there it is. He didn't do it."

"You sound impressed."

She nodded. "And intrigued."

"And so you have come to finish—"

"No!" she stated with such surety that it startled even her.

Jarlaxle stared at her intently.

"No," she said again, quietly. "I have come without malice and with no desire for retribution."

"Because he resisted that which he should not have resisted," Jarlaxle said, and then he was nodding, catching on.

"Then there is hope," Jarlaxle reasoned. "Then within there remains a piece of Drizzt, a piece of who he was, an anchor to hold him from the pressing tides."

"No, he will not find his own way out of his malady."

"You just said—"

"That he did not strike down Catti-brie is quite amazing," she admitted. "And yes, it reveals an inner strength and heart that gives me pause. But that does not mean that the persistent whispers of the delusion will be held at bay."

"He thinks the whole world, his entire reality, is a grand deception designed solely to tear his heart asunder," Jarlaxle asserted.

"The persistent whispers of delusion," Yvonnel repeated.

"And so it follows that if he realizes that his delusion is absurd . . ." Jarlaxle started to argue.

"That clarity cannot hold."

"Grandmaster Kane will show him the deepest understanding of his body and mind."

"And the whispers will continue, evermore."

"He will recognize their lies!"

"No."

"You speak foolishness."

"Your mind is clear and so you expect the same of Drizzt," Yvonnel told him. "Such a typical misunderstanding. He is broken. Something within him is damaged. You can no more expect Drizzt to clearly unwind his twisting thoughts than you could expect a man with shattered legs to run. Just because you cannot see the injury does not mean that it isn't there. Nor is it one that can be cured by force of will, any more than simple determination could mend shattered bones."

Jarlaxle shook his head, trying vainly to deny it all.

"It is an insidious malady," Yvonnel went on with confidence. "A constant barrage of doubt and fear, playing cleverly against all his hopes and dreams." She gave a little almost helpless laugh. "It is not unlike the teachings of Lolth, and how the matron mothers hold the entire city of drow under their spell. Only these particular matron mothers of deception are within Drizzt's head, and they will not relent, and he cannot win, for unlike his earliest days in Menzoberranzan, this time, Drizzt Do'Urden has no place to run."

Jarlaxle clearly wanted to argue but at long last his shoulders slumped. "To think that this is the fate of Drizzt Do'Urden . . ." he said with great lament.

"You admire him," Yvonnel reasoned.

Jarlaxle didn't argue the point.

"And now you are disappointed in his weakness," Yvonnel added.

"No," the mercenary insisted.

"Yes!" Yvonnel shot right back. "You do not like that truth, but your anger at it does not make of it a falsehood. Drizzt is the child who disappointed you, the hero who, this time, did not meet your measure."

Jarlaxle tried to respond, but in the end, he could only lift his hands in surrender.

"Because you cannot understand what is in Drizzt's thoughts," Yvonnel explained. "How could you, when your reason will not flee you? This is the frustration, and yes, the anger, whether you deny it or not. If he just tries harder to hold his smile and keep his thoughts aright, then all should be well, because with you, who are not afflicted, that would be the obvious outcome."

"What would you have me say?" a defeated Jarlaxle asked. "What would you have me do?"

"Drizzt will need our help—mine and Kimmuriel's at the least," Yvonnel explained as the door opened and Artemis Entreri appeared. He gasped at the sight of Yvonnel Baenre.

Yvonnel continued, undeterred, "Perhaps his work with the monks will bring Drizzt to a point of trust enough for him to accept that help, and in that moment—and it will be a fleeting moment, I fear—we must be prepared and we must be quick. That is his—that is our—only hope."

She looked at Entreri then, matching his glare with one of equal intensity. She had long before come to the conclusion that she had lost the best chance to cure Drizzt of his Abyssal malady in that moment—that moment of naked truth—when he had confronted the demon he thought to be Catti-brie. In that moment, watching him through her scrying stoup, Yvonnel had seen the drow thoroughly, utterly, desperately defeated and with nothing left to lose.

That moment was an opportunity, she had thought then, and believed still. She looked at Entreri and tried to recall all the history between this man and Drizzt Do'Urden. Her knowledge was quite extensive, for Artemis Entreri had been in Menzoberranzan those many decades before, when Drizzt had first returned to the city and Yvonnel the Eternal had been the matron mother.

Yvonnel let her stare linger on the human assassin, and she nodded, for perhaps she had an idea.

# PART 3

# The Unlikeliest Hero

THERE ARE MOMENTS EVERY DAY—MORE NOW, I ADMIT—WHERE I feel that I am a fool for my fears, nay my certitude, that this is all a conspiracy of nightmare. Moments of seeming clarity when the preposterousness of all that has happened—the return of Catti-brie and all my friends, the long life of Artemis Entreri—pales beside the preposterousness of my nightmare, for the lengths to which Lolth has gone to destroy me seem beyond all reason.

But then I remember that I have so insulted the Spider Queen that there would be no journey too great for her to properly pay me back.

And I remember, too, the machinations to which Errtu subjected Wulfgar in an effort to cruelly devastate him.

This journey, though, seems grander and on a scale many times larger, for now I am halfway across Faerûn, in my mind at least, to a place I have only heard of in tales.

There is much to admire in the Monastery of the Yellow Rose. The brothers and sisters here are among the most dedicated practitioners I have ever seen. Their adherence to their code and rituals rivals the fanaticism of the Gutbusters or the dedication of the weapons masters of Menzoberranzan. It is a delight to behold, with so many practicing in harmony and building upon each other's gains with such honest contentment—even though the gains of another, Afafrenfere, for example, might well threaten the station of oneself.

Mistress Savahn celebrates Afafrenfere's march up the hierarchical ladder of the Order of the Yellow Rose. She had told me, with joy in her eyes and lightness in her voice, that she has never witnessed such an extraordinary advance of body and spirit as that which Afafrenfere has displayed. Yet he will soon challenge her for her station, and should she lose that fight, she will step down a rung on the order's hierarchical ladder.

I asked her about this, and her answer rang true to my heart: if he could beat her, then he deserved the accolades and the station, and she would have to work harder to retrieve her current place. Afafrenfere's ascent, therefore, would ultimately make her better.

She has found the truth of competition, that there is no better challenge to be found than one a person can make with herself, that the personal competition outweighs any other, and by great magnitude. Simply, the rise of a rival challenges each of us to do better and be better, and that is to be celebrated, not feared or prevented.

This is the opposite of the philosophy prevalent in Menzoberranzan. Indeed, the drow determination to hold back others, even through murder, that the powerful can hold their gains, lies at the heart of that which drove me from the city, for it is a philosophy wholly immoral and limiting.

Here, in the Monastery of the Yellow Rose, it seems that I have found the exact opposite of that empty paranoia. I feel as I felt when I encountered Montolio and learned of Mielikki, except that this time, I see in community practice that which I hold in my heart.

And it is a beautiful thing.

Too beautiful.

As is Kane, the Grandmaster of Flowers, a man who through the deepest meditation and dedication has become something more than a being of the Material Plane. He is at once weightless and translucent, existing in a place of spirit more than anyone I have ever known, and at the same time, weighted and full of solidity. I have come to believe that he could have defeated me at any point in our sparring match, and that he only took his time so that he could gain my full measure by revealing to me that there was a long road of physical perfection yet before me should I choose to walk it.

I have oft noted that perfection of body is not possible, and that the pursuit of it, the journey, is the point more than the goal. In Kane, I have found the closest example of that elusive, unattainable perfection, more so than I believed possible.

And so I am honored to be in his presence, to be tutored by him.

I feel the ground more solidly beneath my feet now, and that is the clue. If this were real, if Kane's advance was true as presented, then indeed I could envision myself following this path.

And so it is clear to me that my enemies have found a way to get me to lower my guard, that they have found a way to tease me with illusions that go to the fondest desires of the heart of Drizzt Do'Urden.

And thus, in those moments when the ground seems most solid beneath my feet, when the preposterousness of my fears seem so much greater than the preposterousness of the reality that led me to those fears, then I must remind myself of that weakening guard and of the price that I will pay when at last I have become fully deceived into believing that this is all real.

Yes, this monastery is the ring of truth that I have ever longed to wear.

Yes, this Grandmaster of Flowers Kane is the epitome of my personal goals.

Yes, I would embrace this, all of it.

If I believed it.

But I do not.

—Drizzt Do'Urden

# CHAPTER 19 ◈

# *When He Met His Match*

MALCANTHET SAT IN THE QUEEN'S ROOM AND CONSIDERED her situation carefully. She had garnered quite a bit of information from her shared time in this body with Concettina, enough to give her a cursory understanding in the ways of the Court of Helgabal and her own predicament—though she was hardly fearful—regarding the frustrated King Yarin.

She wanted more, though, and needed a spy.

The succubus queen casually tossed a log into the hearth. She raised her arm and turned it over and a ball of flame appeared, hovering above her uplifted palm. Malcanthet gave a soft blow and the flame flew down to the log, instantly igniting it.

Malcanthet nodded, determined to thoroughly consider her every move. She knew the dangers. Many of the demon lords had taken advantage of the weakened Faerzress to escape the bonds of the Abyss. Faerûn's Underdark was thick with demons of all types, even the greatest of their kind.

"Including Graz'zt," she whispered with trepidation, her voice smothered by the hiss of the burning wood, which was not yet seasoned.

Graz'zt was not fond of her, and her greatest ally, Demogorgon, had been destroyed in the entryway of Menzoberranzan before she could get to his side. Perhaps Malcanthet should have returned to the Abyss upon learning of that loss, but the promise of fun in her freedom here on the Material Plane had proven too great a lure.

And so she had hidden in the gem and allowed Lolth's own minions to bring her out of the Underdark and to Faerûn's surface. Here she could play, indeed, but she had to keep the noise of her presence limited, else the others would know.

Graz'zt would know.

Malcanthet had no intention of meeting that one here on the Material Plane!

She was about to call to Inchedeeko, had almost begun uttering the words, when Malcanthet realized that she was not alone. She didn't turn her head, but she could envision the intruder anyway, tipped off by the echoes of the memories of Concettina.

Malcanthet stepped away from the hearth and turned, noting the painting of King Yarin that hung on the rear wall of the room. The left eye of that painting was different now . . it was a living eye.

Malcanthet only saw the painting for an instant, not wanting to stare and tip off the spy, but that was all she needed. She knew who was behind that wall, crouched in the secret passage.

She began to disrobe, slowly and seductively. And as she did, she sent her thoughts out to the hidden corridor, the whisper of her spell calling to Princess Acelya. Like a thin stream of smoke Malcanthet's seductive whisper snaked into the woman, filling her with thoughts of the succubus, teasing her with promises, magically calling her to Malcanthet's side.

A few moments later, Acelya walked through the queen's door, where Malcanthet waited.

Charmed, the weakling human woman was no match for Malcanthet's suggestions. When a disheveled Acelya stumbled back out of the room, Malcanthet was confident she had an obedient spy who would tell her everything she needed to know.

Now her work here could begin in earnest. She padded across the room on bare feet and tossed more logs into the hearth, watching the flames grow, letting her thoughts sink into them and fly to her home in the Abyss. Through the flames, she assembled her servants and issued her instructions.

Only one would come through that night, a tiny humanoid-shaped creature with spiky horns and bat wings, its green skin covered with dripping pustules. Malcanthet smiled. She thought Inchedeeko so ugly as to be cute, but she smiled because the little quasit had brought her the requested items.

She slipped her magical whip under the soft mattress of her bed, and considered her favorite toy of all, a large mirror framed in copper, long turned green, and shaped into the grotesque and leering face of a demon, its exaggerated mouth opened wide, the mouth itself serving as the reflective surface. It had been given to her by an arch-lich, on the promise that she would occasionally return it, full of trapped souls, to the lich's tomb, where it could feed on the prisoners—and of course he would then give her another, empty mirror so that she could continue her games.

She hung the mirror next to the painting of King Yarin, then covered it with one of Concettina's many cloaks and added a ward of lightning to sting any who might try to remove that cloak.

It would not be wise to leave such a malignant device open to prying eyes.

If too many were sucked into its extradimensional prison cells, who knew what the mirror might vomit back out?

◆ ◆ ◆

"WE'LL HAVE TO be long gone an' not lookin' back," Ivan said. "They're goin' to know 'twas yerselfs, both o' ye, and yer House, or morada, or whate'er ye're calling the durned thing . . ."

"Hee hee hee," said Pikel, slowing Ivan only a bit.

"Topo . . . err, Topolungo, or whate'er!" Ivan finished, and Pikel hee hee hee'd again.

"We intend to be long gone with Concettina before King Yarin even knows she's not in her room," Regis answered. "Long is the reach of Donnola Topolino, I assure you."

"And I ain't for trustin' Yarin's spies," Ivan answered, "so me an' me brother'll be with ye."

"Me brudder!" Pikel chimed in.

That not-subtle warning didn't bother Regis. He was thrilled at the prospect of having the Bouldershoulder brothers beside him once more, though he was also thinking that the sooner he got them on a boat to the west and on the road to meet up with Bruenor and the others, the better for everyone. Morada Topolino survived by maintaining a low profile, after all, and should he allow the Bouldershoulder brothers to remain with the Topolino gang, it wouldn't be long before jests and whispers about Pikel became common throughout Aglarond.

"They'll be expecting us along the south road," Regis said. "Perhaps we should head north instead."

Ivan shook his head. "Not much north. Farms and spies. Could go west to the mountains and run their foothills south into Impiltur, but that's a long and hard road, don't ye doubt."

"So what do you counsel?" asked Wulfgar.

"Eh, just go south and go fast," Ivan decided. "We can get some miles behind us, and me brother's a good one for hidin' folks."

"Me brudder!" Pikel shouted with alarming volume, drawing a chorus of "shh!" from the other three.

"Ooo," said the green-bearded dwarf.

"Ye get yerself on out into the garden," Ivan told his brother. "We're all to be needin' a fine meal afore we start our run, eh?" He turned to the others and added, for Pikel's benefit, clearly, "None's makin' a finer meal than me brother."

"Me . . ." Pikel said loudly as he headed for the door, but he paused when he saw the other three snap their heads around to regard him. "Brudder," he said quietly, and he added his own, "Ssh!"

◆　◆　◆

NONE OF THE conspirators understood that their volume didn't really matter, since a little demon spy was hearing every word anyway, and so it was no coincidence when Queen

Concettina showed up to visit with Pikel out in the garden just a short while later.

"You know them?" she said to the dwarf's beaming smile, which disappeared almost immediately.

"The halfling and barbarian from Aglarond," Malcanthet explained. "They are friends of yours."

"Umm . . ."

"Come to help you rescue me and steal me away to safety," the succubus added. She put on a most disarming and grateful smile, one that nearly made Pikel swoon, so powerful was the magical charm behind it.

"Ooo," he admitted.

The queen bent low and whispered so that only Pikel could hear. "We cannot run. King Yarin is wary and he is no fool. He knows that the halfling has come for me."

"Ooo." The word was the same, but the tone evoked a very different meaning, this time one of concern.

"Yes, ooo," the queen replied. "I cannot run away to Aglarond, dear dwarf. If I do, it will mean war, and I will not start a war."

"Uh uh," Pikel agreed.

"But I really don't want a headless statue to be my legacy, either," the queen said with a wail. "Oh, Pikel, you must help me!"

"Oo oi!"

"Will you help me?"

Pikel nodded so forcefully that he nearly threw himself over backward in the process.

"The guards at my door are lazy," she said. "They sleep all the time. Send me the big man this night."

Pikel's eyes widened and he gave a nervous "Hee hee hee."

"Yes, I know it is naughty, but I have no choice," Concettina replied. "I will not run and start a war, and likely get you all killed in the attempt. But I must do something. So bring him to me, and I will give the king what he most wants, and perhaps we can all know peace. Will you do that, Pikel? Will you tell your brother?"

"Me brudder!"

Had he been thinking more clearly, it might have occurred to Pikel that Queen Concettina didn't know that he and Ivan were brothers, or that there was no way she should have suspected their little plot so clearly and so quickly. But there was something about the woman's smile that didn't let any of that seep into the green-bearded dwarf's mind, and so he bounded back to his little cottage and the others to tell them that plans had changed.

◆ ◆ ◆

"Be quick an' be quiet," Ivan called down the small spiral staircase. It had taken three days, but finally the dwarf had been assigned as a nighttime sentry for Queen Concettina's room, and so the moment was upon them.

"He's being stubborn," Regis called up as quietly as he could manage.

Ivan rambled down the stairs to find the halfling standing exasperated, hands on hips, with a sour looking Wulfgar leaning up against the wall of the stairwell.

"I cannot agree to this," Wulfgar said. "This is not why I came to Damara."

"Lady Donnola . . ."

"Did not tell me this part of the plan," Wulfgar insisted.

"We came to save the queen, and so now we're saving the queen," Regis replied, but Wulfgar's expression did not soften—quite the opposite.

"You are asking me to father a child and then abandon it," the barbarian said.

"You have spent the last two years in the beds of any woman who would have you!" Regis argued, and Ivan gasped at the volume.

"Shh!" the dwarf scolded. "We're in the king's own home, ye dolt!"

The frustrated halfling nodded.

"That was play, but this is real," Wulfgar said. He believed that he had not been irresponsible, nor had he ever lied to the women he had known in this second life. And yes, to him it had been play, and with proper precautions, particularly after he had met Penelope Harpell, who had shown him more than a few tricks and common concoctions to prevent conception.

"Play that might have . . ." the halfling pressed.

"Enough!" Wulfgar said. "Do not tell me how to live my life, my friend. I have taken great care, and with no illusions. But in this, you ask me to purposely sire a child, and one I'll not ever know."

Regis and Ivan exchanged puzzled glances at the barbarian's steadfast stance, and finally Regis remembered a not-unimportant detail.

"Colson," he said. "You are reminded of Colson." He turned to Ivan. "Wulfgar once had a child, not his own, but one caught in similar circumstance . . ."

"Enough," Wulfgar said again, and indeed, he was thinking very much of Colson, the dear young girl he had returned to her mother when he had left the friends in Mithral Hall in his previous life, so many decades before. He had never seen Colson again after that, and had no idea of what had happened to her. Certainly, her future had looked secure enough when Wulfgar had returned her to Meralda in the mountain town of Auckney, but still, the mystery from that point forward had chased the barbarian back to the tundra and had filled many of his nights with anxiety—and Colson wasn't even his own daughter!

"You know nothing of it," Wulfgar went on. "What you are asking of me is . . ."

"The only way, boy," Ivan interrupted, stepping forward and seeming quite sympathetic. "I'm wishin' it could be otherwise, but ye heared what the queen telled me brother. We can'no steal the queen away without provokin' a war, and sure but that's not what ye're wantin'! Bah, but in that case, when the fields are bloodied, how many won't be knowing their kids no more?"

"This way is not fair to the queen," Wulfgar tried to argue, desperate to find another direction.

"Was her own idea," said Ivan. "And who can be blamin' her? She's to get herself with child or she's to be without her head. There's nothing we can do about that, boy. Well, nothing else besides this. Ye can'no fight King Yarin and ye can'no run, for he'd catch ye, catch us all. And if he didn't, he'd send his army against Aglarond, and that'd be a formidable fight, don't ye doubt. So go on now up the stairs. She's waitin' for ye. Ye'll save the lady's life, and she's a good lady and worth savin'!"

Wulfgar glanced down at Regis, and the halfling nodded.

"And yer boy'll be King o' Damara," Ivan went on. "Or yer girl, Queen o' Damara, and with a Ma who's loving and kind. And ye'll help us all stop a war. And the king's an old man. Nothing stopping yerself from coming back once he's gone to face his crimes."

Wulfgar rubbed his face, trying very hard to justify this entire situation. He didn't want a war and he certainly didn't want the poor woman executed. He thought of her, then, of the pretty young woman he had seen at court. He couldn't imagine her with the wretched and ugly old King Yarin of her own accord, and it was that notion, that her marriage had surely been arranged and for reasons other than love, that finally made him nod in agreement and start up the stairs.

A long while later, Ivan opened the concealed side door of the palace and peeked out into the darkened garden area. Seeing no one around, he motioned for Regis and Wulfgar to slip away into the night, back to the visitor's cottage.

A disheveled Wulfgar staggered out of the palace, hardly able to walk, and shaking his head in confusion with every step, which gave the dwarf and the halfling more than a few chuckles.

"A good thing you didn't take the offer of Jarlaxle's dragon friend," Regis giggled when they were safely away. "I do believe she would have killed you."

Regis grinned up at him, but he didn't see it.

# Chapter 20 ◈

# *The Undisciplined*

H

E DIDN'T HAVE HIS SCIMITARS. HE DIDN'T HAVE HIS BOW.
His magical anklets and armor, too, were back in his private
chamber, far from the training room.

His opponent, on the other hand, carried all of his
normal weapons in the form of his hands and feet, and
had hardened his skin as armor.

Only speed and skill and the balance of a drow warrior kept
Drizzt upright as Master Afafrenfere pressed the attack, sliding
in close and tearing off a series of punches, chops, elbows,
knees, and high kicks.

Drizzt blocked a barrage of punches, drove a forearm smash
up high, and slammed his knee into Afafrenfere's hip. But the
monk spun away too quickly to suffer any damage from the blow,
and used that spin to come around with a leg sweep.

Drizzt tucked his legs up under him, the monk's attack
sliding beneath. Drizzt kept his legs tucked, falling low to the
ground as Afafrenfere set his sweeping leg. He transferred the
momentum across his body to send his other leg snapping up
high—too high for the falling Drizzt, who hit the ground but
quickly popped back up.

Now Drizzt pressed the attack with a dozen shortened but
powerful jabs and a snap kick, none of which got through
Afafrenfere's perfectly angled blocks and twists.

Still, the ability to turn back the advantage and regain the
initiative in unarmed combat against a Master of the South

Wind had the spectators in the balcony above the training room nodding in approval.

The opponents each kicked out, their legs connecting shin to shin between them. Drizzt got the worst of that exchange, and felt unsteady in the knee as he brought his foot back to the ground beneath him. He tried to mask it by coming forward fiercely, but he winced with the first step. That took him a bit off to the side, his attempted left hook coming in too wide.

Afafrenfere ducked that punch and sprang under it, past Drizzt's undefended flank, to land with his back foot even with the drow, his right foot behind.

The monk stabbed his left arm under Drizzt's retracting left, lifting it tight against the drow's armpit and snaking his forearm and hand around, up, and over the drow's shoulder to grab the back of Drizzt's hair.

Drizzt tied to roll and duck away, but the monk was having none of it, stepping more fully behind him with easy balance.

Drizzt elbowed hard to force Afafrenfere out from behind him, to try to again gain some leverage on the left, but the monk had anticipated the desperate attack and so not only accepted the reduced hit by twisting only his torso but managed to snake his right arm outside-in under the crook of Drizzt's elbow.

Straight up went the monk, and Drizzt was locked, his left arm caught up and out by the monk's left, upper arm pinning the drow under the armpit, hand tight on the back of Drizzt's hair, and with his right arm now painfully lifted at the elbow by Afafrenfere's right.

Drizzt had to twist and roll to get out of the lock, but when he tried to maneuver, he again found weakness in his stung right knee, and the slight hesitation allowed Afafrenfere to get around enough to stamp his right foot in front of Drizzt's. The monk lifted and shoved and tripped Drizzt right over that foot. With his arms pinned, the drow had no defense, no way to lessen the weight of the fall. He and Afafrenfere pitched over, Drizzt landing face down, the monk crashing atop him.

The stunned drow, his breath blasted out, had no defense as the monk began crawling up over him, each movement lifting Drizzt's arms more painfully, making him even more helpless.

As his senses came back to him, Drizzt was well aware of the fact that Afafrenfere could easily pop his shoulders out of joint.

The monk knew it, too, and so he let go and leaped away, standing calmly as Drizzt finally pulled himself back to his feet. He faced Afafrenfere, who brought his hands together at his chest and bowed.

He is a demon imposter, humiliating you! the voices in Drizzt's thoughts screamed at him. He took himself through a dark maze of unreason, coming to the conclusion, somehow, that Afafrenfere had beaten him in this manner not to humiliate him but to give the appearance that all was well—for how could such a fight have ended otherwise against a foe so greatly trained in unarmed combat?

Every instinct in Drizzt told him to leap upon the defenseless, bending man and execute a choke hold that would take the life out of him.

He even started to do so, just a hint, before catching himself, before a sliver of sanity grabbed at him.

And so he stumbled away and did not strike out at the man who had defeated him.

But neither did he return the bow, a very basic tenet of the sparring, a fact that was not missed by Afafrenfere or the onlookers.

◆ ◆ ◆

YVONNEL RAISED MORE than one eyebrow in the room when she said to Jarlaxle, Kimmuriel, and Gromph, "He needs our help, and so let us help him."

"Why?" Gromph asked, the question that was on all of their minds.

But before the conversation could go down that deeper road, Jarlaxle intervened. "I am trying to do exactly that."

"And you will fail," said Yvonnel. She looked to Kimmuriel for support, and to Jarlaxle's surprise the psionicist nodded his agreement with her.

"Why?" Gromph asked again.

"Because the healing Jarlaxle attempts with the monks is incomplete," Yvonnel replied.

"Not that," said the archmage. "Why would you care about the well being of a rogue heretic from a fallen House, who has brought nothing but misery to Menzoberranzan?"

"Perhaps I see value in him," Jarlaxle answered. "And perhaps he is my friend."

"Not you," Gromph clarified. "I understand your motivations, even if I think you a fool. But why you?" he asked, nodding his chin at Yvonnel. "What games do you play here?"

"He is the Champion of Menzoberranzan, or did you not witness that glorious victory?"

"He was a spear thrown at a demon, nothing more," the archmage countered.

"Does it matter why?" Jarlaxle interjected. "Your daughter—"

"Do not call her that," Gromph interrupted, and Jarlaxle noted the stare between him and Yvonnel. They were in agreement on this point. It seemed quite clear that their familial relationship was physical only, at least in the sense of father and daughter. That made sense to Jarlaxle, given this strange woman's mental makeup. Was she really more Gromph's daughter, or his—and Jarlaxle's—mother? And of course that didn't even matter, because more importantly, was Yvonnel anything besides the virtual avatar of Lolth, the voice of the Spider Queen as had been her namesake? Yvonnel the Eternal had torn down House Oblodra by channeling the unbridled power of Lolth. Could anything less be said of this Yvonnel's display against Demogorgon?

"What does it matter?" Jarlaxle asked again. "She had come here with important advice—even Kimmuriel agrees with her insights. Do I not owe it to Drizzt to try?"

"I know not what your twisted mind views as your debt to that worthless rogue," said Gromph, "but perhaps you would do well to care more about the motivations of this woman before you. Perhaps she desires Drizzt to be sane when she tortures him to death, or ruins everything that is important to him. Would that not be the way of Lolth?"

That gave Jarlaxle pause. He rested back in his chair and stared hard at Yvonnel, scrutinizing every aspect of the too-beautiful young woman. He approached her advice and offer from every conceivable angle, trying to see Gromph's point, but he couldn't quite get to that place of dark vision no matter how hard-pressed. He had been in the dungeon of House Baenre with Drizzt, Entreri, and Dahlia. There was no reason for Yvonnel to have gone to all of this trouble. She had him then, fully helpless and vulnerable. And if she really was speaking as the voice of Lolth, then she surely could have cured him in the dungeons of House Baenre before murdering him, had that been her desire.

So Jarlaxle let his thoughts stream out wider than merely his focus on Drizzt. Was Yvonnel, perhaps, working a greater plan to punish Jarlaxle, too? And Kimmuriel and Gromph, perhaps? Was her arrival here and were her subsequent suggestions simply a plan to destroy the larger conspiracy against Menzoberranzan, the one that included many males and even Matron Mother Zeerith Xorlarrin?

It made sense on some level, but again Jarlaxle was shaking his head. If Lolth, through Yvonnel, wanted to tamp down this budding movement of drow males and their desire to find some equality within her city, then some devious plot to heal Drizzt only to torment him would be a terrible maneuver indeed.

No, the most likely motivation was exactly what Jarlaxle saw hinted at in Yvonnel's eyes when she first arrived. She was intrigued by Drizzt. She had seen the same possibilities of a wider and grander philosophy, one based on a love of others as much as, or more than, a love of oneself. Drizzt's dedication to a greater cause than his own gain did hint at something from which most drow were starved.

"So let us help him," Jarlaxle agreed.

Yvonnel nodded and smiled. "We need to go to him—I do, at least."

"I will go with you," said Jarlaxle.

Yvonnel considered it for a moment, then shook her head. "I know every step of my plan, and you are not a part of it at this time. No need to complicate anything."

Jarlaxle started to protest, but Yvonnel had already turned to Kimmuriel. "I do not wish you to accompany me . . ."

"I would not," he said, to which she just nodded and kept on speaking.

"But I will briefly need you soon enough, and I might need you again when the moment of truth is revealed. You can travel without constraint of distance and time, so it seems, in thought at least."

Kimmuriel nodded, and without hesitating Jarlaxle slid over his head the silver chain upon which hung a small whistle. He tossed it to Yvonnel. "It is attuned to Kimmuriel," he explained. "He will hear it across the very planes of existence. And it will guide him truly and will allow him to quickly come to your side."

"You can get me to this Monastery of the Yellow Rose?" Yvonnel asked Gromph.

"No."

"I ask you for nothing more than a simple teleportation spell," the young woman shot back. "For me and one other. Surely . . ."

"I do not know this place," said Gromph. "I have never been there, nor viewed it, and so such a spell carries a risk."

"A small one."

"There is no risk so miniscule that I will accept it for the sake of Drizzt Do'Urden," Gromph said. "None."

"I can get you there," Jarlaxle interjected, and looked to Kimmuriel. But Kimmuriel, too, shook his head, and when he thought about it, Jarlaxle understood, for Kimmuriel could not simply warp time and space randomly and without restriction. He could travel to places he knew well, or could follow the call of the whistle with his thoughts across any distance, even through planar barriers. But, like Gromph, he had never been to the monastery.

"How do you feel about riding a dragon?" Jarlaxle asked Yvonnel. "It will take a few days—longer than a teleport spell, surely—but . . ."

"I look forward to the experience," she said. "Secure my passage, and get me an audience with Grandmaster Kane."

◆ ◆ ◆

"HE IS QUICKER than any I have fought," Master Afafrenfere said to Savahn and Perrywinkle Shin. "Even without his magical anklets."

"His display was most impressive," Savahn agreed, and with a grin, she added, "For a moment, I feared that it would not be Brother Afafrenfere who would soon challenge me for the title of Master of the East Wind."

"Drizzt could attain that rank," Afafrenfere replied.

"No, he could not," Perrywinkle Shin said, even as Savahn was nodding in agreement. The other two looked to the Master of Summer, the highest ranking monk of the Order of the Yellow Rose, other than Grandmaster Kane, with surprise.

Master Shin said nothing in response to those looks, just stared at them as if they should be able to figure out his reasoning.

And both nodded, remembering the end of the fight between Afafrenfere and Drizzt, when the drow didn't bow in respect, and indeed, seemed very much as if he wanted to slug the monk in the face.

Physically, the measure of Drizzt Do'Urden seemed unlimited. He certainly could, with years of training, aspire to the level of Afafrenfere or Savahn, and likely to Perrywinkle Shin's rank, as well—perhaps he could become one of the very few to transcend, as had Kane.

But attaining those higher levels of the Order of the Yellow Rose were less a matter of physical prowess and more about the mental and emotional discipline needed to allow a disciple to so perfectly follow the grueling regimens of understanding and of manipulating his or her body.

In this most important area, Drizzt' Do'Urden was sorely lacking.

No one who had known Drizzt before his journey to the Underdark would have ever anticipated such a thing.

◆ ◆ ◆

"How long?" Dahlia asked.

Entreri could tell that she was trying hard to keep the anxiety out of her voice, and the reality that his idea had so adversely affected her pained him greatly. He hadn't even thought about the pain he would cause Dahlia when he agreed to go with Yvonnel—Artemis Entreri simply was not used to thinking of anyone other than himself, not as a matter of course, at least.

And why wouldn't Dahlia be in agony over his decision? She was no coward, of course, and she well understood the value of friends and the responsibilities comrades must share with each other—hadn't Entreri, Jarlaxle, and Drizzt just rescued her, after all? But the woman was finally, after all these years of misery, finding a bit of peace and security. She had resolved her differences with her son, and now Effron was creating his chambers in the growing Hosttower of the Arcane.

And she and Entreri had found each other, both bringing something to the other that eased the pain and gave new insight and perspective.

And now he was leaving, with perhaps the most dangerous drow on the surface of Faerûn, as part of a group that included Gromph Baenre.

"You are not the same since you returned from your visit with that strange Kimmuriel creature," Dahlia stated.

Entreri couldn't deny the truth of that. After the meeting Yvonnel, Jarlaxle, and Kimmuriel had come to Entreri with

Yvonnel's plan—a plan that included Entreri. He would accompany Yvonnel to the Monastery of the Yellow Rose. And to precipitate that journey, Entreri had allowed Kimmuriel into his mind, a most unsettling thing indeed.

"We took a journey together," Entreri tried to explain.

Dahlia was clearly startled by that news. "Where?"

"Not where, but when," Entreri clarified. "Across the centuries, to memories long faded, and ones that now surprise me."

Dahlia didn't understand, but didn't press the point.

"You feel like you owe this to Drizzt," she said when Entreri's pause went on too long for her patience. "I understand."

Entreri shook his head. Her words were rational and logical, and followed, given the purpose of Drizzt's trek to the Underdark where his affliction started. But still, those words sounded wrong to the assassin. This was no debt pulling him to go to Drizzt for the sake of some desperate plan to save the ranger. No, it was something more than a debt, or if a debt, then one, strangely, that Artemis Entreri owed to himself. He thought of a windswept ledge outside of Mithral Hall, of a sewer in Calimport, of a tower chamber designed specifically for him and Drizzt to do battle.

"In that case, I should go," Dahlia said, and still Entreri shook his head.

"Yvonnel asked me, and would not even hear of Jarlaxle accompanying us."

"Why? And why would you trust her?"

"I don't."

"Obviously you do!"

Entreri blew a sigh—it was hard to refute that he was indeed putting great trust in the unusual young dark elf.

"I expect that she has no reason to lure me away, since she recently had me, had all of us, in her possession," he explained.

"What reason would she have to help Drizzt?"

"I cannot begin to know."

Now Dahlia snorted and put her hands on her hips. "I do not wish to be difficult," she said, "but none of this makes any sense to me."

"Yvonnel is convinced that Drizzt needs a great trauma or a moment of high crisis in order for him to allow her spells to heal him," Entreri explained. "And so, is there anyone in all the world better at bringing Drizzt Do'Urden to a place of great crisis than Artemis Entreri?"

His moment of levity seemed to have no effect on the woman.

"It is more a matter of making him face the truth of his despair, making him actually face the depths that he fears inevitable," Entreri went on more seriously, "before he will surrender his stubbornness enough to let Yvonnel, or anyone, help him."

"I am not sure I believe that," Dahlia said.

"Neither am I," Entreri admitted, and he didn't add his realization that if Yvonnel was wrong, he would likely be killed. He instinctively brought his hand to the hilt of Charon's Claw. For years he had cursed this blade for keeping him alive, though he was never really sure if the curse upon him was made from Charon's Claw. In either case, he was fairly certain now that the Netherese blade's hold over his soul was diminished, if not fully gone. To the point, Artemis Entreri sensed that he was mortal again, and what ill luck that was, since for perhaps the first time in his life, he did not want to die.

"You will meet with this great man, Kane, again?" Dahlia asked. Entreri had told her of his previous encounter with the Grandmaster of Flowers, more than a century before, when he and Jarlaxle had adventured in the Bloodstone Lands.

"Perhaps, if Jarlaxle can find a way to arrange it."

Dahlia put on a wide smile, showing Entreri her acceptance and trust in him—and he greatly appreciated that.

"Tell Kane that you're the King of Vaasa," she joked, referring again to that old encounter. "That proclamation should have him running to meet with you."

Entreri surrendered and wrapped Dahlia in a great hug.

"Please don't tell Catti-brie of my departure, or anything of Yvonnel's plans," he whispered when they broke their long kiss. "I do not wish to offer false hope."

That raised Dahlia's eyebrows.

Entreri could only shrug. Yvonnel's plan seemed difficult to him, even ridiculous when he stepped back from it. But it was all they had.

◆ ◆ ◆

DRIZZT ENTERED THE small circular chamber tentatively.

The candle was new, set in the holder exactly as the one Drizzt had seen on his first visit to this place. They had anticipated his arrival, he thought, when he noted the small *fusee* on the floor.

They seemed to know him well.

Too well.

The notion that he was being toyed with, that his persecutors were deriving great pleasure from walking him in endless circles, followed him to his place in front of the candle, and he rolled the *fusee* over in his fingers, unsure if he should proceed. He wanted to take his own measure, but he certainly didn't want to give his captors—and that was how he was now seeing the monks—the exhibition they apparently desired.

But he couldn't resist, so he flicked the *fusee* and dropped into his deep squat as he lit the candle, determined to see this through, to prove to himself at least that he could find a place of contentment, a place of silent meditation, a place where his tormentors and his torment, perhaps, could not reach him.

For the first moments, he felt as if he could hold the pose forever. It didn't seem a trial at all as he relaxed into the full position, hands folded in front of him. He stared at the candle and let the light take him inside—not inside the candle, but inside himself.

The muscles at the back of his thighs began to pain him, burning. He fought it off and stubbornly held his position.

Time slipped past him, irrelevant. He felt the discomfort and fought to go deeper into the candle, deeper into himself. It was his own realization of the pose that was hurting him, he knew from his many hours with Afafrenfere and the others. His muscles were twitching, seeking to hold him perfectly steady. And it was exactly that, the effort of trying to be perfect, that prevented any such thing.

Drizzt let it go, just stared into the candle, just stared into himself. He thought only of his own breath, and let the boredom of that rhythm take him to a deeper, more contented place.

He closed his eyes, but wasn't aware of it. His posture was indeed perfectly balanced and at rest, but he wasn't aware of it.

He found a place of nothingness, and there, a sanctuary, a place of peace.

And Catti-brie was there beside him, so beautiful and warm, and it was wonderful.

And she smiled at him, and her teeth were sharpened, canine and vicious, and she laughed, a wicked, screeching sound.

Drizzt tried to fight the image away, and his legs began to ache once more, the muscles burning again.

He opened his eyes to find the candle, his focus, but the light danced wildly, and that commotion only added to his uneasiness.

His own panting breath was moving the candle flame as he tried to hold something so elusive.

His legs ached and he fell back to sit on the floor, gasping.

The candle had burned somewhat, he noted, much more than in his previous attempts, but still, that seemed a meager accomplishment to the drow, and not one he would ever care about.

He had found a place of peace, the most secret and personal place of peace.

And there, too, he had been invaded by his tormentors.

There was no rest to be found.

Drizzt Do'Urden knew then, even more certainly than before, that he was lost. He slumped back to his small chamber and fell upon the straw mattress, praying that unconsciousness would overcome him and give him reprieve.

◆ ◆ ◆

"YOU DID BETTER with your meditation," Kane said to Drizzt the next day, the grandmaster coming to Drizzt's chamber to awaken him very early, before the sun had crested the eastern horizon.

Drizzt stared at him, not knowing how to respond.

Drizzt didn't care, and he was quite certain at that moment that any words coming out of his mouth would not have pleased this man . . . or demon, or whoever or whatever this supposed Grandmaster Kane might be.

"Were you of the Order of the Yellow Rose, you would now be called Immaculate Brother Drizzt," Kane went on.

Drizzt's expression showed how little that meant to him.

"Well on your way to the title of Master, likely," Kane continued, unbothered. "It is not a high-ranking title, perhaps, but one that few brothers or sisters will ever attain. In you, though, I see that possibility. The discipline is there, though you bury it in unease . . ."

"Enough!" Drizzt demanded. He cut short his next biting retort and shook his head, calming himself, and repeated, "Enough."

"You have trained for decades, and it shows," Grandmaster Kane said, and he, too, shook his head.

"A pity," Grandmaster Kane muttered, and he turned and left.

# CHAPTER 21 ◈

# *Revealed*

T O KILL HIM WOULD HAVE RUINED EVERYTHING, AND Malcanthet was beginning to recognize the potential for enjoyment in this forlorn and ugly little corner of the world. She had only agreed with the Hunzrin plan to bring her to the surface because with Demogorgon destroyed and Graz'zt reportedly stalking the Underdark, it seemed a safer place by far. She had always thought she would return to the Underdark as soon as Graz'zt had gone home to the Abyss—she had many connections in more than one dark elf city, after all.

But now she wasn't so sure. These humans were so easily manipulated . . .

"My head hurts me so badly that I cannot even keep my eyes open," she said, dramatically draping her forearm across her forehead.

"I care not!" King Yarin said, and he grabbed her by the shoulders. "I must have you!"

He tried to shove her onto the bed.

He would have had better luck trying to push over the castle.

Surprised, Yarin looked into his queen's red eyes.

Red?

"I said that I am not up to these . . . duties," Malcanthet said, and King Yarin shrank back and swallowed hard.

Her eyes reverted to Concettina's blue, and she offered an apologetic smile. "I will send for you as soon as I am feeling better, my love."

King Yarin stumbled back then whirled around, staggering out of the room, shaking his head and trying to sort out what had just happened. Malcanthet watched him go past the guards, including the dwarf, who glanced back at her knowingly.

She gave a slight nod to Ivan and closed the door.

"Daring games," Inchedeeko the quasit said when she turned around. "You let the human see the truth."

"He has no idea what he saw," Malcanthet replied.

"And now you bring in the barbarian?"

The succubus grinned wickedly. "I am bored."

"And so you begin trouble? Big trouble?"

"Perhaps," Malcanthet replied with a shrug. "Does that please you?"

The quasit giggled, then scampered under the bed when there came a soft knock on the queen's door.

◆ ◆ ◆

IVAN STOOD GUARD in the hallway, keeping as far from Queen Concettina's room as possible without being away from his post. He leaned on a railing at the landing atop the back stairway, just to the side of the hallway and out of sight of the queen's door. He pretended to polish a bit of a spot from the shining armor that had once—so it was rumored, though few believed it—belonged to King Gareth Dragonsbane himself.

"Oh milady, oh milady, oh milady," he heard from below, the voice growing stronger to indicate that someone, a woman, was running up the stairs.

The dwarf winced—he had thought this tryst extra dangerous that particular night, a nagging doubt that had only heightened given the king's bad humor when he left Concettina's room. But Queen Concettina's nod to him as the king departed could not be ignored, on her word.

"Oh milady, the guards, milady!" the voice said.

Ivan gasped and started for the hallway, but fell back behind the statue in surprise.

"The guards come—take care, milady!"

Acelya Frostmantle, the king's sister, rushed past him, too focused on Concettina's door to even notice him.

"Acelya?" the dwarf mouthed quietly. Her apparent concern made no sense to him. Acelya hated Concettina and made no secret of it. Why would she be running to warn the queen of the approach of hostile guards? And how could Acelya even know of Wulfgar's presence within the room?

Or did she?

◆  ◆  ◆

"MILADY, THE GUARDS!" came a frantic voice, followed by even more frantic knocking.

Queen Concettina was pulling off Wulfgar's shirt, roughly kissing him—then she casually shoved the barbarian away, sending him stumbling across the room.

"What?" he asked, eyes going wide.

"Guards!" came the cry from the door. "Coming fast, milady!"

"You have to get me out of here!" Wulfgar said.

Not waiting for an answer, the barbarian rushed for the window, but the woman was there before him, cutting him off.

"You have nowhere to go," she said.

The door banged open and Princess Acelya stumbled in. "Milady!"

"Shut up!" the queen ordered in a deeper, more sinister voice. "And shut the door, you idiot."

Acelya obediently did as she was told.

"What—?" Wulfgar asked again, but the word caught in his throat when the woman he thought was Queen Concettina turned to glower at him. Her eyes were red and her forehead had sprouted small horns, like a goat's.

"We'll not play this night," she said.

Wulfgar slugged her and looked to the small table beside the bed where his warhammer rested. He started to call for it, but his breath was blasted out as the demonic imposter hit him back—and with the strength of a giant.

He staggered back but she was there with him, grappling with him. He managed to call for Aegis-fang and the hammer appeared in his hand, but to no good use. The false queen held Wulfgar too close for him to execute a proper attack.

He grabbed the hammer with both hands and tried to shove her away but she, too, grabbed the weapon, her hands inside his grip. She gave a sudden twist that brought the mighty barbarian to one knee.

The creature tore the hammer from Wulfgar's grip with ease and tossed it aside before she slapped him so hard across the face he reeled and nearly swooned.

He was standing again, then, caught with one hand on the front of his shirt by the false queen.

"You are fortunate I enjoy playing with you," she said. Then she threw Wulfgar across the room, where he slammed into the hearth and stumbled aside.

He set himself and called upon his years of experience, letting his sensibilities catch up to the unbelievable situation that had so suddenly come over him. He reached for the distant hammer, about to call.

But the creature, the being he had thought simply Queen Concettina, stood at the bottom of the bed, grinning at him. Great bat wings unfolded behind her. She brought her arm around and a dark cord—a whip—swung out at him. Baleful arcs of lightning issued from its length as it snapped, cracking against Wulfgar's arm.

Stunning fires erupted within him, a wave of dizziness surging through him, stealing the word to call his warhammer before he ever uttered it. The dizziness swept through him, leaving numbness in its wake.

His arm fell dead at his side.

The demonic creature laughed and pursed her lips and gave a little blow, and Wulfgar felt a jet of air rush past him. He heard the flutter of a hanging cloak behind him.

The whip cracked again and he shied away, turning defensively and trying hard to hold his footing on weakened legs. And then he noticed the cloak that had been hanging beside the hearth flopping to the side, revealing the leering demon face and the mirror secured within its gaping maw.

Wulfgar saw himself in that mirror only briefly before some strange energy reached out at him from within the item, grabbing him, engulfing him. He felt stretched and understood only that he was leaning in at the looking glass.

The room around him elongated and then he was gone, sucked into the mirror, leaving the demon laughing.

◆ ◆ ◆

"HE WILL COME with me," Malcanthet announced to Acelya, who stared in horror at where the man had been standing.

A commotion in the hallway told them that the guards had come.

"Take me!" Acelya cried.

Malcanthet moved for Wulfgar's hammer, but it disappeared as she reached for it. She glanced back at the mirror, nodding, though surprised that her slave could call for the magical weapon through the extra-planar, life-trapping mirror.

A gauntleted fist pounded heavily on the door.

"In the name of the king!" came a roar.

Malcanthet waved her hand at the door and the wood swelled, tightening it in its jamb.

"Milady, it is Rafer!" Acelya pleaded, grabbing Malcanthet by the arm. "Take me, please!"

Acelya turned for the mirror, but the succubus cupped her chin and would not let her view herself, would not let her be caught within the glass.

"No, dear girl," Malcanthet answered, gently stroking Acelya's face.

◆ ◆ ◆

"DAMNED THING'S LOCKED!" Rafer Ingot yelled. He slammed his shoulder into the door.

"No lock on that door!" another of the guards replied, and he kicked at the door as Rafer smashed into it again. This time the jamb groaned and the wood creaked and cracked a bit.

Ivan didn't know what to do. He kept turning for the stairs and back to the door. He couldn't leave Wulfgar so vulnerable to the guards, but would he be helping the man if it was discovered that he was part of the conspiracy? There was no way for Wulfgar to get out of that room, and found by the king's loyal guards in a compromising situation with Queen Concettina, the barbarian would get a fast trip to the back garden and King Yarin's head-chopper!

Grimacing at his lack of options, Ivan came up behind the mob.

"Show some courtesy for the queen!" he yelled, but they seemed not to hear.

Rafer Ingot did notice him, though, and slapped his hand out in the air in front of the dwarf.

"The axe!" he demanded.

Ivan recoiled and started to argue, but several others grabbed him all at once, and before he knew what was what, Rafer had his axe and was chopping at the door.

Wood flew all about and as soon as the middle board fully splintered, the swelled seams sagged and Rafer shouldered the door again, breaking it in. The brutish man tossed Ivan's axe aside, went for his more comfortable sword, and led the charge into the room. He cried out almost in pain as Ivan, trying to collect his axe in the jumble of rushing guards, heard the snap of a whip.

The dwarf shook his head, confused, and expected to hear the bellow of Wulfgar, and what was he to do when that happened?

He couldn't let Rafer and the others kill the barbarian, surely, or even beat him down; but among this very group of castle guards were men and women who Ivan had come to know as friends.

When he finally managed to get through the press at the door and into the room, though, the dwarf saw that it didn't matter. It wasn't Wulfgar brawling with the guards, but someone—something—all together different.

She looked somewhat like Concettina, only larger, and with horns and bat wings and an awful sparking whip that crackled as it curled and struck with such fury that all those near the snapping tip had to shield their eyes and turn away in painful shock, like from a mage's lightning bolt.

The weapon snapped and the man beside Ivan fell limp right on top of the dwarf, knocking him to the floor. Down there, the dwarf noted Rafer, lying over by the bed, squirming weirdly, shrieking, and trying to reach for his face with an arm that seemed to have no strength at all. The murderous man rolled over and Ivan gasped. That first whip crack had taken out one of his eyeballs. Worse, it still rolled around on his cheek at the end of its stalk.

Ivan tried to get up, determined to leap into the fight, but a flying body hit him and sent him tumbling back to the floor, pinning him against the wall just beside the door. Half a dozen soldiers were down, and a seventh went up into the air in the grip of the monstrous demon's left hand. Casually, carelessly almost, she launched the poor fellow across the room, spinning head over heels like some child's doll to smash through the window, taking the glass and iron lacing with him as he crashed free into the empty night air.

Ivan heard his diminishing screams as he fell the forty feet to the ground.

"Ah, ye beast," the dwarf growled as he stubbornly tried to extract himself.

And then he froze in place, looking at the naked demon, then past her to the back wall, to a green demon face and a mirror. And in that mirror he saw Wulfgar, hands against the glass—the *inside* of the glass. The barbarian's mouth opened in a silent scream as his image swirled and disappeared.

Another pair of guards charged through the door only to be stopped short by the snap of that lightning whip.

The demon—Concettina, or whatever or whoever it was—leaped away, gathering up the mirror under one arm and tearing it from the wall with horrifying strength. Before Ivan could get out from under the body of the lifeless man pinning him, and before the two newcomers could launch at her once more, she was out the window, leaping high, her great batlike wings spreading to catch the winds.

Ivan stumbled to the window sill, staring out at the night. The fiend glided down to the garden then leaped once more high into the night, flying off to the north and right out over the city wall.

The dwarf spun around to survey the chaos of the room. Men groaned, others ran around tending them, and there was even more commotion out in the hall.

Ivan pushed through, exiting the room, and made for the stairs.

"To check on the king!" he snorted to one guard that questioned his departure.

But Ivan lied. King Yarin was the least of his concerns at that desperate moment. He sprinted down the stairs, taking them three at a time, then sneaked and quick-footed his way out of the palace's back door, speeding for the cottage where Pikel and Regis waited.

# CHAPTER 22 ◈

# *Swallowing a Demon*

**O**F COURSE I ACCEPT YOUR WISDOM," BROTHER AFAFRENFERE said. He was obviously fighting hard to maintain his composure, a reminder to the others that though he had progressed so quickly and so high up the ranks of the Order of the Yellow Rose, he was still a young man, and perhaps not so tempered.

"But you do not agree," Grandmaster Kane replied.

"I do!" Afafrenfere blurted. "It is just that . . . I do not know what it is, Grandmaster, except that I am quite fond of this curious drow. I am sure that I owe him a great debt. I was lost and he was among those who found me.

"When the dwarf Ambergris saved me at my first meeting, my battle against Drizzt, and so pulled me from the Plane of Shadow, Drizzt did not have to forgive and accept me. He did not have to help guide me along a more proper road—indeed, he would have been well within his rights, legal and moral, to slay me, or to have me jailed, at least. Yet he did not. He took me into his group and under his eye, and in our travels together, he trusted me, and that was perhaps the greatest gift I have ever received."

The other few monks in the room raised their eyebrows at that claim, particularly given the amazing gifts Grandmaster Kane had bestowed upon this particular brother by possessing him and teaching him as a true and full partner that which others would spend years, decades even, trying to learn—and usually futilely.

But Kane clearly understood Afafrenfere's point. He nodded, offering a genuine smile.

"It has not been that long," Afafrenfere pleaded.

"Long enough to know," said Kane. "We have done all that we can for Drizzt Do'Urden, and it is not enough, but so be it. It is time for him to go home."

"Yes, Grandmaster," Afafrenfere said with an obedient bow. "Shall I tell him?"

"No. Go and fetch him." Kane looked around at the others. "All of you. I will speak with Drizzt alone."

When they were gone, Kane turned to the door at the side of the room and called softly, and Yvonnel came through to stand in front of him.

"I am honored by your trust," she said.

"I know better than to trust the likes of Jarlaxle, and of you, Yvonnel, who I am told is possessed of extraordinary power."

"Yet you accepted the request from Jarlaxle that you grant me an audience, and in this, your home."

Kane shrugged. "Because I am not afraid."

Yvonnel smiled at that. "Can you see into my soul, Grandmaster of Flowers?" she asked.

"I know that Drizzt is possessed of many friends who would willingly die to save him," the monk replied. "Jarlaxle is one of them, I believe, and so in this, I expect that his course is transparent and correct. In any case, I did not lie to my brethren in my determination regarding our confused friend. It is an enigma, this malady that has so ruined a warrior of Drizzt's heart, reputation, and discipline. An enigma and a tragedy. I cannot repair him because . . . ?"

"Because he cannot repair himself," Yvonnel answered, and after a moment, a curious Kane nodded his agreement.

"And you believe that you can?" the monk asked.

Yvonnel clearly wanted to nod, but she wound up shaking her head instead. "I cannot know, but I wish to try."

"Why?"

And so Yvonnel told him of the curse she had put upon Drizzt, and of how he had shocked her by somehow avoiding her trap, through sheer force of will and perhaps something more, something deeper in his heart. She told him of her course now, and of what she believed was the missing piece to the puzzle of Drizzt's affliction.

The monk assumed a pensive stance. "There are two kinds of demons in the world," he explained, quite deliberately. "One you know well, as you hail from Menzoberranzan and are well-acquainted with the Spider Queen, of course. These are the demons of the Abyss, the physical demons, and to some, godlike."

Yvonnel's next snort was telling.

"But that is the lie, I say!" Grandmaster Kane declared with great certainty and atypical emotion. "A lie because we are the gods over these false beings. They exist only because they are the stuff of our shared nightmares. If none worshipped them, if none believed in them, if none feared them, they would have no power. Alas, that is not to be."

◆ ◆ ◆

YVONNEL STARED AT him for a long while, somewhat intrigued, or at least not willing to dismiss what he had said out of hand.

"Two kinds of demons, you said," she replied to the monk after a long pause.

"The other demons are the ones we ourselves create," Kane explained. "They are demons of hate and of fear, and they are very powerful. Though without corporeal form, they are as tangible as any creature in the Abyss. Drizzt Do'Urden has swallowed his demon of fear, and has so given it a nest deep within his heart and mind."

"And such a demon protects itself by creating fear in the host," Yvonnel replied, nodding.

"The Abyssal Plague has caused great tumult in the Underdark, and great despair," she added. "Almost all afflicted will never break free of the twisting cords of its madness, I am sure, because even with the help of a great priest or wizard or psionicist, their demons of fear will prevent them from accepting the healing."

"But perhaps Drizzt is special," Kane remarked.

Yvonnel could only shrug and vaguely reply, "It is in the interest of my people to find a way through this curse."

She had heard so many tales of the disciplined Drizzt Do'Urden—so many of those in Menzoberranzan who had known him and his father would secretly admit that Drizzt would have been among the greatest of weapons masters the city had ever known. And although weapons masters were not very highly regarded, being mere males after all, Yvonnel the Eternal knew that a truly disciplined warrior was no less a work of artistry, no less a complete creature, than any priestess or wizard.

"And if your plan does not work?" the monk asked.

"Then I will take him home to Catti-brie and the others, if I am able," she replied somberly. "If I am not, then I will bring his body home and let his friends properly mourn his death."

"And if you cannot defeat him? Am I to deal with a crazed Drizzt Do'Urden rampaging about the Monastery of the Yellow Rose?"

Yvonnel merely laughed at what she obviously considered an absurd thought.

"And of the other?" Kane asked. "This plan you present is treachery, Priestess of Lolth, and treachery toward such a being most often gets one killed. Or worse."

"I have asked for your help," Yvonnel reminded him. "Are you as formidable as I have heard?"

Grandmaster Kane nodded. "Drizzt will be expelled presently."

"I will await him beyond the fields outside your doors," she said.

Yvonnel left the room the way she'd come in. She was watched very carefully as she moved through the corridors and wide chambers of the Monastery of the Yellow Rose, but the brothers and sisters remained polite and at a distance at all times, except when they rushed in to open a door for her, making certain that her path out was direct.

Outside, Yvonnel crossed the wide field, moving down the mountainside to the forest in which she'd left Entreri and the dragon that had flown them out from Luskan.

She found Entreri alone.

"Where is Tazmikella?"

"She and her sister maintained an estate just outside of Helgabal," Entreri explained. "They left it disguised, trapped, and heavily guarded, but apparently our friend wanted to check on her treasures. She is a dragon, after all."

"The sisters so readily agreed to fly us here that I expected they might have other business," said Yvonnel. "It is probably better that she is not here when Drizzt joins us."

"Kane agreed?"

"He was finished with Drizzt," Yvonnel explained. "He knew that he had failed and that there was little he could do."

A cloud crossed over Entreri's face.

"He has given Drizzt some internal peace," Yvonnel said to soften the blow, "and that is no small thing. But it is as I explained to you—Drizzt's malady is not something he can simply will away. He is wounded, and the wound is real, and it is an injury that cannot be healed unless he is trusting in allowing that healer into his thoughts."

Artemis Entreri understood very well his role in trying to get Drizzt to that point. He wore a grim expression and nodded his agreement, his hands going instinctively to his belted weapons.

"I must soon call to Kimmuriel," Yvonnel said. "I hope."

Entreri nodded again, but then relinquished his grim focus. "There is another matter," he said.

Yvonnel wasn't particularly glad to hear of any complications, and she let her concern show clearly. But Entreri pressed on.

"There is something afoot in Damara, so Tazmikella told me," the assassin explained.

"What? Does it concern us?"

Entreri shrugged. "All she said was that she saw things afoot that we could not, that her dragon eyes revealed to her something concerning. She promised that she would tell us more when she returned from Helgabal."

Yvonnel didn't press the issue, because she really didn't care at that particular moment, figuring that Tazmikella's concerns about some petty human kingdom had little to do with her. She nodded, letting Entreri know that he had done his duty in informing her, and that was the end of it.

"So we just wait here?" Entreri asked.

Yvonnel moved to the edge of the trees, looking back up the mountainside at the main doors of the Monastery of the Yellow Rose. "He will be out soon, I believe," she said. "Do you know your place?"

"Completely."

"Drizzt is not to know that I am here. Do you understand?"

Entreri snorted and Yvonnel turned on him sharply. "You do not understand the sword's edge on which you stand," she declared. "It is very likely you will die this day."

"I know."

"I have cast many spells and can assure you that I do not believe that Charon's Claw, whatever magical longevity it might once have provided to you, is any longer your guardian. The Sundering ended that, if it was ever really there."

"I know."

"It is very likely that you will die this day," she repeated.

"I know."

"Or that you will kill this drow you call your friend."

"I know."

"Do you, truly?" Yvonnel demanded, coming forward. "If you hesitate, if you are anything less than sincere and honest in your battle, then it will all be for naught. You will fail, and die, and Drizzt will gain not at all—indeed, such a miserable failure on your part might doom him forevermore."

"Why do you care?" Entreri growled at her. "Who are you? I was told you were the daughter of Gromph, but he hardly cares—not even enough to teleport us to this place. I was told that you could have been the Matron Mother of Menzoberranzan, the wretched mouthpiece of a demon goddess . . ."

"Beware your words," Yvonnel warned, and in such a tone that Entreri did soften his own words and tone.

"Why would the matron mother care about Drizzt Do'Urden, the heretic, the fallen?" he asked.

"I am not the matron mother."

"But you could be."

"Indeed. With a word. But I am not. That alone should tell you something."

Entreri shrugged and blew a frustrated sigh. "Why do you care?"

"Why do you?"

"You cannot simply answer?"

"Answer your own question. Our reasons, I am sure, are quite the same."

◆  ◆  ◆

THAT LEFT ENTRERI at a loss. He fell back a step, shaking his head, trying to make some sense out of it all. He cared because Drizzt had held up a mirror to him, and had forced him to look honestly into that mirror.

He cared because Drizzt's example had helped Entreri look into that mirror and not loathe who he saw staring back at him.

He looked at Yvonnel more carefully, and this all-powerful drow who could command an army of twenty thousand dark elves, who was possessed of the highest level of divine spells among her race, and could do battle in arcane magic with the likes of Gromph Baenre as well, seemed so small.

Glancing past her, up the hill, Entreri saw a lone figure emerge from the monastery, and when that figure summoned a magical unicorn and began walking it down the hill, Artemis Entreri knew that his moment of ultimate truth was upon him.

"Here he comes," he whispered.

"Remember your place and why you are here," Yvonnel said, and then she was gone, disappearing into the brush.

Entreri summoned his own mount, a nightmare steed from an obsidian figurine, and paced it out onto the road, just in the shadows of the trees, and waited for Drizzt to arrive.

"What are you doing out here?" the startled drow asked when he came upon the man. He appeared quite shaken to Entreri, and had so even before he had noticed Entreri under the trees.

Entreri spat on the ground. "All of this going on about you and you cannot figure out the truth of it?" he asked in a sneering tone. "I am disappointed, Drizzt Do'Urden."

Drizzt leaned back. "What do you mean?"

Entreri slid down from his mount and dismissed the nightmare with a wave of his hand, then motioned, inviting Drizzt to join him.

The drow stared at him curiously, suspiciously, for a bit, then did so, sending Andahar away and leaving the two men facing each other from just a few strides away.

"Why are you here?" Drizzt demanded more forcefully. "Are you in league with—?"

"I need no allies," Entreri interrupted.

"Then this is just coincidence?"

"I do not believe in coincidence," Entreri said, and in such a way that it seemed to strike a deep chord in Drizzt, as if he had heard those same words spoken by this man in just this way so many, many decades before.

And indeed he had, in the tunnels of Mithral Hall when the drow of Menzoberranzan had first come against King Bruenor and Artemis Entreri had walked among Drizzt and his friends in the guise of Regis.

Drizzt shook his head.

"Can you not guess why I am here?" Entreri asked grimly. "Why me? Why this form, this man, this enemy?"

Drizzt winced.

"Who else would you expect as the embodiment of your nightmare?" Entreri said, laying it bare.

Drizzt leaned away, clearly caught off guard.

Entreri drew Charon's Claw, the red blade catching a bit of sunlight and shining awfully. Out came his trademark dagger, and he flipped it over in his hand a few times, letting the jewels in the hilt sparkle in display.

"What do you know of my nightmares?" Drizzt said, trying to regain his composure.

"It is all a lie, right?" said Entreri. He painted on a sinister sneer. "A grand deception to ruin you utterly? Or are you, perhaps, an arrogant ass who thinks himself the center of all the living world?"

He took a step forward and Drizzt took one back.

"I am your nightmare, Drizzt Do'Urden," Entreri announced. "And if there is a grand deception, it is time for your ruin."

"Why?" Drizzt asked, stepping back. "Why all of this? Why the elaborate deception?"

Entreri's smile was perfectly wicked and he recited, "The sweeter comes my victory."

Drizzt staggered as if he had been punched, those words, too, surely echoing in the recesses of his memories of Artemis Entreri.

"Draw your weapons, Drizzt Do'Urden, that we may continue the fight we began in Calimport's sewers," Entreri teased. "Or at least, that was your presumption on that long ago day, yes? Though we both knew it went longer, for my skill mocked your principles, and your very being mocked my discipline. That was our rivalry, remember?"

"That was a very long time ago, in a place far removed from—"

"Not so far, apparently. Draw your weapons."

Drizzt made no move.

"Draw your weapons that you might learn the truth," Entreri said.

"I know the truth."

"Draw, or I will kill you where you stand." There was no bluff in Entreri's words.

Drizzt shook his head, more than ready for this to be over. Instead of drawing his scimitars, he simply held his hands out wide, inviting the assassin's blades.

"Fight for your friends if not for yourself!" Entreri demanded.

"My friends are dead, long dead," Drizzt said.

"Fight or I will torment them for eternity!" Entreri yelled, and there seemed then, finally, a bit of desperation in his voice, an indication that he was, perhaps, not as in control as he desired.

"If you are what you claim, then you will do that anyway," Drizzt replied, his voice filled with resignation.

Entreri composed himself, and put that wicked smile on again. "But I will enjoy it more."

Drizzt steeled his expression and stood straight.

"Coward," Entreri said.

"Kill me, then."

"So in the end, Drizzt Do'Urden is a coward," said Entreri. "You think yourself brave—so ready to die—but you are only ready because you are so afraid of that which you fear. In the end, Drizzt Do'Urden is a coward."

"As you wish."

"As it is," Entreri corrected. "If I strike you down, you will die with uncertainty, with a tiny flicker of hope remaining so that your confused mind leads not to your feared conclusion. And so you are not accepting. No, you are merely surrendering."

He finished with a lazy thrust of Charon's Claw, stopping it just short, but coming around and flashing his dagger hand at Drizzt, just nicking the drow's cheek and drawing a line of bright blood. It was not a serious wound, or appeared not.

But Drizzt's eyes widened in shock and Entreri knew he felt the truth of that awful jeweled dagger as a teasing sense of absolute obliteration, of his very life essence being stolen from him.

For all his despair and darkness, for all the helplessness and resignation that had cowed Drizzt Do'Urden, for all his confusion wrought by the Abyssal Plague, that moment of realization, that sense of utter obliteration, suppressed it all.

The scimitars appeared in Drizzt's hands, Icingdeath and Vidrinath.

"It is past time to end this," Artemis Entreri said.

And on he came, beginning the battle in a measured fashion as he and his skilled opponent fell into a rhythm that was so familiar to them both.

How many times had they matched blades? How many times had they joined blades against a common foe? Working against each other or in concert was much the same, for the harmony and flow of their twists and strikes were so complementary, so anticipatory of the other's movements, that the fight seemed more a dance than a struggle.

◆ ◆ ◆

FROM THE SHADOWS of the trees, Yvonnel watched the contest with true appreciation. Even those initial thrusts and parries, the combatants simply feeling each other's rhythms, seemed worthy of the best of Melee-Magthere.

As the tempo increased with every turn, the sounds of metal on metal became indistinct, like one long screech of steel on steel. With every clever angle of a thrusting blade met by an equally clever angled parry, those initial testing strikes seemed like nothing.

Yvonnel nodded and lifted the whistle to her mouth, blowing it for Kimmuriel. She heard nothing, but trusted Jarlaxle and knew the psionicist would hear.

But would he heed the call?

Yvonnel shrugged. It didn't matter. Kimmuriel would help her, would amplify her message if all went as she hoped, but in the end, this would not be decided by him in any case.

The priestess closed her eyes and cast a spell, sending her thoughts across the planes to the Abyss, to Yiccardaria.

"Lolth grant me this," she whispered.

The handmaiden heard her. Yiccardaria seemed confused, but she was soon on her way to Yvonnel's side.

• • •

DRIZZT'S BLADES SWEPT in with brilliant speed, three times left and right, and three times did Entreri bat those attacks aside—as Drizzt knew he would. It was all so familiar, so in tune, so . . . repetitive. This fight had been waged before, the choreography similar, near exact even, the combatants the same, even two of the weapons the same.

Almost as if on cue, Entreri charged ahead, sword up high, forcing a ducking, twisting disengage from Drizzt, with Vidrinath rushing up to intercept a subtle under-stroke of the dagger.

A roll sent the scimitar for the assassin's chest, but Entreri was too quick, leaning and shuffling back before the blade ever got close.

Across went Charon's Claw, trailing a sheet of ash that hung in the air, and Drizzt fell out to the side as Entreri burst through, weapons flailing and hitting only empty air. But the assassin was not caught at a disadvantage. Drizzt rushed in behind, and Entreri's Netherese blade swept across again as he turned properly to meet the drow, putting another opaque wall between them. This time, Drizzt went through as Entreri went through, crossing side-by-side—so close! And yet even in there, even with the visual barrier, these two knew each other so very well that metal hit only metal, each one thrusting and parrying and defeating the other's advantage.

The wall of ash diminished between them from their turmoil, and as Entreri began to enact another one, Drizzt struck first, engulfing them both in a globe of absolute magical darkness.

And in there, they fought, blades hitting blades, twisting and dodging on instinct and sound and simply from knowing their opponent.

Entreri came out of the globe first, rolling to the side. Drizzt came out some distance away, and with room between them, out came Taulmaril.

"Still a coward!" Entreri said even as he dived back into the globe.

Drizzt's leveled bow followed. He could take the man down, even in that darkness, with a barrage of arrows that could not be blocked or avoided.

But he didn't. Something, the familiarity of it all perhaps, or perhaps his own sense of honor, stayed his hand. He flipped the bow back into his belt buckle and drew again his melee weapons.

He thought of bringing in Guenhwyvar, but on that, too, he demurred.

He would beat this man alone, without tricks.

Going back into the globe of darkness, Drizzt found himself wondering why he was so determined on that point. Entreri wasn't Entreri, after all, but some demonic fiend sent to break him body and soul. Shouldn't he use every advantage he could muster to kill this beast, as he had with Tiago Baenre?

The thought was fleeting, and the pair were right back into it, blades spinning and stabbing. When Drizzt missed a parry and barely escaped serious injury he heard a gasp from Entreri—and used the seeming distraction to drive Icingdeath home.

But the blade was caught and pulled out wide by that vicious dagger, Entreri apparently recognizing his own mistake in making a sound—if it was even a mistake and not a lure, Drizzt decided. And so the drow threw himself forward, going into a clinch with his foe, and drove harder.

Out the back of the globe they went in a tumble, disengaging as they rolled and coming back up several strides apart. Neither was unmarked now, with assorted nicks and cuts.

Drizzt thought of the sleeping poison of Vidrinath—perhaps his enemy would be slowed.

He also considered the reputed festering wounds of Charon's Claw, and wondered if he was already dead.

◆ ◆ ◆

"HE MUST BE cured to properly realize his doom," Yvonnel explained to Yiccardaria. "And the children of Lolth will find the added benefit of understanding, at long last, how to beat the Abyssal affliction."

"It seems a lot of trouble for a mere male," replied the handmaiden in her beautiful, dark elf form.

"Not just any male," Yvonnel reminded her, "but one Lolth has singled out for extreme torment."

"So destroy his beloved and his friends before his eyes," the handmaiden said. "Torture them. Break them and so break him. Then turn him into a drider—it is a fitting end for Drizzt Do'Urden, is it not?"

"He will not—he does not—believe it. Any of it," Yvonnel said. "The Abyssal affliction has dulled him to such atrocities. I could murder his friends horribly in front of him, and he would doubt the reality of it too much for the pain to be absolute. So let us fix him—grant me this."

Yiccardaria looked at her suspiciously. "Though I and you and certainly Lady Lolth have wasted far too much time and effort on this insignificant insect, I will remain by your side until you are finished and Drizzt Do'Urden is properly and finally destroyed," she said.

"Of course, Handmaiden," Yvonnel said with a bow.

Yiccardaria glanced around curiously then, seeming alarmed.

"Kimmuriel Oblodra," Yvonnel explained, for she felt the disturbance as well, "warping distance to come to my call."

"Another heretic!" the handmaiden scoffed.

Yvonnel held up her hand and wore a look of disagreement. "He is Jarlaxle's lackey. Are we to punish him, as well? Would Lady Lolth desire such a thing? And recall that it was Kimmuriel's work with the illithid hive mind that allowed for the defense of Menzoberranzan against Demogorgon. Surely that counts as some measure of penance."

Yiccardaria faded from sight. "I will inquire," she said, vanishing, and even as she did, Kimmuriel stepped into view.

"Them again," the psionicist said, looking past Yvonnel to the battling duo. "This is a song I've heard too many times. Let us be done with this, if you will."

"I will," Yvonnel promised, "when Drizzt is ready for us."

The daughter of Gromph licked her lips in anticipation. Everything was coming together now, perfectly.

She hoped.

◆ ◆ ◆

DRIZZT THRUST VIDRINATH between Entreri's upraised weapons, but across came the red blade of Charon's Claw, driving it aside. The assassin's ensuing move to the left turned Drizzt, putting the drow's back to a tangle of birch trees.

Entreri came in low with his slash and with his dagger instead of his sword. But Drizzt had seen this before. Even as he stepped back and launched his downward attacks on the stooping assassin, he knew Entreri's sword would come up high to intercept. When he tried to re-angle Icingdeath for a lower stab, the dagger came up to drive it aside.

"It will not be a quick kill," Entreri promised, and Drizzt was back in time, it seemed, to a windy stone ledge . . .

On came Entreri, furiously, as if giving lie to those words, exactly as Drizzt knew he would. The attack was blocked, so the assassin went into a spin, blades out like the edge of a screw.

Drizzt complemented the move.

Like competing dust devils in far-off Calimshan's endless dunes, the two whirled and spun, often reversing, always reacting perfectly.

They came out of the twists together, very near each other, and the next exchange proved the most furious yet, scimitars, sword, and dagger working in a ringing blur, metal sliding against metal, both fighters growling and yelling through the pain and exhaustion.

Down low went Entreri's slash. Drizzt hopped it and came in high.

Entreri ducked and came up at a deadly angle, and Drizzt leaned back—so far back, almost to the ground!

And he snapped right back up, double-thrusting low, and down went Charon's Claw to keep the blades too low to score a hit.

Drizzt worked Entreri up high then, inviting the attack. Entreri took the bait and double-thrust low.

Drizzt's scimitars crossed down atop Entreri's blades, and his leg came up, snap-kicking high to painfully clip the man's nose.

But up, too, came the dagger, and it cut into Drizzt's calf and sent the drow rushing away.

Entreri swept Charon's Claw across to create an opaque field of ash.

And Drizzt didn't hesitate.

Entreri thought he had an advantage, thought, likely, that Drizzt had been wounded worse than he actually had been. The drow went through the hanging ash, blades working wildly, expecting to meet Entreri.

But the assassin wasn't there.

Confused, and more than a bit leery, the drow fell into a low defensive crouch, finally spotting Entreri, who stood strangely at ease a few strides away.

Drizzt paced in carefully, ready to resume, moving in fast and close with his scimitars leading. But Entreri lifted his blades as if to block, then threw his arms down and to the side, throwing both Charon's Claw and his dagger into the ground at his sides. The sword sank in and stood diagonally, and the dagger buried in the earth up to its hilt.

"What?" Drizzt asked, stopping just short, both Vidrinath and Icingdeath within a finger's breadth of the assassin's chest.

"Do it," Entreri said.

"What are you doing?" Drizzt's hands began to sweat more than they had during the furious battle.

"If you think me your enemy, then be done with me here and now," Entreri replied. "If I am the bringer of this nightmare you believe around you, then end it and end me."

"You claimed—"

"I told you what you needed to believe, nothing more."

Drizzt hesitated.

"Is it all a lie, Drizzt Do'Urden?" Entreri asked. "Is it all a grand deception?"

"Yes!" he insisted.

"Then who is more likely to be your deceiver than Artemis Entreri?"

"Lolth!" Drizzt answered before he could even consider the words.

"In what better form?"

Vidrinath came in, tearing through the assassin's leather jerkin with ease, cutting into his skin and nicking his rib.

Entreri grimaced and fought hard to stay straight.

"If you believe it all a lie, then I am a lie," Entreri insisted. "If I am a lie, then destroy the facade. Do it!"

"Shut up!" Drizzt yelled back.

"Coward!"

Drizzt glared at him.

"You cannot! Coward!"

"I will!"

Entreri pressed forward and the scimitar sank in deeper.

# CHAPTER 23 ◈

# *The Riddle*

ELLS TOLLED THROUGHOUT HELGABAL, CALLING THE ARMY
of King Yarin to formation and alerting the citizens to hole
up and be wary. All over the city men and women rushed
about, seeking safety or answering the call. Excited children shouted to friends and wagged their fists, enjoying
the break in their normal routines and not quite grasping
the gravity of the situation.

"King Yarin will not leave his room," Dreylil Andrus told the
court wizard, Red Mazzie, when he joined the man in Queen
Concettina's chamber.

The place was covered in blood, and with burn marks all
over—from dripping demon blood, they believed.

"I am surprised he allowed you to leave his side," Red Mazzie
replied. "I have never seen the man so shaken, not even in the
earliest days, when the line of Dragonsbane faltered and a dozen
dangerous people vied for the throne of Damara."

"He is surrounded by many trusted guards," the captain
assured the wizard.

"How fares Rafer Ingot?" Red Mazzie asked. Rafer was Yarin's
most favored bodyguard, even though both Dreylil Andrus and
Red Mazzie profoundly hated the man.

"Dying," Andrus replied. "The demon's whip struck him
and inflicted a festering wound. The priests cannot help him.
He will die in agony."

"A pity," said Red Mazzie, who clearly didn't feel that way at all.

"But the king will survive and is safe enough," the captain informed him. "His chamber is a fortress."

Red Mazzie nodded, but couldn't hide his doubt, and so Dreylil Andrus put on a questioning look and bade him to speak openly.

"We thought the same of Princess Acelya's room," Red Mazzie reminded him. "Has she been found?"

The guard captain shook his head. "Our attention has been here," he explained, and indeed, the unexpected, shocking battle had only recently concluded.

"The creature flew out over the northern wall," Andrus continued, "and away to the north, so we believe. We have many witnesses to this, though we still do not know the nature of the beast."

"A succubus," Red Mazzie answered. "That would be my guess. And a very powerful one to have done—" he looked around and sighed "—all of this." He shook his head, at a loss. "Perhaps half-succubus," he said unconvincingly, for he was clearly uncertain, "and half some other, more powerful demon. I am not well-schooled in demonology, I admit. I prefer to keep my dealing with the lower planes nonexistent."

Dreylil Andrus looked around. "Few would disagree with that sentiment."

"If the creature is gone, how long will the king remain in his private chambers?" the wizard asked.

Dreylil Andrus lowered his voice to a whisper, for other men and women were about the room and the hallway, searching for clues. "King Yarin has been carnally consorting with a demon, it would appear, and it has brought him to a trembling and broken place. To think that he was lying with that beast, perhaps for years . . ."

"Not years," Red Mazzie replied with confidence.

"What do you know?"

The wizard pulled Andrus over by the broken window and produced a gem-studded necklace from his pocket. "Do you remember this?"

"From those filthy dwarves," the guard captain answered.

Red Mazzie grabbed the item by one particular gemstone. "This jewel was enchanted," he said. "I can feel the echoes of its magic. A phylactery, and one that held the demon succubus, I would guess—nay, it is more than a guess."

Dreylil Andrus's eyes went wide. "The king wears a similar item!" He turned to run from the room, but Red Mazzie grabbed him by the arm and held him back.

"I was given the opportunity to inspect the king's matching necklace before he accepted the gift," he reminded, "and I remain confident that there was and is no dweomer upon it. I will look at it again more carefully, however, and yes, we should take it away from King Yarin in any event."

"If that one held the demon, and is now empty . . ."

"It is quite inert now," the wizard assured him. "The dweomer is no more."

"So the queen and the demon share her mortal body?"

Red Mazzie shook his head.

"Then where is the soul of Queen Concettina?" the guard captain asked.

Before the wizard could speculate, a woman cried out from the side of the room, by the hearth, not so far away, and the two men and some others rushed over.

She stood trembling, pointing at the chimney, then down to the hearth, where a pool of blood settled upon the ashes. Dreylil Andrus dropped to his knees and scrambled forward, craning his neck to peer up into the chimney. He came out immediately, looking quite sick.

"Get her out," he told the nearest guard, and he fell back a step.

"The queen!" Red Mazzie cried, thinking the riddle solved.

The guard moved in and began tugging, tentatively and with a most disgusted expression, at the body stuffed up the chimney. A woman's bare arm dropped into view and the man yanked harder. Another guard came over to assist, but still, it took them some time to finally pull the unfortunate victim from the tight shaft. When the broken body fell into the hearth, Red Mazzie and the others knew his error.

"Princess Acelya," Dreylil Andrus breathed.

"But where is Queen Concettina?" one of the guards asked.

"She is not in the necklace," Red Mazzie asserted. "The magic is wholly spent."

"And where is the man we were told was in this room?" another guard dared to remark, and Red Mazzie and Dreylil Andrus both stared at him dangerously.

"Such rumors will allow your head to roll free," the wizard remarked, and the guard—all the guards—shrank back.

"Take her out of here," the guard captain told the woman who had found Acelya. "Wrap her carefully and with due respect for the Princess of Damara."

The woman nodded and motioned to the man who had tugged the poor woman out of the chimney. He stepped over and lifted the body into his arms, gently shifting Acelya over his shoulder.

"The rest of you search the hallways and all chambers about this room," Andrus ordered. "We will find Queen Concettina and any others who might know of this horrible crime!"

"You heard the rumors of the queen's lover?" Red Mazzie asked when the two men were alone.

"The barbarian from Aglarond," Dreylil Andrus replied.

"Icewind Dale, actually, but yes, him. The guards did not come to this room on a call of help, but because . . ."

"I know."

"Then where is he?" the wizard asked.

"With Queen Concettina? Was she even here? Is she even anywhere about? Or was she long disposed of by the imposter demon?"

"Then where is her lover?" the wizard reiterated.

Dreylil Andrus nodded his agreement with that curiosity, and something else occurred to him then. The dwarves and the barbarian were connected in only one way he could think of, in the form of one of his soldiers who, by happenstance, had been on duty this very night in this very proximity and whose green-bearded brother was often seen conversing with Queen Concettina out in the garden. Who had, in fact, been spied out there with the woman just the other day.

The thought did not settle well on Captain Andrus's shoulders. He was quite fond of those dwarves, and considered Ivan Bouldershoulder among his greatest military assets.

But these strained coincidences were not lying to him.

◆ ◆ ◆

THE BODY SHE inhabited could sense the direction of its rightful soul, and so Malcanthet continued her run to the north only briefly before turning due west. With her wings lifting her into long leaps, the succubus covered tremendous ground, and the Galena Mountains loomed large in front of her when the first rays of dawn lit their peaks.

After each long stride, she paused and adjusted, sensing that she was getting close. But of course, the gemstone with the body's true soul was underground, in a deep complex that reputedly ran through the mountains all the way to Vaasa. Malcanthet knew that finding the surface entrance would prove no easy task.

Soon she was in the rocky foothills, moving more carefully, leaping straight up and lifting higher on beating wings to peer all around for some sign of the spriggan clan.

After many tries and with the sun now nearly halfway to its peak, the demon sat down upon a large boulder and summoned Inchedeeko to send him off to search out the smaller crags and crevices. Soon after that, she brought forth more servants, flying chasme demons, and sent them, too, scouring the mountainsides.

Still, it was nearly dark again when Inchedeeko finally returned with word that they had found some dwarves—spriggans actually—in guard positions along one boulder tumble just to the north.

The quasit led Malcanthet to the place, and the succubus, looking very much like a normal human woman, looking like Queen Concettina, actually, walked onto a flat stone in the midst of the guarded area.

"I seek Toofless and Komtoddy!" she called, her words echoing across the stones.

The response came in the form of a boulder flying for her head. She turned away at the last moment, and purposely let it just clip her. That sent her spinning, and she dropped to the stone as if it had been a lethal hit.

Malcanthet remained there, trying to hide her sneers and growls. She heard the heavy footsteps of her assailants nearing, and heard one giant mutter, "Bah, but ye killed her!"

She let the spriggans come closer. One even moved up and kneeled beside her, rolling her to see if she was alive.

He met her open eyes and she looked past him only for a moment to see the other half-dozen brutes climbing up onto the rock.

"Your friend there tried to hurt me," she whispered to that giant, her voice thick with magic. "To make me ugly. You do not wish me to be ugly . . ."

"'Ere, but why'd ye trow da rock!" the kneeling brute yelled, leaping up and spinning to face another of the clan. "Ye stupid goblin!"

"Who's ye callin' a gobbler?" the other retorted, poking a finger at the first.

Malcanthet rolled to a sitting position, smiling at the spectacle.

"Hey, but she's up!" a third behemoth said, but that didn't stop the one who had first gone to her, the one she had charmed, the one outraged beyond all reason at the brute who had tried to mar this most beautiful creature in all the world. So the charmed brute punched the finger-pointer right in the mouth, and tackled him as he staggered backward, the two of them rolling right off the stone.

A couple of others started for the pair to break up the row, but stopped fast at the crack of a whip and the crackle of a thunderbolt.

The giant hit by that whip bowed awkwardly to the side and crumbled to the ground. He tried to rise but flopped like a fish on land, unable to control half his body

"Ah, ye dog!" the nearest spriggan yelled, and threw a stone at the woman's face.

She slapped it aside, and when the brute followed up with a charge to bury her, she extended her free hand and stopped him as surely as if he had run into the side of a mountain. She closed her hand, bending his armor and pinching his skin under it. Then she casually threw him off to the side, launching him spinning through the air.

Her whip cracked again and the next nearest giant's face ripped open. That spriggan, too, dropped straight to the stone, gurgling and rocking in uncontrollable spasms.

"Take me to Komtoddy and Toofless *now*!" the succubus demanded. "Or I will find them myself and present them with your severed heads!"

As she threatened, a swarm of chasme descended over the area, wings humming, grotesque, bloated human faces leering hungrily at the spriggans.

Unsurprisingly, Malcanthet didn't hear any further argument.

❖ ❖ ❖

"Uн oн," Pikel said when Ivan crashed through their cottage door, the dwarf tumbling in and nearly falling on his face.

"Aye," Ivan told his brother and Regis, who was sitting at the dinner table, a full plate before him. "Ye get out, both o' ye. Get out and get runnin'!"

"Oooo."

"Running where?" Regis asked, starting to rise, pausing, taking one last bite, then hopping from his seat.

"Something . . . bad," Ivan stammered, and Regis helped him to a chair. "Something bad and they're knowin' I'm in it, and deep."

"They found Wulfgar," the halfling breathed.

"Oooo," said Pikel.

"Nah, not them, but someone . . . some*thing*, and something bad," Ivan tried to explain. "The queen—she ain't the queen! No, some demon thing."

"Huh?" Pikel and Regis asked together.

Ivan settled and patted his hand in the air to silence them. "Them guards came runnin' like they knew Wulfgar was in there," he explained. "They crashed through the queen's door and found her, or something that looked like her, but with wings like a bat and horns, and with a whip that took 'em—took *us*, down like nothing I e'er seen, I tell ye!"

"Oooo," said Pikel.

"And she had a mirror, and I seen Wulfgar in it!"

"His reflection," said Regis.

"No, him . . . inside," Ivan explained. "And she took it and flew out the window. Came down right in the garden, not far outside from here, but jumped away and flew out over the north wall. She got Wulfgar, whatever she might be, and ye got to get to her, and now."

"We," Regis corrected.

"Me brudder!" shouted Pikel.

"Nah, not me," Ivan said, shaking his head. "They're knowin' and they're comin'. Was meself who let Wulfgar in that room—if they knew he was in there, they're knowin' who put him there."

"You can't know that," said Regis, but even as he spoke, a call of "Ivan Bouldershoulder!" sounded not far from the house.

Pikel whistled at a vine hanging by the door, and the plant swung a length, hit the door, and sent it swinging closed.

"I can put 'em off, but ye got to find out where that thing went runnin'," Ivan explained. "I can tell 'em Wulfgar went in there to expose the demon, and if we can figure where the fiend went, they'll be thankin' me, not cuttin' off me head!"

"Oooo, me brudder," said Pikel.

"Go, go, go," Ivan urged, pushing Regis and his brother toward a large plant at the side of the kitchen, one whose considerable pot had no bottom, by design.

"Go where?" Regis asked. "They're right outside."

But Pikel took the halfling by the hand and reached for the plant with the stump of his other arm. In an instant, even as the cottage door began swinging in, Pikel and Regis were pulled into the plant, traveling down its stem to the roots, then to connecting roots carrying them along and out into the garden.

They came out in the tangle of a lilac bush, and looked back to see Ivan being tugged out of the house, his hands bound behind his back.

"Grr," said Pikel, moving, but Regis pulled him back under the leafy cover.

"The best thing we can do for your brother—"

"Me brudder!"

"Shh!" Regis begged. "Yes, the best thing we can do for your . . . for Ivan, is to find this . . . this . . . this whatever it was that took Wulfgar."

Pikel wagged his head in agreement, but then crinkled his nose as if in disgust.

"What do you know?" the halfling asked.

"Stinky," said Pikel and he climbed out of the lilacs and began hopping in circles.

"They're not that bad," Regis said, contorting out behind him and indicating the lilacs.

"No no no no," said Pikel, and he rushed in a wide arc, then stopped and sprinted to a spot, pointing to the ground and repeating, "Stinky."

When Regis got there, he saw the scar where a patch of garden grass was dead and rotted. He was about to say that it made no sense, as the rest of the lawn was healthy, but then he realized what Pikel was so excited about.

It was a footprint.

The demon imposter that took Wulfgar had left a trail that the plants knew about.

And Pikel could talk to plants.

◆ ◆ ◆

"GIVE ME THE gemstone," Malcanthet insisted.

Toofless Tonguelasher and Komtoddy exchanged nervous glances. How did this fiend know their names? She had asked for them specifically.

She thrust her hand out to Toofless emphatically. "I know you have it in your pocket," the succubus said. "This body senses its rightful inhabitant and leads me to you. I will have it now, or I will tear you apart and take it."

The spriggan was more than twice the succubus's height, but had no doubt that she could do just that, to say nothing of the group of grotesque demons that looked like a cross between a human and a housefly that crawled about the ceiling. Toofless reached into his pocket and produced the gemstone that held the trapped soul of Queen Concettina.

"I need a chamber," Malcanthet said. "When will the drow return?"

Again the spriggans exchanged confused looks, and both shrugged when they looked back at Malcanthet.

"Idiots," she said. "What is the finest chamber in your complex? Lead me there at once, and know that I will scour the whole of this place in the coming days and if I find one more appropriate, I will furnish it with spriggan-skin rugs."

The two spriggans had heard enough of the fight out on the rock to realize that she could, and probably would, do exactly that. So they led the demon off at a great pace to the lower levels of the Damaran side of Smeltergard. They moved swiftly and confidently to a specific room they had been fashioning for themselves.

Its door was iron-bound and made of a rich, green-gray stone flecked with bits of stark red: the bloodstone that gave this region its name. Toofless fumbled with a large key ring, locating the one for this particular door, which he began to insert into the keyhole.

But Malcanthet stopped him, roughly yanking the keychain from his hand and shoving him aside, a push that sent him skidding away. She considered the key, then another that seemed identical, and held that one out to the spriggan.

"Aye, dat one, too," Toofless confirmed.

Malcanthet grabbed the two keys in her hands, held them out to opposite sides, and pulled the ring apart. The torn ring and dozens of other large iron keys bounced noisily to the floor.

"Are there any others that will fit this door?" the succubus demanded.

The spriggans shook their heads vigorously.

"See that I am not disturbed," said Malcanthet. "Ever!"

The spriggans nodded emphatically.

Malcanthet unlocked the bloodstone door and swung it open, but paused before entering to look back at the intimidated pair. "Unless the Hunzrin drow return," she said. "Then inform me."

The two were still nodding when she slammed the door behind her.

Inside, the succubus found a large and roughly oval chamber comfortably lit by lichen and by some glowworms on the ceiling high above. The walls had been scraped and smoothed to minimize the shadows, and a chimney had been fashioned from the lone stalagmite-stalactite formation in the chamber, across from the door just more than halfway to the back wall. Its base had been shaped into an open hearth, with a pile of peat and logs nearby.

She could work with this, Malcanthet thought, scanning the place. Her gaze settled on the right-hand curving wall of the chamber and the most dominant and appealing feature of all: an underground pool some twenty feet across, the water still but clear enough for the demon to see fish occasionally flitting near the surface in the dim lichen and glowworm light.

She wasted no time in hanging her leering mirror over the hearth, facing the door, a suitable trap for any intruders.

She kicked a few logs into the hearth and created a ball of furiously burning flame in her upraised palm, then threw it in. The fireplace exploded into fiery life. And that served as the physical manifestation of Malcanthet's magical gate, which she first used to bring back Inchedeeko. The quasit came bearing gifts: her favorite dress, a black and red affair that crossed at her chest and hips, but was joined at those two places only by fabric on one side, leaving most of her stomach, her legs, and her arms bare.

Seduction was often her strongest play.

Inchedeeko brought her magical rings, her magical bracers, the necklace that stored spells, and her protective cloak.

"Search the pool and see that there are no threats within," she ordered, and the quasit leaped away.

Malcanthet rubbed her fingers and called again to the lower planes. This time, a large, vulture-like demon with a hooked beak and clawed arms hopped forth from the flames.

"Outside the door," she told the vrock. She summoned a second one soon after to stand guard with the first.

She brought in the chasme from the hallway and sent them through the flaming gate in the other direction, back to the Abyss, to fetch her belongings.

"Yes," she said when the buzzing fiends had gone, and she nodded. Already the chamber seemed more comfortable to her.

She could enjoy her visit here.

◆　◆　◆

"Ug," Pikel said to Regis, and the halfling understood to add "ly" to the truncated word.

The two crouched behind a wall of broken stones, staring down at the yawning entrance to a deep cave—a mining operation, they assumed from the piles of dark stone chips and dirt all about the tunnel. Goblins came up every so often, usually bearing another cart full of waste.

As ugly as the goblins were, though, Regis realized that Pikel was talking about the other creatures milling about. Some were giants, some dwarves, and all equally filthy and misshapen.

"Oooo," the pair said together when one giant moved to the side, trembling, his bones shaking violently and cracking with loud popping sounds as he shrank down to become, to their astonished eyes, a dwarf.

"How?" Regis whispered.

"Spriggan," Pikel answered, but Regis had no idea what that might mean except, of course, that Pikel had seen what he had just witnessed: the creature in front of them, other than the goblins at least, could change their size dramatically, from dwarf to giant, and quickly, and with their armor and other items appropriately shifting to accommodate the new size.

The two crouched back down behind the rocky berm.

"You are sure?" Regis asked quietly. "The demon creature went into that cave?"

"Uh-huh."

"Maybe she went by it," the halfling reasoned, trying to avoid having to sneak in there.

But Pikel quickly retorted, "Uh-uh," shaking his head emphatically.

"We should go back and tell the king," Regis remarked.

"Uh-uh," Pikel insisted, wagging his finger at the halfling.

"I don't know how we can get in there," Regis replied. He shifted and peeked once more over the berm, noting the dozens of dwarves and giants. "They've got the place fully guarded . . ."

He stopped when Pikel tugged at his arm, and when he looked at the dwarf, Pikel motioned to some trees beside the rocky entrance, on the side of the mound and down the side of the mountain.

The dwarf winked and led Regis away, taking a circuitous route to the copse. Grasping Regis's hand fully, Pikel started for the nearest tree.

"No, we can't," Regis whispered emphatically. "We might come up in the middle of a hundred of them!"

But Pikel just giggled and cast his spell, and he and Regis went right into the nearest tree and fell into another disconcerting root slide, flowing down through the rocks and to a darker place. They came out the exposed end of one root, some ten feet from the floor, and dropped down hard to a mossy bed.

Collecting himself, Regis took a deep breath of relief to discover that they were alone in this stretch of passageway. But that relief proved short-lived, for the sound of gruff voices came at them from around a close bend.

"Pikel!" the halfling breathed, and he tapped his beret, his form twisting and shifting in aspect and in hue, disguising him with the facade of a goblin.

"Hee hee hee," said Pikel, and before Regis could warn him to hide, and just before the approaching monsters came around the bend, the dwarf giggled and snapped his fingers, and in his place stood a mangy-looking dog, with one of its forelegs stubbed to match the dwarf's arm.

"You can do that?" Regis breathed, his eyes seeming as if they might just roll out of their sockets. Pikel had always called himself a druid, and so he was, and amazingly accomplished at it, it would seem!

Pikel's hackles went up and he began to growl as around the bend came a pair of goblins. They paused, clearly caught by surprise, and both settled their gazes on the dog.

One addressed Regis, though he could hardly understand the guttural language, given the dialect and the speed with which the little wretch was speaking. Regis did pick out the goblin word for "dinner," though whether the goblin was talking about dinner for the dog or of the dog, he couldn't quite be certain.

The latter, he thought, so he responded with a stern denial. Apparently Pikel had understood as well, Regis noted, for that little dog could certainly growl.

The goblins backed away a step, but just a step, and both brought forth mining picks.

Regis grabbed his dog by the tuft of its neck and held up his other hand to diffuse the situation.

"The dog is nervous since she returned," he said in his best goblin, which he knew wasn't very good.

The goblins eyed him suspiciously and did not relax, making him wonder if he'd said what he'd meant to say.

"She," Regis reiterated, and he lifted his arms out to the side to mimic great wings.

Both goblins nodded, and one asked him a question.

"She brought us," Regis answered. He thought the creature wanted to know who he was or why he was here, or, likely, both. "I am to deliver to her this demon dog," he improvised, "but I cannot find her."

The goblins looked at the three-legged dog with clear suspicion.

"Demon dog?" one asked.

Pikel went through a series of strange growls, and it occurred to Regis that he was casting a spell. Then he barked, and spewed a small cloud of stinking green smoke, and the goblins recoiled.

Pikel growled more insistently and ambled toward them.

"Show us where she is," said Regis. "The demon dog won't wait!"

One goblin pointed down and to the left, the other turned and ran off, and the first, as soon as it realized that it was alone, did likewise.

Regis looked at Pikel and shrugged. They couldn't go through the stone, but at least they now had a general direction.

So the goblin who was not a goblin and his demon dog who was not a demon or a dog started off down the dark corridors. They encountered more goblins and even a couple of the strange giants, and Regis always greeted them with, "The lady's dog," after which Pikel would bark a cloud of green, stinky gas, or whisper for all the roots in an area to tremble wildly, or coax some bats to fly around his head, or some other druidic trick that obviously seemed demonic to any onlookers.

With a bit more guidance, they came to a long, wide corridor bordered by several ramshackle doors, and with one large and perfectly fitted door made of bloodstone at the end. Two hulking guards that looked like a cross between a giant vulture and a huge man with great clawed hands and a beaked face that seemed as if it could peck through stone stood on either side. The demons weren't as tall as the giants, but appeared far more formidable, and certainly less persuadable.

"Now what?" the halfling in goblin form whispered to his demon dog.

Pikel bit Regis's pant leg and tugged him to the side, verily pulling him through a door. In that side chamber, the dwarf became a dwarf once more and rushed to the wall nearest their targeted room, feeling about the stone.

"What are you thinking?" Regis whispered. But he hushed fast and slipped very near the dwarf when a large form and several smaller ones passed outside the door. The companions heard female voices then, that of the demon posessing Concettina, they knew, and some others, melodic and lyrical and speaking the language of the drow.

"Pikel, what?" Regis mouthed silently and expressively, desperate to be away, but the dwarf just brought a finger to his pursed lips and stared at the door, then nodded and grinned as he heard the receding chatter. The group was moving away from the room and not toward it.

He went back to the crack in the wall, closing his eyes and feeling about, then shook his head happily.

"What?" Regis asked. "A root?"

Pikel smiled and grabbed his hand.

"It's just a crack!" Regis argued, louder than he intended, trying futilely to pull away.

But Pikel was already into his spell, and his form twisted and contorted and was sucked through the crack and into the root, tugging a terrified Regis in behind him.

The root-walking was disorienting and unnerving enough, of course, but doing so through tiny cracks in solid stone proved perfectly terrifying. Regis spent the entire magical journey with his mouth wide open in an unending, and unheard, scream.

They came out of the stone wall soon after, as if vomited by the rock, their corporeal forms reshaping as they exited the druid's root transit. Both of them tumbled down to the wet stone floor.

As soon as he collected his wits about him, helped by Pikel's "Ooo," Regis realized that they were in the demon's room. To his left was the same bloodstone door, but now from the other side, and hanging to his right, directly across from that, was the leering, demon-faced mirror.

"No!" Pikel whispered harshly and he slapped his hand across to turn the halfling's face as Regis looked at the mirror.

Regis stumbled aside and held up his hand, nodding to show the dwarf that he understood. Ivan's remarks about Wulfgar being in the mirror served as ample enough warning.

"That has to be it," Regis whispered. "The mirror that captured Wulfgar."

"Woofgar," Pikel agreed.

The halfling glanced around the circular chamber, noting the pool and a collection of strange furniture, including human-sized chairs and a table that all seemed to be made of mushroom stalks, and a circular bed with a grand red canopy all shot with golden designs, and with bed sheets the color of blood. The halfling shuddered as he noted shackles hanging from the headboard, and he thought, too, of Wulfgar's remarks regarding the creature they thought to be Queen Concettina.

Regis figured that he owed his friend a huge apology. Then he snickered, despite the desperate situation, thinking Wulfgar would probably thank him instead.

"We take the mirror and get out of here," Regis said to Pikel, who nodded happily.

The halfling untied his fine cape, thinking it wise to cover the glass.

◆ ◆ ◆

PIKEL WASN'T THE only one nodding. In the shadows of a high alcove above the mirror, Inchedeeko heard every word. The quasit, bound to its mistress, telepathically conveyed every syllable to Malcanthet, who was not far away.

"You will excuse me," the succubus queen told Charri Hunzrin and the others who had come to speak with her. "I have guests."

She rushed out of the room, extending her wings and half-running, half-flying down the length of the long corridor. Passing a side passage, she called to a group of goblin miners, yelling at them to fill the hall so that none could escape.

◆ ◆ ◆

REGIS HAD HIS cloak set in place over the mirror, which he and Pikel had lifted from its hooks and leaned against the hearthstone. Pikel slipped off to the side of the room to gather some vines to better secure the cloak for their desperate retreat, while the halfling congratulated himself for such a disciplined performance. Not once had he glanced at the glass.

"We'll get you out of there," he promised Wulfgar, and he thought to call to the man—perhaps the magic of the mirror would bring Wulfgar's image back to the glass for him to see.

He grabbed the edge of the cloak, thinking to lift it just enough to whisper for his friend, but he knew enough about these sorts of magical devices to back away from that foolish course.

A dozen thoughts careened through his mind—would Pikel be able to carry them out of there with the mirror as they had come in?

Could Regis put it in his pouch?

He dismissed that notion almost as soon as he had it, for the mirror and his pouch were apparently both extra-dimensional items, the combination of which, so he had been told, could lead to very, very bad outcomes.

With that unsettling thought in mind, he was doubly glad he hadn't accidentally looked at the mirror and been pulled in.

He sighed in relief then grunted in surprise as the room's door banged open. Regis spun to see a pair of chasme charging his way, and with the demon Concettina out in the hall and coming fast, and a horde of goblins behind her.

He drew his sword and yelled, "Pikel, run!" and wondered what in the world his little rapier was going to do against the charging brutes.

His crossbow wouldn't slow them, he knew he couldn't get to his dagger in time and free up the living snake garrotes, and his rapier would do little more than sting the beasts as they tore him apart. And he couldn't run, so he pulled his cloak off the mirror and fell to the side.

The vrocks skidded to a stop, their beaked faces swiveling, catching their own reflections in the mirror—which caught more than that!

In they went, and Regis staggered aside, running for the chamber's right-hand wall, where he and Pikel had come in. He could get there!

But Pikel couldn't. The dwarf was across the room, running hard behind the hearth and mirror, but the winged demon was in the chamber now, whip in hand.

"Pikel!" Regis screamed, and he drew out his hand crossbow and fired a dart at the succubus. He had no idea if he hit her, and if he did, it surely showed no effect. She cracked her whip into Pikel's side, sending him spinning and falling weirdly and hard with a tremendous "Oof!" and then a long and agonized, "Oooo."

The demon turned on Regis, hissing, her eyes blood red with fury.

And into the room came goblins, dozens of goblins.

"No!" the demon howled, but too late. There were the stupid goblins, and there was the exposed mirror.

Into the glass went a goblin, then a second, a third, a fourth until Malcanthet's Mirror of Life Trapping held a dozen and a half extra-dimensional compartments, and they weren't all filled with her prisoners.

Because when they were full, any additional creature caught by the magic and pulled in would expel, randomly, one of the other prisoners.

And powerful, malicious, cunning Malcanthet certainly had some prisoners she didn't want freed!

Regis ran to Pikel, lying broken near the pool. He slid down to the dwarf's side, begging Pikel to get them out of there.

"Oooo," the dwarf moaned. He tried to reply more fully, but his mouth drooped. Indeed, half of the dwarf, the side where Malcanthet's whip had struck him, seemed quite paralyzed. Regis tugged him to the wall.

In went a sixth goblin, and just an instant before Malcanthet could throw herself in front of the mirror to block any reflection, in went a seventh, the nineteenth prisoner.

And it became again the eighteenth prisoner as the mirror expelled a previous victim.

A hydra.

Huge and reddish in hue, the ten-headed creature came forth in fighting form, its necks swerving about each other, draconic maws snapping at the nearest goblins, biting off hands, arms, even a head before the goblins even realized it was there.

And then they scrambled and fled, but the hydra came after them, heads snaking out in all directions and breathing jets of fire.

"Oooo," cried Pikel.

Regis pulled at him furiously, and goblins came rushing at them. A line of fire washed over them.

Pikel heard scuffling and screaming and a crash of bodies and the hiss of water as the flames swept over him, burning him.

He cried out for Regis, for his brudder, for Woofgar, and he scratched and pulled and squirmed for the wall, reaching for a crack in the stone.

"Idiots!" he heard the demon cry, and Pikel desperately looked for Regis.

But there were just bodies, so many bodies, lying about, burning, and the hydra between the hearth and the door, and the demon at the hearth with the mirror, and some dark elves—oh, could it get worse!—in the doorway and falling back in surprise and terror.

A pair of hydra heads swerved Pikel's way. One swept back to the front of the room and spat a line of fire that dropped a group of goblins trying to get back to the door.

The other spat at poor, helpless Pikel.

In his hand, he felt the tip of a root.

◆ ◆ ◆

DRACONIC HEADS SWERVED for Malcanthet, their jailer, the fiend who had stolen the pyrohydra and thrown it into a nondescript cell for decades uncounted.

But she stood there, hardly amused, holding her mirror.

Perhaps most of the ten heads avoided looking into the glass, but one, at least, did not.

Into the mirror went the hydra once more, and out popped a very confused goblin, standing remarkably near to where it had been when the mirror snatched it in the first place.

It looked at the bat-winged woman curiously.

Malcanthet's whip cut the poor goblin in half before it could stupidly look into the mirror's magical glass once more.

"You may enter now," Malcanthet called to Charri Hunzrin and the others, which now included a group of spriggans, led by Toofless and Komtoddy.

"What was that?" the drow priestess asked.

"Intruders," the demon said, fixing a judgmental stare on Toofless. "Your corridors are not as secure as you believe," she added in withering tones, and the spriggans fell back.

"A fire-breathing hydra?" Charri Hunzrin asked, shaking her head. "Good fortune that you had the mirror in hand!"

"Good fortune that all that came out when the beast was caught was a goblin," Malcanthet corrected. "I assure you, drow, there are worse creatures in my toy."

"I have never seen such an item," Charri said.

"Don't look closely," the demon quipped. "It was a gift from a powerful lich who resides in a tomb in a land you call Chult, who uses the souls trapped within the glass to feed his undeath." She turned her head a bit, as if looking somewhere far away. "I should return it soon for my rewards and get another. Now that it is full, I cannot use it without releasing a prisoner, and some are better left entrapped."

The dark elves backed away, and Malcanthet laughed at them.

◆ ◆ ◆

PIKEL ROLLED OUT into the copse of trees beside the tunnel entrance. He couldn't stand, and could hardly see, his eyes singed from the hydra fires, half of his body still numb from the lightning crackle of the demon's whip.

He could hear the giants not far away, all excited and chattering about some disturbance deep within their home.

"Regis," the dwarf muttered under his breath, and he pictured again the burning bodies all around him in the chamber and could smell that stench still—from his own beard.

How he wanted to go back in there and rescue his friend, and the other one, too!

"Woofgar," he lamented.

But there was nothing he could do. Even if his body somehow healed immediately, what might he do against the likes of that mighty demon?

If he had known the truth of Malcanthet, that she was the succubus queen, consort of the godly Demogorgon, hated rival of Graz'zt, he would have realized that truth even more profoundly and hopelessly.

He tried to walk, but could not. He started to crawl, but it hurt him so. He thought of becoming a dog again, but what good might that do for him with half his side paralyzed?

He cast a spell of healing, and it felt good, but did little, and a moment later, he realized that the exertion of the spellcasting was worse than the healing it had accomplished. So again, Pikel focused on how he might get away and get some help. He wanted to become a bird and fly off, but he only had one arm. A one-winged bird probably wouldn't soar very far.

And besides, his side was dead, killed by the whip, at least for now.

He heard the giant voices again, and realized that things within must be settling down. He was vulnerable, and he didn't have the spell power left to take his druidic root journey.

But he could transform himself again, and so the clever dwarf became a snake. Even with half his body broken, Pikel found that he could slither.

He slithered out of the copse. He slithered down the rocky mountainside, making careful note of the markings so that he could find this place again.

The sun set and still he slithered.

He slithered onto a road and kept going.

Long into the night, he slithered, and then he slithered to the side of the road and coiled up, thinking he would be better in the morning and that he would have his spells renewed and so could slide through the roots back to Helgabal.

But his sleep was filled with nightmares inspired by the magic of the demon's whip. When the rising sun came into his eyes, Pikel found that he was a dwarf once more, that he was worse off and not better. The poison or magic the demon had struck him with had flowed deeper within. He could not pray, could not ask for spells, could not think clearly enough to begin to remember anything or cast anything.

He couldn't even become a snake again.

So he crawled and clawed.

He inched his way along the road, ignoring his breaking fingernails, fighting through his labored breathing as his lungs would hardly answer his call for breath.

The sun went high overhead, a hot summer day full of buzzing bees and chirping birds.

The sweating dwarf crawled.

He wanted to stop, to just surrender, to let himself die and be done with the pain.

"Woofgar," he whispered through lips that would barely move, and he knew he had to crawl.

So he did.

◆ ◆ ◆

SUNLIGHT AWAKENED PIKEL again, but to his surprise and confusion, he was in a bed and not on the road.

A comfortable bed in a clean room. Pain wracked his body, demonic poison biting at him, whispering to him to let go and die.

He turned his head to the window and watched the rising sun and whispered for his brudder.

"Ah, ye're awake!" he heard and he tried to turn his head.

A fat, red-cheeked face came over him, a wide smile and smiling blue eyes. "We thought we'd lost ye!" the woman said. "Oh Chalmer!"

"What, woman, what?" another voice said, a man's voice, and Pikel managed to turn enough toward the open door to see an even fatter face, and one lined by great gray sideburns.

"Ah, so ye made it through another night," the man named Chalmer said. He looked to the woman, who Pikel figured to be his wife. "I'll go get him some soup."

"Woofgar!" Pikel managed to breathe.

"Oh, but he's talkin'!" said the woman.

"Woo . . . woof . . ."

Chalmer laughed. "Or barking," he said. "Ah, but keep him comfortable. He won't live much longer, to be sure."

"Woof . . ." Pikel whimpered, wheezed, and he began to cough.

He looked plaintively at the departing man, and into a common room beyond, with many folk milling about or sitting at tables and having breakfast.

Voices floated in, the sounds of life, and Pikel could only listen.

Chalmer and his wife tried to feed him, but he couldn't swallow and nearly choked, coughing.

So they tucked him in tighter.

"I'll sit with him," the woman informed her husband, and he left the room, leaving the door open, as she bade him.

Pikel just lay still and listened to life, and knew that his own neared its end.

He perked up a bit sometime later, though, when a finely dressed halfling went by the door—Regis!

But no, it was not Regis. He could tell by the voice as the halfling woman chatted with her friend.

Pikel could only catch snatches of their conversation and of others in the room, but held onto them fiercely, wanting to live his last moments aware of the world around him.

He heard of an army mustering outside of Helgabal, and it gave him hope that King Yarin was going to find the demon, and maybe Wulfgar.

He heard about rumors of a dragon flying over the fields to the east, and he smiled, remembering the rumors of dragons that had come to Yarin's Court only a couple of years before.

He heard the halflings talking about some strange goings-on at the Monastery of the Yellow Rose.

"They've let a drow into their order," one said with obvious disbelief, and the mention of dark elves alarmed Pikel—he had seen drow at the demon's chamber in the mines.

"Aye," the halfling woman replied. "But not just any. It's Drizzt Do'Urden himself, I've been told, come from the Sword Coast."

Pikel's eyes popped open wide and he struggled mightily. The woman grabbed him to hold him steady and cried out for her husband.

"He's in his death throes!" she told Chalmer when he rushed into the room, several others crowding in behind him. "Oh, the poor dear."

Pikel fought through the pain. "Drizzit Dudden!" he gasped. "Drizzit Dudden!"

Chalmer and his wife looked at each other, perplexed. "What?"

"Drizzit Dudden?" echoed a halfling voice from the door.

# Chapter 24 ◈

# *The Heretic*

A STARTLED DRIZZT, PANTING FOR BREATH, RETRACTED HIS arm and saw blood dripping from the end of his glassteel blade.

"Why do you hesitate?" Entreri demanded, almost chasing him now, though his voice was pained. "You know me as a fiend! You know all as a grand lie!"

"Shut up!" Drizzt cried, and he came forward to end it, to end Artemis Entreri.

And Artemis Entreri stood straight and closed his eyes, his arms out wide, inviting the death blow.

But it was Drizzt who toppled, right after his scimitars fell to the ground, the drow crouching in agony—and indeed he was wracked by great turmoil and pain. He was sure, so sure, that it was all a lie, a grand deception to utterly destroy him, and yet, in this moment of truth, in this last desperate gasp of defiance, he found that he hadn't the strength to do it. He could not strike down this man he had come to know as an ally.

As he could not before strike down Catti-brie.

And so he was lost, and the black wings of doubt and terror chased him to the ground and held him there, sobbing.

Artemis Entreri stood over him, saying nothing.

◆ ◆ ◆

KIMMURIEL TOOK YVONNEL'S hand and sent his psionic wave out to the slumping ranger, and that wave carried Yvonnel's spell, carried her consciousness.

Her mouth moved, winding a pair of chants, one divine and one arcane, dispelling magic and curing disease. With Kimmuriel's help, she journeyed through the ranger's recent memories, following Drizzt back to the Monastery of the Yellow Rose. At all the points where Drizzt had forced himself to claim deception against the reality around him, Yvonnel assaulted those doubts. They appeared as foggy gray curtains to her, and she easily tore them down and pressed onward, backward in time, to the next curtain of doubt and the next beyond that.

Drizzt's remembered path led them back to Luskan. The thick curtain that had precipitated the attack against Catti-brie was torn asunder, leaving Drizzt naked with the truth that he had almost killed his beloved.

Not some fiend, but his beloved Catti-brie. Just Catti-brie. Really Catti-brie!

They were back in Menzoberranzan and House Do'Urden, and through Drizzt's recollections, Yvonnel witnessed the death of Zaknafein.

And tore the curtain down.

Then back in the tunnels they went, descending from Gauntlgrym on the journey to Menzoberranzan, and there Yvonnel found the initial intrusion of the Abyssal Plague, a wall of confusion, depression, and doubt, an unwinding of Drizzt's reality.

Her spells of healing slammed into that wall, chipping some darkness away, but it was not as easy as tearing down a curtain anymore.

"Give me this, Lady Lolth," she begged, knowing that one standing nearby could answer her prayers.

She slammed into that wall of blackness once more and was repelled—but she held out hope, for it wasn't Drizzt trying to fight her. He was broken, a witness and not a participant, as she had anticipated.

"Yiccardaria," she whispered, and was heard.

A surge of magical strength coursed through her divine spell, spinning and diving like a drill, tossing black flakes aside as it punctured the wall of Abyssal doubt.

And there was lightness beyond, and reality beyond, and memories—trusted memories!—beyond.

The priestess came out of her spellcasting trance and staggered back under the weight of the magic she had evoked. She looked across the way, to the kneeling and sobbing Drizzt, the broken drow.

The torn masterpiece.

◆ ◆ ◆

IN HIS MIND, he was atop Kelvin's Cairn, his thoughts spinning and dulled from the encounter with Dahlia. She had killed him.

But Catti-brie was there, and Bruenor and Regis, rushing to him and to Guenhwyvar, and the warm healing magic flooded through him.

And Wulfgar was there.

Drizzt opened his eyes and gasped until he could steady his breath, staring at Artemis Entreri's feet.

But holding fast to that moment atop Kelvin's Cairn.

For it was real.

All of it.

◆ ◆ ◆

"BRILLIANTLY EXECUTED," SAID a female voice behind Kimmuriel and Yvonnel and both turned to see Yiccardaria's approach.

Yvonnel knew the handmaiden would return, but Kimmuriel gasped.

"Heretic," Yiccardaria said, and that was enough—too much, actually. Kimmuriel fell into his psionics and warp-stepped away.

Back to Illusk, beneath Luskan, Yvonnel figured.

Yiccardaria laughed.

"You could have stopped his retreat," said Yvonnel.

"I am a handmaiden of Lolth," Yiccardaria replied. "Of course."

"But you let him go. So Lady Lolth approves of my work here, and of Kimmuriel's help."

"Or she simply doesn't care about that mind flayer lover, either way," said Yiccardaria.

Yvonnel nodded. "But you—she—granted me the spells to defeat the Abyssal Plague within Drizzt."

Yiccardaria walked up beside Yvonnel and looked to the field beyond, where Drizzt remained on his knees, face in hands, weapons lying beside him.

"Did you cure it or break him?" the handmaiden asked.

"He sees the truth now, the truth that was always there in front of him. That is my guess, at least. His reactions are what I would expect from one of his conscience."

"Good," said Yiccardaria. "Then you have been granted your wish, to heal him that you may make his death all the more exquisite." She held her hand out to the field and the ranger. "I would prefer to watch you turn him into a drider, and I will show you how."

"No."

The simple answer stopped Yiccardaria before she could ever get going. "No? You prefer to simply torture him to death?"

"No."

"There will be no easy death," the handmaiden said. "That is the bargain. And weave no more clever traps for the heretic Drizzt. If you wish him to live for a bit longer, then make of him a drider. If not that, then begin your torture and I will relay his screams to the Spider Queen. They will please her."

"No."

"No, what?"

"No, I will weave no clever plans to destroy him," Yvonnel said. "I will not torture him, or kill him, and certainly will not turn him into a drider,"

The handmaiden stared at her threateningly. "There is no bargain to be had here," she warned. "You will do as we agreed."

"Will I?" Yvonnel asked, and she looked past Yiccardaria and gave a little nod.

The handmaiden swung around, and even called "Kimmuriel!" as if suspecting the two had plotted this blasphemy.

But it was not Kimmuriel Oblodra standing behind her.

It was Kane, Grandmaster of Flowers.

Without a word, with speed the demon couldn't begin to anticipate, the monk delivered a right cross into the handmaiden's pretty drow face, hitting her so hard he knocked her right out of her disguise. She resembled a lump of mud, or a half-melted candle with waving tentacles again, planted on the ground where the drow woman had stood.

She flailed, but those tentacles weren't really aimed, as Yiccardaria was trying vainly to get past the stunning power of Kane.

He hit her again, right and left, and leaped up high to drop a devastating double-kick upon her. He back flipped off her, landing facing her. He unloaded a barrage so brutal and forceful that Yvonnel found herself inadvertently backing away.

The handmaiden never had a chance, never even managed a single block or retaliating swing.

She just sank down to the ground, a bubbling pile of oozing, melting mud.

Kane bowed to his defeated opponent and stood straight, looking at Yvonnel, and the woman knew she was wearing a face full of trepidation. She had never witnessed such overwhelming, controlled brutality, such speed, precision, and sheer power, and especially not from a seemingly unarmed human.

"And now, Lolth will declare me a heretic," Yvonnel said with a shrug. "I am in good company, though."

"Is he really cured?" the monk asked, looking out at the field.

"He did not expel me when I went into his mind with the truth," Yvonnel explained. "He was broken, with nothing to lose and in full crisis."

"As you predicted."

The woman nodded. "Until this moment, Drizzt could not be cured because he could not trust the healer. Now, what choice did he have?"

"Then let us go and see," said Kane, and he led Yvonnel out of the copse of trees and onto the field.

Drizzt was still on his knees, Entreri standing beside him. The drow looked up at the approach of Kane and Yvonnel, his eyes going wide indeed when he saw Gromph's daughter.

"Well met again, Drizzt Do'Urden," Yvonnel said.

Drizzt glanced at his scimitars, lying beside him on the ground.

"Yes, I do believe that you would more easily strike me down than you ever could Catti-brie, or Artemis Entreri, it would seem," Yvonnel said, and those lavender eyes fixed upon her once more.

"You know the truth," Yvonnel announced. "You are cured."

"And?" Drizzt asked, and the woman shrugged.

"And so you are free," Yvonnel replied. "We will get you back to Luskan and Catti-brie. All is well there, and proceeding with brilliant magic and beauty. Yet there is no satisfaction in Catti-brie's eyes, I fear."

Drizzt tilted his head a bit, curious.

"Because of you, of course," said Entreri. "She is heartbroken, but that too is soon to be cured."

"Is it?" Drizzt asked, staring directly at Yvonnel again. "Is this your ultimate or penultimate play regarding my . . . future?"

"I hope it will not prove to be my last adventure with you," Yvonnel admitted, and that made Entreri's eyes widen as much as Drizzt's, which made the woman simply laugh. "But it is the last of this journey we have walked together—yes, the ultimate play. I give to you your thoughts untwisted, your heart trusting, your path your own to choose."

"Why?"

"Because you have earned it, and I would be a lesser and petty thing to allow my surprise at your resilience, at the power of your love, to lead me to jealousy instead of, perhaps, enlightenment. And I am not a lesser and petty thing."

"I am free?"

"Of course."

"With no debt owed?

"None to me." She looked to Kane. "As for the monastery . . ."

"No debt owed . . ." Kane began, but he looked askew at Drizzt for a moment, then changed his mind. "There is one thing I would ask of you."

◆ ◆ ◆

DRIZZT WATCHED THE candle burn out—a full candle, a burn measured in hours and not minutes.

For nearly three hours, he had remained in his stance, his posture perfect, his breathing slowed and smooth, his thoughts blissfully empty. He had never come close to this length of time, not one-tenth of the candle had burned before his previous collapses.

Now the whole of it was melted, and Drizzt felt as if he could go on—and he expected that he would be doing exactly that when Grandmaster Kane entered the room. But the monk motioned for him to stand, and did so with a look of approval, joy even.

"There is no need to go further at this time," Kane said.

"Why? Why is there a limit?"

"There are not six in the order who could see a candle through its burn," Kane explained. "To get to this place, this length, one must hold to pure inner peace." The monk nodded. "I can confirm the words of Yvonnel. You are indeed cured of your malady, Drizzt Do'Urden."

"I am," the drow replied. "And I am anxious to be home." He gave a little laugh. "And at the same time, I am intrigued by this place and these teachings."

"You have many years of life before you. Close no doors behind as you journey on."

Drizzt nodded and followed Kane out of the room. To Drizzt's surprise, the monks had prepared a feast for him, in his honor and in celebration of his cure. Artemis Entreri was there, which pleased him.

Yvonnel was there, which confused him.

Kane sat him right next to the woman, with Entreri on the other side of her and Afafrenfere flanking Drizzt.

"Yes, there is much you do not know," Yvonnel said with a laugh, looking into the doubts plainly etched on Drizzt's face.

"I have left Menzoberranzan behind," she explained. "I suspect that the Spider Queen hates me more than she hates you now."

"You sound pleased by that."

"Amused," Yvonnel corrected. "It will pass. Lolth has more pressing problems than a runaway priestess."

"A priestess no more, I would expect."

"We shall see. Lady Lolth is more complicated than most would imagine. My surprises, like your own, likely amuse her more than they anger her, for they throw her children into chaos. You understood that about yourself, did you not, Drizzt Do'Urden?"

He shook his head, not catching on.

"All the time as you ran from your heritage, to the battles you waged against drow, even when your dwarf friend killed my namesake—a most painful memory, I assure you—you were unwittingly doing the work of Lolth."

Drizzt bristled at that, sitting straight.

"Take no offense," Yvonnel clarified. "You were not serving Lolth, but your actions surely did, for she thrives on strife and chaos and conflict. A harmonious Menzoberranzan bores her and allows her devout followers too much time to consider things anew, and so she will never let it be that way."

Drizzt relaxed, but still couldn't quite manage to blink.

"Perhaps someday we will take it from her," Yvonnel said.

"It?"

"Menzoberranzan," said the woman. "And our own destinies. Is that not something you have desired?"

"You think to lead a revolution?"

"Our lives are long," said Yvonnel. "Who knows what changes a millennium might bring?"

Drizzt was about to make a snide remark that perhaps Yvonnel would fall back under Lolth's spell, but he held the words and instead considered the great changes he had seen in the world over the course of two centuries.

The journey forward was a somewhat circular path, but rarely did it wind up in exactly the same place.

There was always a surprise.

And so it was the very next morning, just as Drizzt, Yvonnel, and Entreri were preparing to leave to find Tazmikella, when a tired and dirty halfling came galloping up the hill on a tired and dirty pony.

"I seek the drow named Drizzt Do'Urden!" she shouted to the monks who stood on the porch of the monastery's grand front door, with Drizzt and the others saying their farewells to the masters of the order. "Or Drizzit Dudden, or something like that!" the halfling added frantically.

"Drizzit Dudden?" Drizzt whispered. It was a curious mash-up of his name, one he had only heard from a single fellow a long, long time before.

❖ ❖ ❖

WE SHOULD BE *away*, Denderida's fingers flashed to Priestess Charri.

*Malcanthet contained the threat,* Charri's hands responded.

*For now. There will be more.*

Charri Hunzrin walked to the ill-fitting door of the chamber the spriggans had provided for her and her entourage. She certainly sympathized with the sentiments Denderida was expressing, but there were other matters in play less favorable to that course.

House Hunzrin had brought Malcanthet to the surface, purposefully so and without the blessing of House Baenre or the explicit guidance of Lolth. It behooved Charri and the others to make sure the succubus was fully contented with their performance, or she would surely report back to Matron Mother Baenre.

"Another tenday," Charri said.

"A tenday in this filthy place," one of the others lamented, and Charri didn't scold her. How could she disagree? She preferred even stinky goblins and orcs to these utterly disgusting spriggans, and it wasn't even a close comparison.

Her fingers flashed to Denderida, *Go to Toofless and secure us a place nearer the surface, and nearer to Vaasa. If trouble comes to Malcanthet, then let Malcanthet and her spriggan allies handle it.*

Denderida nodded, and soon after, the drow were marching fast to the northwest along the tunnels of upper Smeltergard, to areas far less inhabited, and, Charri believed, far preferable.

◆ ◆ ◆

THEY TOOK DIRECTIONS from the Kneebreaker, a fine middle-aged woman named Brouha, but did not invite her to ride along. If she was about to take offense to that, surely her opinion was changed and her eyes opened wide when Artemis Entreri dropped an obsidian figurine to the ground and summoned a black-as-coal, hellish horse—a nightmare—all fiery hooves and smoking breath.

And as the assassin scrambled up onto his mount, Drizzt blew a whistle and a second mount appeared, seeming far, far away. Even from this apparently great distance, though, all gathered on the front porch of the monastery could see the dramatic contrast. This one was no hellish beast but a unicorn, brilliantly white and with a beautiful horn.

One stride, two strides, three strides later and the apparent distance was revealed to be an illusion, or some boundary between the planes. The mount stood tall, shining in the daylight, pacing right beside Drizzt.

He went up to his seat, and as Artemis Entreri offered his hand to Yvonnel, who climbed up beside him, Drizzt did likewise to Grandmaster Kane.

The monk shook his head. "I will meet you at Chalmer's house," he said. "I know the place and would like to do some scouting first."

"Our mounts will not tire and we will ride through the night," Drizzt replied.

"You will not arrive long before me," Kane promised, and he offered the drow a wink.

Drizzt nodded. He had seen too many inexplicable feats from this man to argue the point.

Off they went, riding hard to the northeast, keeping the higher peaks of the Galena Mountains to their left. They bent around to due north as the mountains curved, and soon found the road. With the morning sun, nearly a hundred miles behind them, they came to an intersection of several roads, though most were little more than trails. In that many-corners area, they found a cluster of houses, exactly as the halfling had described.

Drizzt was at Pikel's bedside before the guests in the common room had even begun their breakfasts.

The dwarf's face was ashen. He somehow opened one eye, just a bit, and even managed to whisper "Drizzit Dudden" and grin, though the effort made him slip away a bit more.

"Do something!" Drizzt bade Yvonnel, who stood with Entreri at the door.

"Would you have me commune with Lady Lolth?" the priestess asked skeptically, holding her hands out wide. "She'll not grant me any spells of consequence at this time."

"You have nothing?"

"Minor spells onl—"

"Use them!" Drizzt cried. "All of them, any of them!"

Yvonnel nodded and moved to Pikel's side. Just in examining the dwarf, she understood that she could offer nothing more than the temporary relief of those minor spells that required no intervention from the goddess or her handmaidens.

She looked closer at the dwarf's wounds. Somewhere deep in her memories, deep in the memories of Yvonnel the Eternal, she recognized this wound. She had seen it before, she was certain, though she couldn't quite place it.

But she understood the nature of it.

She cast a few minor healing spells, which seemed to make the poor, battered dwarf relax a bit.

"Perhaps I can do more than I believed," she told Drizzt. "This wound is rooted in magic, and, like much of the Abyssal powers, is as much arcane as it is divine."

She cast again, a different sort of chant, a magic-user's cadence and not that of a priestess.

Pikel breathed easier and opened his eyes.

"Drizzit Dudden," he said more clearly, and with a genuine smile.

Drizzt and Yvonnel changed places once more, with Yvonnel whispering into his ear as they passed, "It is temporary. He will likely be dead before this day is passed and there is nothing I can do."

Drizzt absorbed the words without letting his smile break completely, and he knelt beside Pikel and took the dwarf's hand.

"Woofgar," Pikel said, shaking his head.

"Woofgar?"

"Woofgar! Woofgar, and Regis," Pikel said.

"Wulfgar?" Drizzt cried, and he turned to the others.

"Shh," said Pikel, and he began to cough.

"Give me some time with him," Drizzt bade the others, and they left the room, closing the door to let Drizzt hear Pikel's tale.

◆ ◆ ◆

DRIZZT EMERGED FROM the room hours later, shaking his head at the startling revelations. He recounted what he had learned to Yvonnel, Entreri, and Kane, who, not surprisingly, was there as well.

It was a short story of a complex of dwarves who could become giants and a demonic winged woman who stole the identity of the Queen of Damara and now had "Woofgar" entrapped behind the glass of some magical mirror deep in the bowels of the mines.

"That's all?" Entreri asked.

He nodded.

"You were in there the entire morning!" Entreri protested.

"Have you ever had a conversation with Pikel Bouldershoulder?" Drizzt asked sharply, and his lavender eyes flared with some inner anger, or inner pain, that warded any further questions.

The ranger sighed, and he could hardly believe that he had found his old friend in this time and place, as Pikel's life neared its end, and he could believe even less that he had lost another dear friend, poor Regis, once again.

But then one more detail of Pikel's rambling did occur to Drizzt. "He said there were dark elves in the dwarven—or giant, or whatever they are—caves."

"Drow?" Yvonnel echoed, and that notion resonated with many possibilities for her. "Did he say who?" she asked, leaning forward.

"He got a fleeting glance, no more. They were priestesses of substantial rank, though, I believe. Pikel described the gown of one, and if his memory is correct, it is nothing I would expect any but a noble daughter to wear."

Yvonnel nodded. It was beginning to come together for her then, particularly given the claim of demonic possession taking the queen.

"What can you tell me about this Queen of Damara?" she asked Kane.

"Queen Concettina," he answered. "There is quite a bit of talk about her on the roads about Helgabal."

"When?" Entreri asked skeptically.

"Last night, when I was there," said Kane, and Drizzt was not surprised.

"That's a hundred miles to the east," Entreri protested, but Kane just nodded.

"King Yarin has mustered his army," the great monk went on, "though they know not where to go. The rumors say that Queen

Concettina was stolen by a conspiracy, one involving a demon, a barbarian from Icewind Dale, and a halfling from Aglarond."

A slight breeze would have knocked Drizzt over.

"Do you know the history of King Yarin's wives?" Kane asked, and when none replied, the monk told them the tales of Drielle and those who had come before her, of the king's embarrassments and the executions and the statues in his gardens wearing pigeons as heads. He finished by explaining that Pikel had worked in those very gardens and went back to the conspiracy that was being whispered in the area of Helgabal regarding the conspirators.

"The halfling and the barbarian, a demon and a dwarf named Bouldershoulder," Kane finished, and he and the others turned as one to the door of Pikel's room.

"Then they will come for him," Entreri reasoned.

"No," Drizzt explained, for Pikel had expressed some related fears to him. "Not Pikel, but his brother, Ivan, who is likely in the king's dungeons even now, if not already executed."

"Go and give the king's army direction," Yvonnel told Kane.

"I have to go straightaway to the caves," Drizzt said, "or I would go with you to speak for Ivan Bouldershoulder, as fine a dwarf as I've ever known."

Kane's expression told Drizzt that he understood the subtle undercurrents of that remark, and that gave Drizzt hope. It would take more than a dungeon door and a few jailers to hold back Grandmaster Kane.

"To the caves, then!" said Entreri, and he looked at his ranger friend and offered a grim and determined nod.

"I have a few other things I must attend, for all our sake, though expect that I will meet you there," Yvonnel told the pair.

"Take some rest and some food before you leave," Kane bade them, but he didn't heed his own advice before he rushed out of Chalmer's hospitable house and ran off so fast down the eastern road toward Helgabal, Drizzt doubted that Andahar could have kept pace with him.

✦ ✦ ✦

"WE'RE GOING TO go get Wulfgar," Drizzt assured Pikel a short while later, after a brief respite. "And we won't forget Ivan, I promise."

"Me brudder," Pikel whispered, his voice very thin, and his grip—Drizzt held his hand—weak.

"Rest easy, my friend," Drizzt said, patting his hand. He looked back through the opened doorway, where Yvonnel waited. She had promised to use every healing spell she could muster on Pikel again now that she, too, had found a bit of rest.

In the common room, Drizzt ate a small meal with Entreri as the two plotted their course, figuring that if the information Pikel had given Drizzt was accurate, and Kane's directions correct, they could find these caves before nightfall.

Yvonnel returned from Pikel's bedside soon after, gave a little nod at the pair, and moved to a side room the innkeeper had offered, fetching a waiting pitcher of water from the bar as she passed.

"Divination," Entreri explained, and Drizzt nodded.

"I expect that she knows something, or many things, that we do not," the drow answered.

"There is a lot happening," Entreri replied, and he gathered up his weapon belt and strapped it around his waist as he headed for the door, obsidian figurine in hand.

A few moments later, the pair thundered along the road to the north, toward the foothills.

"Revenge for the dwarf," Entreri told Drizzt when their pace slowed and a narrow trail climbed, exactly as Pikel had described it to Drizzt.

"And for Regis," Drizzt replied. "One you know well."

Entreri could only shrug, for there was little he wanted to say regarding the halfling friend of Drizzt Do'Urden. In another life, Regis had lost a finger to the blade of Artemis Entreri, and that wound had reappeared on his new body, curiously.

"You would have liked him, had you found the chance to know him better," Drizzt told the man. "There was so much more to Re . . .Rumblebelly, than most could ever see."

"And Wulfgar?"

"Aye, certainly so."

"Then let's get him out of the looking glass, and go get the dwarf's brother away from the king," Entreri said. "I find that I am liking this King Yarin less and less with each tale of him I hear."

"From all I can tell, you are not alone."

◆　◆　◆

LATER THAT SAME day, as night began to fall, Yvonnel paced the room anxiously after several failed scrying attempts. She was looking for a demon, but gained little assistance from the Spider Queen or her minions.

Yvonnel told herself that that lack of cooperation had less to do with her current status with Lolth and more to do with Lolth's wise decision to keep herself away from the demon princes and lords and queens she had loosed upon the Prime Material Plane.

After regaining her composure, she returned to the bowl of water and cast again her spell of clairvoyance.

Through the powers of the pool, her vision went to the Galena Mountains, her magic following the same trail the dwarf had described to Drizzt. She had already seen the entrance to this complex, guarded by giants and dwarves, but had become lost in the maze within, with no sense of demonic energy to guide her.

So this time she entered and called upon the enchantment to guide her to not the demon in possession of Queen Concettina's body but to the Hunzrin drow.

She could only hope that they were still around.

And so they were, though far, far along the tunnels to the north, gathered in a room and plotting over some maps laid out on a table. She recognized Charri, First Priestess of the mercantile House, and another she thought to be Denderida, a well-known scout. The other three women in the room were clearly of lesser stature.

Yvonnel listened in on their conversation and nodded knowingly as they plotted about distributing beautiful jewelry to the surface to unsuspecting kings and queens, jewelry most poisonous to the wearer for in its gems and baubles would lurk a demon, ready to take control, as Malcanthet had done to the Queen of Damara.

Yvonnel fell back from the bowl.

"Malcanthet," she whispered, nodding, for that had been her fear when Drizzt had recounted the dwarf's tale. Yvonnel the Eternal certainly knew the Succubus Queen, and her memories of the extensive power of that Abyssal denizen were not lost on the new Yvonnel.

She had suspected that it was this particular demon when Drizzt spoke of the magical, life-trapping mirror. In days long past, Malcanthet had entered such a bargain with the lich Acererak to fill one of these most vile toys with souls and return it to Acererak's tomb.

Malcanthet was a known consort of Demogorgon, and so it followed logically that she must not have been far from Menzoberranzan when the corporeal manifestation of the Prince of Demons had been obliterated. And the Hunzrins had ushered her safely away, so it would seem.

Or perhaps, not so safely.

Yvonnel produced a scroll from her bag and unrolled it on the table beside the bowl. She remembered Gromph's refusal to teleport her to Damara to find Drizzt, when he had reminded her of the risk of teleporting to an area little known and unprepared and had insisted that no risk was too small for him to accept it for the sake of Drizzt Do'Urden.

Yvonnel looked back from the teleport parchment to the bowl. Transporting herself magically to an underground location, particularly one she knew only through brief scrying, was more difficult by far, for if she came in too high or too low, the stone would take her.

Coming back to corporeal form inside a stone wasn't a pleasant way to die.

For a moment, she couldn't believe that she was even contemplating this dangerous spell for the sake of the heretic Do'Urden.

But that was for just a moment, and with a growl of determination, Yvonnel went into the arcane chant, felt the energy building all around her, and stared into the bowl, examining the image of her destination.

She stepped out of the spell, to the shock of five drow women, right between Charri Hunzrin and Denderida.

"Does Matron Mother Quenthel know that you have brought a demon queen from the Underdark and to the surface of Faerûn?" she asked pointedly before the shock of her arrival could even begin to be appreciated.

Charri Hunzrin's eyes widened and she fell back as Yvonnel pressed forward, the dangerous young Baenre's face barely an inch from the startled gaze of the Hunzrin priestess.

The priestess stuttered and Yvonnel leaned in closer, her eyes flaring in direct threat.

"Lady Baenre," another of the Hunzrin clan began to protest, and Yvonnel snapped her head around and silenced the impudent child with a withering glare.

That break allowed Charri Hunzrin to compose herself enough to remark, "Our designs on transporting demons to the World Above via the gemstone phylacteries was known to the Ruling Council."

"Including the Succubus Queen?" a skeptical Yvonnel asked.

Charri fumbled unsuccessfully for an answer.

"Would not Lady Lolth desire such a thing?" Denderida offered. "It is the spread of chaos and the removal of a threat to Menzoberranzan in one swoop, for surely Malcanthet was not pleased with the destruction of Demogorgon."

"She told you this?" Yvonnel asked, letting her gaze drop over the scout.

Denderida shrugged, but Charri added, "It is a reasonable assumption."

"Or perhaps she was afraid," Yvonnel said, turning back, but now remaining far enough away to let the conversation continue without the overwhelming intimidation. "And perhaps with reason."

"Surely if we could defeat Demogorgon . . ." Charri began, but Yvonnel cut her short.

"There were other powers lurking in the tunnels of the Underdark more frightening to Malcanthet than the drow," she said. "And what reason would we have to wage war on the Succubus Queen, who has long been an ally of the greatest noble Houses?"

The way she said it created concern in those around her. Had they stolen away a potential Baenre ally in a time of dangerous upheaval without informing the matron mother?

Charri Hunzrin swallowed hard.

"We meant only to foster chaos," she said.

"And to profit from it," Yvonnel added.

"Is that not our edict?"

"Perhaps, but now your edict has crossed my path, and I am not amused," Yvonnel said. "Tell me, how will you put your demon back in her cage?"

Charri, Denderida, and the others all looked around nervously. There was no way they could do that, of course. The five of them combined, perhaps even with the reputed powers of the daughter of Gromph bolstering them, would be no match for Malcanthet.

"We cannot," Charri admitted weakly.

"But you will," Yvonnel declared, and she began to mutter under her breath.

"But Lady Baenre, that is impossible!" one of the lesser priestesses said, right on cue.

Yvonnel finished her spell, and cast her hand out at the young priestess, who was barely more than a child. The magic fell over her, and she shrieked.

Then she croaked—where she had stood squatted a bullfrog that began turning this way and that in utter confusion.

"You will do exactly as I instruct," Yvonnel warned Charri, turning to encompass Denderida and the others with her threat as well. "If you misspeak a single word, a single syllable, a single inflection, then I will destroy you, and all of House Hunzrin as well."

She focused on Charri. "Are we in agreement?"

The woman swallowed hard, but didn't immediately answer, so Yvonnel stepped to the side and stomped on the bullfrog with her boot, splattering it on the stone floor.

"You doubt me?" she asked the gasping Hunzrins. "Would you like to call to a handmaiden of Lolth, Priestess Charri, and ask her for a spell of resurrection for your young lady?"

"I cared nothing for her," Charri answered unconvincingly.

"Are you afraid to try?" asked Yvonnel. "Because if you do, when Lolth does not answer your call, you will know you are doomed."

Charri Hunzrin seemed as if she might simply fall to the floor.

"You are fortunate, for I have a plan to correct your errors," said Yvonnel. "And if you execute this plan as I instruct—*exactly* as I instruct—then you will find the power to restore your . . . friend. And you will know that you are back in the favor of Lolth, and can rest easy that the secret of what you have done here will not go to the matron mother or the Ruling Council or any others who might take great exception to the transportation of a demon queen from the city without permission."

Her voice lowered ominously as she asked again, "Are we in agreement?"

Charri Hunzrin nodded.

"Every syllable, every inflection," Yvonnel warned again.

# CHAPTER 25 ◈

# *Overmatched*

T HE SOUNDS OF AN ARGUMENT LED DRIZZT AND ENTRERI to a rocky bluff overlooking a flat stone in front of the yawning opening of a large cave. Down beside the stone, dwarves and giants, looking very similar other than the obvious size difference, grumbled and spat and threw bones, gambling over the items that had been stripped from a pair of giant bodies lying in the dirt to the side of the stone. Those mostly naked corpses had been there for a couple of days, at least, and apparently some wolves had feasted on them in the night, strewing their limbs and entrails about.

Entreri tapped Drizzt on the shoulder, then pointed to a higher ridge just beyond the opening. Several giants stood up there, pointing down at the game and laughing.

"Too well guarded?" Drizzt whispered. "Perhaps there is a side entrance."

Entreri scoffed and shook his head. "Remember the duergar?" he asked slyly.

Drizzt nodded and smiled, and rarely had he been this excited for an upcoming battle. His mind was clear, his heart strong, his determination full and solid, and he had Artemis Entreri by his side.

"Fast under the cave entrance so they can't rain stones upon us," Entreri remarked.

"They will come down, and if they have allies waiting within the cave, we will have no way out," Drizzt warned.

"Yes, we will," Entreri replied, drawing his blades. "Only it will take a little longer."

Another nod, another smile, and Drizzt thought it time for him to bring in a powerful ally. He pulled the onyx figurine from his belt pouch and whispered for Guenhwyvar.

◆ ◆ ◆

SHE COULD SEE nothing through the perpetual gray fog.

"Is this death?" poor Concettina Delcasio Frostmantle asked for perhaps the hundredth time since she'd been thrown from her body and into this strange prison, or afterlife, or whatever it might be.

"Am I a ghost?" she asked when she pushed through the fog to a wall, and there she thought she could see out into the world she had left behind.

"Help me!" she cried as loudly as she could.

She pressed her face closer and through a distorted lens could see what she thought to be the wall of a compound, or of a town, perhaps. Beyond it, an orange flame flickered, though she couldn't see the fire, just the haunting reflection of it in a cave.

The woman shook her head. It made no sense, or would have had to be a gigantic cavern if that was indeed the wall of a castle or compound or city in front of her.

Straining, she peered even closer, or maybe it was just that she found a clearer spot through the translucent material. Concettina got the most curious impression that she was within some strange chamber inside of a giant chest. Were those gold and silver coins around her?

But they were gigantic!

"I go mad," she whispered, turning away.

She spun back just in time to see a gargantuan hand coming for her, a plump hand with four fingers. She had the sensation of falling, but like everything in this strange afterlife, she really didn't fall, couldn't fall, for even her solidity, it seemed, was an illusion.

But the hand was not an illusion. It closed over the translucent wall.

Concettina threw herself at that wall and knew she was there, though she could feel nothing solid.

Still, she screamed. For all her life, she screamed.

Even when she realized she couldn't hear her own voice, that her scream was as intangible as her form. Broken, terrified Concettina screamed.

◆ ◆ ◆

"REMEMBER THE DUERGAR?" Artemis Entreri asked with a wink, and Drizzt could only grin.

The pair swooped down upon the unsuspecting spriggans like a whirlwind, closing upon the giants with dizzying speed, leaping and turning about each other, four blades working in deadly concert.

Drizzt drove a giant back with a double-thrust of his scimitars, and in that move shifted both to his left hand. He spun, putting his back to the behemoth and setting his legs firmly as it charged in. Then he dropped his free right hand out and in front of him.

In ran Entreri, taking that foothold and leaping as Drizzt shoved to send him higher.

The giant blinked and lifted its arms, but too late, and Charon's Claw gashed its throat as the assassin sailed past.

And Drizzt ran between its legs as it stood there quivering, his scimitars taking out the tendons at the back of the giant's ankles.

Side-by-side, the companions met the next two in their path, dodging blows and countering with speed and precision, though not getting near enough to score any solid hits.

Just as the giants began their attacks anew, Drizzt went left, Entreri right, both turning as they seamlessly crossed, each leaping out to the side.

And the spriggans turned, too, and right into each other, face to face.

Both took a dozen stabs and slices before they realized their error—and a dozen more before they could untangle enough to do anything about it.

And Drizzt and Entreri ran past.

The drow dived, a heavy stone crashing down in front of him. He turned to the ridge where the other sentries stood. A second spriggan had a stone up high over its head, ready to launch.

But Guenhwyvar leaped first, crossing past the giant's face and taking a considerable amount of that face with her in her clawing descent. The giant turned as she passed, howling in pain and throwing its stone—right into the face of the other spriggan.

Separated now, Drizzt found himself straight up against a spriggan with a sword longer than the drow was tall. A few lumbering swings got nowhere near to hitting the speedy Drizzt, but this one was clever. As it began another apparent sidelong slash, left to right, it halted its momentum and turned the other way, sweeping its left leg across to try to trip up Drizzt.

But Drizzt leaped straight up and tucked his legs, and the giant's kick was too low to catch him. And in that leap, he sheathed his scimitars, pulled his buckle-bow, and set his arrow.

And in that descent and before he touched the ground, as the giant tried to bring its blade back in once more, Drizzt let fly. The sizzling lightning arrow slashed up under the behemoth's chin, through its mouth, and into its brain.

It staggered back a stride, then another, and fell over dead.

And Drizzt rolled to the side to avoid another thrown stone and came up facing the ridge, where giants frantically tried to ward the panther and another hoisted boulders that rained upon the attackers.

Off went the lightning arrows, one after another. The second shot took the thrower in the arm just as it lifted the next stone up high, and that stone fell free and crashed down against its face. The giant brushed it aside, but the next arrow was there instead, driving into its cheek and throwing it back against the mountain wall behind the ridge.

Drizzt kept firing, and he whistled.

To the side of him, Entreri, too, called out. He spun farther from Drizzt, his red-bladed sword cutting down a goblin. He turned right past it, driving his dagger into the chest of a dwarf stupidly thinking it could sneak up on Artemis Entreri.

The next group in line—a pair of goblins, a dwarf, and another giant—slowed when Entreri's nightmare appeared, stomping fire, snorting smoke, and charging them with abandon.

Andahar charged across the flat stone at Drizzt's call, gliding past the drow, bearing straight for the cave opening.

Goblins dived aside, but a giant spriggan dared to block.

The moment the tip of Andahar's horn came out its back, that spriggan recognized its mistake.

"You need to make me one of those!" Entreri said as Drizzt put Taulmaril away and drew his scimitars once more, the pair following the path opened by their magical mounts.

Another group waited just inside the cave opening, but those few who managed to dodge the charge of the nightmare and the unicorn found themselves in the midst of a blade storm, scimitar, sword, scimitar, dagger coming at them too swiftly and in too perfect unison for them to begin to respond.

Drizzt and Entreri went into the darkness side by side. They had to dismiss their magical, powerful mounts.

But they were not alone. Guenhwyvar, her paws bloody, bits of spriggan stuck in her teeth, padded past them, her hunger unsated.

◆ ◆ ◆

As they made their way through the upper tunnels of Smeltergard, heading back toward the Damaran entrance, Yvonnel considered and reconsidered her plans. If the ruse was detected, she would be in serious danger and everything would fall apart for her and the others as well.

Even her Hunzrin escorts failed to understand the gravity of this moment, of this creature they had loosed upon the World

Above. This was no mere succubus, the likes of which were nowhere near as formidable as even a pit fiend or a balor.

No, this was the Succubus Queen, a demon princess, a being just below those demon lords that had swept into the Underdark. If Drizzt had all of his companions by his side and Yvonnel could summon her father, and Jarlaxle and Kimmuriel, and maybe coax Grandmaster Kane to join the fray, then perhaps they could wage a battle against Malcanthet.

But that force could not be assembled, surely not in the time allotted. This conflict had to be won with guile and fortitude.

Not that much fortitude, Yvonnel convinced herself as she considered the polymorph spell and her vulnerability. She needed a patsy.

"Who leads these ugly dwarves?" she asked. "Or are they giants?"

"Spriggans," Charri Hunzrin corrected.

"Of course," said Yvonnel. "And who leads them?"

Charri and Denderida exchanged nervous glances.

"Truly?" Yvonnel asked, and she produced a flask from her hip bag and shook it around as a reminder, the frog guts and entrails bloodying the sides of the glass.

"Toofless and Komtoddy," Charri quickly said.

Yvonnel winced, thinking that sounded like a bad dwarven drinking song—and indeed there actually was one of a similar title: "Toothless and Hot Toddy."

"Take me to them," Yvonnel instructed. "One of them will become very beautiful this day, for a time, at least."

Again the Hunzrins exchanged doubtful, skeptical glances, but the flask was still in sight and so they veered for the chambers shared by the spriggan leaders.

◆ ◆ ◆

"Yach, but ye stupids just keep yers eyes peeled," the dwarf told the goblin patrol. "Can'ts be doing the only lookin' meself!"

The spriggan stared back at the wide-eyed goblin nearest him.

"What?" the dwarf asked before he caught on that the goblin was looking past him.

He spun around.

He died.

The goblins scattered as Drizzt and Entreri charged past the falling dwarf, those at the back whooping, confident that the unfortunate wretches up front would slow this unexpected duo enough for them to scatter to the tunnels.

But the duo was a trio and Guenhwyvar leaped over those first lines to land among the few trying to flee, claws tearing, teeth catching legs and ripping them apart.

It wouldn't have mattered anyway. Drizzt and Entreri came through the front lines as easily and swiftly as they burst through Entreri's ash walls.

In mere moments, only one was running free, the others dead or dying.

Out came Taulmaril, but before Drizzt could set an arrow and let fly, a missile flew past him, catching the goblin mid-back and throwing it down to the floor.

Drizzt considered the throw, the jewel-hilted dagger sticking from the twitching creature's back. He glanced over at Entreri.

"Get me one of those bows," the assassin said, going for his dagger. "Perhaps you'll find occasion—rare occasion—where you beat me on the draw."

The drow shook his head and looked around. He couldn't deny Entreri's efficiency.

They went fast down some empty corridors in the lower levels, for Pikel had indicated that the demon, the mirror, and Wulfgar were at the very bottom tunnels of the complex. On several occasions, they heard the scuffling of rushing footsteps—more goblins and spriggans running for the surface.

*Let us hope that the demon, too, has gone to investigate the fight at the door,* Entreri said to him, but not aloud. The assassin used his fingers, signing in the silent drow language perfectly.

Drizzt nodded his agreement, then motioned to the side. Guenhwyvar's ears had gone flat, the panther peering intently at an upcoming intersection where this corridor ended and broke both left and right, with flickering light coming from both directions.

They crept down and peered around the corner. To the left, more ramshackle doors lined the corridor, but down to the right they noted a pair of giants standing beneath lit torches set in sconces on the wall, flanking a most remarkable bloodstone door, just as Pikel had described.

*Twenty count,* Entreri's hand flashed to Drizzt, and the assassin slipped around the corner, blending in beautifully with the shadows.

And where there were no masking shadows, Entreri used Charon's Claw and made his own. So skilled was he that even Drizzt, with his Underdark vision, lost sight of the man before he had silently counted to ten.

The drow counted on, setting an arrow to Taulmaril.

"Silently, Guen," he whispered to the cat, then swung around the corner, leveling his bow at the giant on the left.

Entreri had crossed over, though, and that giant fell silently, a red blade going across its throat as the assassin dropped upon it from the ceiling.

Drizzt swung Taulmaril and let fly for the other, his arrow burrowing into the spriggan's chest and knocking it back against the wall.

Entreri moved to finish the task, but fell back as a ball of feline muscle and claws flew past him. Guenhwyvar landed against the behemoth's chest, her jaws settling about its throat, choking off its screams.

By the time Drizzt reached the end of the corridor, Entreri's fingers had worked carefully along the door jamb, the assassin falling to his knees before the lock.

*There could be a magical trap,* Drizzt warned.

Entreri just shrugged. What else were they to do?

He had the door unlocked in moments, turning the last tumbler tentatively, grimacing as if he expected to be blown up by a fireball.

He looked up at Drizzt, whose fingers flashed, reminding him not to look into the mirror.

With that thought in mind, Drizzt sent Guenhwyvar back the other way, to guard the corridor.

The drow pulled Taulmaril from his belt buckle and set an arrow.

Entreri grasped the door handle.

The companions nodded.

◆ ◆ ◆

THE RUMORS OF an invasion met the drow group as they neared the more southern reaches of Smeltergard. Yvonnel did well to hide her smirk at the whispers. From the frantic words of those fleeing goblins they interviewed, it seemed as if some group had exploded into the place and left a line of carnage in their wake.

The news only made Yvonnel push the Hunzrins on faster, fearful that Drizzt and Entreri would soon face the likes of Malcanthet.

They found the spriggan leaders in their dwarf forms soon after, in the room the two shared.

"Smeltergard has been attacked," Charri Hunzrin stated when she entered.

"Drow," Komtoddy answered.

"And have you killed these drow?" Yvonnel asked.

The spriggans blanched and fell back, both shaking their heads emphatically.

"Theys went low, way down," Toofless said. "We thinks them friends o' our guest."

"Hardly," Charri Hunzrin started to say, but she stopped and glanced over at Yvonnel suspiciously. She had made no mention of any other actions against Malcanthet.

Yvonnel ignored her and stepped right past her to stand in front of the spriggan leaders. She spent a moment studying each, taking their measure. The little one with the gum-mouthed lisp seemed slimier, to be sure, while the other was more muscular.

"I have a job for you," she told Komtoddy.

The dwarf looked past her to Charri Hunzrin.

"So now ye're to be orderin' us about, eh?" Toofless said to Charri.

"This is the very great Matron Mother of Menzoberranzan," Charri warned, indicating Yvonnel. "You should take care your words, Toofless Tonguelasher, for none speak more fully for the Spider Queen herself than Matron Mother Yvonnel Baenre."

Yvonnel let the mistake pass, for it served her, clearly, as both spriggans stood straighter and seemed, then, more attentive.

"You," Yvonnel said, indicating Toofless, "be gone from here. If you are wise, you will gather your minions and flee to the north. Your work in Helgabal has sent the king's army against you, and they come with many powerful allies. The attack on this place has only just begun, and it will not end well for any of your clan caught here."

Toofless looked at Komtoddy, licked his lips, and started to inquire about his friend.

But Yvonnel's scowl cut him short, and with another look at his friend, one more of better-you-than-me than any sympathy, Toofless scampered for the room's door.

"You can transform into a giant?" Yvonnel asked a clearly nervous Komtoddy.

He nodded tentatively.

"Do so."

The spriggan crossed his arms over his chest, but his only direct response was to match Yvonnel's glare.

"Toofless Tonguelasher!" Yvonnel called, turning to stare at the spriggan just as he was about to leave. She held up her hand and motioned for the dwarf to return.

"Show your friend what will happen to him if he disobeys me," Yvonnel instructed when Toofless arrived by her side.

The spriggan looked at her curiously, at a loss.

And Yvonnel hit him with a lightning bolt, point blank, that lifted him and sent him flying across the room into the hallway, and there splattered him, bits and pieces flying all over.

The chamber—the entire complex—shook under the power of that blast.

Yvonnel calmly looked over at Komtoddy.

As the spriggan's bones began to pop and elongate, Yvonnel moved over to a weapon rack and pulled forth a large sword, one suited for a giant. She could hardly lift it by the hilt, so she let the point drag on the ground as she began casting once more, running one hand the length of the blade, pressing it left and right.

More enchantments followed before she finished and turned, grinning, to the Hunzrins and the now giant Komtoddy.

"I am going to make a hero of you," she explained. She stepped aside, revealing the sword, which now appeared more slender but more formidable, with a blade that was wavy and not straight.

"A hero?" Charri Hunzrin breathed.

"The Dark Prince," Denderida replied.

"Come now, my toy," Yvonnel said to the dwarf. "What is our name?"

The spriggan moved over tentatively. "Komtoddy."

"I have work to do with you, Komtoddy. Your skin needs to shine like polished black stone, and you need more fingers, and more toes."

Komtoddy turned an alarmed and pleading look to Charri Hunzrin, but she backed away, shaking her head.

Yvonnel was already spellcasting once more.

◆ ◆ ◆

ENTRERI THREW OPEN the door and dived through, rolling off to the side, drawing his weapons as he went.

Drizzt was right behind him, leaping across the threshold, levelling Taulmaril at that woman standing beside the hearth—beside the mirror!—looking back at him.

When her batlike wings extended, Drizzt let fly.

The arrow soared for her chest, hit a magical shield, and exploded into thousands of harmless sparks.

Drizzt sent another, and another, and another, to similar non-effect, while Entreri executed a rolling and diving charge, and the demon responded.

Her fireball filled the room, hissing on the surface of the small pool off to the right, sweeping out at Drizzt and engulfing Entreri. Drizzt dived, replacing Taulmaril and drawing Icingdeath and Vidrinath as he went. He winced as the flames and smoke dissipated. A heavy steamy fog billowed back from the water. Entreri stood and lunged for the demon.

But the assassin hit only steamy air. The woman was gone.

Entreri called to Drizzt, "Where is she?"

"Keep moving!" Drizzt warned, finally spotting the demon on the other side of the hearth from his friend.

"Left!" Drizzt cried, starting for her.

A whip cracked in the air just in front of him, its lightning spark throwing Drizzt backward, his hair dancing from the shock.

Stumbling to regain his balance, he spotted Entreri again, circling behind the hearth, closing fast.

But she was gone again, straight up with a beat of her powerful wings—and likely some magical enhancement—and the assassin rushed out under her with nothing to hit.

Out came Taulmaril and off went another arrow, Drizzt tracking and letting fly repeatedly, determined to burn through that magical shield.

The demon laughed at him and bellowed forth a cloud of thicker smoke, filling the room with a heavy haze.

Down she came, whip crackling, filling the room with a sulfuric smell.

Drizzt and Entreri coordinated by yelling out to each other. Drizzt put a globe of darkness over by the door, and the demon's whip snapped at it, lightning crackling. And so Drizzt saw just enough of her. He reached deep inside himself, deep to those abilities he had known in the Underdark, to those innate drow abilities that resonated strongly within him. He cast a limning faerie fire upon the fiend.

The blue flames didn't burn, but they outlined her enough to minimize the distraction of her fog.

She turned and cried out—Entreri was upon her.

Drizzt went in the other way, stabbing hard and scoring a hit as the demon leaped straight up once more.

Both men dived away, getting a second fireball for their efforts.

Drizzt came up and Entreri staggered to the side. "I'm all right," the assassin insisted, but his voice was scratchy, his cough real—that blast had surely stung him.

Drizzt started for Taulmaril once more, but saw the demon diving back down, straight for Entreri.

Drizzt cried out for Guenhwyvar, and charged to intercept. He came in hard enough to stop the demon from finishing his companion, who was still staggering from the fireball. Instead, the demon slapped Entreri, sent him flying, and spun on Drizzt, winding her whip out his way.

He was too quick, and accelerated past the reach of the awful barb at the end of the whip.

But this was no ordinary whip, and was more a matter of the demon's will than her sweeping arm. She called that barb back in.

Just before he reached his target, Drizzt felt the bite in the middle of his back, and the full power of a baleful Abyssal stroke of lightning exploded within him. For a moment, he realized that he was flying, and he saw the wall coming up fast. But strangely, he felt nothing, nothing at all, when he slammed face-first into that wall.

He bounced back and was caught by the fiend and pulled in to her side. Dragging him as if he were weightless, she charged after Entreri.

And she bit Drizzt's neck, and he felt his life-force being pulled from him.

The demon fed.

◆  ◆  ◆

"THIS IS MADNESS," Charri Hunzrin dared to complain as the procession made its way along the corridors of Smeltergard, descending for the room the spriggans had given to Malcanthet.

Yvonnel stopped and stepped in front of the impertinent Hunzrin priestess. "You understand, of course, that this is your only chance to avoid the wrath of the matron mother," she said.

"You think to fool the Succubus Queen?" Charri protested. "You think to fight her?"

"Of course I do not!"

"Do you think to ask her politely to leave?"

"Foolishness," the Hunzrin priestess said, shaking her head.

"Perhaps," Yvonnel admitted. "But foolishness with which you will cooperate." She held up the jar of frog guts once more and shook it. "Every word, every syllable, every inflection," Yvonnel warned in no uncertain terms.

Charri Hunzrin looked to Denderida for support, but the scout wisely merely nodded at Yvonnel's reminder.

"We will get through this," Yvonnel promised them. "And House Hunzrin will be free to continue their trade with the surface without restitution for this one error in judgment—an error that will go no farther than this group, House Hunzrin, and House Baenre."

That brought a suspicious look to Charri's face, exactly as Yvonnel had hoped. The woman would never believe charity from the likes of House Baenre, and certainly not from the daughter of Gromph representing that House. But the hint that their little secret would go no farther lent credence to some larger plan, some service or allegiance, likely with a Hunzrin ally like House Melarn, that was more consistent with the Baenres' desires.

And so Yvonnel's lie was stronger.

"And I will lead Smeltergard!" added the six-fingered, six-toed, six-horned, obsidian-skinned Komtoddy, in a voice clear and beautiful and resonant.

Yvonnel smiled at him. "You may keep this form if you so desire," she said. "You are quite beautiful."

Komtoddy laughed.

He had no idea what unintended consequences might come with that apparent gift.

◆　◆　◆

THE SECOND FIREBALL had hurt him. He felt scarred in his throat and had to work hard to draw a full breath. But he couldn't stop.

Artemis Entreri rushed around the front of the hearth, taking care to avert his eyes from that horrible mirror.

He saw the demon, moving to the right side of the room, near the pool, putting distance between herself and him, Entreri knew.

Then he saw Drizzt.

The assassin's heart fell. She had her teeth in Drizzt's neck and he wasn't fighting it. He wasn't doing anything, just hanging limp, as if dead. He wasn't even holding his scimitars any longer, having dropped them back behind the hearth.

The demon looked up at Entreri and spread her wings like a crowning eagle. Her face was covered in Drizzt's blood, and so was the side of Drizzt's neck and chest.

And still he didn't move.

A flicker of hope appeared, a black flicker of flying hope, as Guenhwyvar charged into the room and sprang at the demon.

With a feral growl, Artemis Entreri charged right behind.

He heard the crack of the whip, the retort halting him, but he started in once more, wincing. The cat had been struck directly and crashed to the floor, skidding as if she would slide right into the demon and Drizzt. But the panther slid through the pair, becoming an insubstantial mist, dissipating back to her Astral home.

With a single snap of that awful whip, this fiend had destroyed the mighty panther!

And now Entreri saw the whip reaching out at him, delicately, dangerously, arcs of black lightning following its curling sweep.

At the last moment, so the demon could not alter the angle of the strike as she had done with Drizzt, Entreri sprang over the whip and into a roll. He didn't get hit, just barely escaping, but the thunderous retort did sting him and send him farther along his way.

He rolled to his feet, pivoted, and threw himself into a straight run at the demon.

Out came the whip, and again, at the last moment, Entreri fell aside, narrowly avoiding that brutal crackle. Now he was closer, though—too close for the demon to execute a third strike. Charon's Claw cut fast for the demon's open left side. Her arm came out to block—and she took the hit with her bare flesh.

Bare flesh and magical enchantments, clearly, for such a stroke from that red-bladed sword should have severed her arm with ease. It did draw a deep gash, but the demon seemed not to care. The hit didn't slow her, and Entreri had been certain the sword's life-killing sting, a product of the lower planes, would have little effect on her.

The demon smiled, mocking him, and continued her swing. Entreri was shocked by the strength of that backhand, so powerful it halted him in his rush and sent him staggering back. His shoulder went numb and Charon's Claw flew from his grasp and splashed into the pool.

He leaped right back in close—what else might he do?—and grabbed on for all his life.

He didn't stab with the dagger, not right away, because he saw one desperate chance.

But he knew that chance would almost certainly cost him his life.

So be it.

The demon's hand grabbed him with frightening strength and he felt as if his shoulder was being crushed. But Artemis Entreri held on. He grabbed Drizzt's nearest arm, hanging limp and lifeless, and forced his dagger into Drizzt's hand, his own hand closing over it, guiding it to stab the demon in the belly.

She slugged Entreri hard, sending him flying away, crashing down near the hearth. Barely holding on to consciousness, the assassin crawled, desperate to reach Drizzt's scimitars.

The demon roared and Entreri thought his life surely over. He threw himself to the weapons, grabbed up Icingdeath, and rolled to face his doom.

But the demon wasn't roaring at him, nor as much in shock and pain as rage. The dagger had punctured, just a bit, and drank, drawing the demon's great life-force and transferring it to the wielder, giving Drizzt just enough awareness to hold on for all his life.

The demon's eyes widened in horror. With a growl, she bit down on Drizzt's neck again and began drawing forth his life, feasting on it as he feasted on hers.

They moved around in circles in some sort of macabre dance, and the sheer horror of the spectacle had Entreri gasping through his burned throat and mouth.

"Now," he told himself, thinking he had one chance, and he scooped up Vidrinath as well and leaped to his feet.

But there was no opening. The demon convulsed, a great exhale and shove, and sent Drizzt flying limply to the side to hit the floor and roll about like a dead seal caught in the surf.

The demon's eyes and smile widened, all the more garish because of the blood covering her face. She didn't seem seriously wounded, and Entreri knew that he was doomed.

She strode for him deliberately and determinedly, slowly, that gruesome expression taunting him.

But then she stopped and straightened, and looked confused. She spun, and her newest attacker moved with her, staying behind her.

A halfling, dripping wet, held a beautiful rapier in his hand, its tip bloody from the stab in the demon's back. It hadn't done much damage, clearly, and the halfling looked panicked as he struck with a different weapon—and not a three-bladed dagger.

Entreri stared incredulously as Regis brought a flat gemstone up against the small hole he had poked into the demon's back.

Around came the demon, and Regis tried to flee but wound up flying, along with the gemstone and the rapier, at the back of her hand. He crashed down hard, cried out in terror, and ran for the pool, leaping for the water and disappearing under it just as the whip cracked and lit the surface with a sheen of sparkling lightning.

The demon, furious now, spun back on Entreri, who tried to get to her once more. She lifted her whip for the killing stroke.

Entreri dived back, rolling repeatedly, trying to put the hearth between them.

But the strike didn't come and the demon lurched and walked weirdly, stumbling. She cursed, but the words were garbled, her mouth twisting awkwardly as if she couldn't control herself.

She stumbled into a run, angled for the door, and crashed out of the room. Just outside, she roared in outrage.

Entreri wasn't about to give chase.

# CHAPTER 26 ◈

# *Courage*

SHOULD HAVE TAKEN THAT WEAPON, MALCANTHET SILENTLY cursed herself. She couldn't form actual words as she staggered along the corridor, veering from wall to wall. That awful dagger had hurt her more seriously than she wanted to believe.

The soul of Concettina was back in the body, fully aware and fighting wildly to hold on to her corporeal reality. Each step became forced and difficult as the division grew sharper, the battle more fully engaged.

Possession of another was a difficult thing even in the best of circumstances, when the victim was caught by surprise, but this would be no easy struggle. More than just the body of Concettina, that dagger had drawn at the life-force of Malcanthet herself, and she felt the pain as Concettina vied for control.

This would not do. Not at all.

They stumbled and they fought through a series of passageways, mouth twisting in indecipherable screams, legs stiff, and gait awkward.

Malcanthet just had to hold on a bit longer, until she could find an unsuspecting host.

The woman crashed into a door, which fell open and left her stumbling through and falling face down on the floor. Both Malcanthet and Concettina, sharing the body's ears, heard the collective gasp of surprise and recognized the shouts and hoots that followed as those of goblins.

And they were just a woman now, a feeble, broken human, so it appeared, and one barely dressed.

A goblin came over and grabbed the thick blond hair and yanked the woman's head up and back.

The smelly creature, holding a wicked, serrated knife, was not alone. Its dozen friends in the chamber, recovering from the shock of the unexpected intruder, seemed no more disposed to decency than this wretched and filthy thing.

◆ ◆ ◆

"DON'T LOOK IN the mirror!" Regis warned Entreri. "Don't look in the mirror! Bad things in there! Very bad, very bad!"

The halfling was gasping, out of breath and out of sorts, and clearly overwhelmed by his ordeal, which Entreri expected was much more than this last battle here with the demon woman.

"We were told you were dead," he replied as he rushed past Regis to drop to his knees beside the body of Drizzt. He lifted the drow's head in his hands, thinking to say goodbye, but to his surprise, Drizzt wasn't quite dead.

"Something! Anything!" Entreri yelled, and Regis, after carefully placing his cape over the mirror once more, came running.

"Drizzt!" Regis cried, reaching for his magical belt pouch.

He produced a small flask and put it fast to Drizzt's lips, pouring the liquid down his throat.

"I didn't even know he was here," Regis gasped.

"She threw him," Entreri said grimly. "She destroyed the cat."

"Guen," Regis mouthed, placing down the empty flask and grabbing a second from his pouch. That, too, went to Drizzt's lips.

"Where did you come from?" Entreri demanded.

"The pool. I dived into the pool. There was a hydra, or a dragon with many heads, breathing fire. I had nowhere to go."

"That was days ago."

"I only came up for air when I had to—a couple of times, no more."

"What?" the assassin asked incredulously.

Regis shook his head, having no desire to explain his genasi heritage at that desperate time. "Who told you I was dead?" he asked.

"The dwarf, Pikel."

"He lives?" Regis asked, incredulous. "He escaped? Oh, Pikel!"

Before Entreri could respond, Drizzt coughed—a pathetic and wheezing thing, but a sign of life, at least. The ranger opened his lavender eyes and took in the scene before him, two faces hovering over him, the two who had saved him.

"Drizzt!" Regis cried, and he put the flask back to the drow's lips, wanting him to get every drop of the healing potion.

"Can you move?" Entreri asked.

Drizzt's eyes turned to regard Entreri directly, but he made no other movement than that, not even a slight shift of his head.

"Collect his things," Entreri ordered. "Help me get him over to the wall by the door."

"What's wrong with him?" a desperate Regis asked, and he sucked in his breath, finding his own answer. "The whip! Oh, that horrid whip!"

He went for his pouch, for another potion of healing, but he knew it was useless.

"Why are you here?" he asked Entreri.

"I came with Drizzt."

"I understand that much, but why are *you* here?" Regis asked again.

Entreri snorted. "You know how they say that when you get older, you get wiser?"

"Yes."

"They're wrong."

Regis handed Icingdeath to Entreri, who slid it into the sheath on Drizzt's right hip.

"We have to get out of here," the assassin said.

"But Wulfgar's in there," Regis replied, pointing to the mirror.

"I know, but I don't think we can take it with us."

"But . . ." Regis searched for some answer. "If something goes into the mirror, something else comes out."

"What comes out?"

"The fire-breathing hydra-dragon thing came out."

"Lovely."

"I don't know how it works," Regis admitted. "But I heard the demon tell the drow—"

"The drow?"

"There are dark elves down here—priestesses from Menzoberranzan, I think."

Entreri had been told as much back at Chalmer's house, but he was hoping against hope that Regis meant a drow, a single priestess, Yvonnel. That didn't seem to be the case.

"She said that the mirror was full," Regis explained, "of prisoners, I assume, and so whenever another is entrapped, it will throw one out."

Artemis Entreri rubbed his face and sighed. "And Wulfgar is in there?"

Regis nodded.

"You are certain?"

The halfling hesitated for just a heartbeat, then nodded again.

"Stay here with Drizzt," Entreri ordered. "Make him comfortable."

"Where are you going?"

Entreri moved to the door and peered out. With a look back at Regis and Drizzt, he left the room, closing the door behind him.

◆ ◆ ◆

THE GOBLINS CHATTERED about what they should do with this gift that had fallen through their door, this helpless woman.

It didn't matter, though, because they didn't understand.

The first to realize the error was the goblin with the knife nearest the woman, holding her by the hand and waiting for confirmation from its friends that it should hurt her or kill her.

Malcanthet had come to understand that she would not easily, or quickly, regain control of frantic Concettina's corporeal form. The human understood the pain, now, and the horror of being dispossessed from her own body, of being invaded by another being.

Malcanthet accepted that reality, because she didn't need Concettina's form any longer, not to inhabit it, anyway.

So the demon exited, her soul flying free for just a moment before sweeping into the body of the unsuspecting goblin.

The creature leaped up and fell back, confused. It was not a very smart creature, nor strong of will, and Malcanthet overwhelmed it, terrorizing, scaring, striking mentally.

The meager creature never had a chance, and Malcanthet had control almost immediately, enough so to break the corporeal bonds of the goblin form, to take that flesh and bone and reshape it, basking in the pain as bones twisted and broke, and grew.

Then two women were in the room, a sobbing and broken Concettina and a taller and more solid, black-haired woman, who grinned wickedly as horns sprouted atop her forehead, and as her backbone crackled, sprouting wings that unfolded, tearing away the ragged clothing the goblin had been wearing.

The other goblins fell all over each other trying to get back from the mighty fiend.

Malcanthet pulled her whip from Concettina and cracked it in front of the goblins—and how they ran!

The succubus laughed. She reached down and grabbed up Concettina by the hair, hoisting her with frightening ease. She plucked her rings roughly from the woman's hand and pulled free her necklace, then took back her favorite dress.

She roughly threw the now-naked Queen of Damara back to the floor.

"You are fortunate that I may need you in the coming days," she said above Concettina's sobs.

Malcanthet used her foot to spin the broken woman around, back at the door. "Crawl," she ordered.

Concettina sobbed.

Malcanthet grabbed her by the hair and yanked her forward. "Crawl, or I will drag you."

Poor Concettina, barely reoriented back in her body, agonized from the battle with the demonic intruder and the wounds of the fight Malcanthet had waged, pushed herself up to her hands and knees, wobbling.

The whip cracked in the air, the thunderous report shaking the poor, terrified woman.

Out into the hall they went, Malcanthet taunting Concettina continually, threatening her, telling her all the things she would do to the woman once she didn't need her anymore.

They had gone a long way from Malcanthet's chambers in their joined, dizzying run, but after a moment, Malcanthet recognized the area and knew the way to the room of the spriggan leaders. So she guided Concettina on, and like an old and weary dog, Concettina crawled.

Her hands bled, the stones ground her poor knees, but still she crawled.

She crawled and she cried, and around the corner came several other women: dark elves, horrible drow.

"What is happening?" Charri Hunzrin asked, glancing from the true form of Malcanthet to the bloody and beaten woman in front of her.

"You tell me," the demon demanded.

"Intruders have come to Smeltergard," Charri explained. "And more are on the way. You should be gone from this place. Long gone, for House Baenre is aware of your flight to the World Above, and they are not pleased."

The Succubus Queen scoffed. "Children of Lolth, do not presume to tell me what to do," she warned.

"They speak wisely," came another voice from behind the Hunzrin contingent, and a fifth drow woman stepped into view. "I am Yvonnel . . . Baenre," she said. "The daughter of Archmage Gromph."

"Then you should thank me," Malcanthet retorted, hardly seeming impressed or fearful. "For by my hand is Lolth's most hated heretic destroyed."

Malcanthet smiled when she noted the newcomer's slight wince.

"You should leave," Yvonnel said evenly. "Be far gone."

"Do you presume to order me about, child of Lolth?"

"It is a prudent warning," Yvonnel replied, her voice growing stronger. "Your presence here is not unknown, to House Baenre and to powerful enemies you have made in this land. An army approaches, and with mighty foes among its ranks."

"The pathetic king?" Malcanthet asked. "Good, I wish to see him dead." She kicked Concettina, just because, tossing the woman to the side of the passageway to crash against the wall where she groaned and cried. Then Malcanthet stepped over and grabbed her up roughly, with frightening strength, and slammed her down on the floor in front of her.

"And others," Yvonnel said. "Others have noticed much about your presence as well. Do you know me, Malcanthet? I am Yvonnel, who led Menzoberranzan to the demise of Demogorgon."

Malcanthet hissed and lifted her whip arm.

"I came to find you, to offer you fair warning," Yvonnel retorted and didn't back away.

"You think to destroy me?"

Yvonnel shook her head and shrugged. "You know the games we all play," she explained. "We choose our sides among constant war."

"And you choose against me?" asked the incredulous succubus.

"In a war against him?" Yvonnel asked, her tone equally incredulous, and she turned and led the succubus's gaze down the hall beyond her to a far corner where smoke billowed and a tall, black-skinned, demonic humanoid appeared, all smoke and haze and fire, and with a huge wavy sword.

Malcanthet's eyes went wide. "Graz'zt," she breathed.

Yvonnel smiled. The Hunzrins fell aside, clearing the way for the possibly titanic fight.

"You have made a great enemy this day!" Malcanthet warned Yvonnel. With a feral growl, the succubus lifted her foot and crushed it down upon poor Concettina, grinding her against the stone.

"Look over your shoulder forevermore!" Malcanthet yelled, but she didn't crack her whip at Yvonnel, and didn't charge. She wanted no part of Graz'zt.

Malcanthet spun and cast a spell, splitting the very air open wide as if it were a door, and through it she went, disappearing from view.

Back to the Abyss, Yvonnel knew, and she breathed a great sigh of relief.

"Heal her!" she told Charri Hunzrin, pointing to Concettina. The priestess balked.

"We will need her, you idiot!" Yvonnel scolded. "Heal her! And you, go and get that idiot spriggan out of my sight before I reduce him to ash," she ordered Denderida, who rushed off to see to Komtoddy.

Yvonnel rubbed her face and tried to sort out her next move. Drizzt was dead, so said Malcanthet, and the young woman could hardly believe the great pain that news had brought upon her.

"Take me to Drizzt," she said softly, to Charri Hunzrin, though the priestess was deep into spellcasting and clearly had not heard her.

◆ ◆ ◆

REGIS STARTED WITH fear when the door burst open and a goblin came stumbling through. He relaxed almost immediately, though, for right behind the little wretch was Entreri, sword drawn.

The assassin shut the door, took the goblin by the scruff of its neck, and fast-walked it to the mirror, which was covered by a cloak. He nodded to Regis.

"Are you sure?" the halfling asked. "There are bad things . . ."

"Do you want to get out of here, or don't you?"

Regis put down what he was holding, an onyx panther figurine. He had been contemplating recalling Guenhwyvar to see if the Astral Plane had helped heal the damage wrought by the demon's whip, but held off.

"If the journey home helped Guen, perhaps we can get her to take Drizzt with her back there," he explained.

"I doubt it."

"We have to try!" Regis moved over to the other side of the demonic mirror, stepping off to the side and behind it so he didn't accidentally look in.

"We have to try everything," Entreri agreed, and he, too, moved behind the mirror's edge, though he kept his sword upon his prisoner.

"Tell me what you see," he ordered the goblin, and Regis pulled the cloak aside.

The goblin looked at Entreri, glanced over at Regis, then seemed transfixed by its own image in the looking glass.

Then it was stretched, pulled into the mirror, caught by the magic, and so another prisoner came forth, materializing in front of the glass.

A lizard.

A big blue lizard, longer than ten of Wulfgar's strides, with a dozen legs and curving horns and a giant crocodilian head. It hissed, the sizzle of its voice echoing off the chamber's walls. Without looking into the mirror, it leaped to the stalagmite hearth and rushed upward with frightening speed, twelve legs scrambling as it ran a circuitous route to the room's high ceiling.

Regis and Entreri, of course, fell back.

"What in the Nine Hells is that?" Regis cried.

"Get me the bow!" Entreri yelled at him.

Reptilian eyes stared down at him. The great crocodile maw snapped open and a burst of lightning shot forth, barely missing the running halfling and making the whole room leap under the concussion of the explosion.

"Forget the bow!" Entreri yelled, scrambling the other way for cover. Creatures with such breath weapons—dragons, though this was no dragon Entreri had ever seen!—were rarely affected by that which they breathe, and Drizzt's bow shot arrows of lightning.

"I will kill you!" the lizard yelled.

"It can talk?" both Regis and Entreri said together.

"How dare you put me in that looking glass?" the lizard cried, and it came rushing down the stalagmite with terrifying, dizzying speed, hitting the floor in a run for Regis, who dived into the pool. It spun with startling agility for a creature of that size, and caught Entreri just before he got to the room's door.

"We didn't put you in the mirror!" Entreri gasped, rolling his weapons in his hands—a sword and dagger that seemed feeble indeed next to the clear power and size of this monstrosity. "We let you out!"

The lizard hissed in his face. "Why?"

"We seek our friend, who is also in that mirror," Entreri explained. "Captured by a demon succubus."

The lizard backed off a bit. "Yes," it hissed, extending the word for many heartbeats. "I remember her now."

The enormous crocodile head nodded—such a strange sight. "Where is she?"

Entreri nodded at the door. "Somewhere out there, in the caves."

"Caves?"

"Tunnels," he blurted. "Many. Do you mean to kill her? We can help . . ."

"I will stay as far away from that creature as I can!" the lizard promised, and it moved to the door, pulled it open cautiously, and peered out.

"Who are you?" Entreri asked. "What are you? I have never seen such a dragon."

The lizard scoffed—and who had ever seen a lizard scoff?—and slipped out the door.

Entreri ran to the spot and saw the creature disappearing around a corner far ahead, moving fast. He fell back into the room and closed the door, falling against it with a profound sigh of relief.

"What was that?" Regis asked a few moments later, climbing out of the pool.

"Good to know that when the fight begins, I can count on you," Entreri said dryly.

"You thought to fight that?" Regis replied, and the assassin could only shrug. If he had been on the other side of the room, he would have been under the water faster than Regis.

Entreri almost turned his head to the left, to look directly into the room. "Cover the mirror," he said to Regis, and he put his hand over his eyes to make sure he didn't slip up.

"The creature was too smart to look back into the glass," he said. "So we are left right back where we began."

He rolled around and opened the door.

"Where are you going?"

"Same place I went last time," Entreri answered.

"You can't be serious!" said the halfling, "You mean to do this again?"

"Do you want your friend back or don't you?" And he left the room.

◆　◆　◆

"STOP SNIVELING," CHARRI Hunzrin said to Concettina.

The woman, healed by the drow priestess, stood trembling and crying, overwhelmed and horrified.

"Leave her alone," Yvonnel scolded. She cast a spell, summoning a small chest to her side, and pulled it open revealing many clothes. Rummaging quickly, she tossed a robe to the naked human, and said, "You are safe now."

Charri Hunzrin gave a slight but noticeable growl of disapproval.

"Take me to Malcanthet's chamber," Yvonnel ordered Charri.

Concettina gasped and fell back, the mere name of her possessor stealing her strength.

"The demon is gone and not to return," Yvonnel told her. "It has found another body, and you are safe."

Charri Hunzrin started past Yvonnel, her expression showing that she was not pleased by these events.

"No, wait," Yvonnel reconsidered. "You, all of you of House Hunzrin, are done here. Leave this place now, with all speed."

"Gladly," said Charri.

Yvonnel noted Denderida, who was far more worldly and understanding of the truth of Yvonnel Baenre than the First Priestess of House Hunzrin, wincing at Charri's attitude, her body language warning Charri to contain her aggressiveness.

"Down the foothills to the south of the Damaran exit is a road," Yvonnel said evenly, threateningly, and she moved a bit closer and locked Charri's eyes with her own. "That road will take you to a small hamlet. In the house of Chalmers, you will find a dwarf, Pikel Bouldershoulder by name. He is gravely ill, stung by the whip of Malcanthet."

She paused, noting hopeful recognition on the face of Concettina.

"Heal him," Yvonnel ordered.

"A dwarf?"

"If he dies, and I learned that he died after your arrival and failure, then return home to Matron Mother Shakti and assure her that her House will soon face the wrath of Baenre," Yvonnel calmly explained. "In full."

Denderida winced again, Charri's bluster disappeared.

"You—"

"Shut up," Yvonnel interrupted. "Get out of this place and heal the dwarf."

Charri Hunzrin stood as if slapped, but Denderida came up quickly and grabbed her by the arm, tugging her aside and back up the tunnel.

Komtoddy turned to follow.

"Not you," Yvonnel told her demon impersonator. "You will take me to Malcanthet's chambers, at once!"

The Graz'zt lookalike clumsily rushed to comply.

◆　◆　◆

ENTRERI SHOVED THE goblin ahead of him, in front of the cloaked mirror.

"Are you sure?" Regis asked.

"Get me the bow," Entreri replied.

Regis moved over to Drizzt's limp form and fumbled with the belt buckle until Taulmaril came into his hand. He grabbed up the magical quiver and brought both to Entreri.

On a nod from the assassin, Regis brought his rapier tip in at the goblin's throat, holding the creature helpless while Entreri switched weapons and set an arrow.

"The demon said there are worse things in there than the hydra," Regis warned again as he took his position by the side of the mirror.

"We're not leaving him."

"But we could take the mirror and release the captives with more allies around," the halfling offered.

The assassin stared at him hard and motioned for him to pull the damned cloth aside.

With a sigh, Regis complied. The goblin, on a glance, was yanked into the looking glass.

Another form appeared in front, a vulture-like demon Regis had seen before.

The halfling fell back and pulled his hand crossbow.

Entreri shot the thing in the face, scorching and cracking its beak.

The vrock leaped at Regis and the desperate halfling drew out his dagger, broke free the side-blades, and threw the living snakes, one, two. Those magical snakes worked fast, slithering up around the demon's neck, and the specters appeared as expected, tugging hard.

But the vrock was too strong to be yanked to its back, and the magical garrotes barely slowed it. Nor would they choke it—demons didn't need to draw breath.

Regis realized his error, cried out, and continued to retreat—he wouldn't go into the pool, though, and leave Entreri alone.

He realized to his horror that he couldn't get there anyway.

Dagger and rapier in hand, he set himself, taking heart when a second arrow crashed into the demon, lurching it to the side.

Thinking it distracted, Regis started forward, but fell back as a black wall appeared in front of him, between him and the demon. He didn't sort it out until Artemis Entreri rushed in front of him and leaped through the ashen, opaque barrier.

Regis could see furious movement behind the cloud, and the shrieks of the vulture demon echoed deafeningly about the cave walls.

The halfling ran around to the side, not daring to go blindly into the furious fight, and by the time he came in sight of the combatants, the vrock was down. It leaned on one arm, trying to get up while Entreri battered it with his mighty sword and the twin specters behind it yanked at their garrotes.

The demon finally went down and Entreri fell back, blades pointed at the specters. "What have you done?" he asked.

Regis calmly walked over and poked the ghostly figures, one then the other, and they winked out of existence. He held up his now single-bladed dirk and shrugged.

Entreri nodded. "I need to go find another goblin."

Regis started to argue, but the assassin's voice cut him short. "Cover the glass."

Entreri returned almost immediately after Regis had set the cloak, prodding a goblin in front of him.

A few moments later, that goblin went into the looking glass, and another goblin appeared in its place.

"Look in the mirror!" Entreri ordered the thing, Taulmaril set to blow it out of existence.

"No, please!" the creature pleaded.

"Your only chance at living," Entreri warned. "Look in the mirror!" He lowered the bow and shot a lightning arrow between the feet of the shying creature—and had another one set before the goblin recovered from the shock.

"Now!" Entreri demanded.

The goblin disappeared into the looking glass.

And out came Wulfgar.

# CHAPTER 27 ◈

# *God and Life*

ON'T TURN AROUND!" ENTRERI YELLED AT WULFGAR, NOT as a threat but as a warning.

"The mirror is behind you!" Regis explained, and he tried to throw his cape over it once more, partially covering it, at least. "If you look into it, you'll be caught once more."

"Where am I? What is this place?" Wulfgar demanded.

"Go to him," Entreri ordered Regis, and he hoisted the mirror off the wall and started to the side.

"What are you doing?" the halfling asked.

"Artemis Entreri?" asked Wulfgar, and his voice changed when he looked past the man, who was heading for the pool. "Drizzt!"

He swept up Regis in his wake as he sprinted to the back wall and the prostrate drow, who appeared lifeless. Wulfgar slid to his knees and cradled Drizzt's head in his hands.

"What is this?" he said desperately.

"The demon . . ." Regis started to explain, but he lost his voice when he saw Entreri throw the mirror into the pool.

"Damn her and her vile toys," the assassin answered to the incredulous expressions of Regis and Wulfgar.

Regis shook his head, each movement growing more frantic.

Wulfgar, though, went right back to Drizzt, holding his friend close. There was no strength there, and he rightly feared a profound, mortal wound.

"Not in there," Regis said to Entreri, standing, forcing Wulfgar's attention once more. "No no no."

"What?" asked Entreri, tossing the cape the halfling's way.

"There are fish in there," Regis stammered. "Living fish."

Entreri paused, Wulfgar looked up.

And as if on cue, the water began to bubble and a huge shadow appeared under the rippling water.

Steam wafted off the water.

"Run," Entreri said, stepping back.

Wulfgar scooped up Drizzt and slung him over one shoulder then followed Regis for the door.

A red hydra head appeared above the water, blowing fire back into the pool, the liquid hissing and steaming in protest.

"Oh, run!" Entreri said more emphatically.

Regis got to the door first, and fumbled to open it—and fumbled more when he looked back, to see the hydra and the creature the hydra was apparently battling.

It floated out of the pool then, a giant eyeball, it seemed, but with a toothy maw full of long teeth, and many stalks of smaller eyes atop it.

Regis spun and tried to exit, but he hadn't pulled the door far enough open and he just slammed into it, pushing it closed.

Wulfgar shoved him aside, threw the door open, and rushed out of the room, Regis under one arm, Drizzt over the other shoulder.

"Put the little one down and ready your hammer," Entreri told the barbarian, sprinting past him up the corridor.

Behind them, the corridor shook, lightning boomed, fire crackled, water sizzled, and there came a screech more profound than the hydra's, more dragon-like, and they knew a third combatant perhaps worse than the other two had joined the battle.

"Just run," Regis kept saying and he tried hard, but unsuccessfully, to stop looking back over his shoulder.

Following Entreri, they turned many corners and traversed many corridors, almost all too narrow for the hydra or a dragon, at least. That brought little comfort, though, and less still when they came into a wider passageway, a main artery to the upper tunnels, and found a giant demonic humanoid billowing smoke and wielding a wave-shaped greatsword.

"Does it never end?" Entreri asked, and then he realized that the behemoth was not alone, that a familiar woman stood beside it, and he thought that the succubus had returned.

But there came a command to hold and Yvonnel rushed out from the shadows to the side. She shoved the giant to the side, or tried to. When she couldn't move him, she just told him to get out of the way.

"I found you," she said with relief. "This is Queen Concettina, truly. Malcanthet is gone, but we should leave this . . ."

Her gaze fell over Drizzt.

As Wulfgar gently placed him upon the floor, she fell over the broken drow. "Oh no," she wailed.

"The demon's whip struck him," Entreri explained.

"Help him!" Regis demanded.

Yvonnel hadn't found the power to begin to heal Pikel's wounds, and Drizzt's seemed far more profound.

"Oh no," she said again. She closed her eyes to concentrate, whispered a spell and cast it. A minor wave of healing washed over the fallen ranger.

And she opened her eyes and realized that she had done nothing of consequence.

"Oh, the Hunzrins," she said, and silently cursed herself for dismissing them too quickly. "We must catch . . ." she started to say, but a slight gasp from Drizzt stopped her, turned her to him.

From the memories of Yvonnel the Eternal, this Yvonnel knew well the final rattles in the breathing of a dying person. They could not catch Charri Hunzrin and the others in time.

Yvonnel stood and paced, slapping her hands over her eyes and crying out to the Spider Queen.

"Lolth, hear me!" she begged, casting a spell of communion. "I know you care for him!"

*You know nothing, child,* she heard in her head, and to her horror, Yvonnel recognized Yiccardaria's voice.

She knew then that she was doomed, that they were all doomed.

Yvonnel went to Drizzt, shoving the others aside, and cradled his head. "Would you let him die like this?"

"Would you give yourself for him?" came a disembodied and gurgling, watery voice, filling the corridor.

Wulfgar, Regis, and Entreri formed a triangle, shoulder-to-shoulder, back-to-back, around the terrified Concettina. The three had their weapons out, though all sensed how futile such implements would likely prove.

"Would you give yourself for him?" the voice, Yiccardaria's voice, said again, and then Yvonnel heard in her head, *Summon me if you wish him to live.*

"You ask me to die . . ." Yvonnel whispered.

*I did not say you would die.*

"You did not say I would not!" Yvonnel answered.

*No, I did not,* the magical voice agreed. *Choose now.*

Yvonnel looked to Drizzt, then to the others, and said, "Run. For your lives, be as far away as you can."

"I'm not leaving him," Regis said, moving behind Drizzt.

The others joined him, forming a line across the hall, and Concettina, clearly at a loss, fell in behind them.

"I have no time for . . ." Yvonnel started to reply.

"Do as you would," Entreri told her. "We are not leaving him."

With a sigh, Yvonnel rushed back up the tunnel a bit and began spellcasting, a mighty dweomer to open a gate to the Abyss.

She fell back and held her breath as the black gate flickered and filled, and Yiccardaria came through, in her natural and grotesque form, a pile of mud waving tentacles.

The handmaiden stopped there and gestured back at the portal, adding her own magic, and the black gate flickered and filled again.

And something else came through.

And she was beautiful beyond compare, mocking the trembling drow woman in front of her, who gulped and gasped and fell to her knees.

And the drow woman became a giant drider then, just for a moment, just so that the other witnesses would understand the truth and be afraid.

"We're dead," Entreri whispered.

Concettina fell to her knees and wept.

Regis's dagger fell to the floor, his hand too weak to hold it. The tip of his rapier, too, scraped the stone.

"You surprise me, child," said the Spider Queen. She seemed amused.

"I . . . I . . ."

Lolth laughed at her, then hissed and waved a hand in front of Yvonnel's face.

Something roiled within the daughter of Gromph, rising like bile. At the very last moment, she recognized it for what it was and she spun to face Drizzt and verily vomited a spell at him, a mighty spell that washed into him and physically moved him with its sheer magical energy.

He rolled over, coughed, and leaped up—awake, healed, and facing Entreri, Regis, Wulfgar, and the sobbing woman beside him. Their expressions clued him into turning around.

Then Drizzt nearly fell over again.

"As you asked," Lolth said to Yvonnel.

"Take me," Yvonnel whispered.

Lolth snorted and Yvonnel was magically thrown aside, toyed with by a mere thought from the mighty Queen of the Demonweb Pits, and slammed into the wall, where she cowered.

"At long last, Drizzt Do'Urden," the Spider Queen said.

Drizzt stood straight at her and did not blink.

"Are you not afraid?"

He didn't blink.

"Perhaps I tire of your insolence," Lolth said. "I demand your fealty."

"I cannot give you that."

"Denounce Mielikki!"

"She is not mine to denounce," Drizzt admitted, and a crack in Lolth's omnipotence appeared then when a cloud of confusion briefly colored her face.

"I can destroy all that you love," Lolth warned.

"So I have come to expect," said Drizzt.

"Do you know the pain I could give you?"

"I do," Drizzt answered before she even finished.

"Good," she purred.

Drizzt squared his shoulders.

"And you can avoid that, all of it," Lolth said. "And your friends will be spared, even your precious Catti-brie."

Drizzt winced at the mention of his beloved wife. But as soon as he swallowed that shock, he understood that anything and everything she promised or threatened was irrelevant to anything and everything he might do. Lolth was too far above him in every way. She would do as she pleased, whatever his course, and he could no more influence her actions than he could lift Faerûn out of the oceans.

"Kneel to me!" she demanded, and it carried magical weight that shoved Drizzt to his knees.

"And how dare you look upon me without my permission!" she cried, and a second blast of magic forced his gaze to the floor.

But in there, against the magical suggestion, Drizzt Do'Urden saw a single light, a candle in his memory.

He looked up at Lolth.

He moved through the magic and stood.

"So much can I take from you," she warned. "Worship me!"

"What you ask is not mine to give," he explained.

Lolth sneered and waved her hand, and the corridor behind Drizzt filled with thick webs, lifting his three friends and Concettina from the floor, catching them fully and holding them fast.

Drizzt glanced back at their gasps, unable to resist, and he saw them, trapped and helpless, and saw, too, the thousands of small spiders gathering on the ceiling.

"Worship me," Lolth calmly demanded.

"How?" Drizzt asked innocently. "I cannot control that which is in my heart, and that which is in my heart is not aligned with the way of Lolth."

Lolth growled, a most feral sound, and behind Drizzt, the clatter of spider legs increased.

And his friends began to cry out in pain, voices muffled by webs, agony obvious.

They were being eaten, every one, by tiny spiders.

"I will have you, Drizzt Do'Urden," a grinning Lolth promised.

"No," Drizzt said simply.

Behind him, Entreri managed to mutter between grimaces and groans, "Not what she wanted to hear," but Drizzt barely registered it.

He found the candle in his thoughts, dropped into his meditative pose, and there found peace, removed from the scene.

Because there was nothing he could do, nothing he could even pretend to do. Long ago had Drizzt Do'Urden come to understand the truth of this "worship," that it was not strained, that it was not even given, that, truly, it was not even accepted.

It just was, a way of heart and belief and shared joy.

It could not be created.

It could not be coerced.

It could not be altered.

It just was.

Drizzt removed himself from the pain around him, went away with his thoughts to a place where he could not hear the cries. He felt a twinge of regret, a momentary wave of guilt, but he fast suppressed it.

There was nothing he could do. This was Lolth, a goddess. Drizzt could pull Taulmaril from his belt and shoot her in the face and the arrow would not come close to hitting her—or of hurting her if it did. This was no dragon in front of him, no normal demon, not even Demogorgon. This was something all together different, something all together greater and beyond.

So Drizzt went away, and so removed from the scene was he that he was genuinely surprised when he was grabbed by the tunic and hoisted up into the air with horrifying strength and frightening ease.

The sounds behind him had greatly diminished, not a cry of agony, not a scuffling spider leg. He wasn't sure how long he'd gone away, and he feared they were all dead behind him.

The soft sobbing of a woman—Concettina—gave him a tiny flicker of hope.

"I am not just pain," Lolth said to him, her face very near his, and in a voice very different. "I am pleasure."

And she kissed him, urgently, passionately, and a thousand fires of tickling electricity coursed through him, teasing him, tempting him.

She pulled him back and smiled alluringly. "On a word, it is all yours."

But Drizzt shrugged and shook his head.

Lolth dropped him to his feet and he fell back as if struck. For a moment, in the angry eyes of Lolth, Drizzt imagined a horrible death flying for him.

But she calmed, and laughed.

"I do not just take away, Drizzt Do'Urden," she said. "I can give as well. Call to your panther."

Drizzt hesitated.

Lolth held out her hand and he followed the motion to look behind him. There was a pouch on the ground there, right in front of the webbing and his trapped, but very much alive, friends. His pouch, he realized, which held the onyx figurine.

"I can bring her myself," Lolth promised, and Drizzt didn't doubt it.

He called to Guenhwyvar and watched the mist form and coalesce. And the panther was there, and Drizzt felt his heart fall.

Guenhwyvar flopped pitifully, her body not answering her demands. She whimpered and fell over and tried to right herself, but to no avail.

Drizzt could hardly stand the sight. He thought to pull Taulmaril, not to shoot Lolth but to put Guenhwyvar out of this misery.

"Guen, be gone!" he begged.

"No," said Lolth, and the panther did not disappear. "I'll not allow that."

Drizzt turned to regard her, then began to fall into his crouch once more, to go away.

But Lolth cast a spell past him, and he turned to see Guenhwyvar restored.

The panther crouched and issued a growl.

Lolth laughed at her and waved her hand, throwing Guenhwyvar back into the web, where she, too, was caught fast.

"See?" she asked when Drizzt turned back to her. "I am not without my gifts. I am much more than simple pain and torment."

Drizzt conceded the point with a slight nod.

"Worship me," she said. "Know my love."

"No. I cannot, and you know I cannot."

Lolth licked her lips, the slight wetness shining alluringly. "I can give him back to you," she said.

Drizzt swallowed hard, suddenly afraid.

"You know that I can."

"Zaknafein denied you," Drizzt said, simply because he had to hear it spoken aloud. "He is not with you."

"Would that matter?" she asked, not denying his retort. "I can give him back to you. You know that I can."

Her grin showed Drizzt that she believed she had him then.

But she did not. Because she could not.

"I cannot give you what you want," he said simply. "I could not worship you whatever your gifts, your pleasures, your threats. Such a thing is not to be given. I could serve you, and so I shall if that is your price, so long as that service is not at the expense of an undeserving innocent. Never that."

He considered his own words and shrugged. "Or no, not even could I do that, I expect."

"You would let your friends die, you would let your beloved Guenhwyvar wallow in agony, you would turn away from the thought of seeing Zaknafein, simply because you do not believe in the gods?"

"Or because I believe in something greater still," Drizzt said. "Something that speaks to justice and that which is right."

Lolth scoffed at him and pointedly said again, "I can restore Zaknafein to your side! All you need to do is offer your fealty to me."

"If you ever expected anything like that from me, you would not have taken Zaknafein from me in the first place, nor the many others you have taken to your torment."

He looked back over his shoulder, to Artemis Entreri hanging awkwardly and clearly in pain, his face red from spider bites. And despite it all, Artemis Entreri returned a smile.

"And if ever you hoped to convince me that you seek to change, to go to these places of justice and that which is right," he said with confidence and clear strength, "then you would have restored Zaknafein to my side long ago. Without condition."

Lolth narrowed her eyes.

"You would have me lie? To what end?" Drizzt asked. "Fear is not fealty and worry is not worship."

Lolth's demeanor changed again. Her laughter seemed lighthearted, which made Drizzt believe the final blade was about to fall.

But she looked to the side. "I gave to you a great gift," she told Yvonnel.

The young woman shrugged.

"Look at her," Lolth told Drizzt. "She is but a few years old, and yet she is imbued with the wisdom and memories of the very eldest of my children. And power! Oh, great power that comes from me. But where is Yvonnel's gratitude, I wonder?"

Yvonnel didn't answer, and Lolth snickered.

"You amuse me," she told Drizzt, told them both. She grabbed Drizzt again and forced another kiss, though again, for all her magical enticements and hinted promises, he did not kiss her back.

*"Drojal zhah obdoluth dorb'd streeak,"* she whispered, though all in the corridor heard. *"Lueth dro zhah zhaunau dorb'd ogglin."*

And she was gone, and the gate was gone, and the webs were gone, and the five captives dropped back to the floor.

"What did she say?" Regis was the first to ask.

" 'Existence is empty without chaos,' " an unnerved Yvonnel translated the first part.

" 'And life is boring without enemies,' " Artemis Entreri, who spoke fluent Drow, finished.

"What does it mean?" the halfling asked.

Drizzt and Yvonnel looked at each other but neither had any idea.

Drizzt was about to offer some comforting words to his little friend—they were alive, after all, and that seemed quite an improvement over expectations—but before he could begin to talk, a commotion of air and sparkling lights came through the tunnel wall not far from Yvonnel, who fell back defensively.

Those lights coalesced, sparkling and spinning, then seemed like a rabble of butterflies dancing on unseen current before settling to the floor. And down there, the mat of colors expanded, rose, and Grandmaster Kane stood at the fighting ready in their midst.

He looked around and relaxed, seeing no threat—though he kept a wary eye on the strange, obsidian-skinned creature farther up the hall.

"An illusion," Yvonnel told him, nodding at her spriggan creation.

"The army of King Yarin has come, and is outside these tunnels," Kane informed them. "The Order of the Yellow Rose stands beside them, and with a dragon beside us." He looked at the halfling down the hall and added, "And the Kneebreakers."

"The demon that possessed Queen Concettina is gone," Yvonnel told him, indicating the woman who stood beside Wulfgar. "She is free."

"We are all free," said Drizzt, and Yvonnel nodded.

"I cannot go back there!" Concettina blurted. "Oh, please, take me from this place!"

"That, of course, was our intention," Grandmaster Kane said. "But it won't prove an easy task, for right outside of Smeltergard King Yarin and his forces are in full control, and he has ordered the queen, and Wulfgar, arrested immediately for high treason. And he already has a pair of conspirators, dwarf brothers, in chains.

"A fair and open public trial was all that the king would offer, and that after much discussion," Kane went on. "To you others, he would give no more than open threats—threats backed up with batteries of archers leveling bows our way."

◆ ◆ ◆

"PIKEL IS WELL," Regis informed Drizzt, Entreri, and Yvonnel as they sat at a table at an inn in Helgabal a few days later. "Fully recovered. He said that dark elves came to him in a dream and took away his pain."

Drizzt and Entreri, of course, turned to Yvonnel.

"I'm a good friend to have," was all she would reply to those inquisitive stares, and she was glad that Charri Hunzrin had heeded her demands.

"This whole thing is going to be ugly, though," Regis went on. "My Kneebreaker contacts nearest the king's guards have told me that Yarin has been pressing Kane for more arrests, including myself. He's been talked down from that, but he's determined to get some revenge for the embarrassment done him in his own house."

"Wulfgar is in trouble," Drizzt reasoned.

"And Ivan," said Regis. "Though I've heard rumors that Pikel will be set free. A bargaining chip with Kane, who is resisting him, but who has little open influence in the city these days. It is likely, they believe, that Ivan will be spared the guillotine. Wulfgar, too, but only because King Yarin has been informed that executing Wulfgar would likely lead to a massive dwarven army assaulting his walls, one led by King Bruenor Battlehammer himself."

"And Concettina?" Drizzt asked. "Surely she cannot be blamed for anything done under demonic possession."

"It's more complicated than that," Regis replied, and he explained the story of why he and Wulfgar had come to Damara in the first place, recounting Concettina's fears before all of these crazy events had taken place.

"He has the excuse he wanted," the halfling concluded.

"What a wonderful thing are the laws that serve the whims of the powerful," Artemis Entreri said with a snort and a disgusted shake of his head.

"We do not plan to let that happen, I hope," said Regis.

"Not without a fight," Drizzt replied, and Yvonnel nodded. "I'll go to Kane."

"And I to Tazmikella," said Yvonnel.

"And I to get a drink," said Entreri, and he got up from the table and moved to the bar.

◆ ◆ ◆

KING YARIN WAS unnerved. He had discovered a great demon in his bed, had viewed the shattered body of his sister Acelya, and had lost his most trusted murderer Rafer Ingot. Powerful forces had been stirred in Damara, including the monks, of whom he had little experience and no fond regard and who were led by a dear friend of the legendary King Gareth Dragonsbane himself.

He surrounded himself with guards, many ranks deep, and would not leave the castle. He called upon his trusted networks and set spies in every corridor of the place. He moved his bedchambers to a small room with a single heavy door, no windows, and thick stone walls, then each night filled the hallway outside with rows of soldiers.

No one could get near him.

As had believed so many pashas in far-off Calimport.

The last thing King Yarin saw were the eyes of his killer, staring down at him dispassionately from above the pillow that was tightly pressed over his mouth.

◆ ◆ ◆

DREYLIL ANDRUS WAS awakened before the cock crowed the next morning. Bleary-eyed, the guard captain told his wife, Caliera, to pull the bedclothes up high and staggered fast to his door, recognizing the insistence of the knocking. He threw it wide to find Red Mazzie, who looked like he, too, had just been awakened, standing in the hall, other soldiers milling about outside.

The wizard, grim-faced, entered the room and shut the door.

"What time did you leave the guard post in the king's corridor last night?" Red Mazzie asked.

Dreylil Andrus looked at him curiously, and the wizard nodded at the very telling hesitation.

"I was not there last night," Andrus replied.

Red Mazzie chuckled. "Yes, you were."

"He was here, all night," Caliera Andrus insisted.

"No, you went there just after the toll of the midnight hour," the wizard corrected.

When Andrus started to argue, the wizard interrupted, "Many saw you, and were looking for you for guidance when they discovered that King Yarin was dead."

Dreylil Andrus fell back in shock. His wife gasped.

"How?"

"It would seem that his heart succumbed to the tensions of the times," Red Mazzie said, but in a sarcastic voice reflecting what they both now knew for certain.

"Perhaps it would be better if you remembered that you were there last night," Red Mazzie added, and in no way was it an accusation. Rather it was a plea, because if the king was discovered to have been murdered, it would throw Damara, Helgabal in particular, into a state of frenzied interregnum that would serve neither of these powerful court officers nearly as much as an orderly succession. The king had no heir, no family at all now that Acelya was dead.

"We should quickly erase all charges against Queen Concettina," Andrus said, trying to think it through.

"As Captain of the Castle Guard, you now legally serve as magistrate to her trial," Red Mazzie informed him.

A bell tolled, a somber note.

The men patted each other on the shoulder and Red Mazzie departed. Dreylil Andrus went for his uniform, knowing that this would be a long and difficult day, with many orders of weighty business before him.

"What does it mean?" asked his shaken wife. Like so many others of Yarin's court, Caliera Andrus had little love for the king, but still her eyes rimmed with tears, weeping for Helgabal if not for the man himself.

"It means that today is a day of sorrow and tears and preparation," Dreylil Andrus answered past the lump in his throat." He steadied himself with a sigh. "But that tomorrow will be a brighter day by far. The king is dead, long live the queen."

◆ ◆ ◆

THAT FIRST BELL toll, before dawn, awakened Regis. It took him a long moment to realize where he was, for he was not in his bed but sitting on the floor of his room at the inn, still fully dressed from the night before, including his weapons.

No, not fully dressed, he realized when he scratched at his tousled hair.

A moment of panic had the halfling scrambling about until he noted his precious blue beret, the hat of magical disguise that had allowed him to get through the giants' lair unmolested, lying on the floor nearer the door.

When he got to it, he found it scrunched down, as if it had been sat upon or stepped upon . . . or slid under the closed door.

Regis tried to remember the events of the previous night. He had been in the common room with Drizzt and the others. A couple of glasses of wine, a mug of ale . . .

How did he get back to this room?

He couldn't remember.

The bell tolled again. Somewhere off in the city, a rooster crowed.

◆ ◆ ◆

THOSE SOLEMN BELLS tolled in Helgabal throughout the next morning, lamentations for the passing of the old king whose heart, it was said, had broken under the duress of the recent excitement.

Calls began immediately for Queen Concettina, the woman who had survived the demon and escaped its foul possession, for the hope of Helgabal and all of Damara, and cheers filled every street when the Captain of the Castle Guard, the Court Wizard at his side, announced from the balcony overlooking Castle Square that Queen Concettina had been declared innocent, the victim of a heinous demon that she had expelled through her goodness and force of will.

Drizzt, Yvonnel, Regis, and many, many others, breathed a sigh of relief as events fast-unfolded that morning. The whispers mounted that the trial, and so the subsequent fallout, would be avoided. Wulfgar and Ivan would be rejoining them that very day, Grandmaster Kane came in and told them soon after.

And so they would all be together.

Well, not all, for, strangely, Artemis Entreri was nowhere to be found.

Indeed, it was not until many days later, when Drizzt and Yvonnel climbed down from the back of Tazmikella on the field in Luskan near the huge and growing Hosttower of the Arcane, when Drizzt caught sight of the man again, standing at his tent flap with Dahlia, watching Drizzt sprint across the field to the waiting arms of Catti-brie.

For just a moment, as Drizzt spun his beloved wife in a great hug, Drizzt and Entreri locked stares from afar and shared a slight knowing nod.

Drizzt understood what Entreri had done.

So be it.

The world was a complicated place.

# CHAPTER 28 ◈

# *The Snow Is Deep, the Woods Silent*

IVAN BOULDERSHOULDER RECLINED IN A HAMMOCK ON THE balcony of a quiet room at the back of the Ivy Mansion on an early summer day in the Year of the Rune Lords Triumphant, or 1487 by Dalereckoning. Below him, birds chirped, hummingbirds hummed, and bees buzzed happily in the most amazing gardens of Penelope Harpell.

Never had those gardens looked better, and all because of the work of Ivan's doo-dad brother, who was down there every day, hopping about and singing to the plants, casting his spells and singing and dancing with the birds and the bees and the squirrels and the trees.

Yes, even the trees, which animated to his calls for a dance, much to Ivan's chagrin.

But it was Pikel's calling and his work, after all, as this was Ivan's work, standing—or rather, lying—guard in front of the anteroom, recently constructed against the back wall of the place with a threshold of three long, narrow stones, two upright and one laying atop them.

"Pikel!" Catti-brie called. "Come along. We mustn't keep King Bruenor waiting."

"Oo oi!" Pikel replied.

Ivan rolled himself out of the hammock and straightened his armor and fine clothing. He licked his fingers and shaped his hair more tidily.

Catti-brie and Drizzt arrived shortly after, Drizzt in his black leather armor and forest green cloak, his weapons sitting comfortable at his hip. Guenhwyvar was beside him, which made Ivan giggle, knowing how the cat always loved to tease King Bruenor.

The dwarf only regarded Drizzt and the cat for a moment, though. Catti-brie, with her white gown and black lace shawl stole his breath.

What a fine couple, he thought, and he hoped the whispered rumors were true.

Pikel was dirty, disheveled, and laughing when he arrived soon after, and the source of his mirth became obvious a moment later when Penelope Harpell and old Kipper entered, followed by a pair of floating discs that held casks of fine Longsaddle wine, the most coveted product of Penelope's years of labor in her gardens.

Drizzt and Catti-brie exchanged grins and nods at the sight of the woman, and their silent gossip wasn't lost on Ivan. Penelope was stunning, too, in a splendid blue gown that hugged her tightly and accentuated every flattering feature.

Ivan, like Drizzt and Catti-brie, had not been to Gauntlgrym for several tendays, but Penelope had been traveling there regularly, working with Gromph and the other wizards in their controlled releases of the primordial's fires—and, reportedly, on another project, little of which was currently known.

"Ye're sure I can leave it?" Ivan asked.

"It will be fully secure on the other end," Catti-brie told him. "For just this night, it will be all right."

She turned to Penelope with a questioning look.

The woman nodded confidently and walked to the door, motioning for Ivan to unlock it. "Gromph is certain," Penelope said to the others before entering.

"So am I," said Kipper, reminding them all that he had been the lead wizard on this part of their work with the primordial. After all, this type of magic was his personal specialty.

"Here we go, then," said Penelope and she took out a sheet of parchment—where she had concealed it in that revealing gown, Ivan could only guess. She cleared her throat, and began reciting a most arcane spell.

It was in the ancient Delzoun language of Gauntlgrym, but Ivan nodded knowingly, recognizing the words for "friend" and "ally" and the quick pledge of "kith and kin."

The base of the upright stones began to glow, orange flames swirling, like the reflection of a fireplace in thick glass, even though the stones were not reflective, and surely not translucent.

The flames climbed the pillars, reaching the apexes at the same time and crossing the top beam to meet in the middle. The moment they joined, they intensified, and all in the room could feel the heat. A sheet of flames filled the threshold.

Drizzt's hand went instinctively to Icingdeath. "Are you sure that we need no protection?" he asked.

Old Kipper laughed and walked past him, right into the flaming doorway, and disappeared, his disc floating in behind and similarly vanishing.

"Oo oi!" said Pikel, and he verily tackled Ivan, bull-rushing him into the fires before him.

"This should be a fun night," Penelope said to Drizzt and Catti-brie, and they weren't about to disagree.

Catti-brie squeezed Drizzt's hand and led him in. He felt a brief moment of warmth, a brief sensation of movement, and then exited a similar stone gate into a room he knew to be off to one side of the great throne room of Gauntlgrym, more than a hundred miles away.

"Elf!" a beaming Bruenor, who was waiting for them on the other end, cried happily, but his expression quickly dropped. "Bah, but why'd ye bring the durned cat!"

"Hee hee hee," said Pikel.

The area had been significantly reworked. Mithral now reinforced the walls of this smallish room, and the door, magical and secret, was wholly made of the hard metal now. Portcullises and new mithral doors had been added outside the room as well, along with defensive positions all around the corridors leading to the throne room.

Now that the magical gate was working, the dwarves had made sure that any enemies coming through uninvited had nowhere to go.

A wide smile crossed Drizzt's face when they entered that throne room, for a feast had been prepared for this day—and such a feast! Thousands of dwarves were already seated, along with many halflings, including Regis, who bounced up to his friends arm-in-arm with a most lovely halfling woman, and offered the long overdue introduction to Donnola Topolino.

"I had heard you would not arrive in time," Catti-brie said to the halfling couple. "And that thought broke my heart!"

"Hard riding," Regis replied.

"There were many arrangements to be made for such a journey," Donnola added.

Drizzt took in the room again, focusing on the halflings, and he realized to his surprise that he recognized some of those in attendance as members of the Kneebreakers of Damara. Before he could question that, however, he spotted another guest of King Bruenor, and he nudged Catti-brie to direct her gaze to Wulfgar.

The couple exchanged knowing nods, and understood then Penelope's choice of attire.

And Wulfgar was there, and Drizzt and Catti-brie nodded and glanced at Penelope, who had already taken a seat at a table near to Bruenor's main table, next to Gromph.

"The work here is remarkable," Drizzt said to Bruenor.

"Bah, but ye ain't seen nothin' yet," the dwarf promised and he started for the outer door, gesturing for them to follow. "Come along, all of ye, and see."

The cavern outside of Gauntlgrym's main door had been shaped beyond recognition. The underground pool had been cleaned, both magically and through hard dredging, and low lights all around it showed the flickers of many fish in the water.

Indeed, on the railings of the bridge that spanned the water sat several dwarves with fishing poles, bobbers floating below them.

Just past the other end of the bridge, beyond the lake, loomed another new construction: a giant platform of some sort, with ramps climbing up left and right, and both running out for the far end of the cavern.

"I'll get ye the pole I promised ye later, Rumblebelly," Bruenor promised with a wink. "We bringed in knucklehead, too, from Maer Dualdon."

Regis wore a wistful smile, but neither he nor Donnola seemed surprised by any of this, and Drizzt got the distinct feeling that they were in on the surprise.

"Truly remarkable," said Drizzt.

"Bah, but ye ain't seen nothin' yet!" Bruenor said again, more boisterously, and he started over the bridge, under the new raised platform and then across the main cavern floor, past the shaped defensive stalagmite and stalactite fortifications and to an area where a tremendous construction project was well underway.

Two new tunnels led out of the cavern, angling steeply upward.

"Next cart's comin' in soon," Bruenor explained, motioning to the tunnel on the left, and looking there, the others noted that rails had been set, from within the tunnel and all the way to the platform near the lake, bordered by low walls that had allowed them to escape notice until Bruenor had pointed them out. Interestingly, those rails disappeared into water along that left-hand run, and the four tourists could only shrug.

Even more interesting, when they looked back to the right, across the way, they found another set of rails coming from the platform behind them. But as this line neared the second tunnel, those rails went up and rolled over, and continued out of the cavern on the ceiling of the second tunnel.

"What?" Drizzt and Catti-brie asked together, and Regis and Donnola laughed.

"They sound just like us," Donnola said.

"Aye, and good!" said Bruenor, leading the way for his clearly impatient friends. "I told 'em to wait to set the next length."

At that tunnel, they saw many dwarves working, but they were standing on the ceiling, upside down.

"Harpells," Catti-brie immediately figured.

"Aye, was their idea, and a fine one," said Bruenor. He gave a sharp whistle and a group of dwarves a little farther up the tunnel but standing on the floor and not the ceiling jumped into action. Singing a song for cadence, they hefted and carried a length of metal rail farther up the slope, just beyond where the rails on the ceiling ended.

Then they rushed back and another stepped forward, a human, a woman, and it took Drizzt and Catti-brie a moment to recognize Kennedy Harpell, who turned back and offered a friendly wave.

Then she looked ahead into the tunnel and cast a spell, and those new rails the dwarves had placed fell upward to clang against the ceiling.

"Be quick, boys!" yelled the leader of the dwarf gang, and they rushed past Kennedy, flipping over as they plunged into her dweomer, falling to their feet some eight feet or so to the ceiling. There, they went to lining up the rails with the rest of the track and setting them firmly in place with long spikes.

"Team's only got a short while to get up . . . err, down, there to set the rails in place, then get out afore the spell dies," Bruenor explained. "They can lay a hunnerd feet a day on the upside, but Gromph can only make it lasting at ten feet a day."

"Lasting?" asked the drow.

"Fore'er," Bruenor said with a proud grin.

"You're building an upside-down tunnel?" Drizzt asked incredulously, for he seemed the only one of the four who could find his voice.

"Yep," said Bruenor. "Callin' it the Causeway."

"Wait," Catti-brie interjected, "so a cart can roll down from the surface—" she pointed to the tunnel on the left—"then roll back up to the surface?"

"Easier than pullin' it," said Bruenor.

Somewhere up the left-hand tunnel, a cowbell began to ring.

"Ye might want to move back a bit," Bruenor told Donnola, who was closest to the low wall of the left-hand run.

The ground began to tremble, and moments later, a cart full of dwarves came screeching into the cavern, rushing along back toward the lake. Water sprayed from the wake of the wheels out both sides over the low walls, the drag slowing the cart so that it barely began the climb up the ramp to the platform. There it clicked over some gear, which locked it in place so that it wouldn't roll back.

The dwarves who'd been fishing moved to a ladder and went up to the platform, and began turning cranks that carried the cart up to the top where the newcomers could disembark.

"By the gods," breathed Drizzt.

"She's a beautiful thing," Bruenor agreed. "We're goin' to have to pull it all the way back up the same tunnel it came down, for now, but we'll have the return run finished afore the summer's end, don't ye doubt."

"How did you even dig these?" Drizzt asked.

Bruenor shook his head.

"Passwalls," Catti-brie explained, nodding. "That's why Penelope has been here so often of late."

"And all forever," said Bruenor.

Drizzt leaned over the small wall and watched the work of the dwarves affixing the rails to the ceiling far ahead. He tried to imagine riding a cart upside down on the ceiling of a tunnel, rolling up to a steep hill to the surface above.

He had seen a lot of strange and incredible things these last tendays, including the Prince of Demons and the Queen of the Demonweb Pits. He had felt the power of Menzoberranzan combined within him and released to destroy mighty Demogorgon. He had ridden on the back of a dragon across half of Faerûn and had met and been tutored by a man who had transcended his mortal coil.

And now this.

And he found, and was glad, that he was still surprised.

◆ ◆ ◆

BRUENOR SAT TO his left, Catti-brie to his right. Wulfgar was there, Regis was there, Jarlaxle was there. Guenhwyvar curled up on the floor behind Bruenor, as if to warn him that she might wish a softer bed even if dwarves were not all that much softer than a stone floor.

Almost everyone he cared most about was in that room, singing and toasting and feasting and laughing and looking ahead to a future that seemed so full of promise that Drizzt's heart felt as if it might burst from overflowing.

He had met Lolth and had denied her—had she really accepted that denial? But even if not, then what did it matter? In his heart, Drizzt had, at long last, found complete peace, had walked his road into a circle of understanding and acceptance for this world and his place in it.

He looked to this strange young woman named Yvonnel and didn't quite know what to make of her. He considered her as the scales of justice, with Menzoberranzan itself on trial, and while he wasn't convinced of her honesty as magistrate, he saw within her greater hopes than he could ever have imagined.

Had he passed the torch to her?

He laughed at the notion and squeezed Catti-brie's leg, just to feel the solidity, the reality. He could hardly believe the dark road he had just walked, lost in doubts that now, to his healed mind, seemed so completely absurd. His world had come to a place of peace and goodness, surrounded by friends and love.

A flicker of warning flashed in his thoughts then, but he laughed it away.

The sound of silverware tapping glasses and mugs began to ring about the great hall, calls for a speech by the most excellent host.

Bruenor cleared his throat and rose. "I'm too busy eatin'!" he said to many laughs. "So "I've asked another to speak for me."

He sat back down and, to Drizzt's surprise, Regis rose from his seat and climbed up on the table, lifting his glass high.

"My friends, my family," he said, gathering his thoughts. "It has been my greatest pleasure to connect the homes I've known, to introduce to Clan Battlehammer and the Companions of the Hall, my other family, Morada Topolino!"

The halflings whistled and the dwarves cried "Huzzah!"

"To Wigglefingers, and to Donnola, my love and soon to be my wife!"

The announcement sent the cheers to new levels.

"To Doregardo and Showithal of the heroic Grinning Ponies!" Regis cried above the cheers. "To Tecumseh Bracegirdle and the legendary Kneebreakers!"

"Huzzah!"

"To Penelope and Kipper and all the Harpells!"

"Huzzah!"

"You are all invited to our wedding!" Regis declared. "All of you, and all of Clan Battlehammer!"

"Am I to be insulted?" Jarlaxle yelled, dramatically.

"You, too!" Regis replied. "And your dark elf friends!"

It took a bit longer, but the "Huzzah!" did arise.

"Do you think you might leave behind your weapons?" Regis quipped to much laughter.

"Do you think we would need them?" Gromph replied to that, silencing the mirth—until the archmage grinned and lifted his glass in toast.

Possibilities, Drizzt thought. Possibilities.

"Let's do it now!" one dwarf cried from the back.

"I'll bring the beer!" another promised.

"King Bruenor's shield!" a third reminded the gathering, and laughter shook the room.

But Regis changed his aspect, lowered his glass and his gaze, his shoulders slumping a bit.

"You may reconsider your laughter and your response, for I have an admission to make, and it is one of great treachery," he said.

The room went silent.

Drizzt studied his friend carefully, hesitatingly, but Bruenor noticed his look and offered a reassuring wink.

"For I have planted a spy within your midst these last few months, one paving the way for some great changes that will come to this land." He motioned to the side, and Pikel Bouldershoulder stood up on his table and cried, "Oo oi!"

"Our friend, my spy, Pikel here, has been in secret contact with me and with Donnola for these last months, making preparations, and promising the finest of wine for the celebration of our wedding. And judging from what he has brought this very day, I doubt him not." He motioned to Penelope Harpell and the cheers erupted anew in appreciation of her vintage.

"So, silly halfling, do you mean to presume that King Bruenor will abandon his throne to travel halfway across Faerûn to celebrate the wedding day of his dear friend?" Jarlaxle asked loudly, and, it seemed, rudely. A hush fell over the gathering, and only the sly grin of Regis tipped Drizzt off that this interruption had been practiced and coordinated within Regis's toast.

"Bah, I'm going nowhere!" Bruenor harrumphed. "Me own bed's where I'll be sleepin'!"

"And your bed will be waiting for your hairy arse that same night, my friend!" Regis promised.

"Are you planning a flame-gate to Aglarond?" a horrified Catti-brie asked them all. The creation of the gates from Gauntlgrym to other points, like the Ivy Mansion, was a tremendous undertaking, both in process and in implication.

Drizzt knew her words were not pre-planned, and were surely heartfelt.

Even Bruenor blanched at the thought. "One gate for yerself in Longsaddle, and one more to Mithral Hall!" he insisted. "And might be one to Icewind Dale, but that's for another time."

"Why then, my friend, we will have to bring Morada Topolino to you," Regis explained. "All of it!"

He jumped down and Donnola Topolino took his place atop the table.

"Tonight we announce Bleeding Vines," she explained. "A new home for Morada Topolino, on the back doorstep of Gauntlgrym, on land granted my family by generous King Bruenor!"

Stunned silence became overwhelming cheers and boisterous huzzahs and resounding chimes as glasses and mugs tapped enthusiastically.

"And Bleeding Vines will serve, too, as home base for the Kneebreakers and the Grinning Ponies, who have decided to join their forces to patrol the Sword Coast, Neverwinter to Suzail," Donnola announced.

"The Causeway," Catti-brie quietly remarked, and Drizzt chuckled, because indeed, those tram tunnels led up to the rocky vale, the back door of Gauntlgrym.

"Ever know better traders than a bunch o' halflings?" Bruenor asked. "Even Jarlaxle there'll have his hands full with Donnola's tricksters."

"You taste the wine Lady Penelope Harpell has brought this day," Donnola added to many cheers. "She has spent years developing the grapes, indeed, but only recently has she found the missing ingredient to perfection. And she has agreed to share this ingredient with us, that the wine of Morada Topolino will be known and cherished throughout the Realms, cultivated in both Bleeding Vines and Longsaddle."

"Seems we've got conspirators all around us," Drizzt whispered to Catti-brie.

"And this ingredient?" Donnola asked. She hopped down from the table and scurried over to Pikel and kissed him on the head. "Him!" she explained.

"Huzzah!" one dwarf cried, but he was cut short by Ivan Bouldershoulder.

"No!" Ivan yelled, silencing all. "Not huzzah." He looked to his beaming brother and yelled, "Oo oi!"

And all the room, in unison responded, "Oo oi!"

Drizzt leaned back and took full heart that his world had come to a place of peace and goodness, surrounded by friends and love.

◆ ◆ ◆

BRUENOR ENDED THE feast before the next dawn by blowing the cracked silver horn in tribute to one who was not there.

All paid solemn homage to the specter of Thibbledorf Pwent.

The great hall, the throne room of Gauntlgrym, began to empty soon after, or, in many cases, began to resonate with the contented snores of stuffed dwarves.

None noted the ghostly mist that breezed through the chamber, past the throne and to the statue set on a ledge on the wall in front of the royal seat. The lava rock entombing the body within had cracked, and the ghostly mist crept in.

And then returned, more substantial, floating to the Throne of the Dwarven Gods.

And there did Thibbledorf Pwent sit, and it was not the fighting specter produced by the horn.

The vampire looked up at his own sarcophagus and mused . . . was there a way?

The Throne of the Dwarven Gods did not reject him.

THE SNOW IS DEEP, THE WOODS SILENT, SAVE THE CREAK AND GROAN of naked trees, the mournful north wind, and the occasional howl of a Bidderdoo.

Tomorrow is the first day of the Year of Dwarvenkind Reborn, and Guenhwyvar, my dear companion, never have I looked forward to a year more.

And why not, for there is so much good that will be done, and so much joy that will be realized.

Regis and his friends will have their town fully in place, the Causeway completed, the grapes planted, and so the growing alliance of the northern Sword Coast will strengthen even more.

The Hosttower nears completion, its wizard complement as diverse as Effron, Gromph, and Lady Avelyere. It is no threat, but another source of stability, working so closely with the Ivy Mansion that Penelope maintains a grand workshop and library there. Jarlaxle's continued transformation of Luskan is a wondrous thing to behold, a hopeful road being walked.

Can I say any less about my own anticipated journey? You and I will continue our good and exciting work of catching the Bidderdoo werewolves and bringing them into the Ivy Mansion so that Catti-brie can help them control their feral impulses and make them more akin to their namesake.

Master Afafrenfere arrived the day after last we spoke, Guen. He was defeated by Savahn in their challenge, but is of good spirits, and Kane sent him on the road to find me and offer more insights into the ways of the Yellow Rose. It is a personal journey I welcome!

How the world has turned, bringing me back to a place I once knew and with a perspective to live it again more pleasurably.

A place I once knew, but that is so very different now, as the Companions of the Hall have become, so it seems, the Legions of the Hall.

And that number will grow, my friend.

I thought it was a burp from Catti-brie, a sudden shift, but no, it wasn't a growling belly.

It was a foot, Guen, a perfect little foot, the foot of my daughter or of my son, perhaps. A perfect foot.

What steps will that foot take, I wonder? What roads wandered, what adventures found, what goodness left in its wake?

My road has come fully home now, and I am surrounded by all that I love and cherish—and now so without fear. Catti-brie is beside me and so I am happy.

You are with me, and so I am happy.

Regis has his settlement on the door of Gauntlgrym, and so I am happy.

Bruenor is the rightful King of Gauntlgrym, and with the Hosttower renewed, the dwarven city will long outlive him, and so I am happy.

Wulfgar is all about, and ever smiling—perhaps he will become King of Damara someday, or more likely he will find his road ever winding and full of adventure—and often, I hope, with me beside him—and so I am happy.

And Artemis Entreri . . . I do not know where to begin. Never did I imagine that in the end, I would come to see him in this manner. Has he found redemption and atonement? That is not for me to decide, for I know not the depth of his crimes or the full darkness that once clouded his heart. But I know now what he has become: someone who can look into a mirror. Someone who can smile.

It is striking to me that I care so much—perhaps the sun does shine brighter after the darkest night, after all—but truly, when I look upon him now, I am satisfied. He came for me, at great risk. He stood by me, and Regis, in the darkness of Malcanthet's lair. He is no one I would need pull to Port Llast to help the settlers now, for he would offer to walk beside me.

To believe in redemption is to believe in hope and rescue from any darkness.

And so I say, and they are not words I must force: "Artemis Entreri, hero."

—Drizzt Do'Urden

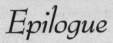

# *Epilogue*

J ARLAXLE SCRIBBLED HIS NAME ON SOME MANIFESTS AND work orders, the clerical functions of running a city like Luskan. The mercenary truly hated these duties, but at least he had Beniago to keep his own attention to such mundane chores to a minimum.

And despite the heavier load of parchments this day, Jarlaxle couldn't help but be in a fine mood. All was progressing wonderfully. The Hosttower had many levels, many rooms, and many inhabitants, the ties with both Gauntlgrym and Menzoberranzan strengthened every day, and those few people Jarlaxle cared about on a personal level were safe and prospering.

At this moment, however brief it would probably be, the world was good.

There came a soft knock on his door, and Jarlaxle was surprised as he looked up to see Yvonnel walk into the room.

"I thought you were off to Icewind Dale," Jarlaxle said, leaning his chair back on two legs, folding his hands behind his head, and throwing his booted feet up onto his desk.

"I found an interesting side road," was all Yvonnel replied.

"To finish an interesting year, no doubt."

"To meet a goddess? Yes, interesting is a word I would use."

"Speaking of that one, your spells?"

"They remain as strong as ever," Yvonnel informed him with an honest shrug. She was as surprised by that as she clearly expected Jarlaxle to be.

"You pray to her still, then?"

"No."

"Then why? How?"

Yvonnel shrugged again, and Jarlaxle came forward in his chair a bit, staring at her, intrigued.

"He faced her," Yvonnel said. "Toe to toe. Without fear of her. Fully at peace with whatever tempest she might bring."

"Drizzt?"

"He thinks he can remake her," Yvonnel said, shaking her head with every word. "He will never admit it, I expect, but he thinks he can reform her."

"Of course he does!"

"Her! Lolth!" Yvonnel said incredulously.

"Of course!" Jarlaxle explained. "That's why he fights. Hope gives him meaning. That's why we love him. Still, you must admit that the gods are practical above all else. If the hearts of their followers change, their power will be diminished if they do not follow. Divine paradox, I think."

"Her!" Yvonnel said again, laughing helplessly and shaking her head. She gave a slight nod, then glanced back out the open door and nodded to someone out of Jarlaxle's sight.

Another drow, a man, walked in through that door.

Jarlaxle nearly fell backward over his chair, then, compensating, fell forward and only caught himself by the edge of the desk, his jaw open, the mercenary speechless for one of the very few times in his long life. He closed his uncovered eye and stared through the magical eye patch. Then, certain, he threw back the eye patch so he could fully see the man.

He knew what he was seeing, but didn't know what to do, and for a long-held breath, didn't know how to feel, what to feel, what to think . . .

His mind whirled backward in time, to dances in the streets of Menzoberranzan, to so many battles, singing songs and weaving a deadly symphony of four blades.

Arms joined, swords side-by-side, with his most trusted—his *only* trusted friend.

He leaped over the desk in a rush, caring not for the ink bottles and parchments and knickknacks flying all about. He hit the floor in a stumbling run up to the newcomer and threw a great hug over the man then almost immediately shoved him back to arms' length so he could stare at him some more, needing to know that this was real.

"I wish to see my son," the man said.

And it was real. The tears came rushing to Jarlaxle like the tide on hurricane winds, and he didn't even try to hold them back. Voice breaking, he fought for the words.

"You will be proud."

◆

# SEARCHING FOR HARD-TO-FIND TITLES?

Your favorite Dungeons & Dragons® novels
— including new and hard-to-find titles —
are now available in print, ebook, and audio.